A Pirate's Mistress

He stood back drinking me in from the tips of my toes to the top of my head. "Never have I seen such perfection," he said. "And you stand so proudly."

I reached up and put my arms around his neck. I pressed my naked body against him. I murmured sweet lies: "I am proud because you've wanted me!"

"I love you, darling, and I've longed for you an eternity."

"Two years isn't an eternity," I said.

"It was to me," he whispered, kissing my eyes, my nose, my lips, and my throat as he carried me to the bed. "How delicate you are. How sweet and innocent."

Wanton as any strumpet, I delighted in every fiery touch of his fingers—forgetting my father, Lady Neilson, and the murderous ways of the pirate who loved me. But when it was over, the first thing that came to mind was a prayer: *God help me for surely I am condemned by all that is holy.*

Also by Lorinda Hagen:

SUMMER OF '32
IN LOVE AND WAR
SOMEBODY'S DAUGHTER,
　SOMEBODY'S WIFE
NEVADA
AMY JEAN
BANNERS OF DESIRE
SWEET SINNER
DESTINY AND DESIRE

BOLD BLADES FLASHING

Lorinda Hagen

LEISURE BOOKS NEW YORK CITY

For Elizabeth Worland

A LEISURE BOOK

Published by

Dorchester Publishing Co., Inc.
41 E. 60 St.
New York City

Copyright © MCMLXXIX by Nordon Publications, Inc.
              1983 by Dorchester Publishing Co., Inc.

All rights reserved. No part of this book may be reproduced or transmitted in any form or by any electronic or mechanical means, including photocopying, recording or by any information storage and retrieval system, without the written permission of the Publisher, except where permitted by law.

Printed in the United States of America

Part 1

One

LONDON—1761

Lady Neilson was among those who came to the house to see about my welfare; perhaps she felt duty-bound to look after the daughter of the man who had saved so many of her horses the previous year. I appreciated her kindness, especially when she asked me to come to her own estate until my father returned. And she added in carefully phrased words, "My dear child, I understand you've been living here in the cottage all alone for more than a fortnight. Therefore, we must consider the possibility that your father will never return, hard as it is to even think of such a thing. If you do not come with me, how will you live? How can a gently brought-up young girl of fourteen survive in London? I honor and respect your father as a man as well as a skillful animal doctor. For his sake, you must let me give you a home until he either returns, or..." At that point, Lady Neilson was unable to continue speaking. I'm sure the tears that filled my eyes contributed to her own feelings of sadness and distress, for she was a woman of boundless compassion as well as great beauty.

"But my father would *never* abandon me," I answered as bravely as I could. In my heart I knew he would never leave his only child to fend for herself. "Surely he will return very soon."

The Lady shook her head. "I know how well he loved you, Garnet. For that reason alone, I fear for his safety, even his life. It is not easy for me to speak of the possibility that your beloved father has met with foul play, but we must be realistic. He loved you beyond life itself. During the time when our horses were falling dead in the fields he spoke of your beautiful mother in a most heartbreaking way, and more than once he mentioned that you are her image, both in outward looks and in your actions. Such tenderness toward a daughter is a rare and lovely thing. Won't you come with me? At least for the present, Garnet. I cannot bear to think of the adored daughter of George Shaw in need. Your father has provided quite well for you and you're not accustomed to going without the niceties. How will you keep yourself fed?"

"I am almost a woman, Lady Neilson," I replied, "and even though I've not wanted for anything, I've learned to cook and I've learned how to take care of a house. I've looked after myself and also my father for my entire life." I gestured toward my surroundings. Our serving woman had given me notice a few days after my father disappeared, for she couldn't work without her wages. "I've cleaned these rooms myself." The remains of my meal of codfish and ale were still on the table, the only thing that marred the orderliness, but if Lady Neilson had not arrived at that very moment I would have cleared away the plate and silver. "The rent is due on the cottage within a few days, but surely my father will have returned by then. And I have a few bob left with which to purchase my meat and bread."

The beautiful Lady Neilson gave me a small purse. "I owed your father this amount, Garnet, and I planned to settle with him this week. Now I will give it to you in his stead, and you may give your landlord his money from it." She smiled, and took my hand. "I am resigned to your decision to wait for your father's return, but you must promise me that if he does not come back within a fortnight you will come to me. You have been sheltered, and some say you've been spoiled, but that is not for me to say. If you find it necessary to come to Neilson Hall, you will be the daughter of the house. My sons are grown and I have always yearned for a daughter."

The women who had congregated before Lady Neilson arrived spoke to the Lady of the dangers to a young girl all alone, without a father to protect her. They meant well, I am sure. They were the same women who had sometimes been outspoken to my father as they gave him advice because he had no wife. We had enjoyed a very special companionship, my father and I. As they continued to speak worriedly of the fate that might befall me, I recalled how my father had laughed as he told me a few months earlier that some of the good dames resented his decision to remain a widower.

"Garnet is as soft as a princess," said Dame Clements. "How shall she do when it comes time to wash out her clothes, for she's never so much as washed a pair of her own drawers? Nor does she know how to build a fire, and you know as well as the next one, My Lady Neilson, there are times when the best of the serving women allow a fire to die. She will burn down the house in an attempt at building a fire so she can cook her own victuals."

Resenting the idea of being talked about as if I could not hear, or were too stupid to understand what was being said about me, I answered stoutly: "I know the arts of housewifery as well as any other maiden of fourteen. I'll not let the fire go out."

"But she has no one to defend her honor!" Dame Clements was a widow lady all these long years and not content with her lot, according to my father. She had been quite bold with her concern for my poor, womanless father and his poor, motherless child for as long as I could remember. "It's different with me," she went on in her high, piercing voice. "For I've two stout nephews who make their home with me. London is full of thieves and cut-throats. And a much worse danger for a small maiden like Garnet Shaw is that of menfolk who think nothing of downing an innocent lass and upping her skirts. Pray, Lady, what shall we do if she turns up with a brat? Look at the size of her. So small she barely casts a shadow."

Lady Neilson appeared to give Dame Clements' words some somber thought. At last she said she would send around one of her most trusted manservants to watch out for me. To guard me while I slept. Then, before she left, she turned to the good ladies and favored each one with her charming smile, saying, "Garnet is her mother's daughter, I understand by the words of her father, the horse doctor. She's as fair as a flower. But there is steel in the girl, for all that. She's her father's daughter as well, for George Shaw was not the man to cross. There will be no more talk of sending Garnet to a foundling home." Turning back to me, her dark eyes were sad. "And my child, you've made me a promise. I hope and pray to the good Lord Jesus that your father soon returns. He may have taken sick of a sudden, and not been able to get you word of his whereabouts. And I've heard talk of men falling prey to a lapse in memory. Of awakening and knowing not who they are, or where they've been. My Lord Neilson will see to it that a search party gets underway for him and if he is in London County, you may rest assured that he will be found. But if he does not come home or is not found within another fortnight, you will take up your abode with me." For a moment, Lady Neilson cupped her hand under my chin, forcing me to look up, and into her eyes.

"I promise, My Lady," I said. And then I experienced a most strange thing. From the backs of my heels to the nape of my neck, I felt a chill. It was awesome. For along with the chill came a loathsome foreboding as I heard a voice that was neither within me nor without, but somewhere in between, speaking clearly: *"The Lady Neilson will not live another day."*

How many times I've rebuked myself for not speaking out! How many hours of darkness I've spent in wishing I had given her the warning, for I knew it was a warning. Either that or a dire prophecy, and if these words I sensed were a foretelling of what was to come, then anything I might have said would have gone for nothing since what is to be will be. Still, I may grow old and grey and go to my grave before I will forgive myself for keeping silent.

Excuses are mere bird-droppings on the sands of sorrow and a conscience that is not at rest. My father had forbidden me to speak of the strange things that came to me without will or warning. It was all right, he'd told me, to tell him what I heard, or what I saw, but if I told others of the secret garden where bursts of unbidden ideas or warnings came, he feared I would be considered daft. Or worse, be accused of witchery. He was never visited with strange notions that came from a source outside himself, but he respected those who were gifted—or cursed—with it. My mother had the second sight. She was born with it, as I was, and her own mother and grandmother before her were said to have often been visited by unlearned knowledge. In truth, my mother forecast her own death. As I was growing up, my father told me more than once of her hysterical fear of animals. It was a fear he found hard to live with since he was a doctor of animals who enjoyed the respect of royalty when it came to healing their horses, their mastiffs, even their goats, cattle, and lambs. He could look at a favorite hunting dog that ailed and tell right away what it needed to be healed. Five minutes with a blooded horse and he knew exactly what to do to get it back on its feed. But my mother would have no animal around the house for she knew, or at least seemed to know, that her young life would end because of an animal.

"She knew. Knew, and avoided as the plague all creatures who did not walk on two feet. My Mary was an angel on this earth, but not long for it," my father repeated again and again.

A chipmunk sprang out from behind some fallen timbers as my mother went out to feed the chickens, which were two-legged creatures and gave her no fear. According to my father, the chipmunk attacked her. It bit her ankle and held on, while she stood in the chicken yard and screamed and screamed and screamed. He rushed out of the house and into the garden where he killed the little beast with his own two hands. Had to, for it would not release the grip it had on my mother's ankle. Within three days her face was swollen and purplish, and her body had taken on the look of rotting wood. When it came, her death was a mercy, but my father worshipped her memory and I never doubted him when he stated solemnly that if it had not been for me, a baby of seven months, he would have joined her in death.

Yes. I have wished a million times over that I had given Lady Neilson a warning. Dame Clements awakened me with a knock on the cottage door the very next morning with that look upon her face of one who feels the importance of bearing ill-tidings. It is a gruesome look of utter solemnity, the gurgling grin of delight only thinly hidden, the tone of voice not quite able to conceal the ghoulish joy in being able to tell of disaster:

"My Lady Neilson was murdered in her own bed as she slept, and isn't it a pity? Oh, dear, and she was always the soul of goodness. The good die young, and that's a fact, but to think one of *her* standing should come to such a foul end! They say her throat was cut from ear to ear, and let us hope death came so quickly that she didn't feel a thing. And they say that Lord Neilson is quite beside himself. Stricken with grief and shock, and had to be sedated with opium. Before he took to his bed he offered a reward of five hundred pounds to anyone who can give solid evidence against the culprit who killed her." A sly smile flickered for a moment on Dame Clements' face, but only for an instant before she went on to say in a near-whisper, "But there's some that say he did her in himself. Gossips, of course, and not a halfpenny of truth in it, but it goes to show that even the high muckety-mucks are not immune from the gossipmongers."

"Surely he had no reason to want his wife dead," I said, the first utterance I had been capable of after unbarring the door to allow Dame Clements into my house.

"I'll fix us a spot of tea, Garnet," said Dame Clements as she bustled into my kitchen without so much as a by-your-leave. "You look fair done in by the news yourself, but then you knew Lady Neilson well, seeing that your father and her were so close."

I was light-headed with shock and the memory of my premonition was coming down on me in thick, black waves of guilt because I had not warned her.

"They say he was jealous," announced Dame Clements as she stirred the coals of my hearth and added a few fagots. "One of those silent ones, what you've got to watch. Of course you and I know, Garnet, dear, that your father was not the kind of man to diddle another man's wife—especially the wife of a *lord*! But where there's smoke, there's always fire, or so I've heard, and they say Lord Neilson is the very one who did away with your father. Bided his time, then did in his Lady."

For the next few moments, my mind went blank. Dame

Clements continued to babble away, first putting the lie to the gossipmongers, then throwing in a few doubts of her own. The kettle began to boil and I watched her as if I were seeing everything through the eyes of another as she dipped her hand in the tea canister and dropped the tea into the briskly boiling water.

"There, now," she said as she reached into my cupboard for bread and butter. "I've gone and upset you, but I wanted you to be prepared, Garnet. My heart is as big as the whole out-of-doors." She put two cups down on the table and seated herself across from me. "You'll be hearing the talk, and I thought to myself that I must come right off and tell you myself, so that you'd be hearing it from a friendly mouth. But of course," and she paused to blow on her tea before she drank, then met my eyes across the table, "I don't believe a word of it myself, and neither must you. Fools' talk. That's all there is to it. Imagine the Lord Neilson spiriting away the very man who saved hundreds of his prize horses from certain death! I don't know why people want to be so mean and vicious."

I sat there woodenly, wishing time could go backwards to the day before, or even weeks ago, before my father disappeared.

"Drink your tea, Garnet," prodded Dame Clements.

"We had been to town," I said, speaking of the last day I saw my father. Never mind that I had already told the story of that day to my neighbor many times over, I could not help myself. "Father bought our noon meal at the Golden Calf. After that, we went to the market and I purchased a length of velvet for my new cape. Father stopped at the skinner's to buy me a few pelts, for he believed the winter would be severe."

All the signs of a bitter winter were on the land, he'd said, and father was one to go by nature's signs. The tree bark was tight and darker than usual. The woolly worms were already wearing their dark winter coats, and it only mid-October. All the burrowing animals were securing their winter homes early by storing nuts in their hidden nests early in the season, and even more important to my father was what he referred to as the preparation for a cold, hard winter that was being done by the birds. Those that wintered over in England instead of flying away to the warmer regions were already in the process of lining their nests with extra straw, bits of wool they'd stolen from the clothing being aired for the winter. And so my father had insisted that I have new winter boots, lined with fur. A muff of soft ermine for my hands was purchased at the General Market on Caledonia Road, along with enough ermine skin to line the hood of my cape. For himself, father obtained a quantity of lambs' wool, which I would use to line his great coat. And he bought a new beaver hat, too. He and I had made a day of it in town, laughing and talking as our hired coach sped from marketplace to marketplace. I teased and begged to be taken to the theater that night after dinner, but father said I was too young to clap eyes on such worldly displays. He said there was a woman named Eleanor Davies who wore tight-fitting breeches on the stage of the Covent Gardens Theater, and he added that he didn't care how old I was or even if I was a married woman with children of my own—he had better not catch me in a theater where women flaunted themselves in such lewdness.

After we had our supper at The Grapes, father took out the necklace he had bought for me at a shop on Bond Street, quite without my knowledge. He'd looked at me with such glowing love when he handed the package across the table. Such wonderful, warm, fatherly love when he said, "Garnet, my life, my love, I do not like to refuse your small requests. Like your mother before you, you ask so little of me. But I cannot take you to a place where women show themselves improperly, and so I give you this as a peace offering."

I unwrapped the package and gasped at the sparkling crimson bib necklace. Each one of the gems outshone the other. There were seven strands, the smallest beginning at the center of my throat and the final one hung with a diamond encrusted pendant that was fashioned in the shape of a lily. There were ear bobs to match. "Oh, father!" I looked at the dazzling necklace in awe, unable to express my gratitude.

"Your mother gave you the name, Garnet," he said softly. "And I held out for Lileth. It was my intention to give you something special for Christmas this year, but I couldn't resist it when I saw it today, and of course I couldn't wait to give it to you." Smiling ruefully, he added something to the effect that he would be hard-pressed to give me anything as valuable for Christmas, or on my birthday, which was in January. "Garnets were her favorite stones. She believed they held life within their depths."

"Father, this is all the Christmas or birthday present any girl could expect," I said quickly. I knew our circumstances. We were not rich, and even though I had no idea how costly the necklace and ear bobs were, I had sense enough to know they were worth a small fortune.

Sitting there across from Dame Clements, I wondered why I had had no premonition concerning my father's disappearance.

"If he is dead," I swore, "then surely I would *feel* it!"

"Your sainted mother would have known," answered Dame Clements. "The combination of Romany and Gaul in her blood would have told her. But you are not your mother, Garnet. And you're naught but a young girl. Now that your would-be benefactress is dead, you must look to your old friends for help." With covetous eyes, she looked around the nicely appointed cottage. "I could allow one of my nephews to go home to his mother, who is poorly anyway and could do with a strong young man about the place. My older nephew, Wilburn, thinks highly of you, Garnet. If you were properly wed to him there would be no wrong in the sight of man or God if you slept with him in the one bedchamber where you've slept alone all these years, and I could make do quite nicely with your father's chamber."

In spite of my shock and sorrow over the death of Lady Neilson, added to the heavy burden of worry over my father, my ability to think clearly did not fail me. Dame Clements' cottage was a mere hovel compared with our own. Her floors were earthen, while ours were wood. Her two loutish nephews slept on straw pallets on the floor, while she kept the only bedchamber for herself. It was a mean little room without a window, much smaller than our keeping room. I did not give her the satisfaction of an answer to her preposterous notion.

"How much did Lady Neilson give you yesterday?" Dame Clements' slate-colored eyes met mine and in their depths was unmitigated greed.

"One hundred pounds," I answered truthfully. And then I lied: "And I have already taken it to Mr. Christianson, at the Bank of England, who has taken care of my father's finances for as long as I can remember."

Looking disappointed, she asked when I did it, and I informed her that I had gone to the bank straightaway, immediately after Lady Neilson left. And I added, "So if someone comes to the house with the intention of taking what is rightfully mine since my father had the money coming, they will be badly disappointed. I have kept out only five bob."

"It's just as well, I suppose," said the woman as she looked mournfully into her tea cup. "And actually, I'm that relieved, for a hundred pounds is a lot of money to have in the house." She frowned as she bit into a morsel of bread. "Now, tell me again about the night your father left you in the tavern."

"Why?" Her curiosity had always astounded me, but aside from that, I had repeated the tale so many times I was quite sure she knew the details as well as I.

"My nephew, the older one who has taken a fancy to you, is in thick with the constables. Wilburn plans to go to his friends and make a statement on your behalf concerning your father's disappearance, and well you might thank him for his pains, missy. No use in you heaving a long sigh, for Wilburn is a fine figure of a young man and as smart as a whip, too. Having a hundred pounds in the bank and a few sticks of furniture does not make you into a young lady of noble birth. Without a husband, you could lose all of your worldly goods. Better you should give over everything to Wilburn as soon as you're married, and the quicker you consent, the better off you'll be."

Ignoring the part about consenting to wed Wilburn, I said, "My father was looking out the window of the tavern where we had just dined and where he had given me this garnet necklace, when he shoved back his chair and said he must cross the street to the Owl and the Pussycat to speak to a farmer about a debt. He said the farmer was long past due in settling up the account, and there he was, entering the tavern. The farmer had not hesitated one whit to get my father up out of his bed in the middle of the night to help out with a difficult calving just a week before, and he'd promised to pay up the next day."

"And did he mention the man's name?"

"No. He did not. He told me to stay where I was, and ordered a pastry for me. I finished it, ordered more tea, and still he did not come. I waited for a very long time." To my dismay, my eyes filled with tears as I went back over that hour and a half of waiting and wondering what to do. It seemed silly, for even though I was young, I was old enough to know that crying doesn't help. After I had regained my composure, I spoke of going to the owner of the tavern and explaining that I must go across the street, since I was worried about my father. The tavern keeper didn't mention the sum my father owed him for our dinner. He merely said my father was an honorable man, and he also tried to get me to allow him to send a lackey to the Owl and the Pussycat since it is not a place of good repute. By then I was too upset to think of the proprieties, and I insisted on going myself."

"But Mr. Shaw wasn't there." Dame Clements made a statement.

"No. He was not there; the tavern keeper said he'd been there, but he went out the back door, after talking to a man who had stopped in for a spot of ale. He left with yet another man, who had come up to him and spoken about a horse that was down and couldn't get up."

"So you went back to the tavern where you had supped and waited for another hour or more. Then you came home."

"That's right, but I would appreciate it very much if you would ask your nephew not to go to the Constable."

"Why not? You've nothing to hide."

Without meeting her eyes, I made up a white lie. "It's just that I don't care to add to the rumors that you've just now told me are rampant." My true reason for asking her nephew to refrain from checking into the matter on my behalf was simply that I did not like Wilburn Foy. Nor would I consider

15

marriage with him. He was attractive enough, but he could neither read nor write, and he spoke roughly, and had no manners at all.

"Wilburn is willing to do anything to help you, Garnet. After you are his wife, you'll be grateful to have a strong shoulder to lean on."

I stood up and slammed the palm of my hand on the table so hard that the teacups jumped and clattered. Looking down at Dame Clements, I shouted, "I am not a piece of goods to be bargained for, to be purchased by the first buyer! I will not marry Wilburn. I will not marry *anyone*, unless I find someone I can love as well as my father loved my mother!"

"You'll get into trouble with notions like that," screamed my neighbor. "Love isn't for the likes of us. It's for the *gentry*! Why, even then, the husbands and wives don't love one *another*! They tie the knot in order to keep the money and the land in the proper *families*. To form a combination to increase their powers. If they love at all, they love out of wedlock. You're smart in some things, Garnet Shaw, but you're mighty dumb in others."

"So be it!" I glared at her as I calmed down and spoke coldly. "But I'm not so dumb that I don't know when someone is trying to beat me out of my possessions and the little money I have."

Dame Clements got clumsily to her feet, muttering about ingrates who bite the hands that offer to feed them, about thinking of me as her very own daughter all these years. And then she said something for which I knew I would never forgive her: "Like father, like daughter. All these years we've lived side by side, and him without a woman, me without a man. But no, the likes of me's not good enough for him. Got to go diddling around with a proper Lady. Well, he ended up by getting both of them killed, and for all of me the same thing can happen to you, my proud beauty."

Livid with rage, I opened the door, yelling at the top of my lungs. "Out! Get out of here with that lying tongue of yours!"

Until that very moment I was not aware of my violent nature, and when I realized how close I had come to picking up anything at hand and bashing in my neighbor's head, I was both alarmed and ashamed. Excuses again! I had been through days and days of agonized worry, not knowing if my beloved father was dead or alive, which may have contributed to my lack of control. To have his name besmirched by one of Dame Clements' ilk was enough to madden me. I had long enjoyed the reputation of being Mr. George Shaw's sweet little daughter. Never before had I so much as raised my voice in anger. But I had shouted at her. Wanted to kill her. Actually lusted to see her blood.

As I tried to pull my shattered nerves together by sitting down to a cup of fresh tea that I had brewed for myself, I kept pushing away the horrid words that came to me from out of nowhere:

If you didn't partially believe there was some truth in her wicked accusations about your father and Lady Neilson, you would not have allowed yourself to go so crazy.

Again and again, I denied the awful possibility that my father and Lady Neilson might have been...enjoying a relationship that went beyond that of animal doctor and Lady of the Manor. Scenes drifted through my head with the speed of lightning. The day he took me to the imposing stone house on the hill—never before had he taken me with him on his calls, and I had been surprised when he told me to dress in my plum-colored gown because he wanted me to look my best. It did not seem unreasonable for me to visualize my doting father as one who would take his adored daughter to the home of the woman he cared about. His nature would have ordered him to let the woman he cared for gaze upon his cherished child. He had said, "Put pink ribbons in your hair, Garnet."

Indeed. He *had* wanted me to look my best.

Yes. And they had exchanged long glances. Whether they were loving glances or not, I had no way of knowing. At the time, I didn't give them a thought. I remembered asking about Lord Neilson. The Lady had said he was out of town. We had sat down to high tea, and I was enraptured by the shell-thin cups, the delicate band of gold at the rims, the Neilson crest on the saucers, even on the napery. The scones were flaky and rich, and Lady Neilson had touched my hair once and said, "Your father has told me your mother was a great beauty, with golden brown hair and enormous eyes almost as black as night. A wonderful lady who left him bereft. And he has said you favor her. It is good that you were left to him to fill the emptiness of his heart."

It seemed strange to consider the idea of a man speaking to his lover of his dead wife—but then, my father had loved my mother and it would have been like him to speak of her.

Another scene brought a quick cry of anguish to my lips. My father and I were in a carriage that would take us to Picadilly Circus. Just as the carriage came to a stop, a handsomely painted coach went by at high speed, and I was frightened by a face that peered at me from behind the parted curtains. It happened a week or two before father disappeared. As I tightened my hold on my father's arm, I said to him, "The coach that went flying by, father—an old man stared out the window at me, did you notice?"

"That was the Neilson coach," he answered nonchalantly. "Lord Neilson is feeling poorly, I understand. You've nothing to fear from him, daughter. A man in pain sometimes looks as if he could bite a man's head off. I doubt that he even saw you."

"But he's an *old* man! Lady Neilson is much younger and so lovely!"

"He's some years older than his Lady, but I wouldn't say he's old."

Father had sounded so reasonable. With a twinkle of amusement in his eyes he reminded me that just a year earlier I had looked at him and asked him how it felt to be an old man. It was true, but during the year that had passed I had matured. My father was handsome and dashing at thirty and nine. Tall, slender, kind...I had closed my eyes and shuddered at the idea of the lovely blonde Lady Neilson being intimate with an old, fat, ugly and wrinkled man.

"No!" I picked up my empty tea cup and threw it against the stone hearth. Without thinking or planning, I left the house, unable to withstand the doubts and questions that battered at my very soul.

From the time I left until I came to myself mingling with hordes of people in the disreputable Newgate district, I don't remember a thing. God knows how long I wandered about, how many blocks I covered as I walked along. I asked myself what I was doing there, among the crowd that had apparently gathered in order to see a man hanged.

I moaned, looked down at the ground, anywhere but the gruesome scaffold. A woman cackled in my ear, brash as brass as she asked another woman if she thought they'd hear the prisoner's neck pop. Another one, smelling of rancid grease and onions, ordered me to move. I was obstructing her view. "I get a real big rush of happiness when I see 'em hung," she said. "Ain't no chit of a girl goin' to stand in front of me."

Feeling sick, I made my way out of the crowd, receiving several jabs by elbows and getting my feet stepped on many times. When I walked into the first tavern I came to, I was dizzy, and having a hard time of it to stand erect. A steadying hand came out of nowhere and held my arm.

"Easy, my darling," said a wondrously melodic voice. I looked up, startled, into a pair of hypnotic blue eyes, a long, slender nose that was certainly aristocratic, and a smiling mouth. Before I could say a word, the man who possessed the most handsome features I had ever seen, even in my dreams, leaned down and kissed me full on the lips.

God help me. I responded.

Two

My world spun crazily as my hands came up to push at the man who held me so tightly. A part of me wanted to cling to him in an attempt to keep that moment forever, while another part of me seemed to be standing by and looking on with disapproval, full of righteousness.

There were so many people crowded into the tavern, most of them standing and milling around, and during those wild moments of that unexpected embrace I was aware of other hands that pushed against me from all sides, uncaring, unaware of what was taking place. Still another pair of hands was rough against my right shoulder while a shrill woman's voice shouted in my ear.

"Get away from him, you little tart! Get your filthy hands off Lord Muldoon!"

When the kiss was over, and whether it was ended by my own actions, the strange, pouty-faced woman's, or the man who held me so fleetingly, yet so wondrously, I was never to know—suddenly the place was in an even greater turmoil, with all manner of voices raised in some kind of mad, weird chant that was accompanied by the stamping of feet and the clapping of hands.

Sweaty men and women crushed in on me, mostly men. The scent of powder and perfume mingled with vinegar and garlic. Smoke arose in the air from birds roasting on spits, and all around me were rough men, tawdry women. Fearing for my life, I tried to find an opening in the sea of human flesh that surrounded me, and for a moment I feared that I was being deliberately trapped. After a while, when I had slipped past the wild mob and made my way to the door, I realized that the revelers were merely massed together, intent on their own pursuits, and my presence was just a happenstance, for no hand held me back.

Before I stepped out into the sunshine, however, I couldn't resist a backward glance into the crazily swaying, laughing, joking crowd in search of the handsome stranger who had kissed me. Even so, my face was flaming as I hurried down the street, mindful of my upbringing, my head spinning with recriminations along with a vow to be more careful in the future. My father had warned me about certain taverns where unsavory characters congregated. No matter that I had been shaken. I should have stayed clear of a place I knew nothing about. Yet with my scolding inner voice came another shameful idea: *For one who had been so positive that she could take care of herself, I had not turned in a passable performance. Not only had I inadvertently stumbled into a den of iniquity, I had behaved foolishly, even disgracefully, by allowing myself to be kissed by a stranger.*

Across the cobbled streets the crowds that had come to watch the hanging had begun to disperse, but with reluctance. My footsteps quickened for I did not want to become engulfed in the high-spirited, excited mob that had congregated to see a human being die on the gallows. My father had deplored the lustful joy of those who found sport in such things, I remembered. He'd spoken of them as dangerous, as if the people who came as spectators to a public hanging became a part of a living, breathing mass that was barely human. "They come away," he had said, "in a state of high expectation. Something shameful comes over them when hundreds of people mass together to witness a man's death." He had likened the mass-behavior to stampeding cattle—mindless, untamed and violent—and he had referred to the spark of reason that separates the humans from the animals, saying that spark is absent for a time just after an execution.

My footsteps lagged as I walked along the streets, and I realized I was both hungry and bone-tired. I had no way of knowing how long I had walked along in a semi-daze after I left the house, but judging by the hunger pangs, several hours must have elapsed since I had eaten. A look at the sun told me it was past midday. Dame Clements had come early in the morning to awaken me from my rest. Although she had eaten bread, I had not, which meant that my supper of the night before was the last time I had partaken of food. At last I was in a neighborhood that I recognized, and the little shops that lined the streets sent tempting aromas of cooking meats and baking breads into the air. My mouth watered as I neared a chocolate shop where fine ladies were arriving and leaving. I entered, feeling suddenly weak and shaken, and no wonder. The clock on the brick wall was just then striking the hour, and it was two o'clock in the afternoon. After I had selected a bun stacked high with bits of meat, I chose a sweetmeat and a mug of chocolate, which I took to a corner table, barely able to sit myself down before I began to devour the food. When the last crumb of the sweetmeat was no more than a lingering delight on my tongue, I arose to buy another cup of chocolate, only to find my way barred by a tall figure in immaculate attire and a knowing smile on his face. It was the stranger who had kissed me.

Staring at the handsome man, I was unable to do a thing but stand there with my mouth open. The pouty-faced woman had said he was a lord, I remember thinking. But she was no longer at his side. He was quite alone, and smiling down at me as if I might be a choice morsel displayed inside the shop.

"The little maid of the Boar's Head," he said with a dazzling smile. "And with nutmeats on your cheeks, a mustache of chocolate on your upper lip."

"You followed me," I said accusingly, the empty chocolate cup in my hand.

"On the contrary. My presence is a mere coincidence, but I find it a happy one. Allow me to replenish your mug. You're a slender little minx, obviously in need of sustenance." His voice was melodious, his eyes capable of stopping a bird in mid-flight with one glance, or so it seemed to me at the moment. "What is your name?"

Against my will, I answered him. "Garnet. Garnet Shaw."

"You are lovely. A jewel in a cinder patch. I find it strange that a beautiful young creature who is obviously no serving girl should be walking about the streets of London all alone. Stumbling into questionable taverns and risking her lovely young neck. Do you not know the dangers on the streets, Garnet Shaw?"

Tears filled my eyes at his gentle rebuke. In my misery, I nodded and looked down, away from him, anywhere but into his strangely compelling eyes. My hands were trembling and if he had not taken the chocolate mug from me I would have dropped it. At last, I said, "I know full well the dangers of the streets, sir—"

"I am the young Lord Muldoon. Jonathan is my given name. How does it happen that you have no serving woman with you? No guardian of your person on these crowded streets?"

"I have no one, and I have recently suffered a severe shock," I answered truthfully. And then my sense of what is right and what is wrong came to my rescue. With dignity, I said, "But I have recovered, and by your leave, Lord Muldoon, I shall be on my way. As you have guessed, I am not a street woman, nor am I a person to be accosted inside a chocolate shop."

He touched my cheek, and the place where his finger caressed me turned as hot as coals. "God's eyeballs," he said in a near whisper. "Never have I seen such a fetching piece. Such sooty lashes, such glorious skin. A fresh and succulent berry in the midst of rotting fruit!" He sighed. I curtsied. He bowed. I walked away with my head held high but my heart, I was sure, forever changed.

No matter that I was a step above the serving class, the titled gentry was not for the likes of me. A pussycat may look at a queen. A lord may dally with a seller of brooms or a flower girl, and a lady may enjoy herself with a groom or a chimney sweep, but I was not brought up to cheapen myself by becoming a titled gentleman's toy. My doting father had taught me to read and write. The library in our home was filled with books and I had been privileged to learn many things that most young women of my station would never know. Therefore I knew of the powerful Lord Muldoon, whose holdings covered the entire County of Northampton.

Fine linens were made in and around the city of Wycombe as well as the most delicious of breads, wines and ales. Cord fabrics from Warwick Town added to his coffers. The soaps from Coventry were so fine and so expensive that they were used by the Queen and her ladies-in-waiting, and everyone who knew anything was aware that Ely was the undisputed home of fine leather goods. Lady Neilson herself had mentioned that her saddlery came from Ely, and she was the most renowned horsewoman in the County of London.

As I set my feet on the path toward home I reminded myself of all those things, but I also knew a sense of bitterness at the way things were. No. Absolutely not. Young Lord Muldoon was not for the likes of me, but by all that was holy, I would not have Wilburn Foy. It was not fair, I raged in silence as I trudged along the darkening streets, to have touched the tip of my tongue to honey and at the same time to know that I would never again taste it. But I was damned if I would accept weak gruel. No use in being silly. No sense in wasting time on thoughts of what might have been, but it was difficult to keep myself from yearning after the one man I had seen in my short life who had been capable of lifting my heart and setting my senses to reeling. At the time, my life did not seem short, though. At fourteen, one does not accept the realization of one's own immaturity. I had read the great literature and deep in my heart I expected the kind of romantic love that I had found in the books, although at the time I didn't realize it. All I knew was a deep sense of injustice. I might as well have been a scullery maid, or a street urchin, when it came to dreaming of love with a lord.

It occurred to me that it was grossly unfair of my father to bring me up to expect what I could never have, for he had known as well as the next one that there is no breeching the gap between commoners and the gentry. I kicked at a pile of fallen leaves in my frustration and rage, and for the first time I understood the meaning behind Samuel Pepys' comments that ignorance is bliss. Better to have remained as ignorant as a peasant girl than to set myself up for something that could never be mine.

By the time I reached home I had settled myself down somewhat. In spite of her uncanny ability to know much of the future, I had been told that my mother was uncommonly sensible and my father, who had admitted that he was a dreamer, had often commented that it was probably a good thing for the both of us that I had inherited my mother's logical mind. As I entered my house I counted my assets. I was fourteen, healthy, reasonably attractive and not without funds, so I should be counting my blessings. If I could keep myself out of trouble by showing my neighbors that I was capable of taking care of myself I would not be forced into a marriage with Wilburn Foy—or anyone else that I detested. Lady Neilson had given me one hundred pounds. No mean sum, but on the other hand, it would not last me forever. Even if I lived frugally, a hundred pounds would soon dwindle away if I dipped into it often.

Frowning, I sat down at the table and tried to fathom where my father might have put any other monies he might have had at the time of his disappearance. He'd never been one to be saving, and he'd spent quite a bit during our last day together, I reminded myself. Sadly, I looked at my hands. They were soft and well tended, for every morning and every evening I rubbed them well with a compound my father made from lanolin and oil of bergamot. But I could sew a fine seam, and I could do embroidery work that was the envy of everyone who looked at it. Many had remarked that my embroidery was fit for the gowns of royalty. Perhaps I could augment my slender resources by calling upon my father's wealthy clients and giving them a sample of my work.

It seemed reasonable to believe that I could eke out a living in such a way. Since I had been keeping his accounts for the past four years I knew their names and where they lived. We had never owned a horse of our own, or a conveyance, but I could get about the streets of London and environs by hiring a rig, just as my father had before me. But I could not go unaccompanied. That was out of the question. Not only would I be endangered by footpads, cut-throats and thieves, I would be the target of gossip and speculation. In no time at all, I would be considered a harlot. Already, I had risked all kinds of dangers by rushing headlong into the streets after the disturbing discussion with Dame Clements.

Very well, when morning came I would risk setting out on foot once more by going to the street where Thelma lived. She would come back and work for me, I was sure, for she had been tearful when she left. She could continue to work as always by gathering fagots for our cooking fire, taking care of the marketing, and sharing the housework and cooking. More important, she would accompany me on my rounds. If she had promised to stay on with her present employer, then I would be forced to find someone else. Meanwhile, I must make ready my wares if I intended to sell my services as a seamstress.

For the next hour or so, I busied myself by going through my own gowns and selecting the most impressive to show to prospective customers. After all those long days when I spent most of my time feverishly pacing the floor and wondering what had happened to my father, it was good to be busy, but not once did I mentally consider the idea that he would not, someday, return. It was unthinkable to dwell on the possibility that he would not. No matter the crushing awareness that had descended upon me earlier in the day that there was a grain of truth in the gossip about a liason between the animal doctor and the Lady Neilson. I couldn't allow myself to think about it. Nor could I allow myself to give in to the urge to fall into daydreams about the dashing young Lord Muldoon. Every time I saw his handsome face before me, I quickly closed my eyes and concentrated on the task at hand. I was to be a businesswoman, I reminded myself sternly. Little girls of five were sent out on the streets to sell flowers. Little boys of the same age made their daily rounds as chimney sweeps, and many of them worked long, hard hours in the mines. I was lucky. I would not have to apprentice myself to a weaver, or a baker. Winter was coming on and I would have to buy coal for my fire. I no longer had my father to depend on, so I must fall upon my own resources, but I was fortunate to have a talent to fall back upon, I kept reminding myself.

When darkness fell, I lit a candle, ate a bit of bread and cheese, brewed a pot of tea and looked with satisfaction at the display of beautiful gowns I would show as proof of my skill with the needle. To me, each one of the garments that were draped around the room was more fetching than the other. The flickering fire and the flame of the candle caused the beads on the peacock blue gown to shimmer. The white silk with the masses of violets I had so painstakingly embroidered gleamed. The velvets, the satins looked opulent. There were other items, too, that would show the world I was an expert in milady's fashions. Satin slippers for the only ball I had ever attended were encrusted with glittering green glass to match the green ball gown of corded silk.

A smile played about my lips in spite of my sorrow and worries as I remembered how my father had extravagantly insisted that I purchase the fabric and set to work at once, as soon as he came home with the invitation. The ball was to be held at Kildeer Mansion, in celebration of Lord Kildeer's marriage to the Lady Katherine Spurgeon. She was his second wife, his first one having succumbed to smallpox several years earlier. How excited my father had been, and how droll, too! It was almost as if he were there in the same room with me, speaking the words over again:

"It is to be the occasion of the season, Garnet. The Lady Katherine is very young. Sixteen, to Lord Kildeer's fifty and three, but he will be more than a match for her, you may lay to that. And she is as pretty a girl as I've ever seen, except for you and your mother before you. They're an old and respected family, but Lord Spurgeon has accumulated so many gambling debts that the family is in dire need—else the Lady Katherine would not have been promised to a man old enough to be her grandfather."

Lord Kildeer's stables were the finest in all of England, according to my father. Even better than the King's own, but of course he would never have dared to say such a thing to anyone but his daughter. His horses were another matter, however. They could not begin to compare with those which were bred by Lord and Lady Neilson. "Too short in the cannon, too fat in the hock," he'd said with high disapproval, "but there are those who favor one breed over others, and they'll continue to breed their unfortunate choice forever and ever."

It was a mere eight months ago that we attended the ball.

Looking back, it seemed much longer, but only because so many dreadful things had happened during the last fortnight. It was cold that night. February was raw and bitter, and the fog had come in the day before, casting all of London Town in a dense pall that was made worse by the clouds of acrid smoke from fireplaces. As I prepared myself for sleep I looked backwards to that night when we had set out in the coach, father wrapping me from head to foot in blankets against the cold.

We had attended. But we didn't mingle with the titled guests, nor did we dance. Everything was proper right down to the last napkin ring, and proprieties negated the animal doctor and his daughter doing any active participating. But it had been enough to be there and see the magnificent sights. Bejeweled and wigged gentlewomen vied with one another for the limelight, but all of them paled alongside the gorgeous Lady Katherine, who had become Lady Kildeer at four o'clock that afternoon.

"She is beautiful," my father whispered, "but not as beautiful as you."

I was sure he was wrong. The Lady Katherine had golden hair piled high on her head, and like mine, it was unsullied by powder. My father disapproved of young ladies of just-past-thirteen indulging in paints, but he allowed me to use a scent. Her eyes were a peculiar, very startling shade of aquamarine blue, and her gown exactly matched her eyes. Mentally, I made a note to include the flamboyant, but of late scandalous, Lady Katherine Kildeer in my itinerary of prospective clients. I cared not a whit who she was sleeping with. Lord Kildeer danced to her every tune. He fawned over her in public and followed her around like a puppy dog, which he had done at the ball. And my father's assumption that her elderly husband would be able to keep her content had proved wrong. She had taken a lover. They went out in public, sometimes with the old lord in attendance, but just as often the Lady Katherine and the young groom, John Pembroke, kept their own company. At a fair in July I had seen them kissing as they stepped down from Lord Kildeer's handsomely outfitted coach. Then the lord himself had appeared, looking at his young wife and her lover with a kind of crushed expression in his watery blue eyes, and then—so help me—he smiled. And patted his wife on her golden head just as if it were a very natural, even delightful thing for her to be doing.

"He's daft over her," my father had said. "Lost every one of his brains." Then he'd confided in me that the old lord slept alone while the Lady Katherine slept with her groom.

I had looked at him in surprise. "Who told you such a thing?"

"Lord Kildeer. He said it was enough to have her there in the house, so he could look at her. So he could touch her face, and run his fingers through her golden hair."

Against my will, I recalled the night of the ball and the glance that had been exchanged between my father and Lady Neilson. They had not spoken a word to one another, but I had seen her look at him, and just at that moment I looked at him and saw what I realized, there in the darkness of my bedroom, was a look of exceeding joy mixed with sorrow. And in the silence of the room my voice was loud in my ears as I cried out, "Oh, God! Oh, no!"

It was then that I accepted what a part of me had known all along, but refused to acknowledge. My father and the late Lady Neilson had been lovers. And that ruined old man had either killed him or had him killed, just as he had killed his wife.

Lord Neilson was not cut from the same cloth as Lord Kildeer.

I went stiff as a board, my senses throbbing with the instinctive knowledge of my heart. Dead! He was dead and I had no choice but to face it. All along, I think I had known. But the mind does not always allow us to comprehend knowledge, especially if it is painful. For several hours I remained rigid as I silently mourned my father. It didn't occur to me to bring charges against a lord. There was no proof. I was a mere child. No one would come forth to help me bring him to justice, and it was not the first time a man had taken deadly steps in order to remove the horns from his head. Down through history, Kings had killed their Queens with amazing regularity for having committed adultery, and usually they murdered the Queens' paramours. Publicly, by execution, or privately with poison or some other means—it didn't matter. It was done by royalty and members of the upper classes. Except for a week or so of raging gossip and speculation, no penalty was ever paid—not even if the woman happened to be innocent.

It wasn't until dawn had begun to barely lighten the sky that I slept, and then I was as dead to the world as I felt my father to be. At ten, I awakened in a state of urgency, only dimly remembering the grand plans I had for the day until after I had been up and about for a half hour. When I saw all my finery laid out in the dining room, I remembered, and hastened through a sketchy breakfast before I left in search of Thelma.

What was done could not be undone. Vowing never to admit my realization of the night before concerning my father, I prepared to set forth. A glance inside my purse showed me I must reach into the secret cache, for I hadn't the price of a conveyance, and the residence on Yardley Lane where Thelma had found work was better than three miles away.

"Oh, no!" Dumbly, I looked into the empty square where I had put the pound notes Lady Neilson had given me. It could *not* be empty!

But it was empty.

An hour later, I came back to myself after giving vent to the madness that had consumed me when I found myself bereft of the pounds I had so confidently expected to see me through until I was on my own. Only with great difficulty did I recall the hour that had passed, and even then I knew I had been so lost in madness that I remembered very little of it.

Strands of my hair were wrapped around my hands where I had pulled at it frantically as I ran from room to room. There were claw marks on my arms where I had scratched at myself like a crazed, trapped animal, and rents in the frock I had donned so confidently as I prepared to journey forth, where I had torn at it with my fingernails, or even bitten at it with my teeth, for all I knew. I could remember screaming insane things at the four walls of the kitchen. And flinging myself against doors and furnishings. At one point, I was sure I had cowered on the floor, my back against a bench, my head buried in my hands as I contemplated various ways to kill myself.

But I stamped my foot and swore. No. I would *not* kill myself. I might kill someone else, but not myself. After I had wiped the blood from my arms, washed my face, done up my hair and donned a fresh gown, I opened the front door and looked across the way to Dame Clements' cottage. As I covered the distance, I ground my teeth together, visualizing myself in the process of clawing the woman's eyes out. My hundred pounds had been stolen. Only she could have discerned the hiding place, and of course she'd not believed my story of taking the money to the bank. And I would get it back, or I would kill her.

Three

The house was empty. By the looks of things, the Clements family had made a hasty departure, because several items of clothing were strewn about on the earthen floor and there was even a five pound note among the debris. I snatched it up and looked at it through a red glare of rage, stuffed it down the front of my bodice and continued to look around at the leavings of thieves who had fled in the night. While I slept, they'd all left. Or maybe they'd packed up their few necessities and run with my money before I had even come home on the afternoon before.

When I wasn't cursing myself for being a fool—God knows I should have realized the scum they were, had sense enough to know Dame Clements would have put two and two together and realized I'd not had time to put the money in the bank—well, when I wasn't flailing at myself I was mentally cursing the absent, thieving Clements family. However, the human condition is full of unexpected quirks, and even as I yelled and screamed and used all the street words I had overheard, but kept my father from knowing I knew, I began to laugh. Maybe it was the laughter of one who is demented, but even now when I recall that dreadful time a smile of amusement comes to my lips. A cat caused it. A black and white cat that had probably strolled in through the wide open door to see what she could see. She swished her tail back and forth and looked up at me with a bemused expression, but it was more than the look she wore that sent me into gales of laughter. It was the thing on her back. I had seen Dame Clements wear that food-stained, filthy old stomacher at least a hundred times. She had no sense of style at all, for she wore it over just any old kind of dress, mixing colors indiscriminately as well as fabrics. Anyway, it was entirely out of date with its embroidered panels, orange tassels, and fringe of silver.

Speaking aloud to the cat, I said, "You look much more exotic, little tabby, than Dame Clements did when she wore it, although it's for the belly, not the bottom." Somehow, the cat had become entangled in the tattered ribbons. Her quickly swishing tail and her lithe movements had caused the outlandish garment to slide backward, tassels falling gracefully over her behind parts, adding a certain flair to the whole picture. And so I laughed. I fell to my knees and finally had to put my hands down on the dirt floor in order to keep from falling flat on my face as I howled. Tears streamed down my face. My side ached, and I still laughed. And all the while the cat continued to stare at me with a solemn expression on its face, a sedate demeanor, as if I wounded her dignity by my convulsive laughter.

Nothing of promise had been left in the Clements household except for the five-pound note. As soon as I could squelch the high-pitched giggles that pealed forth against my will, I arose and walked unsteadily back to my own dear house.

Five pounds. I sat on the floor and stared at it in much the same way that the tabby cat had stared at me. It wasn't much. Not enough for what I wanted to do—but oddly enough, I felt relieved after my uncontrollable laughter had run its course. I also felt silly, because I was still inclined to burst out into laughter, and there was nothing, absolutely nothing for me to laugh about. I was alone in the world, with five pounds to my name. There was precious little food in the house, winter was coming on, I was practically destitute. A glance at my fine costumes gave me little hope. I knew the location of the pawnbrokers, but I doubted if I would get a fraction of their worth, and further, if I put my clothing up for collateral, I would have no proof of my worth as a seamstress.

All right, then, I would keep three of the very finest

costumes I owned and pawn all the rest. The garnets were warm at my neck and I touched them lovingly before I threw fagots on the fire. Until then, I hadn't given the jewels a thought, but surely they would bring much, much more at a pawnshop than my frocks. But it distressed me greatly to think of parting with my father's last gift. I wasn't in the humor to try to persuade myself that I would only leave the garnets in the pawnshop for a little while—just long enough to get on my feet. If I did not come back to claim them within thirty days *and* with the amount of money I had borrowed, plus interest, they would be sold. I knew all about such transactions. Once, during a period of near-famine, my father had pawned his boots and a few of the instruments he used to help with the birthing of calves. He had never redeemed them. It sickened me to think of losing the beautiful necklace, but I had nothing else. My mother's jewelry had been buried with her. I had a little enameled watch that was worn on a ribbon around my waist, but it had not worked for several months. So the garnets must go, for I could not eat them.

It took but little time for me to prepare myself for my distasteful business. Although gentlemen of fashion were wearing their hair long and careful waves or curls when they chose not to wear wigs, ladies were going through a period of studied carelessness in their hairdress. I wore mine loose and flowing, so all I had to do was comb it. For the street that day, I chose a raspberry-colored silk overdress with the skirt pulled back to expose an ivory underskirt with raspberry-colored flowers embroidered down the front and along the hem. The petticoat was embroidered as well, and of the same color as the underskirt. Although the neckline was not cut high, it was not over-revealing. I wanted to look as if I came from a home that was affluent enough to have gifted me with a splendid garnet necklace, but I didn't want to look overdressed. My mules were satin, and of the same fabric as the overdress. Since we were quickly approaching the season, the streets were packed with the young dandies who were already strolling along to show off their finery. My costume was sedate compared with the beribboned, belaced men of fashion with their towering wigs, their tasseled walking sticks and canes. I saw several men carrying muffs, even though the weather had not turned cold enough to warrant them, but then I remembered it was now fashionable for men to comb their hair in public, so I supposed they used the little pockets inside their beaver muffs for their combs. Such simpering! Such posturing! And the trail of scent was almost odious. My father would never have dressed himself in such outlandish attire, nor would he have preened and prinked so. Suddenly I found myself recalling the immaculate white lace, the stunning black coat of the handsome man who had kissed me on the day before. I doubted very much if he would deign to present himself in public as a popinjay.

Random thoughts fled as I entered the pawnbroker's shop on Lombard Street, for I was very much aware of my tender years and fearful that I would be asked to bring my parent or a guardian. The man said nothing alarming, however. He merely took the necklace, still warm from my flesh, and looked at it as if it were paste. I was trembling inwardly.

After a long while, he said, "I can give you a few bob. Seven is my limit."

"But the workmanship is exquisite," I said with as much determination as I could muster. His offer made me feel as if my insides were about to spill out on the floor. "And those are beautiful garnets. The diamonds on the pendant are big, too."

"It's a pretty little trinket, but there's not much demand for jewelry this year. You ladies have turned into sparrows and even the courtesans seldom wear a bauble. I'm doing you a favor to give you seven bob."

"But it's worth far more than that," I protested. "I just can't—"

"Take it or leave it, little lady," the man said as he pushed the sparkling gems toward me. "I'm being fair and square with you. Even if I give you seven bob, I'll not make out on it since it will have to sit around and collect dust until the ladies begin to deck themselves in baubles again." He shook his head, and added, "Faugh! Dame Fashion has each and every one of you at her mercy. Well, what do you say, little lady?"

"No!" Grabbing the precious necklace in my right hand, I turned and stumbled blindly from the shop, dismayed at the sudden tears in my eyes. I was sure my father had paid at least twenty pounds for it, and probably much more. Unmindful of the jostling crowds, I fastened it at the back of my neck as I walked along the street, intent on finding another pawnbroker. I thought I remembered one a few doors down, but either the proprietors had moved elsewhere or I was mistaken. When I finally found the shop, I was exhausted, for it was a long, long walk and my feet hurt. Out of breath, I had to pause for a moment before I could state my business. And then I had no breath at all, for when I reached to unclasp the necklace, it wasn't there.

No use in going into the dreary details of the next few weeks except to say that the five pounds I had so carefully pinned inside my bodice was gone, too. The streets of London teemed with thieves and I had been careless. Carefully I hoarded my small store of provender, forcing it to last for many days. Fortunately there was about a quarter of a pound of tea in the canister, for after the last crumb of food was gone I was forced to subsist for may days on weak tea with nothing for sweetening. On the fifth day of going without food, I filched a bun from a bakery and had it half gobbled down when I was apprehended as I ran down the street, both terror-stricken at what I had done, and still determined to assuage my consuming hunger. I swallowed the last morsel just when the policeman grabbed my shoulder.

"You'll come quietly, miss," he said in a low voice. "There's a law agin' takin' that which don't belong to you and you were seen, fair and square." In the depths of his eyes was a sorrow, or so it seemed to me. His next words underscored his sadness. "A lass dressed in finery, more is the pity. Silks and plumage fit for a queen. Surely you've fallen on bad days to risk being jailed over a bit of a bun."

"I was hungry. I've pawned all my clothes save for the dress I have on my back," I cried out. "But the men who run the pawnshops weren't fair with me. What am I to do to fill my empty stomach?" In spite of myself, I burst into tears as I sobbed out all my pent-up frustrations. "They're unfair. The lot of them. Far more guilty than I am of theft. And I had a necklace, but it was stolen from my neck, along with the small amount of money I had left to my name after I was robbed. And I'm an orphan girl to boot, without a friend in the world."

The baker man came running up on his little bowed legs, his fat jowls trembling as he vilified me for a thief. He said a man couldn't make an honest living, that he was sick and tired of having his baked goods stolen the minute they were out of the oven. The law man pleaded my case, pointing out that I was a starved little wench who had fallen on hard times, but the baker was adamant. He cared not a whit, he said, whether I lived or died. He wanted to make an example of me, then mayhap all the other thieving wretches who stole his wares would take heed. Again, the law man begged for my mercy, and his hand on my shoulder was more of a caress than a clutch.

He said, "Look at her and take pity, kind sir. She's as skinny as a wraith. The penalty for stealing is thirty lashes, be it a first offense. A few blows with the cat's tail and this little thing will draw her last breath."

"I'll have her flogged and be damned to you," grated the baker. "And I'll watch her take her punishment with my own eyes, and publish her screams in *The Public Ledger*! For my part, I don't care if she falls dead with the first lash of the whip."

A crowd had gathered. There were a few shamed faces, a few who looked as if they felt pity in their hearts for a small girl who had been caught at thievery, but for the most part they looked gleeful, and many a guffaw rang out in the cold, clear November day.

The Constable gave me a sad look. "I'm sorry, lass. I don't suppose you have a friend who'll pay the fine. Ten pounds, else I'll have to take you to Bailey Criminal Court."

I gasped in disbelief. Ten pounds seemed an incredible sum to pay for one measley little bun! Not that it made any difference, for I didn't have a penny to my name.

During that moment of quiet, while the crowd listened to see if I would name someone who might pay me out of the jam I was in, a strong, authoritative voice rang out. "I'll pay." Surprised, I looked around and saw a tall, robust stranger stride through the mob of onlookers. He appeared to be close in age to my father and he was head and shoulders taller than anyone I had ever seen. A giant of a man, and dressed in the attire of a gentleman, too. All I could do was stand there with my mouth open as I stared and stared. Never in my life had I seen the man before.

He removed several banknotes from his purse and gave them to the baker, who looked as startled as I. As soon as the fat little man with the bow-legs had the notes safely in his hands he bowed slightly, looked somewhat mollified, and gave my savior a sickening smile. "Your daughter, sir? Please accept my most humble apologies for bringing this disgraceful situation to a head but I'm sore pressed to make an honest living and I've been pushed to the end of my wits by thieves. Young ones and old ones alike take my goods, with never a thought for the price."

"Take the blood money and be damned," roared the gigantic man. "No, she's no daughter of mine, but she could be if I had one. Get out of my face." To the Constable, he said, "Release her, you hear? Unless you're of the same filthy ilk that'd see a wee little lassie flogged, and it plain as day that's she's starvin'."

The law man removed his hand from my shoulder. "Believe me, sir, I had no heart for this miserable bit of business. The girl is little more than skin and bones, but I believe I recognize her, too. She's the daughter of—"

"But the law is the law." The baker was bound to get in the final word, which almost cost him a cuff on the head by the big, burly man who had given him the pound notes. He scurried on back in the direction of the bakery while I looked up into a pair of hazel eyes under heavy grey-blond brows and tried to voice my heartfelt thanks.

"Come with me, lass," the man said before I could say a word. "I'll put you on the outside of a substantial meal."

The Constable's glance was searching. "Have a care, miss. In this world you don't get something for nothing. The gentleman came to your defense. Now he wants to feed you. Be wary, I say, for many a sweet, pure lassie has found herself locked up in a room with nothing to look forward to but being an old man's plaything."

"I've no stomach for little girls," roared the tall man. "I

mean to give her a good, hot meal and send her on her way, nothing more and nothing less. Come along and see for yourself if you doubt my intentions."

"I've got a job to do," answered the law man. "But unless I'm mistaken this girl is the daughter of a man I respect, and I'll be watching to see that she doesn't come to a bad end by your hand or anyone else's."

My defender sneered and his words rang with sarcasm. "Sure and it's plain by your actions that you planned to look after her. You'd have taken her to Old Bailey where she'd be flogged after her hearing."

"No, sir. I planned to take her there, true. But only until I could go home and get the pounds to satisfy the baker's charges against her." The Constable held his ground staunchly. "If you'd tell me your name, sir, perhaps I might show a little trust. The girl is almost of the gentry, and it's clear that she's fallen upon bad times. I'd not like to see things get worse for her."

"I'm Solomon Merryweather." A glint of respect for the minion of the law shone for a moment in the big man's eyes. "I own land in County Fife and a goodly fleet of fishing boats as well. The lass reminds me of an old, lost love. She could be her daughter, for there's a marked resemblance to my poor, lost Geraldine, who went to her Maker these many years ago. I mean no harm to her. I'll feed her, provide her with a few pounds and let her tell me why she was brought to this low estate. I'll not harm one hair on her pretty head, and I swear it on the grave of me old mother, may she rest in peace."

The Constable opened his mouth and took a step backwards. "Solomon Merryweather, is it? Then I'll be begging your pardon, sir. That is, if you can take me to someone who will vouch for true and certain that you're who you say you be."

The enormous man tipped back his head and roared with laughter. Then he pointed to the tavern across the street. "We'll go there, then. The three of us, for there'll be at least a dozen and a half men who will tell you my name."

Looking impressed, the Constable nodded. "Come along, gal," he said to me. "This may be your saving grace after all, and I hope so, for a fact."

Almost as soon as we were inside the dark tavern, several men left their places at drink or food and came forward to clap Solomon Merryweather on the shoulder or back. They called him by name, and treated him with deference suitable for a member of the upper class, and I soon realized why. It turned out that he owned the tavern, a circumstance that took the wind out of the sails of the Constable. With many a beg-your-pardon and much bowing and scraping, the minion of the law said he would be on his way. Turning to me, he warned me to steer clear of the baker's shop and to see to it that I didn't steal in the future.

"Now, lass," said the elegantly-dressed gentleman as soon as the Constable was away, "we must fill you up afore you fall into a swoon." With much hustling and bustling, the serving woman prepared a fine table for two, and in a hurry. It had been so long since I had tasted proper food, or even looked upon it, that I fairly drooled as the meat pasties were set in front of me.

"Eat hearty," prodded Mr. Merryweather. "But go at it easy-like in the beginning, mind. An empty belly that's gone a long time without victuals will sometimes send it right back up the old gullet."

The serving wench brought a dish of sliced oranges encrusted with sugar, a baked hen, a bowl full of buttered and salted nuts and a whole loaf of crusty bread just taken from the oven. Mr. Merryweather slathered great slabs of butter on the hot bread and washed his down with a tankard of ale as he enjoyed the sumptuous meal with me. After my empty stomach had once adjusted to the shock of food, I was able to eat more than my share.

During the meal he spoke to me at length about his dead sweetheart, repeating what he'd said to the Constable about my marked resemblance to her. "She was named Geraldine, and she looked so much like you it was uncanny when I saw you. Fair gave me a start, it did, when I caught a glimpse of you runnin' hellbent for leather down the street and stuffin' that bun in your mouth, the law hot on your heels! If she'd lived, poor darlin', Geraldine could have had a daughter about your age. But the plague got her just two days before we were to be wed."

His eyes grew misty as he went into detail about the way

his Geraldine had looked. "A face as fair as any Madonna that's been sculpted by the masters, I vow. Heart-shaped, just like yours, and a pair of eyes on her that were emerald green, where yours are brown. Hair just that same shade of near-black, though, and thick and full of life, it was! She was born in Drogheda, across the Channel. Just sixteen summers old, she was, when she went to heaven. I was wonderin', lassie, if you could be a cousin, or some other kin to her. She was of the Galloway Clan, the father by the name of Clearsy."

I said I doubted if there was a bit of kinship between me and his Geraldine, for my mother was born in England, just as my father was, and neither one had ever spoken of any relatives on the island of Eire. "Originally," I added, "a long time ago, both families migrated to England from Scotland. My mother's maiden name was Somerset. But her folks before her had been in England for many generations." With the instinctive bitterness that possessed me every time I thought of the woman, I recalled Dame Clements' words about my mother having Romany blood as well as Gaulish. But I said nothing of this to Solomon Merryweather, for I was positive there was not a shred of truth in what she said. My father had spoken too often of the family origins.

The meal ended with a most satisfying cup of chocolate topped off with a generous dollop of cream for me and another tankard of ale for him. Then Solomon Merryweather leaned back and gave me an unfathomable look. At length, he said, "And now, sweet little Garnet with the big brown eyes, whatever shall become of you? I've fed you, but I hate to turn you loose with naught but a meal inside your belly and a few pieces of gold. You'll get yourself into a peck of trouble once the gold runs out, and I'll not be here to get you out of it. I sail tomorrow. What brought you to such a state that you were forced to steal a bun? Mayhap I can rectify some wrong that's been done you."

"There's no way anyone can rectify the wrong, sir," I said. "Unless you have the power to bring back the dead." With the taste of sweet chocolate on my tongue, I launched into the events of the past few weeks and brought myself up to the present.

"By the toenails of God, lass, you've come up against the

wall for fair." There were deep creases around his eyes that turned into laugh lines when he smiled, but they deepened and caused his face to take on a grim look when he was solemn. "I could let things lie where they are and maybe you'd be the better off for it, but I can only try to put myself in your shoes, tiny though they be and ridiculous as the idea seems. So I feel beholdin' to tell you what I know of Lord Neilson: He's plenty capable of doing a man in if he had reason to believe the man in question had made him into a cuckold. Not that he'd do it himself, mind. No, he'd hire him an assassin and make sure his nibs was sitting someplace in plain sight of mighty fine witnesses when the dastardly deed was done. He's got the reputation for having cut down a young man a few years back. Not that the young man was foolin' around with the Lady. It was a commoner that came smellin' around his brother's daughter, the poor young man was found with his head all bashed in. Victim of a ridin' accident, they said. But when a man of wealth and power sets out to end another man's life, girlie, there's not much of a contest. Now, 'though it pains me, I think you'd rather know for sure and certain than to stew and fret, always goin' to sleep wonderin' if there was a bond between your father and the Lady. There was. I knew your father, and a fine man he was, too. It was a little over a year ago when he came to my ship to doctor a—well, an ailing seaman that didn't exactly want to go to a doctor of men. I caught a glimpse of you, then, too, Garnet. Your father brought you to the shore in a fine rig. I believe you were wearin' a blue dress, and you waited while your father came aboard and took a leg off my seaman. That was all I saw of you, just a little girl in a blue dress, for I was aboard and didn't come ashore."

I smiled. "And you assisted my father with the surgery. I remember the occasion well, for I asked my father why a sailor wouldn't want to see a regular doctor. He said the poor man was in some kind of trouble with the law. And he often mentioned that time he went aboard the... wasn't the name of the ship *The Bonnie Lassie?*"

"Indeed it was. You've a good memory, young Garnet."

"My father often wondered if the man recovered."

"He recovered right well. Wore a peg leg and got around

as well as if he'd never had to have the bad one taken off. He'd hurt it at sea, and it was rotten to the core."

"Then you are the Captain of *The Bonnie Lassie*?"

"I was, Garnet. Until she went down five months ago. Only four men and myself survived."

"The peg-legged man went down, too?"

"Yes." Merryweather made the sign of the cross. Then, as if remembering the former conversation, he went back to it: "And I saw your father on another occasion, too. He was in the company of the Lady Neilson, and they were far, far from London." He sighed deeply and shook his head in regret. "You wouldn't guess it to look at me, but I've a soft streak in my heart for those who love. Look upon your daddy as a man who loved, and loved well. And I can give you a small bit of satisfaction in knowing he died all of a piece, not a little bit at a time. A hired assassin doesn't take the time to make a victim suffer." I'm sure he was alarmed at the quick tears that burned my eyes and fell down my cheeks, for he immediately made great, loud, soothing sounds and bumbled around in an attempt to get me to stop. He reminded me of a big, friendly bear.

"Poor lassie," he said as if greatly worried. "Almost a gentlewoman, but not quite. Educated, cultured... what in the devil am I to do with you?"

I looked down at my hands, my throat all constricted with my misery. "I'm not... your responsibility. I'll... maybe I could work as a serving wench somewhere. Perhaps in this tavern?"

Eagerly, I looked into his eyes as he seemed to mull over the idea. At first there was a flicker of approval, but only for an instant. "No," he said at length. "You're refined. And you're beautiful. I'll take you to sea with me. You'll be the daughter I might have had if my darling Geraldine had lived. The Captain's daughter. How does that set with you?"

"You mean you never took a wife, then?" I was stalling for time. More than anything else in the world I wanted to cling to the man who sat across the tavern table from me. To go with him and become the same as his daughter, for I was afraid. All alone in the world, not knowing where I would sleep at night, not knowing when or where I would find food to eat... and yet I held back. In all of my fourteen years I had never been out of London County and the idea of going to strange places was frightening. And I had never been on a ship. In all honesty, I had never even set foot on a boat of any kind and I had heard tales of people being stricken with seasickness so debilitating that they must be confined to their beds for many days.

More than that, though, and this in spite of all his kindness to me, I was afraid that Solomon Merryweather had an ulterior motive. Before my father's disappearance it would never have occurred to me to question kindness. But so many dreadful things had happened to me of late that I was unable to believe the man was all he appeared to be. The words of the Constable seemed to ring in my ears. I did not want to find myself at the mercy of a man who had openly admitted that he was old enough to be my father and I had read penny novels about the absolute control a Captain has over his ship.

"No, I never took a wife," he answered with a smile. "But I've had my good times with the ladies and you may mark it down that I've not had my last one. I've always loved 'em, bless their hearts, especially those who are free with their favors. Not that my Geraldine was. She was a virgin and an angel on this earth. Too good and sweet for the world, which was why she was taken so young. Only the good die young, you know. I've never professed to be good, so I'll live to see my four score and more. But I'll be good to you, Garnet. I'll look after you, see to it that you have the best of everything, on land or on sea."

"But what—" I wondered how I could phrase my question delicately, without coming right out and letting him know what was really on my mind. I changed it quickly to, "But how could I ever repay you?"

"You can read to me. I've an ear for a good story. Not that I'd be askin' for you to do anything in payment for board and keep, but you've been well brought up, my gal, and it doesn't take a man of learnin' to see that. Yes, you'd want to feel like you're pullin' your own weight. So you can read to me, for I've never learned either readin' or writin'. And you can see to it that my London house is fixed up all well and good.

When we're on the high seas, mayhap you can soothe the feverish brow of the men if they should come down with a sickness. But I'll not be expectin' you to share me bed, lass, so if you've got that on your mind, forget it. I've a woman full grown to take care of my needs in that quarter. She's Belle d'Arcy, a mixed breed of a woman that's half-French and half-Irish. A good-hearted soul and not bad to look at, but she don't know a thing past the bed. I always had a yen to learn about other lands. Where they are is something I already know, but I'd like to know about the people that live there—and if there's a grain of truth about the things they're sayin' about the New World."

"I've heard it's a land of hardships," I said.

"And *I've* heard it's a land of milk and honey. Gold anywhere you look, and free for the pickin' of it up. Summertime all the time. Oranges and apples everywhere. Tobacco crops and cotton, they say the earth is as bountiful as mother's love, not that I've ever a thought of bein' a planter."

"I understand it's a big land. So maybe the oranges and apples grow all the year 'round in a part of it while the other part is frozen over all the time. Like Greenland."

"Mayhap we'll see it bye-and-bye. Meanwhile, I'll get you a bed for the night here in the tavern. In the morning, you'll have made up your mind." His face lit up as a medium-tall woman came to stand at his side. She was buxom, comely, but quite vacant of eye. Before Mr. Merryweather made the introductions, I guessed that she was Belle d'Arcy. She smiled at me and neither blushed nor said a word of protest when his big hand caressed her breasts. I turned crimson, but neither of them appeared to make note of my discomfort.

That night I shared a bed with a sixteen-year-old vicar's daughter and her four-year-old sister. The mother and the rest of the female children of the family slept in the other two beds in the room. The accommodations were not the kind I had read about in penny novels or dreamed about. It was my understanding that an inn provided sleeping rooms that were private, but of course a great deal of what I knew had been gleaned from reading. The vicar's wife told me there were more capacious rooms to be had, but they were very dear, and only for the gentry, or for royalty.

It was a restless night. The four-year-old girl wet the bed, for which crime the mother gave her a beating with a stick. I was horrified, for even though I was awakened by the unexpected drenching that came in the middle of the night, as well as somewhat discomfited, I understood that the child had not meant to do it. Again and again and again the sickening thud of the stick fell against the little girl's tender bottom, even against her pitifully thin little back. And all the while the mother shouted at the poor girl, who screamed each time she was whacked. In the darkness, with all the other little children cowering in their beds like shadowy ghosts, it was a scene right out of a bad dream.

After that, my nerves were in such a state that I couldn't get back to sleep. The muffled sobs of the little one in the bed with me did little to soothe my seething emotions and every minute or two the mother would call out in her strident voice, "Shut up! No use in you feeling sorry for yourself, you were a naughty girl!" After a while, the tot fell into an uneasy doze, but awakened with a shudder that shook the bedstead, fearful that she'd done it again since she sat up and screamed that she'd not meant to.

The cocks were crowing by the time I slept, but I knew by then what I would do. I would go with Captain Merryweather. The alternative was a home for orphaned children. But I would be sheltered there for only a few months, for when I reached fifteen I could no longer expect to receive charity. After that, I would be apprenticed as a domestic servant, or even worse, I could be apprenticed to a baker or a merchant, or set to sewing gloves or making boots. The sharing of the room with the vicar's wife and children was what made up my mind for me.

When I was very young a thirteen-year-old girl named Amanda came to my father's house and begged for shelter and mercy. She had been indentured to a blacksmith who had branded her on the shoulder because she forgot to use the bed-warmer on his bed one night. Her wound was all festered and the poor young creature was half out of her mind with delirium when she came to us in the middle of the night. To my young eyes, the scars that the hapless girl bore from countless beatings were even more shocking than the ugly wound which had brought her to our house. Her legs were so scarred that there wasn't a place one could lay a finger without touching one. As I lay there in my sleepless bed of straw I made up my mind that I would not become an indentured servant. It would be my lot to have a mistress not unlike the vicar's wife, I was sure. A woman who was cruel to her helpless child would be doubly cruel to a servant. During the time the woman whipped the little girl it was all I could do to keep myself from springing on her—big, heavy woman that she was—and tearing her eyes out. Since I had felt like that about someone else, I knew my own nature well enough to know that if I lived after a beating such as Amanda had taken, I would kill my tormenter. And then I would most certainly face the gallows. No. Far better for me to take my chances with a man who seemed kind and charitable. A man who already had a grown woman for his baser needs.

And so it came about that I was ready and waiting for Solomon Merryweather when he came down to the morning meal with the woman, Belle d'Arcy on his arm.

As long as Solomon Merryweather lived, he kept to the letter of our agreement. And I kept to mine. Unfortunately, he didn't live long enough to see me into young womanhood.

Four

The Gentle Kathy measured more than eighty feet from the keel to the highest point of the poop deck. It was a beautiful ship, especially in full sail, and I was never seasick for a moment, and neither was I homesick. Captain Merryweather referred to his ship as a "free trader." Made of heavy oak timbers, it was kept in fine shape by a crew of men who seemed to love the sea as much as the Captain loved the ship. Almost from the beginning, it was apparent to me that Solomon Merryweather loved the ship in the way most men love a woman. He would walk along the foredeck and touch the railing in the way he never touched Belle d'Arcy. It would be a lingering kind of touch, as if his fingers were reluctant to leave the fine feel of the smooth wood.

Belle loved the Captain. She was a simple woman. Perhaps simple-minded, as well, for her conversations were vapid and consisted of nothing beyond what her eyes could see or her memories reminded her of. "The Captain is in a good mood today," she would remark almost every day. Her world revolved around him and she would see that he had the most select pieces of whatever meat was prepared, the best of the wines. Sometimes she spoke of frocks she would like to have, or baubles, and she spent a great deal of time at painting her face, but she was always anxious about the results and asked me often if I felt she had applied too much paint around the eyes, or too many beauty patches, or not enough. She worried about the havoc being wrought by sea and sun to her face, and always went about heavily veiled, if she ventured outside on the deck. "My hands," she would say in dismay as she looked at them ruefully. "Will you look at the wrinkles! A woman shows her age by her hands." She used a mixture of whale oil and boiled milk that she rubbed into face and hands three times a day, and she spent long hours in front of her mirror devising different ways to dress her heavy tresses.

"If he has taken you to raise as his daughter, then I suppose in a way you are also mine," she said to me on the third day out. "But of course he will never marry me. I wish I knew a way to make him love me as I love him. He tells me you know how to read, that you've had an education. In the books that you read, does it tell a woman how to make a man love her? You know, I would give my very life for him."

Belle fawned on me. I tried to like her and I also told myself to be grateful to her, but I could not force myself to like her. She didn't resent the long conversations the Captain and I had concerning the voyage. We were on our way to Amsterdam, laden with wood, coal, and iron. We would return with furs, precious stones, perfumes, and art objects from the Far East, which would be waiting for us in the prosperous port in Amsterdam. Captain Merryweather's mind was filled with all sorts of fascinating stories of the olden days, for his father before him had been a merchant seaman and he had begun traveling with him when he was but a lad of eleven years old. I hung on his every word, but Belle yawned and often interrupted by asking him questions that had nothing to do with the conversation—like the time she wanted to know if he thought the neckline of her gown was too daring.

"Too daring for what, my dear?" He was a patient man.

Belle primped her hair. "Oh, I don't know. I guess I just wanted you to notice me."

The Captain knew the name of every star, every constellation. If I gave him an education in history and geography and taught him to read and write during the two years I spent with him, he more than repaid me by his instruction in astronomy and the actual business of running a ship. Although he could not write letters, he had a genius with numbers, and with pride he showed me his bookkeeping system. It was as neat as a pin and he could run his eyes down a column of figures and there it would be, all added up as if he had labored over it as I had to, carrying my numbers on paper where he did his all in his head.

Solomon Merryweather swore I took to the sea as if I had been born to it, for I loved each day aboard better than the preceding one. *The Gentle Kathy* carried a small crew, and for the most part I liked them all. Jack Lawson was a lad of fourteen, but he'd taken his first voyage with Captain Merryweather before he reached the age of twelve. Speed McClintock was the quartermaster, Seaman Stanky his right-hand man. Of them all, I liked First Mate Russel Millar best, and by the same token, I had a hard time being civil to the rigger, Jules Sarpston.

Sarpston was a quiet-spoken man who kept to himself and caused no one any harm, but there was something about him that I mistrusted, perhaps his shifty eyes. One time, at the end of the second year I spent with the Captain, Jules Sarpston came upon me under cover of darkness and pressed his lips to mine. I instinctively pulled away, and the sound of my resounding slap against his cheek was as loud as a clap of thunder. He said, "I meant you no discomfort, Mistress Garnet. It's just that you're so sweet. So lovely." His whispered words, no doubt meant to charm me, had the opposite effect. I yelled at him, and the Captain came running, but Sarpston ducked around a barrel of rum. I will never know how Captain Merryweather knew it was his rigger who'd accosted me, for I didn't tell. But he did know, and for his pains Sarpston was given a severe beating. The fact that he never forgave me turned up much later.

Old Cooty was the only member of the crew who dumbfounded me. If he had another name, or if he had a particular job to do, I never knew of it. There were periods when he was as mad as any man can ever be, this wizened old man with snow white hair and a body that resembled nothing so much as a rack of bones wrapped in seamen's garb. Other times old Cooty walked about smartly and conversed as if he might have been a scholar. When I questioned the Captain about Cooty's duties, the Captain merely smiled and said he owed his very life to the old man, that as long as he lived he would see to it that the poor devil wanted for nothing. Strangely enough, during Cooty's periods of normalcy, he was a remarkable hand at the helm and his navigational skills, according to the Captain, were the best in the business.

Together, Old Cooty and the Captain taught me to take my turn at the wheel, but it was the Captain who took it upon himself to give me lessons in navigation, for Cooty was inclined to go off his mind when he was looking at charts, which was disconcerting at best, for when he was not himself he often spoke a foreign language. Sometimes he had to be constrained, for he often thought he was a bird, which meant he believed he could fly.

The voyages passed with incredible speed. For two years, we spent more time at sea than in Captain Merryweather's London Town home, but when we were in town the time passed every bit as fast for me because I was interested in what I was doing and took a great delight in acting as housekeeper. There were servants in the town house, so I had no actual work to do, but it gave me pleasure to plan interesting meals and sometimes go to the kitchens and prepare a special dish myself. During one of our short stays in town I happened to learn that the servants were taking advantage of their master's absences from home by padding the household accounts. When I pointed this out to the Captain he informed me that I was a puzzling bit of fluff. "You look like a delectable little female, and you know how to turn on the charm well enough," he said admiringly, "but at the same time you've a mind as sharp as any grown man's." It was on that day that he confided in me that he was going to make me the beneficiary of all his holdings.

I couldn't bear to think of life without the big, gruff-appearing man who had become a second father to me and told him so. He reminded me that life was short at best and always perilous, and though he planned to live for a long, long time he felt it would be wise to provide for me in case he was wrong. "And I've another reason," he assured me. "As you've seen for yourself, poor Belle isn't quite bright, but as you've also no doubt seen for yourself she's provided me with a deal of comfort. If I left her an inheritance she'd soon fritter it away or let some sharp operator winnow it from her. I mean to do right by her, but she's not capable of looking after herself. So you'll have to make sure she's provided for, just as any good daughter would do."

Perhaps the dear Captain had a premonition that he hadn't long to live. I will never know whether he did or whether he had simply reached a point in his life where he felt he must take steps to insure that his loved ones were provided for in case of his death. He listed his holdings, and they were considerable. The tavern, a small house in the borough of Hackney and a theater on Drury Lane were his as well as the ship and the large house in London. "I've worked hard for what I've acquired, and I'd not want the vultures in Parliament to make away with it," he said as he handed me a leather-bound book. "What you hold in your hands will show you what I've done with my profits, Garnet, but since I can't write down words, you'll have to make notes for yourself. So sit down and get that look off your face that shows all too plainly you're afraid I'm about to meet my Maker. What I'm doing is only sensible."

I sat across from him and looked at the neat figures, none of which meant anything to me. He explained that he had a certain amount of money deposited with the Bank of England, and the total at the bottom of the fifth page showed the present balance. Then he went on to explain what the numerals on the other pages meant: "Each year, I give a certain percentage of my net worth to the London Hospital, Bethlehem Royal Hospital, the Theater Guild, and the Foundling Home for Abandoned Children... well, I felt it was only right. Why should you look so surprised?"

"It's the fund for the children and widows of miners," I said. "You helped to institute the pension fund. Now I remember reading about it in the publications, Solomon Merryweather. You were referred to as a philanthropist, and I can see why."

"All these things, Garnet, I want you to continue in the event of my death. The more I think on it, the more I believe Providence took a hand in seeing to it that I happened upon you when I did. I should have married and had me a fine family. Since I didn't, I've the next best thing, a girl with the mind of a man all grown and educated. Welladay! Tomorrow I'll take you to my barrister and have him put everything in order."

The following day we went to town but found that Mr. Wherry was at home with the bloody flux, according to his assistant. The Captain said he was of half a mind to go to another man, but he changed his mind when he realized a different barrister would require a lot of time and numerous explanations, whereas Mr. Wherry had been taking care of his affairs for many years, so the whole thing would be much simpler if he waited. There was little time as it was, for we were due to set sail the following morning at sunrise, winds being favorable.

"Next trip back to London Town, then," said the Captain.

We sailed for Antwerp as planned and for the first ten days made good time, for the weather was fair, the winds dependable, and the sea benevolent. On the eleventh night we almost capsized under a sudden storm, but we weathered it well except for the First Mate, who came down with a case of the ague. Because of getting himself chilled to the bone, avowed the Captain. But when I went to look in on Mr. Millar I felt uneasy. A red rash covered the left side of his face and he was restless and quite unable to hold his arms and legs still. They thrashed about almost as if they were on strings and being jerked by a master puppeteer. The poor fellow's eyes were all glazed over as he tossed and turned in his delirium.

Throughout the time we were docked in Antwerp the First Mate kept to his bed. After we were loaded with the customary precious gems and other merchandise as well as the gold that was payment for the supplies we brought from England, Seaman Stanky came down with the same ailment that brought the First Mate low.

"It's not the ague," I said to the Captain that night over dinner. We were alone, for Belle had complained of a headache, and lack of appetite. "I don't know what it is, but they all have an ugly rash on their faces. The young boy, Lawson, seems to be touched in the head with it. Do you think it's possible that the cook is giving us tainted food?"

"Not on purpose, lass." The Captain looked thoughtful,

and he turned his face to one side in what I later looked back upon as a strange way. He said his cook had been with him for years and years, that he was to be trusted.

"I didn't mean I thought he was trying to kill us," I ventured. "It's just that—well, I've seen a lot of strange maladies, but I've never seen anything like the way the seamen have been taken. Maybe we should stay close to land for a while. Just long enough to make sure everyone is going to be all right."

"We can't do it, lass. They'd be up in arms against us in a trice if they learned that we're carrying sick men aboard. The Dutch are a fanatical people concerning sickness. No, we'd best set out for home. Seemed to me the First Mate was some better when I looked at him an hour ago."

The second day out on the return voyage to London, I was standing at the Captain's side when he gave me a strange look and said, "I'm right grateful to whatever fate it was that caused me to be there on the street when you were in trouble. And I'm pleased that you've learned to navigate a ship. I'm feeling poorly, m'girl, but don't worry. I've always been a hale and hardy man, but I—" He put his hand to his cheek and under the rays of the setting sun I saw the tell-tale fiery rash that had manifested itself on the others who had taken sick, Belle among them. Worse, and even more frightening, his hands and arms jerked spasmodically. "Take the wheel, love," he said. "Seems like my eyes aren't doing just right."

I took the tiller and the Captain fell to the floor where he jerked convulsively while I screamed for help. Guiding a ship through the seas with the strong and knowledgeable Captain at my side was one thing, but being at the helm all alone was quite another. I was petrified with fear, both for myself and the crew. Worse, I was terrified that the Captain was going to die before my very eyes.

Young Jack Lawson came in answer to my screams, but his face was deathly pale and I could see that the fourteen-year-old boy would be of little value when it came to helping either the Captain or myself. "First Mate has croaked," he cried out as he stared at the jerking Captain Merryweather with fear-blinded eyes. "And the Captain's Lady is fair having fits, and there's blood in her puke. We're doomed, Mistress Garnet. Ever' man Jack of us. Doomed aboard a ship of death, and not even a Father to say a few words to the Lord in our defense."

"Get Captain Merryweather to his cabin," I yelled. "And get someone up here to take a hand at the wheel!"

"Mistress Garnet," whispered the boy in despair, "There ain't nobody left what knows how to push a great big ship like this through the waters, save for Cooty, and he's in the crazies again. They're all taken down with the sickness, save for you, me, and old Cooty, what ain't got a lick of sense and only here out of the kindness of Cap'n's heart."

When I looked down, I saw Captain Merryweather in what appeared to be his death throes. His arms flailed the deck and his back arched rigidly. Flecks of blood were in the spittle at the corners of his lips. But even in his agony, he was calm. "Get us home, love," he cried out. "Get us all safely home. If I don't make it, take care of Belle."

He didn't make it. God knows how long he had suffered without saying a word to anyone that he was stricken. Judging by the rash that almost covered his entire body by the time he could no longer withstand the dreadful tremors and keep the malady hidden from the rest of us, he must have had symptoms at about the same time the First Mate was stricken.

For a time, it looked as if young Jack Lawson's prophecy was accurate, for one by one, the crew's symptoms worsened. The Captain died during the night. Just as the first brilliant crimson of the sun began to rise, Belle d'Arcy came stumbling from below and fell in a heap at my feet, where I was numbly hanging onto the tiller. She looked up at me out of a wretched face and vomited a stream of blood that was as red as the rising sun, and then she was utterly still. The cook had died before nightfall and the rigger was screaming in agony, even as Jack Lawson and I slipped poor Belle's body into the sea to join the others who had perished before her.

The rigger was wild and Jack Lawson and I together could not restrain him. It was as if the deadly malady had addled his brains, for he was a quiet man before he took sick, but a raving maniac in the throes of it. There was nothing to do but get him into chains after he tried to plunge a knife into old Cooty when the old man was trying to spoon a little broth into him. Jack Lawson informed me that the First Mate had gone crazy before he died, too. Belle had retained her senses, but at the end, the cook was as mindless as a cuckoo. Strange, I mused as I hoped I was keeping on course, that the sickness affected everyone alike as far as the rash was concerned, and the loss of control of the limbs, but it went directly to the brain of some, while it didn't others.

I still couldn't shake the notion that whatever had caused the dread sickness was in the food, but of course I had no way of knowing what it might have been until the worst of it was over, and even then nobody knew for sure. I didn't catch it and neither did Jack Lawson or old Cooty. Seaman Stanky suffered with only a mild form of it. He broke out in a rash and had slight tremors, but he survived, just the same. I had not eaten a bite of bread since we left London, and neither had Jack Lawson, and the reason was simple. Neither Jack nor I liked the taste of rye bread. Nobody knew whether old Cooty had eaten the bread or not. He couldn't remember. But when Seaman Stanky recovered enough to talk with some sense, he said he'd not felt just right about that bread because it had a musty taste. A thin clue, at best, but enough for me to issue orders to throw all leftover bread and the makings overboard. For the remainder of the journey we would be on short rations, but I felt it was better to go hungry than to take a chance on all of us dying. *The Gentle Kathy* carrying a load of corpses.

When we left the dockyard in London there were ten aboard. If we were lucky enough to get back, we would be four in number. But I tried to count my blessings and keep a stiff upper lip, even though I had no idea how I would fare if and when we were safely back at home. Captain Merryweather had planned to provide for me. Well, he'd not done it, due to circumstances not of his own making. I doubted if I could convince his solicitor that he had planned to make me his heiress—in fact, I wouldn't even try. It would be useless, and I faced the fact that I was right back where I had started two years earlier—alone in the world and penniless. The days were long and the nights longer. Fortunately, the sea remained calm enough for me to rest from the tiller at times, but first I had to teach Jack Lawson the little I knew about navigation. Things got better by the seventh or eighth day when the rigger was recovered enough to take the helm, and I slept long hours, for I was suffering from sheer exhaustion. When I awakened my brain was dull from deep sleep, but my senses turned acute when I understood the way things were. Young Jack Lawson's demeanor was no longer pleasant when I came face to face with him. He gave me a leering grin when I asked him to go below and fetch me a spot of tea and his voice was downright nasty when he said, "Get it yerself."

I stood there for a moment, aware of the placid sea, the slight lift and sway of the ship. "Perhaps I misunderstood you, Jack."

He swaggered, and hitched his breeches up a notch or two. "Ye heard me a'right, me fine lady. Things has changed sommat since ye took to yer bunk. Me and the rigger has took over this ship, and Stanky had no choice but to agree. Ye'll go below and do the work of any woman captive. Fix us some vittles and be quick about it. You was in a'right with the Cap'n, but the Cap'n is feeding the sharks by now. Rigger and me has decided to take the cargo along with *The Gentle Kathy* to a distant port for wages due and other things."

I could have argued the point by saying I would see to it that everyone was paid in full when we docked in London. Instead, I merely nodded, lowered my eyes, and turned dutifully toward the galley. In all truth, I actually scurried away in an excellent imitation of a weak and frightened female who knew good and well who was in charge of the situation, but if I thought out my actions I did so without my knowledge, for I was frightened. Still, I was not cowed into submission as I pretended to be. By the time I reached the galley I had conceived of a plan. Where it came from I do not know except to say that the survival instinct was surging through my flesh and bones, and more than that. I would regain control, and then I would take the heavily laden ship to a port far away from London. The goods we carried in the hold were expected, but the payment would not go to me, oh no! It would go to the estate of Captain Solomon Merryweather and in time the bulk of it would go into the coffers of England.

As I went about the task of preparing food, I spared a moment of thanksgiving to the wily Jules Sarpston, for the rigger's plan to dispose of the goods at a distant port was admirable. But I would die before I allowed him to take it from me. Morally, I reasoned, I was the rightful owner, for Solomon Merryweather had made it clear that he intended what he had to be mine. Legally, I didn't have a leg to stand on, and I knew it. But just as the survival instinct was strong in me, I also seemed to have acquired both avarice and greed. As I fried batter cakes and stoked up the fire for the beans that were already cooked, but cold, I mentally surveyed my chances. Jules Sarpston was clever. He was also born with a tendency toward cruelty in spite of his soft-spoken ways. Captain Merryweather had told me of an incident wherein the rigger had tortured a cat. No doubt he would take pleasure in torturing me, but first he would have his way with me. More than once I had felt his dark eyes travel up and down the length of my body after the time he kissed me, and naked desire burned in them. He could navigate, and he was far more knowledgeable of the sea than I. The charts were confusing to me in spite of Solomon Merryweather's patient tutoring. Still and all, I would have to make do without the rigger's skills if I meant to live long enough to look upon land again. Young Jack was still too much of a lad to have come up with the idea of what amounted to mutiny, but he was knave enough to go along with it. Old Cooty was a nothing. He spoke very little, and when he was crazy he had no loyalty to anyone. In all truth, I wasn't even sure he realized Captain Merryweather was dead. He spent most of his time sitting on the foredeck fooling with the ropes and I remembered that he'd shown no emotion when we slipped the Captain's body overboard. Therefore he would be no help to me, but he would not hinder me, either. He was just there.

Unfortunately, the best of the lot had died of the mysterious disease. The ones who had survived were the misfits—the kind of men who took to the seas because they'd not made a place for themselves on land. But they had no love for it, and they would spare no kind thoughts to the memory of the man who had hired them on. There was no way of knowing whether they'd go along with me or stick with Jules Sarpston and I considered it prudent to take it for granted that they'd uphold a man when the opposition was a sixteen-year-old girl.

When I dropped the croton oil in the batter cakes my hand shook in spite of my determination. The bottle was there on the shelf, together with the other medicinal herbs and nostrums that were kept all together for any ailments the crew might suffer during the voyages. I had seen it often enough and it was clearly labeled. Having been brought up by an animal doctor, I knew a good deal of the ills of cattle and horses. Although the plant was of tropical origin, many ladies were entranced by the exotic markings and colorings of the leaves and had instructed their gardeners to use the plants as attractive borders. A horse that happened to nibble at the foliage of the plant from which the oil was extracted could sicken and die, which probably meant that a mere drop of the oil would render a strong man helpless. I didn't want to kill anyone; no, that was not my intention. All I wanted was a crew of helpless mates, laid low by a powerful purge, and the leader of the mutinous action among them. Looking ahead, I planned my moves. I would tell young Jack Lawson that he was a fool if he thought the rigger would share the booty with him once they dropped anchor. "He'll kill you," I fancied myself saying. "And he'll kill me long before that. He's a man who won't share a thing with you or Stanky, so put him in irons and I'll get you back to land in good health."

With Jules Sarpston in irons I would stand a chance. He was a born leader, that much I knew, but I was also aware of the fact that the other two were born followers, and Old Cooty would present me with no trouble any more than he would give aid.

Sweat broke out on my forehead when I realized I might be instrumental in the deaths of every man aboard. My father was not a pious man, but he had brought me up to know the difference between right and wrong, and I knew it was wrong to commit murder. I feared that an Almighty Being would punish me if I took another's life. However, I reminded myself, I was also born with a God-given right to live. But I hesitated, even as the batter cakes sizzled. At last, I threw them all out the porthole save for those which I would personally serve to Jules Sarpston.

When I brought him his plate, Jules gave me a pleased look. "I'm glad to see that you've decided to be sensible," he said as he looked at the food. "A girl who's been pampered isn't always easy to tame."

"It isn't that I've become tame," I managed to say with an uneasy smile. "It's just that I have sense enough to know when I'm licked." My lips jiggled and my mouth was very dry. I felt as if my eyes were giving away my guilt as he wolfed down the batter cakes and fried fish, for no matter how hard I tried, I couldn't look him directly in the face.

"You're scared out of your wits," he said.

I nodded.

"I don't plan to kill you, Garnet," he said in his deceptively gentle voice. "Not if you're good to me. What you've got between your legs isn't much different from any other gal's. I know it ain't been used much, if any at all, but on the other hand, you could do a lot worse than me for your first. I've a way with a maid that makes them sit right up and holler for more." He smacked his lips.

"Wh—where," I said hollowly, "do you plan to take the ship? And the—goods we carry?"

"To a place called Ormuz. That's in Persia." He gave me a lazy, teasing smile and touched my hair. "They'll pay dearly for a girl with your looks. And I'll do very well with the goods with which we're laden. Tell me, now, sweetheart—can you blame me for taking advantage of something that was thrown, so to speak, in my lap? I nearly died aboard this tub, and I know what did it, too. I'm not a man who is lacking in smarts, you know. The Quartermaster was careless when he checked his supplies. It's as plain as those fish jumping out there in the ocean what brought all but four of us to the end. You and the lad didn't like rye bread, so you wouldn't have it. The rash, the crazy actions, the jerks, all of it. It's caused by a mold in rye. Other grains, too, no doubt, but rye is the greatest offender and it attacks different folks in different ways. Some call it St. Anthony's fire on account of the rash that breaks out on the skin. It's a disease akin to erysipelas, but far more deadly. So it turns out that the good Captain and the Quartermaster made a mistake and a number of good men and true went to their watery graves. I narrowly missed it myself, but since I did it's no more than fair that I do as I see fit. Almost like it was supposed to be, now wouldn't you say so, Garnet Shaw?"

"Please," I forced myself to say since he showed no symptoms of falling prey to the croton oil. "Do whatever you like with me. I'll be your slave!" I flung out my arms and fell to my knees in supplication as I begged him not to sell me to the foreigners.

He continued to smile and after a while he said, "We'll see. I always kind of had a soft spot in my heart for you, seeing that you're so pretty." He smacked his lips and yanked me up by the hair of my head to belch obscenely in my face. "Go to your cabin, and don't dally about it. Get into your bunk, your clothes off and all naked, so I don't have to tear your rags from your body. I've a mind to sample the goods before I sell it." So saying, he roared for Jack Lawson to take a hand at the tiller.

As I fled, I wondered if the bottle I had believed to contain croton oil was filled with something harmless, like olive oil. Before I went to my little cubicle, I dashed into the Captain's quarters where I armed myself with the first weapon I laid eyes on. It was a dagger but quite small. The rigger was already wearing the Captain's fine and oranate ones. I supposed he considered the small one I yanked from the sheath too insignificant to bother about taking.

Within seconds, his footsteps pounded outside my frail door. He was singing a lewd song and once he was inside my quarters it was obvious that he had undressed as he made his way below, for he wore nought but his breeches. He carried a jug of rum and smelled strongly of it, as well as sweat, which came as a stench to me as he neared my narrow cot and flung himself on top of me. He laughed, but it had a strange sound to it, for it was without humor. A bleat of surprised protest followed.

"Damn my eyes to hell and back," he cried as he rolled away from me. "What a bastardly trick Nature has pulled on me to give me a call just now." For a long moment, he stood there at the side of my cot, his eyes rolling oddly as he clutched his belly. Then he grasped his middle even more tightly and bent double, moaning and swearing. Great droplets of sweat stood out on his forehead. He groaned and writhed around on the floor, his face waxen and his sweat wetting his hair as he shrieked for mercy.

From my father I had learned much about certain medicines. The croton oil was not guaranteed to kill him. Sometimes it did and sometimes it didn't, if a man reacted the same as horses and cattle when they ingested the leaf of the plant. I had a reasonable idea that the oil itself would cause a more harsh reaction, but when I dropped it into the batter I had no way of knowing how much it would take to kill him, or even to lay him low long enough to render him helpless.

He stared at me in a way that would have wrenched my heart with pity under different circumstances. "I'm burning on the inside of me," he whispered. "Help me, for I'm nigh to death."

"I know nothing of what ails you, man," I answered. "And anyway, why should I help you when you've made it clear what you mean to do with me?"

He had reached the point where he was willing to bargain, but even if I could have eased his pain I would not, for a bargain made in terror is not apt to be kept. Hideous sounds were coming from his stomach, and he reeked of an abominable odor. The dagger was hidden under the bed coverings, but I held it firmly. For all I knew he would recover from the purge, violent as his symptoms seemed. He was so weak he could not move from the floor, but if the cramps came to an end and he survived, I was doomed, for his words showed he realized I had put something in his food.

He ground his teeth together and in between shuddering convulsions, he said I would pay. And pay, and pay. "A little bit at a time, I'll kill you," he muttered. "First your fingers. Then your toes. Oh, it'll be a hard death, my girl. You'll get to the point where you'll beg me to put an end to you mercifully and swiftly." He spoke in jerky phrases interspersed with long, jagged sighs and harsh cries of pain, but his meaning was clear enough to me to cause me to dispense with any thoughts of sympathy. Yet I had to force myself to do it. And I could not make myself look at him when I plunged the knife between his ribs. Luckily for me, he was weak. Too weak to raise a hand in his own defense when I pushed and pulled at him until his back was to me. Even then, I had to close my eyes when I plunged the knife into his sweat-drenched back. He groaned. Surprised because I had expected a scream, at least a token struggle, I opened my eyes, withdrew the dagger and shoved it in again. He jerked each time I rammed it in to the hilt, but except for that initial groan, there was no further response.

Weak with terror at what I had done as well as the horrid act itself, my legs were trembling so hard I had a difficult time getting to my feet. He lay in a sodden mass, the blood from the wounds I had inflected spurting upwards in a crimson fountain. But he didn't move. For a while, I didn't either, for I was incapable of doing anything. The husk that was left of him trembled a few times and then stopped, as if a puppeteer had tired of pulling the strings.

Spilled blood and watery feces combined with the acrid smell of sweat to create a stench so fetid that I could not bear to stay where I was without retching. Slowly, half in fear that the body would come back to life and repay me for my act of violence, I backed away. From my mouth came involuntary little whimpering noises as I inched my way to the Captain's quarters. I went there for myriad reasons. For solace and surcease. A respite, if only for a few moments, for it represented a solidarity, a kind of comfort, even though the man who once spent a good portion of his time there was no longer living. I also went there in order to repair my ravaged countenance, knowing I must present an expression of one who is very much in command, although at the moment I was not even in command of my senses enough to think of clothing my nakedness. It was not until I caught a glimpse of my body in the mirror that I realized I had left my clothes in my own cabin. Before I could begin to think of returning to the death-room I had to pull myself together. Splashing water on my face helped. Combing my hair and doing other things that were everyday and commonplace served to renew my courage enough to allow me to cover myself with a length of cloth and sprint across the narrow hall, but only the dangerous state of my nakedness under the cloth spurred me on enough to once more open that door.

The rigger's body had not changed position. The eyes, already glassy, appeared to follow me across the few feet of space while I snatched up my undergarments, shoes, gown, and the brace of daggers that Jules Sarpston had claimed for his own. Without allowing myself another glance toward him, I again fled across the hall where I dressed inside the Captain's quarters and sat down on his bed for a while until I could force my teeth to stop chattering.

Only when I was positive that I was calm and in control of myself did I allow myself to go above, to Jack Lawson who stood at the tiller. Speaking crisply, as casually as I could, I said, "You'll attend to the body of Jules Sarpston." I had the point of one of the daggers in his back, just enough to let him feel the danger. "And I'll hear no more mutinous talk. I am in command of this ship and I have taken over the Captain's quarters. You'll do as I say, Jack Lawson, and you'll spread the words to Stanky. The two of you have much to learn. I've bested the rigger and I'm quite capable of besting you and Stanky, if you give me any trouble."

The lad turned, gave me a wide-eyed look of terror and went to his knees. "Don't hurt me, Mistress Garnet," he whined. "I only did as Sarpston told me to on pain of death, for he swore he'd cut me up in little pieces if I didn't go along with him."

"Stop your sniveling and lying," I shouted. "Get to your feet and go to the cabin where the scoundrel Sarpston planned to use me ill. I've no mind to keep his stinking corpse aboard."

Although my words were brash and loud, my heart was faint, and my legs continued to threaten to give way beneath me. I was thankful for the long skirts that hid them from the view of anyone who happened to be watching me as I pretended a boldness I certainly did not feel, but it was within the next few moments that the old gently-bred Garnet Shaw expired and the new one came into being. At the time, I didn't realize that by acting a part that was necessary for my survival, I was in the process of being reborn. In time, I learned to pretend so well to be a different kind of person that it became automatic. In other words, by pretending to be strong and fearless, I became so.

Lawson returned within several moments, his face pale, his eyes stricken with fear. "He beshat himself, Mistress, as he died. I took the liberty of cleaning the cabin with lye water and a goodly portion of sea water, hoping it would be your wishes for me to do so."

"Well done, lad." I looked at him narrowly. "From now on, you will refer to me as Captain Shaw."

"Yes ma'am. I mean, Yes, Captain Shaw."

"And you find that coward, Stanky, and inform him that I am the Captain of this ship."

"Yes, Captain!" Lawson cleared his throat. "I—I've already done so, ma—Captain. The crew is properly humble, Captain."

"Very well." I cleared my throat and looked into the everlasting sea, feeling every bit as lost and frightened as the boy who stood before me at attention, but knowing I must not show my true feelings or I would lose all I had gained. "I am naming you second-in-command. You are my First Mate, and responsible for the ship and crew. Take over, Lawson, for I must go below and chart my course."

"Begging your pardon, Cap'n, would you mind telling me where we're bound? According to all signs, the shores of England are opposite the way we are heading."

"I'll tell you in good time, Mate," I said coldly. For I had not the faintest idea where we were bound. For that matter, I hadn't a notion of where we were, but I felt vaguely, and for no tangible reason, that we were not on the original course, but heading toward some great unknown. As I entered the Captain's quarters again, I closed my eyes and breathed a short prayer that night would come soon and fair skies would continue, for I sorely needed the stars to guide me.

Keeping my fears to myself, I maintained a stoic calm throughout the balance of the day. When panic climbed high, I considered my resources and talked myself into believing my dangerous plan would work, but much depended on Cooty's returning to sanity. In short, I had rejected my earlier idea of going to a distant port to trade the goods *The Gentle Kathy* carried for gold. Instead—and *if* Cooty regained his senses and kept them long enough—it would be to my advantage to return to England. To go straight to the port of Harwich from which we had sailed. Somehow, I must convince Cooty that Captain Merryweather had instructed me to take the ship back to London after he was taken ill at Antwerp. I doubted very much if the old man knew his benefactor was dead, and Cooty never remembered a thing after a period of madness. *If* I could make the authorities believe the late Captain was still living, and *if* Cooty regained his senses, I could continue on just as Captain Merryweather had done in the past. Go and come, just as he had. Within a year I should have a healthy stake of this life's worldly goods. After that, I would settle down to a life of respectability. Find myself a suitable husband and start a family. It was a plan of ifs, all strung together out of desperation. But if . . .

That night after the stars came out, I pored over the charts by candle light until my eyes burned and the anxiety that at first was nothing more than a wave of dismay turned into a full-fledged terror. If I understood the maps and charts, I was halfway across the Atlantic Ocean, and heading for God knew where. Sleep was not to be mine that night, for every time I tried to close my eyes I saw the unrelenting vastness of the sea.

The next day, old Cooty began to whistle a chantey along toward evening, a well-known sign that his period of madness was ending. Shortly after that, he came to me where I was at the helm and said in a matter-of-fact voice, "I've been off me rocker again, luv. Now, I've searched high and low and I can find the Cap'n nowhere about."

I said, "He took sick, Cooty. Back in Antwerp, where he had to stay. And he ordered you to take *The Gentle Kathy* home."

"And Belle?"

"She's with him," I answered through dry lips.

"Seems like we're sailing with a short crew."

"Some of the men died, Cooty, of the sickness that caused the Captain to stay in Antwerp."

He drew a long breath. "Then... it wasn't just a part of the sickness? I mean, I didn't imagine that a number of dead were lowered into the waters?"

"No, Cooty. It wasn't just a part of your sickness. The rigger said the sickness was caused by mold in the rye."

"Aye." He gave me a penetrating look. "I've had it meself many years ago. Went down into the shadow of death with the fiery sickness. Imagined all sorts of things was goin' on, and liked to have tore up the whole ship I was on at the time in me madness." He gave me a rueful grin. "At least when the crazies come on me in me old age I don't do 'owt to cause any harm. Just sits there, I does, not knowin' who I be or where I hail from. Then, when I begins to come out of it, it's kind of like a curtain begins to part. Whenever I see that-there curtain beginnin' to open up all around me, I knows it ain't there and never was there, and I knows I been down at me bottom-side again. How many of the crew got took by the sickness?"

I gave him the names and included Jules Sarpston among them, planning to get to the rest of the crew and tell them what story they were to feed the old man before they had a chance to tell him the truth, including my decision to keep it quiet about the Captain's death. Then I said, "I've done the best I could, Cooty, but I fear we're far off our course. Will you go to the Captain's quarters and take a look for yourself?"

"Yes, lass." He turned and walked away, all bent over with age and what I suspected was grief for the dead mates. But then again, he might have doubted the ready lies that sprang to my lips.

I never saw Cooty again. Whether he jumped overboard in a fit of deep sorrow, was murdered by one of the survivors of our ill-fated crew, or died a natural death and was then heaved overside by one of them will remain a mystery to me until the end of my days. I waited and waited. Jack Lawson came to spell me at the helm and I went below, planning to find Cooty and ask him if he had reckoned our position, but I already had a premonition that he was lost to me forever.

Strange about those sudden glimpses of the future. I knew in advance that Lady Neilson would die, but I had no such experience about the disappearance of my own father, no such privilege concerning the theft of the hundred pounds, no previous warning about the disease that swept through *The Gentle Kathy* and took so many lives including that of Captain Merryweather. But I felt uneasy when old Cooty went below, and long before Jack Lawson came to take the tiller I experienced a terrible wrenching of my heart that was accompanied by a vision of a big, black cloud with old Cooty's face growing dimmer and dimmer inside of it until it disappeared altogether. About an hour after I had concluded that he was not aboard—and finally questioned the crew and got no satisfaction—I experienced another vision.

As things turned out, it was incomplete and in the strictest sense of the word, a false vision, for inside my head I saw a big white angel descending from heaven to settle on the sea at the side of *The Gentle Kathy*. Perhaps I wanted so desperately to be delivered from my dilemma that I brought the vision about myself, for the big white angel was merciful and kind, sent down to help a sixteen-year-old girl who knew in her heart of hearts that she was not heading back toward England, but lost on the high seas. One never knows in these instances, and I've always felt if humans could just have the power to call up a vision on order, we would never come to grief.... Providing, however, the vision is true and proper in all respects.

For instance, if I had known in advance that daylight would find me in even greater peril than I had been, I would have ordered Jack Lawson and Seaman Stanky to set sails in an entirely different direction from that which we were moving. Instead, I accepted the picture of an angel of mercy descending on us as truth of what would come. I had even begun to accept my fate, for although I did not want to return to England under the escort of another ship—which was what I took the portent as meaning—I knew I stood little chance of surviving lost on the open sea. If a ship of the Royal Navy brought us home I could not carry out my plan of keeping the payment for the voyage for myself, but I was practical enough to realize that a goodly sum of money would not stand me in much stead if I were dead. And so it happened that I was joyful when a beautifully gleaming snow white ship hove into view on the following morning. Even more grateful when I heard the thrilling call from the deck of the other vessel, "Ahoy, *The Gentle Kathy!*"

Dimly, I could make out the name on her prow. It was *The Dancing Lady*. She was a dream of a ship, four-masted and trim of line, graceful as a sea gull. When her pure white sails caught the orange glow of the rising sun I gasped with pleasure. My joy was short-lived, for the following moment brought a blast that exploded *The Gentle Kathy's* side. Before I could recover from the shock, there came a broadside from what sounded like dozens of salutes from fowling pieces. A second volley from the blazing pieces was ragged and awesome as it grazed *The Gentle Kathy's* deck. It brought up a spray of splinters from the wood and slashed through canvas.

"Mother of God and all of her sweet angels," screamed Jack Lawson, "we're under attack."

My echoed words may have sounded like a question, but they were not. I repeated his words because they sounded so silly. Any fool would know we were under attack by the other ship. Alas, I was unable to grasp the situation and spoke just as stupidly as Jack Lawson because I was in a state of panic. It had never occured to me that it was a pirate ship. In the beginning of my association with Solomon Merryweather I gave the danger of pirates a good deal of thought, but since we'd had no trouble during the past two years I no longer worried. During that shocking moment of the first barrage, I could only think that somehow the authorities had learned of my plans to dispose of the ship's coffers. That they had come to apprehend me and see to it that I received suitable punishment. Within a split second, I realized that nobody in this world could have known of my unlawful plans since I had not spoken of them aloud. But by then Jack Lawson was screaming at the top of his lungs that we were going to be taken by pirates.

Another thunderous cannonade tore a hole in the wounded *Gentle Kathy* that sent her spinning. I ran for shelter in the bulwark, but the choice was by instinct, not intellect, and a bad choice to boot. Muskets and pistols were firing from the deck of the beautiful *Dancing Lady* and the shots hailed down murderously all around me, enough to send an entire crew to their Maker. They tore through canvas and cut away at the grapnel lashings—the rattle and bang of the metal as it zipped and ricocheted enough to awaken the dead.

I screamed. Then I laughed hysterically, for one lonely musket slammed back at the schooner. It was Jack Lawson, his piece a bleat like a lonely lamb in the midst of a thunderstorm. Then came the silence, every bit as frightening as the firing, for with the quiet came the hopeless knowledge that they thought we'd given up. We hadn't given up at all, for except for Jack we'd not tried to defend ourselves. We'd been taken by surprise, for truth, and there's no contest between a crew of four and a party of twenty to thirty buccaneers.

I bobbed my head up and almost swooned at the sight of them as they swarmed over the side, all of them dark and grinning, all of them breaking the unearthly silence as they cried out what I could only perceive of as a victory shout. They poked about with their cutlasses as their footsteps pounded against the flooring of the doomed *Gentle Kathy*. And it was plain as day that they were disappointed to find no hearty seamen to run through!

Their conversation was loud and triumphant as they clomped through the silent *Gentle Kathy*, most of it in a foreign tongue that I couldn't make out. But I could understand the scream of terror that was torn from Jack Lawson's lips, poor Jack who dropped his piece to the deck, seared as a rabbit. Miraculously, he was uninjured, with pieces of broken spar all around him. And I—well, I didn't even know I had left the place where I had run for cover. Yet there I was, running like the furies of seventeen hells toward the slashing cutlasses, the uproarious laughter of deadly-eyed pirates who played with poor Jack like a cat plays with a mouse. But they were far worse, for they were nine in number to one of Jack. Already, they'd lobbed off his right ear and the blood gushed forth like new wine as Jack cowered, his hands trying to protect his head.

In my hand I held a four-pound pellet. In my roaring inferno of rage I must have looked silly indeed, a small girl with dark hair flying, lips drawn back in a savage snarl, my hand with the pellet raised threateningly as I advanced on the grinning, blood-lusting knaves.

"Leave that boy be!" My voice whipped through the laughter of merry-making pirates, at least loud enough to cause them to give me a glance of surprise.

"I'll kill every last mother's son of you," I blasted forth in my impulsive anger. And I kept on advancing, until I was within two feet of them. I with my cannon fodder, they with their gleaming, wicked cutlasses.

They laughed, of course. But my temper had exploded and I didn't have sense enough to realize that any one of them could have cut off my head with a lazy lash of a cutlass.

"You damned big bullies!" I continued to go forward into that nest of vipers. "Can't you see he's just a lad? Why don't you pick on someone your own size? He wasn't doing a thing to you. We didn't try to fight back; we're a ship with naught but a skeleton crew and his only sin was a few weak blasts from his weapon!"

My spate of idiotic words were cut short by the crack of a pistol. I almost jumped out of my skin. Then I turned around to see what had caused the roistering crew of cut-throats to stand at attention, their expressions suddenly contrite. A man strode toward where a hapless boy stood touching the place where his ear had been—and there a ridiculous girl remained transfixed, hand held in the air, nine stalwart men turned shifty-eyed and quiet. The rasp of my indrawn breath was the only sound in the utter silence.

"Disperse at once," ordered a cold voice. "The ship is on fire and listing badly. Get on with the business, or we've wasted a goodly portion of fire as well as time."

The pirates obeyed immediately. They averted their eyes and looked properly chastised as they moved away from Jack Lawson with the ashen face and bloody head. Not one backwards glance by any one of them, either, not even in my direction.

For myself, I was immobilized, but not speechless as I glanced at the immaculately attired man who was obviously the master of the ship that had dealt the killing blows to *The Gentle Kathy*. "The young Lord Muldoon, is it?" My voice was harsh with bitterness. "You look very grand in your spotless white breeches and matching coat. Why, there's not a bit of grime on your stock. Impeccable dress, I believe they call it. Quite fitting for the son of a lord. Too bad you have a face that shows all too clearly you're also the son of a whore, and if your features didn't show it, then your profession would."

Jack Lawson gave me a baleful glance. "Don't worsen your position, I beg—"

His words were cut short by a deep and pleasant laugh, and the pirate captain bowed deeply in my direction. "A whore she was not. But like you, my mother was beautiful. She was also innocent, until my father deflowered her. A Spanish peasant she was, and fetching to the stinking old goat who happens to be my father." He gave me a long, hard look out of his strangely colored eyes. Then he took my hand and said softly, "The rest of your mangy crew, ma'am—I'll not kill them as long as they mind their manners and I'll not allow my men to harm them, either."

Gesturing toward Jack, I stamped my foot and yelled, "That boy's missing ear is proof enough that you cannot control those animals."

He shrugged. "The lad still has his life. And you, my lady, have yours. The excitement of boarding gets into their blood, but a word from me calms them."

"I would as soon keep my ears," I shrieked.

"I may have your tongue, for I have no patience with a woman who hasn't enough sense to know when she's met her master. Even such a lovely one." His grip on my hand tightened, but I refused to wince, or to cry out. Speaking calmly, he said, "Make things easy. Where is the rest of your cowardly crew?"

For answer, I spat in his face.

Five

With incredible speed and efficiency, the pirate crew removed the goods from the hold of *The Gentle Kathy*, and I watched it all from the deck of *The Dancing Lady*. At my side was the handsome pirate captain, gentle and kind as a loving brother. When I spat in his face he merely gave me an exasperated look, and later, as he was leading me away from the ship he had taken, he said, "I'll forgive you for your action, little lady. 'Twas the act of a cornered animal. I admire a spirited wench, but see to it that you don't spit in my face again."

"*The Gentle Kathy* has been my home for the greater part of two years," I replied acidly. "I hardly think you could expect a woman who has just had her home taken away from her—shortly to become a part of the bottom of the sea, by the looks of her—to be *grateful*!"

"I don't expect gratitude," he said reasonably. "Nor do I expect you to suddenly turn tractable, even though I could have sent you down with that old tub. But I'll have respect from you, which means you do not turn on me like a vixen whose cubs have been threatened. Happy Jack Muldoon is the name I go by when plying my trade. And yours is Garnet..."

"Garnet Shaw, for whatever difference it makes."

He sighed. "It doesn't make much difference, really. But life is easier when things are pleasant. You're my captive. It matters not to me whether you're a princess or a serving wench, and if you hadn't chosen to tell me your last name—which I did recall, after you'd said it—I could have picked one for you and insisted you answer to it. This is my ship. I own it, I run it, and I'm the undisputed master of all hands aboard, including you, trinket. I'm telling you this to set you straight, since you obviously are laboring under the impression that the Hand of God is going to soon come down out of the sky and deliver you from your situation. No Hand of God is going to save you, understand? You will continue on to the New World with me, since that's where I'm headed."

I looked up at his handsome face and saw hardness, unmitigated cruelty in his handsome profile. "I've no choice? Is that what you're saying?"

He shrugged and gestured toward the sea, then toward his band of cutthroats who were scrambling over the side, and just in time, for *The Gentle Kathy* was all but submerged. "You could choose a watery grave, I suppose. But it'd be a shame. A terrible loss." His smile blazed for a moment, and once again I saw the warmth and genteel features of a gentleman born, reminding me of the time in the tavern when he had kissed me. "You're young and beautiful. You're made for loving, and it is seldom that I find a delightful young woman aboard the ships I take. But if you choose to jump overboard, to drown, that's your business. I'll not be dogging your every footstep."

"I want to live," I cried. "But it isn't *fair*! You've taken my goods, sent down my ship, brought me and the few hands who survived the sickness aboard your own, no doubt to kill us all."

He raised his eyebrow as he looked at me intently. "*Your* ship? I was under the impression that *The Gentle Kathy* was owned by Solomon Merryweather. And what were you doing in these waters? Merryweather never sailed so far from his regular course that he allowed himself to be wide open to attack. And how does it happen that a mere slip of a girl was in charge?" Again, his gleaming white smile flashed for a moment. "Ah. I know. You've been his little lady love."

"I have *not*! Captain Merryweather befriended me after my father—when I was all alone in the world, without home, hearth, or food. He knew my father, and took pity on me, an orphan of fourteen years. That dear, good man passed away at sea along with his—lady friend, Belle d'Arcy, and most of the crew of *The Gentle Kathy*. I was in the process of taking the ship back to London when you attacked it."

"You were far from England's shores, trinket."

I stamped my foot and yelled. "And don't call me 'trinket!' You *know* my name!"

"Of course. *Garnet*." He appeared to savor the taste of the name on his tongue. "A fitting name for a rare jewel among women. Come. I will show you to your quarters."

"Jack Lawson is just a lad. And Stanky and McClintock are good seamen. You'll not kill them, will you?"

"Certainly not. If they're able seamen, they've nothing to fear. We can always use another mate or two." He took my hand, and I did not pull it away, but followed him obediently since he'd said he was going to show me to *my* quarters, not his. A hint of admiration was in his voice when he said, "So you were bringing *The Gentle Kathy* back to England after the ship was visited by death. How did it happen that the able seamen aboard allowed you, a woman, to take command?"

"I am not without resources," I said coldly. "And anyway, everyone knew I was Captain Merryweather's... ward." It occurred to me that I was treading on thin ice, for the men who had been taken from *The Gentle Kathy* knew I had not exactly taken over the helm out of the goodness of my heart. From my point of view, the situation had demanded that I commandeer the ship since an attempt at mutiny had been made. But those three survivors who were now on *The Dancing Lady* with me knew that I had killed Jules Sarpston, and even though I had done it in self-defense, I had no way of knowing whether my three mates would agree with my motive for ending a man's life. For all I knew, they would inform their new Captain that I had committed murder on the high seas, which would place me in the same moral category as my captor. I was harboring no illusions concerning Lawson, Stanky, or McClintock's loyalties. Anything they might have to say that would make me look guilty would be in their favor. Figuring it was good sense to bide my time and see how the wind blew as far as the mates were concerned, I decided to ask some questions of my own:

"How does it happen that you call yourself Jonathan Muldoon, the young Lord Muldoon, when you're in London, but you're Happy Jack here and now?"

"Jack is a nickname for Jonathan."

"Yes, but that doesn't answer all I meant by my question."

"I don't choose to tell you my life's history."

"But that's not fair at all! I answered you directly when you questioned me!"

His smile was full of doubt, and the tone of his voice was nasty: "*Did* you now? Well, I'll not gainsay you, but I doubt very much if you've told me anything you didn't want to. You're a sly little vixen and bright enough for a woman, but something tells me you're keeping a great deal back. And that word, 'fair.' You've mentioned it for the second time within two minutes, which is puzzling. Surely you're not naive enough after living sixteen years to believe life is the slightest bit fair!"

The steps we descended were steep and narrow, so instead of answering, I lifted my skirts and concentrated on my footing. Through my mind swirled visions of slave ships that I had heard about and read about. I fully expected the hold to be filled with men and women in chains. A dirty and stinking hole where human life was worth only what it would bring in the slave market, and I would join them in their misery.

"You've lovely gams, Garnet Shaw," he said with a teasing smile.

"What you're really thinking is that my legs are strong and sturdy," I said. My voice was hard in my attempt to hold back the tears of fear that threatened me with each downward step I took.

"No. I wasn't thinking that at all. What ails you now?"

In spite of myself, I sobbed, when I had not wanted him to have the pleasure of knowing how terrified I was. "I know all about pirates," I shrieked. "From the ship, you'll take me to an auction block where you'll sell me to the highest bidder along with the rest of the enslaved. You'll strip me down and stand aside to brag about my good health. Spread my lips apart to show off my sound teeth, and you'll point to my heavy hair which is a sign of good health. I pray to God that I sicken and turn weak as water, for it galls me to think of bringing you a high price when you've stolen me."

"Oh, balls. I don't run a slave ship, Garnet Shaw. Whatever gave you that idea?"

"We're going down and *down*! You plan to stow me along with the rest of your plunder!" Several of his scurrilous crew were creating a lot of bumping and thumping as they stowed the crates they had taken from *The Gentle Kathy*. They'd gone down just ahead of us.

"*The Dancing Lady* is not fitted out like the average ship."

"But you put your plunder in the hold," I countered as I pointed to the noisy crew in the process of doing just that.

"Some of it. But I've also a few extra cabins below."

"Full of bilge water, no doubt."

"Why are you deliberately trying my patience?"

"Well, what in the devil would *you* do in my circumstances?" I blazed. "Do you expect me to bow down in supplication and fawn upon the person who has taken me captive? Give you *thanks*?"

"I would have the good sense to wait and see what was going to happen before I jumped to the conclusion that I would be mistreated. Tell me. Have you always been unreasonable?"

"As a matter of fact, I was always considered a sweet and dutiful daughter. I didn't even know I had a temper until... a dreadful thing happened to me." Unreal, I thought, to be conversing in such a manner with a black-hearted pirate, but my answer had slipped out involuntarily, and there was no taking the words back.

"There's nothing wrong with having a temper. In fact, a person who is lacking one is not long for this world. But there's no sense in always looking upon the dark side." He flung open a door and I gasped in amazement. He smiled down at me from his height of almost a full twelve inches above me. "There, now. Not at all what you pictured it, is it? No shackles, no fetid stench of blackamoors on their way into slavery. Surely we'll be comfortable in these splendid quarters."

"It's—it's beautiful!" The room was spacious, in spite of the low ceiling. It afforded a number of luxuries, including ornately carved chests, a thick rug that looked authentically Persian, bronze statuary, a full-sized bed that was draped with an exquisitely embroidered silken coverlet and brilliant with color from a number of satin pillows. A doorway appeared to open into another room, but was covered with lattice in a way that obscured my view. An altogether charming room, with the possibility of another opening from it, but the richness and elegance meant nothing to me for he had said *we* would be comfortable. I had feared such an outcome all along, second to being sold into slavery. My face grew hot as a crimson blush stained me from neck to forehead.

"I don't forget a face," he remarked softly. "Nor the feel of soft, tender lips. Look at me, Garnet Shaw."

I raised my face, but not my eyes, for my mind surged with shame.

He touched my face and continued to speak as if he were gentling a skittish horse. "It was no coincidence that I came upon you, for last night was not the first time I followed the wake of *The Gentle Kathy*."

Above the bed were ruffled lace hangings, gathered together at each post and fastened. I looked at them, thinking of the time to come when the hangings would envelop the soft, deep bed, but I found no delight in my thoughts, for the *we* he'd spoken of did not mean I would recline in that bed alone. I said, "Solomon Merryweather would have been more than a match for you, had you attempted to take over any ship he commanded."

"It was not his ship that I particularly wanted, although it would have made no sense to leave a sinking vessel intact with her load. But you're right. I hold respect in my heart for few men, but the late Captain was an exception. I would never have attacked any ship he commanded. Not because he could have bested me in a battle, for we far out-numbered him. Strength and power always wins in the end. It was you I wanted, Garnet. The nights have been long, and cold and empty since I tasted the nectar of your lips." He led me to an intricately carved chair that was cushioned well and covered with dark blue velvet. I sat, since it was obvious that he wanted me to, but even though he could force me to sit down, he could not force me to change my opinion of him. Rapidly, I assessed my situation. I had killed once. It had not been easy, and ever since, my sleep had been disturbed by horrid dreams in which I stabbed Jules Sarpston over and over again, only to awaken in a clammy sweat. Mayhap the second time would be easier, but I would have to look sharp around me for a means with which to do it, and an opportunity, too.

"If you wanted me, why did you not come out from under the rock where slime of your ilk resides and state your case?"

He laughed, then took a twin to the chair I was sitting in, which was opposite me. "You know very well I would never have stood a chance, Garnet. Your Captain Merryweather was a stickler for all that is right and holy. It's no secret that the bastard son of Lord Muldoon has taken to plundering the high seas. Merryweather would have sent me packing."

"How can you chance showing yourself on the streets of London if it's no secret, then?" Again, my words came unbidden.

"I no longer take such chances. Two years ago, my activities on the sea were not as well-known as they are now. Besides, I had a mission to accomplish on that golden day in October when I was treated to the most delicious sight my eyes had ever beheld, the most delightful kiss my lips had ever tasted."

Contemptuously, I yawned in his face. Then I said, "The speech of Ireland is on your tongue, but you've no need to go to such great lengths to charm me, sir, for charm me you never will. I am at your mercy, and you may enjoy whatever you intend to do to the fullest, but do not expect me to go soft in the head over a blackguard."

"Yes, I saw you and kissed you and never forgot you," he said as if I had not spoken. "Then I got a glimpse of you one day as you leaned over the railing of *The Gentle Kathy*. We were two ships that passed in the gloaming, and the rays of the sun slanted across your dark brown hair, turning it to a shade of fiery russet. A woman stood at your side. A woman rather fusty in appearance, and I took her for Merryweather's woman. Right or wrong?"

"Right. She was Belle d'Arcy."

"Dead of the same sickness that took the Captain?"

I nodded.

He poured from a decanter of wine that rested on the table at the side of his chair. Two silver goblets gleamed richly as he lifted them both, stood, and handed me one. More of his plunder, no doubt, I assumed, as were the rich furnishings in the room. But I accepted the wine, for I was thirsty. He looked at me as he raised his glass. "You've had a bad time of it. Now I will drink to your future, which will be much better if you stop fighting."

"Drink to whatever pleases you," I said with a shrug. "Obviously, I'm in no position to stop you from doing as you wish, but if you think you were doing a kindness by claiming my ship and taking me prisoner, your idea of kindness is very strange indeed." The wine was full-bodied, but not cloying. It slid down my throat like honey.

"You responded to my kiss that day in the tavern, I swear it!"

"You took me by surprise. I was a maid of fourteen, and had only recently lost my father." I gave him a cool and level glance. "Perhaps in my grief my response was natural enough, for he was a very affectionate man, and I was accustomed to his embrace."

He threw back his head and roared with laughter, a most disconcerting reaction to the barb that I had believed so clever. When he was recovered, he said, "Swift of wit as you are, I admire you. But you'll never make me believe that you clung to me and kissed me with such fire because I reminded you of your father. Unless you had an incestuous relationship with him."

For a moment, I considered flinging the remainder of my wine in his face, but it was too good to waste and I was still thirsty. Instead, I allowed his nasty suggestion to go begging for an answer.

"Surely it isn't hard for you, a young woman who was brought up as the darling of her father's house—educated and pampered—to believe that a man can love a maid after naught but a look and a stolen kiss."

"How do you know so much about me?"

"I told you, I made inquiries."

"But not of Captain Merryweather."

"Certainly not. I'm no fool. It's common knowledge on the streets of London that he paid your way out of jail out of the goodness of his heart. A man does not suddenly appear with a young girl aboard his ship and in his London house without folks knowing of it. No person that I talked to knew your name, but several said the late Captain knew your father. Some believed they were friends. I was also told that your father was a doctor of animals, but nobody knew your name." His manner changed as he gave me a dark look. "In all truth, I desired you and planned to have you for my own. But I hung back out of deference to your Captain. Did, that is, until I saw the bloody corpse of a seaman heaved overboard a few days ago."

All the blood drained from my face and I felt exactly the way a captured butterfly must feel, although there were no visible nets.

"You killed him." He made a statement, flat and bold, as if he knew it for a fact. Then he leaned forward and fixed me with his strangely penetrating gaze. In spite of myself, I could not look elsewhere but into his eyes. Our glance was unbroken for a long moment, until I began to wonder if I would live out the rest of my life locked in a limbo wherein I wanted to deny that I had taken the life of another, but could not. At last, our glance was broken, and to my shame I was the one who looked away first.

It was a strange, almost mystifying experience that left me weak as a kitten. Almost as if I had been running as hard as I could, against a strong and relentless wind. During that space of time, I had seen my own reflection in his eyes and I shuddered as I fancied that he had absorbed me all of a piece—that aside from capturing me physically, which he undeniably had, he had also stolen my soul and my mind.

His words were gentle. Surprisingly so. "The seaman tried to rape you. That's why you killed him."

I jerked violently. "How could you know?"

"Because it was in your eyes. They're very expressive."

"You did something to me! I don't know what it was, but somehow, you looked inside my head and read that knowledge!"

"Words cannot express how very glad I am that you bested the beast," he said with a smile.

Again, I turned to scorn and hatred to shore me up. "Why are you glad? So I would be unspoiled for you, when you take me?"

"Stop trying to talk yourself into hating me. What you feel is fear, not hatred. And I promise you this: From me, you have nothing to fear, but without me you have much to dread. I am the master of this ship and I am in total command of it and my crew. You are far tougher than you look, but if you carry out your half-formed plans to have me join the man you killed in self-defense, those same men who bow down to my every command would quickly become what you called them yourself. Animals. To me, you are a lovely young woman who was born for love and loving. At my hands you will know the greatest joy a woman is privileged to know, for I do not love lightly, and I am generous in all things. At their hands you would be used without mercy, without the slightest shred of concern for your feelings. You would be handed from one savage and humiliating scene to another, until you were broken and bleeding, and death would be welcome, even sought after. But that would not be the end of your suffering, Garnet, not by a long shot. Once they had reduced you to a spiritless creature, they would sell you to a house where you would be submitted to even worse depravities. Do I make myself clear?"

"You're saying that I must not kill you, for if I do, I'll be at the mercy of your men." I attempted to smile, but my lips trembled mightily, although my voice was defiant. "But why do you tell me such things? You've pointed out to me already that I am small and defenseless. And I have no weapons." Ruefully, I thought of the Captain's daggers. Either taken as plunder or sent down with *The Gentle Kathy*.

"When a man is embroiled in the pleasure of love, his brains don't function. Because of your ungentle nature, your hair-spring explosiveness, I thought it best to lay my cards on the table before I become vulnerable."

"We're moving." The motion of the ship was undeniable.

"Yes, but that is beside the point. It should also have been expected." He stood. "Have I made myself clear?"

I nodded, both unwilling and unable to speak.

"Then I will take my leave of you." He gestured toward one of the chests. "In there you'll find suitable attire for the Captain's lady, together with a few baubles for your pleasure."

At last I was able to speak again, and my words were vehement. "You can't buy me with baubles!"

If the devil himself is able to smile, surely he lent to Happy Jack Muldoon that smile for a moment, for that was exactly the way it looked. Quietly, he moved across the expanse of rich, thick carpeting and quietly he assured me that it was not his intention to buy me. At the door, he turned and looked at me full in the face. "A man does not purchase that which he already owns." The smile returned to some semblance of humanity. "We will dine within four hours. I will send bath water and after you have bathed, perhaps a nap will sweeten your disposition."

When he had closed the door behind him, I resisted the impulse to throw the heavy brass vase that adorned one of the tables at it. Instead, I burst into tears and flung myself face down across the soft and inviting bed as soon as I'd bolted the door.

Some minutes later, three knocks sounded. A quick look into the full-length looking glass told me my eyes were red and my face swollen. My gown, none too clean to begin with, was badly wrinkled. Altogether, I presented a sorry appearance, but there was nothing I could do about it. Anyway, I cared little about how I looked when it came to presenting myself to a pirate, especially an underling—a lackey who was sent with the water Jack Muldoon had promised.

For a moment, I was tempted to remain silent. To not bother opening the door. But common sense told me the arrogant pirate captain would batter it down, or cause his criminal band of mates to do so. By the looks of him, he seldom turned his soft hands to any kind of work. His white attire was unmarred by any kind of stain. Not even a bit of dust was on him. But the cabin was equipped with a porthole, and for a moment longer I gave it some thought. It would be easy for me to open it and wriggle myself through that opening, but I disliked the look of the greenish brown water that boiled against the glass. For the time being, I put those thoughts from my mind.

I opened the door and stared in shock at the person who stood in front of me. A woman, when I had expected a man or a boy. She was plump and pretty, but past her prime some twenty or more years ago with a goodly bit of grey in her blonde hair and a number of wrinkles upon her smiling face. "Well, miss, are you going to stand there barring my way, or are you going to let me by? This pitcher is heavy when empty. Now it is full of boiling water and I'd be pleased if you'd stand aside so I can fill your tub. Oh—I'm Becky. Welcome aboard, mum."

Touching my hand to my unruly hair, I did as she asked, feeling wretched, unkempt and put upon. It was one thing to allow a rough, crude cabin boy—pirate to see me at my worst, but quite another to be the object of a knowing gaze from the depths of another woman's eyes. "Forgive me," I said. "You took me by surprise, for I didn't know another woman was aboard."

"Yes. Well, I'm aunt to Happy Jack, having been born his father's half-sister. Aunt Becky, he calls me, and you may do the same, child." She hurried into a tiny compartment where I heard a resounding splash of water, and returned immediately to give me a more-than-passing glance. "So you're the one. My my, but you're pretty as a spring sky, all right, even with your eyes red from crying, though younger than I thought. It's time my nephew settled down and stopped frittering away his best years fawning over strumpets." With a nod of her head as if she approved whole-heartedly, she left, calling over her shoulder that she would be back in a thrice with more water.

While she was gone, I ducked behind the latticed partition and found a chamber pot with matching lid. Painted roses bloomed on both pieces. There was a white, furry pelt on the floor that looked as if it might be rabbit, but for all I knew it was ermine. One corner was filled by a porcelain tub that was big enough for me to sit down in if I drew up my legs, and a marble-topped table held a prettily decorated pitcher of cold water. I had just treated my nose to a sniff of the elegant soap, soft as silk and scented with an exotic perfume, when the woman who called herself Aunt Becky returned with another pitcher of steaming water.

"That's a heavenly smell," she said off-handedly. "His own scent, and some might go so far as to say it's womanish of a man to enjoy the good things of life like perfumed soaps, but you'll find that my nephew is all man, lovey. It's just that he likes to be clean and neat. Can't stand to have a speck of dirt on him, and exults in the good life. I can't say as I blame him, either, after all he's been through. His father put him on as stable boy when he was just a lad. Jack swore on his love for his dead mother if he ever got the smell of horse dung off his skin and out of his nostrils that he'd never be dirty again, and he's not." She beamed.

The steam arose from the tub after she'd poured the second pitcher of hot water in, and the fragrance in the moist little room was almost overpowering.

"I dropped a bit of oil in your bath, mum. Makes the Captain's quarters smell ever so nice, but it's a fine treatment for skin, too. Make you all soft to his touch, and he does love the scent of bergamot, but there's more than that. I said to him, I said, 'Jack, dear, you'd have made a good chemist,' for he's always mixing this and that. Makes his own wine, too, and I'll bet you appreciated the fine bouquet of that bottle that was waiting for you."

"Sweet geranium," I said, sniffing in the perfumed steam that rose like a wraith from the tub. "I suppose the lemony smell is the bergamot, but am I not right about the sweet geranium?"

She nodded. "You've a fine nose on you, child, for you've hit it just right. Now I'll leave you to bathe alone."

"Wait." I held out my hand, wanting to detain her, but wanting also to do a little talking myself. "Are there other women aboard?"

"No, dearie. Just you and me, and for all these years my nephew has been plying the seas, it was just me. It'll be a happy change for me to have another female aboard. The boys says I talk too much, but I say I only do so because they don't listen."

85

"But they... I've always heard that pirates live in deadly fear of being drowned at sea and all other kinds of mishaps if a woman is on their ship. I mean, aren't women supposed to bring bad luck with them?"

"Sure, and that's the way the lot of them used to feel, but I was here first and here I will stay, too. As long as the light of my life wants me with him, and I hope he always does."

"You mean you were sailing with him when he... became a pirate?"

The woman looked at me with disappointment. "Why, child, my Jack is no pirate. His men are, that's true enough, but that boy never sullies his hand or heart by taking that which ain't his."

"Oh." I formed a smile, and nodded. "Now I understand."

"I thought you would. And once again, I want to tell you how happy I am that he has chosen you." Her greying eyebrows lifted archly. "Oh, he's besotted with love of you, darlin'. For two years I've heard him speak of little else except the delightful girl he kissed in a tavern."

It was all too clear that Aunt Becky was as besotted with adoration for her nephew as she vowed he was of me, and I suspected that she was slightly daft to boot, for a person who thinks clearly would realize that it mattered not whether he lifted a hand to take that which did not belong to him, he was a pirate through and through since he owned and operated the ship and gave orders to seize and plunder.

As soon as she was out of the room, I bolted the door again and stepped into the little cubicle to bathe, adding just enough cold water to make it bearable. It had been a long time since I had enjoyed the sensuous pleasure of a full bath, for *The Gentle Kathy* afforded few frills, although she'd been a seaworthy and magnificent vessel. The hot water was soothing, the scented oils a caress on my skin. Before the water could cool, I scrubbed myself briskly with the finely milled soap and a sponge, then wet my hair. The suds were thick and white and foamy. So much so that I was forced to rinse my hair with the remaining cold water in the pitcher. I shuddered, but after I stepped out and dried myself, I felt both rested and exhilarated. Ready to face whatever came, and oddly enough, I was no longer frightened. The plump little woman might be a touch dotty, but it was a comfort to know she was there, for I doubted very much if Happy Jack Muldoon, or the Young Lord Muldoon, would harm me with a devoted auntie on board.

After I had wrapped myself in the long, downy-soft dressing gown that I found in the bathing room, I stretched out on the bed to rest my eyes for a moment. Within what seemed but mere seconds, I awakened to a knock on the door and the cheerful voice of Aunt Becky calling out, "Dinner within the hour, lovey!"

I was famished. I was also surprised to realize that I had slept all that time, but a look at the gleaming golden clock on the wall opposite the bed showed me that I had. From the trunk, I selected a pale pink gown of finest silk moire. It shimmered under the glass-enclosed candles that I had to light in order to see my way around, and after my eyes grew accustomed to the mellow golden light I realized that the frock had been woven in a way that made it change colors as one moved. The shimmering quality changed from a deep, flaming red to a frosty baby pink to coral. With my ivory skin and dark hair, I felt the color was complimentary, but I was somewhat affronted by the daringly low neckline.

As I looked at myself in the mirror, I blushed when I saw the full rise of my breasts, the deep cleavage. "No!" I spoke out loud as I yanked the beautiful gown over my head. I would not allow myself to dress as a harlot, even though it was enchanting.

As I sorted through the numerous frocks a blue one caught my eye, but the fabric and sheen of the pink one had seduced me. Another look at the pale blue silk showed me that the cut was far less revealing. The sleeves ended halfway between wrist and elbow, and they were edged with a creamy lace with interwoven threads of fiery green and vivid orange. The underskirt, prominent because of the way the overskirt was pulled away, was cut from the same luminescent fabric as the edging. It clung to my figure and accented my slim waist but it did not make me feel indecent because the neckline was square and modest enough to cover all but the suggestion of curves.

A few minutes in front of the mirror and my hair was

dressed to my liking. It fell free and naturally, although it was still slightly damp and tended to curl more than usual. Frowning, I looked around for something to tie at the back, to lift it away from the nape of my neck, where it felt heavy and unpleasantly wet. A selection of ribbons reposed in a tray on top of a chest. I chose a creamy satin one, and that would have been the end of it had I not chanced to glance into the other tray, and there I was, seduced by the glow and glimmer of opals. I had long adored opals with their magical sparks of fire, their radiant glow of green and blue. For a long moment I stared at the single strand of jewels, each stone as big as the end of my middle finger. I was sorely tempted. There were earrings, too—long, entrancing, and perfect with the gown I had selected. But I turned away, my lips firmly compressed and lowered in disapproval. I had informed my captor that he could not buy me. If I gave in to the temptation, it would look as if I had changed my mind, or at least was willing to give the matter a second thought.

The Lady Neilson had worn opals. She was said to never be without them, but I had been guilty of coveting them. With a pang of sorrow, I remembered how I had begged my father to buy me opals, but he had refused out of hand, saying opals were unlucky for those who were not born in October. "They are her birth stone," he'd said. And she wore them the day she came and gave me a hundred pounds, for I remembered the flash of fiery colors at her throat and they were as big as...

The cold winds of logic caused me to shudder violently as I stepped back to the chest where the opals lay. They gleamed as I held them in my hands and remembered Happy Jack Muldoon's statement about being in London on business the day I wandered into the tavern and he kissed me.

"Business." I whispered the word with a shaky breath, wondering exactly what kind of business. Was he there as hired murderer of Lady Neilson as she lay in her bed? My heart was in my throat. I didn't want to even consider such a far-fetched idea. Not in my present circumstances. Not at all, for it was too frightening to think of that handsome man in the act of slipping silently into a woman's bedchamber, unsheathing his knife and slitting her throat from ear to ear.

But I could not keep myself from looking backwards to that time two years earlier when I had been out of my mind with worry and grief. He had been in London, for I had seen him with my own eyes. "Oh, God!" Again, I spoke aloud, unable to keep the horror of it all inside me, for I had turned the stones over to look at the gold with which they'd been set. If I had ever doubted that my father was in love with Lady Neilson, I no longer did. On the back of one of the earrings, etched by a fine hand, was proof. L. to CN. F. G. S. The letters could only mean one thing: Love to Constance Neilson from George Shaw.

All right. They had loved. Tears stung my eyes, but I blinked and blinked to keep them back. Loving was considered sinful if it came about between a man and woman who were not wed. Yes, I realized that well enough, but loving was a natural emotion and my father had been faithful to the memory of my mother for many a long and heartbreaking year while Lady Neilson was tied to a vile old man who was old enough to be her father. I could excuse them whether the church could or not. But what of a man who did murder? I dropped the jewels as if they were truly on fire instead of just appearing so. The evidence was there, in that lacquered tray. No doubt the necklace had been on her throat when he crept into her bedchamber as she slept all unaware. A man without scruples would not hesitate to take them. The man who had hired him to do the awful deed would not have dared raise a hue and cry over their disappearance.

Then and there I vowed to avenge the woman my father loved. By doing it, I would also avenge my father. For all I knew Happy Jack Muldoon was guilty of his death, also. I had the evidence of his guilt in killing Lady Neilson in the opals. My hands were icy cold, my face aflame with the fever of my fury. Some day, somehow, I vowed, I would return to England. To London. If that ruined old man still lived, I would fix his clock along with his hired assassin's. If I had my way, they would hang together. And I—squeamish as I was about the sight of a man on the gallows two years ago—I was not the same sweet girl I had once been. My mouth twisted into a cold smile as I visualized myself standing and applauding with the rest of those who turned a hanging into a gala affair.

Two knocks sounded at the door. I answered at once. "Yes?"

"I have come to escort you to dinner, Garnet." His voice. Quiet and well modulated, a sign of the gentleman he pretended to be when he was not scavenging corpses after the kill.

Regally, I walked to the door and gave him what I fancied was a ravishing smile. "I'm ready, Captain."

"You're beautiful." He stood in the doorway for a moment, his eyes appraising. Then he walked to the tray of baubles and unswervingly took out the opals. "Far more beautiful than I had dreamed you would be in one of the costumes I had selected for you, but of course you would be delightful in a canvas bag. Turn around. Your complexion and that particular gown will complement these jewels."

I fluttered my eyelashes and smiled again, knowing the dimple at the corner of my mouth would flash flirtatiously for a second. "If you like." I pivoted around and held myself quiet long enough for him to clasp the opals beneath my hair.

As we walked sedately to the dining salon, I accepted his arm, along with his flow of compliments. Among other things, he remarked that a bath and a rest had done wonders for my disposition.

Forcing a lilt to my voice, I said, "I was unstrung, as well as exhausted. Things came into a better perspective after I slept. After all, I could have fallen into worse hands. At least you're cultured and handsome. And—" I almost choked over the next words, but he didn't seem to notice, because he was quickly succumbing to my flattery and a man who is drinking in words of his own praise has no room in his head for speculation about avarice and cunning. "You were right when you said I responded to your kiss. I've thought of you often during these past two years." True enough. I had also dreamed of him, only to awaken and ask myself why I had dreamed of a man I had seen only twice—the time he'd kissed me, and later, when he was in the chocolate shop. But I didn't want to pile it on too thickly. Another time would be better for me to coyly admit that he had walked in the night-shine of my dreams.

The dinner was extravagant, and everything was prepared with great care and finesse. The wines were superb. Even if they had been sour as vinegar I would have imbibed freely, however, for I was not looking forward to the night I would spend in his arms, and having my senses dulled would help.

At the doorway, he looked down at me intently. I looked back, invitingly. "Am I to understand that you've accepted the idea of sharing the bed with me?"

I reached up and touched his cheek, feeling more than a little giddy, yet very much in control. "Ohhh, my! I think I could find a better choice of words. I'm...thrilled. And honored."

To my surprise, he lifted me in his arms and carried me over the threshold. My laughter was tinged with real mirth when he put me down and said he adored me, but he was too busy undressing me to know the difference between the genuine laughter that pealed forth just then and the polite pretense at it that I had forced throughout the lengthy meal. I was laughing because I was learning much about the tall, dark man who believed he had tamed a vixen. And I was thinking of the future, taking satisfaction in the realization that there are many ways to kill a man. It pleased me because I was going to do it a little bit at a time, and because he would never feel a thing or know what I was about until that moment of my revenge. Then he would know, and a man of his pride would be scalded at the knowledge that my pleasure in his company was all sham.

When he removed the necklace, I was both relieved and bereft. The opals had lain heavily against my throat, but I had found the sensation agreeable for it helped me in my resolve. They had also felt warm, and it had been almost cold in the dining hall. When he took them off, I felt naked. Far more naked than I had felt when he removed my garments. When he dropped the jewels into the lacquered box they made a little clicking sound, like a rattlesnake about to strike. I smiled in the secret knowledge that I was the rattlesnake, but it seemed fitting that it was the Lady Neilson's opals that made the sound.

He stood back and appeared to drink me in, from the tips of my toes to the top of my head. "Never have I seen such perfection. And you stand so proudly. Amazing."

"Why should I not be proud?"

He laughed. "Are you saying you've captured the eye of the most eligible man on the ship? That's hardly a compliment, my dear, considering the crew."

At least he had a sense of humor. It would be hard enough to continue my masquerade, but a man or woman who cannot see the funny side of things makes life even more tedious than it is at best, and there would be little "best" for me for a long, long time.

I reached up and put my arms around his neck. Pressed my naked body against him. Against his chest, I murmured sweet lies: "I am proud because you've wanted me. Because I caught your eye so long ago. And you cared enough to fill the trunks with garments that are just my size."

"We'll be married as soon as we drop anchor, Garnet. We'll walk out into the freedom of the New World where we'll find an official to say the words."

"Married!" I almost fainted. Marriage was not a part of my plans. Fat chance a wife would have of bringing her husband to justice!

He was stripping off his fine linen waistcoat, and stopped with his fingers on the top string as if stunned. "You sound as if you don't like the idea of marriage."

"No! I mean, *yes*! I was just... surprised, that's all." Remembering how he'd appeared to read my mind when he'd stared so deeply into my eyes, I lowered my lashes. "I mean, you're a gentleman born. The son of—"

"A scum," he finished for me. "And I'm a bastard, don't forget. But I love you, darling Garnet, and I've longed for you an eternity."

"Two years isn't an eternity."

"It was to me. I couldn't do a thing when I tried to find pleasure in the flesh of willing maidens. But now—" He looked down, and my eyes followed his glance. Then I was almost jolted out of my act, for what I saw was not the way I had pictured the way of men. With my own hands I had laid out Captain Merryweather, but he was dead. Even Sarpston in the heat of his passion was a dying man, and I had given his manly protuberance only a fleeting glance for I had been intent upon the kill. As I backed away, I wrung my hands together and whimpered. "I can't. I mean, you don't expect me to be able to... I mean, you're far too big! We would never fit!"

"You were made for my love, and my love includes possessing you, dearest girl."

My eyes were big and staring. I'm sure the whites were bigger than the irises under the glow of the candles. "But it will surely be the end of me." I was against the wall. Naked as I was, I was edging toward the doorway, my fear overriding the dangers that lurked out there. My hand contacted the ornate door knob when he sprang forward and gathered me into his arms.

"Oh, you little innocent darling," he murmured into my hair. He kissed my eyes, my nose, my lips and throat as he carried me to the bed. "How delicate you are. And how sweet and innocent. I'm not a brute, dearest Garnet. What you fear most will not take place until you tell me you want me, that you are ready for me."

God! He had that way about him that was capable of charming the fear right out of a girl. As he spoke softly, gently, I found myself submitting to him. And God in heaven, I even became so engrossed in the thing at hand that I forgot all about my father, Lady Neilson, the proof of his murderous nature that was etched on the opals. In short, I surrendered wholeheartedly, and never so much as blinked an eye when I cried out to him at long last, "Now. Oh, yes! Now!"

He took me, and there was a quick burst of pain, but it was nothing compared with the consuming lust he had so skillfully built up in me. I was a woman possessed by the demon of desire. Wanton as any strumpet, delighting in every fiery touch of his fingers, and when it was over, the first thing that came to mind once I was capable of thinking clearly was a soul-searing shame. *God help me,* I prayed, *for I am surely condemned by all that is holy.*

Six

I hated Jack Muldoon. Yet he was capable of fascinating me and there were times when I couldn't get enough of his love. Days and weeks passed in a roiling, rushing turmoil. Time went by quickly for the most part, but each hour was an agony that dragged by during those times when I was morbid and confused, and so dispirited and filled with self-loathing that I was almost immobilized. One morning I might awaken in his arms, the length of my body pressed against his as I slept and know an aching desire for him in spite of a night of love-making. The next morning I could just as well awaken as far away from his despicable body as I could get, consumed with a sense of despair and my mind filled with hell's rushing rivers of torment that had filled my dreams. During those times when I hated him, I would go about with my features cold and withdrawn while I savored my plans for the future—for his future. I would hug my hatred to me as I envisioned the way he would react to my public accusations once we were back in London. But by the time dinner rolled around I was often eager to see him, especially if he had neglected me in favor of playing cards with his men or overseeing work on the vessel. Sometimes I had to pretend affection but too often I was not acting at all when I smiled and fawned over him.

He treated me with utmost kindness and respect for the most part. I was the darling of *The Dancing Lady*. When he came to the great cabin each day when twilight began to fall he would invariably take me in his arms and words of his undying love would tumble from his lips. Then we would select my dinner gown. He enjoyed dressing me as if I were a doll, and I not only allowed him to do so, I reveled in it except for those times when I was stricken all over again with the knowledge that he was a diabolical savage who was guilty of all sorts of heinous crimes—and I was as guilty as he. Sensitive to my every mood, he grew concerned during those periods when I despised him, but of course I could not be truthful with him. He would ask, "Are you unwell, dearest?"

"No. Of course not," I replied each time. "I am feeling very well."

On those occasions he would narrow his eyes and look at me strangely, complaining that I had withdrawn from him again. One time he said, "It's as if you stand before me as a shell, complete in all your enchanting beauty, but empty inside, and devoid of life."

I yearned to tell him that was exactly how I felt, for I had been betrayed by my own willful body, my emotions. I was a traitor to the memory of my father, and to dear Lady Neilson. Again, I had resolved to put my weaknesses away. To continue with the part that had begun as a role I was playing, of course, for to turn away from him would make him suspicious. But in the future, I vowed to remain true to myself and my plans, to not allow his wicked, deceiving charm to quell my restless heart. During those times I was sure that my wayward, wanton desire for him was a thing of the past, for even when I looked him full in the face I felt nothing but disgust. It occurred to me that I might have been possessed by madness for a while, which would explain my runaway reactions to a man who was an admitted pirate—and probably much, much worse. If so, I felt reasonably sure that the madness was over and done with, for several days went by in which I wanted to bite the lips that kissed me, break every bone in the hands that caressed me. Once again, I was beginning to feel respect for myself.

After several days of forcing myself to please him, he suggested that I might be in need of a more bountiful diet. Turning on a smile, I asked, "What on earth are you talking about? The food is excellent. Far more bountiful than the fare on *The Gentle Kathy*." It was true, too. There were fresh vegetables in the hold, all kinds of fresh and dried fruits, sea food and meats that had been set aboard in a frozen state and kept that way with ice surrounded by sawdust. The ship's kitchen was spotless. Aunt Becky did not see to the preparation of the food herself, but she made inspections several times each day and exercised her vast store of knowledge in culinary arts.

"You have these spells," he said, "when your eyes lack luster. Perhaps you are homesick." He sat down and pulled me onto his lap. Although I shuddered at his touch, I didn't pull away. In a gentle voice, he said, "You've never spoken to me of your home except to say your father is dead."

And you may well have been the one who ended his life, too, I wanted to say. Turning so I could look into his eyes, I said, "I didn't tell you he was dead. I said I lost him."

He didn't blink an eyelash, but looked perplexed. "I suppose I took your statement as meaning that he had passed on."

I felt that the moment had come for me to ask questions of my own, but I would have to go slowly and catch him unaware. "My father and I were eating dinner in a tavern when he chanced to look across the street and saw a man who owed him a considerable amount of money. He left me to finish my meal while he spoke to the man about his indebtedness. I waited for a long time. Finally, I went to inquire and was told by the tavernkeeper that my father was summoned by someone with a sick animal, he thought. He had left the place by the back door. He didn't come back."

"Not ever?" Happy Jack Muldoon's strange colored eyes showed only concern and pity. But I had no way of knowing how to read what went on behind those eyes and his expression could well have been contrived. With practice, I had learned to put whatever kind of expression in my eyes that I chose. "You mean to tell me," he continued when I hesitated too long about answering. "that you never saw your father again?"

"Not ever."

His lips brushed my forehead. "My poor darling. And you were just a child."

"Yes. And hungry, too. Without a ha'penny to my name."

He could not bear to see me unhappy. My tears sent him into anguish, unless he was feigning as I was.

"So please understand that when I appear to be distant, it's because..." I hesitated, and snuggled closer to him, in order to put my ear next to his heart. The reading I had occupied myself with all my life had mentioned the tendency of a liar to experience a quickening of heart beats and an increase in volume. Speaking just above a whisper in order to hear his every heart beat distinctly, I said, "A neighbor told me it was rumored that my father met his death at the hands of an assassin."

His voice was a deep rumble, but there was no change in his heart beat. "An assassin? But why? Who would want to murder a doctor of animals?"

"The husband of the woman he loved."

"My dear. My angel. But there may be no truth in rumors. Women love to gossip." Still no difference in the steady sound within his chest. He patted my shoulder. "Your mother. You told me she died many years ago. A man... has certain needs, but if your father cherished you, and I'm sure he did, I doubt very much if he told you of his paramour."

"I knew nothing of it until after he disappeared, and then I wasn't sure. Looking back, I can see that my father sheltered me. After my neighbor told me about my father's lady-love, I began to look at certain things that had taken place in the past with a different eye. She—his lady came to me and gave me money. It was stolen from me afterwards, but she gave it, just the same, and said she owed it to him for his services. In time I realized that she probably owed him nothing, but she wanted to help me because she loved him, and I was his child. She was murdered on the very night after she came to my house."

His arms held me more tightly. At last I said, "Her throat was cut as she slept. She was Lady Constance Neilson."

Steady heart beats. Neither faster nor slower. Not louder, either. But his voice was sympathetic. "You were a lost little lamb." He was silent for a moment, then he repeated the name, Neilson, thoughtfully, and asked, "Was she wife to Lord Neilson of Neilson Hall? I suppose she was, of course. I saw fat old Lord Neilson once, many years ago. He came to my father's house when I was a lad, but he didn't have Lady Neilson with him. I think... there was a sordid tale making the rounds at the time. It was whispered among the servants that he had paid for the murder of a young man. His daughter's suitor, I believe, or maybe it was his niece who was in danger of marrying beneath her. I disliked the old frog even before I heard the ugly story, and felt he was capable of anything."

"It's dreadful to realize that men of wealth and title can have a person killed and get away with it."

"As I said before, little darling, there is nothing fair about this life."

"It was believed by those people with whom my neighbor spoke that he had hired his wife's killer to do the job, that he had learned of her assignations with my father."

He sighed deeply and my head rose and fell against his chest. "Yes, it's quite possible. As I remember him, he had mean little eyes, and his entire demeanor gave the impression of one who is rotten to the core."

"But how can a man dare to go out into the street and hire an assassin?" I persisted, disappointed because he had not reacted to anything I had said.

"It isn't necessary for a man to go out into the street, Garnet. There is a place in London where one may purchase anything. Little boys and little girls are sold to men, and sometimes to women. If the child is lucky, it suffers little or not at all. Too often, they are used most hideously, and often they are tortured to death. One can purchase older girls and boys, too, as well as poison and drugs. Available in these places are men for hire, and they'll do anything if the price is high enough, including murder. But there are also young men and old men of what is generally accepted as good breeding. They kill for lust and excitement, wearing masks as they let themselves into the house where they are paid to ply their deadly trade." His voice was cold and deadly, as well as sad. Then his manner changed, along with the tone of his voice. "I've said it before, Garnet. I'm very grateful that Captain Merryweather came to your rescue, for you might have found yourself in one of those places where human life has no value and children are bought and sold."

I drew away from him, unable to control my anger. "How can you sit in judgment on others and you a pirate? And what about *me*? You took me by force!"

His outrageously charming smile lit up the room. "Oh. Did I now? Seems to me you were ready and willing."

"I don't mean that! I mean you took me off *The Gentle Kathy* by force. And regardless of what your Aunt Becky says, your hands are not lily white. They're bloody as hell, for even if it's true, what she believes, and you've never killed anyone yourself, you've ordered your men to kill."

"Aunt Becky wouldn't believe her own eyes if she saw me run a man through."

"There! I knew it!"

He laughed out loud, and said, "Your color has come back. I would much rather have you yelling at me and full of spirit than listless and empty of life."

He had worked his magic again. Cozened me until I was back to normal again, and without my knowledge had me submitting with joy to his caresses. Seething, I pushed my hands against his chest and got to my feet.

"Where are you going?" He looked up at me, his eyes bright.

"I'm going to dress for dinner, of course."

"Wear the yellow gown," he ordered. "With the amber necklace."

"Very well." I removed a gossamer silk yellow gown and pulled it over my head, then turned like a willing child so he could help me fasten the hundred or more buttons. As he glasped the amber beads around my neck, I fingered them idly, but spoke scathingly. "I suppose you think a woman enjoys wearing fine clothes and jewelry, but each time I lay eyes on your baubles I wonder who you murdered in order to get your bloody hands on it."

"I've never killed a woman."

"You lie. I'm sure of it." I looked down at the cunning little slippers that he'd selected for me to wear with the pale yellow gown. They were brown velvet, with gold heels and a strip of gold filigree across the toes, and they fit me as if they'd been made for me. "The poor lost lady who once owned this gown, these shoes, the amber beads—no doubt you took her from a ship as you took me, used her until you tired of her, then cast her overboard. Unless you killed her as she slept, for gold."

"Such notions, Garnet. The gown, yes. It was in a chest that was plunder from a galleon. I'll admit that. But there was no woman aboard. The ship was heading for Spain and the gowns were part of the trousseau for a senorita, or so I was told. The slippers, too. But the amber belonged to my own mother."

My head high, my eyes haughty with disbelief, I said, "Oh, absolutely. You're a lying, thieving murderer, Happy Jack Muldoon, and I—" I realized I had gone too far, and hastily pasted a smile on my face. "Forgive me," I said as we left the cabin. "Sometimes I become carried away by my imagination."

"In all truth, the amber belonged to my sainted mother, and so did some of the other jewels. The rubies, a sapphire bib necklace with matching bracelet and earrings, all those were my mother's."

"But the diamonds, the opals?" I could not resist asking, but of course I could not know whether his answer would be true or false.

"The diamonds came from a pawnbroker's shop on Lombard Street, and I purchased them from him honestly, if cheaply, for he was hard pressed for—"

Whatever he was about to say was cut off in the middle because of a sudden call from the lookout, a call that was both eerie and exciting. "Sail ho!"

At least two dozen voices answered the shout at once, including that of Happy Jack Muldoon. "Where away?"

"Far astern, mates. To starboard!"

We pounded up the narrow, steep ladder to the deck, which shook mightily as men raced aft to take a look. Jack Muldoon pulled me along by the hand, and together we climbed up on a cannon carriage where I looked out and saw a distant ship scudding along under full sail. It looked to me as if it were taking a north-easterly course, but because of the purpling shadows cast by the setting sun I didn't trust my eyes.

"A schooner, by the shape of her," said Jack Muldoon.

He took out his spyglass and pulled it out with a deft movement, then peered intently toward the other ship. "Chances are that she's fully laden," he said in a voice that was heavily threaded with excitement, "for she sits low in the water." Then he shouted and the hair at the nape of my neck crawled when I saw the ghoulish grin on his face just before he cupped his hands to his mouth and yelled in a voice loud enough to wake the dead. "All hands stand by! Stand by to come about!"

"You're not going to try to take that beautiful ship!" I cried.

He looked down at me with an expression of contempt as he snapped, "Of *course* we're going to take her. Does a parson read from the Bible? Does a blacksmith shoe horses?"

"But . . . I'm afraid!"

"No need to fear for yourself. Go below at once and remain there until I come for you."

"But I don't want to be aboard a ship on which every crew member is dancing to the tune of plunder. Listen to that savage cheer of them as they prepare to seize that lovely ship!"

"They're delighted at a chance for a scrap. Now, do as I say. I don't want you in the way."

"You go to hell!"

He laughed. "I probably will, Garnet, but not right now." He left me there as if I meant no more to him than a keg of rum. His voice came back to me loud and clear as he shouted out an order to his quartermaster to bring the small arms from the hold, and then his footsteps thundered above as he yelled at the helmsman to put the rudder hard over.

A great, ruddy-faced man almost knocked me down as he prepared to lay the cannon where I stood in his way. "Get below, damn it," he snarled at me. "That is, unless you can lay a cannon."

It may have been my imagination, but it seemed to me that we were growing closer already to the billowing sails of the schooner. Another mate fell to and began to strip the canvas jacket from the cannon. Together, he and the first one heaved it into position, but they didn't raise the hinged gun port in the bulwark, which gave me hope. Perhaps they wouldn't try to take the other ship after all. But my hopes were dashed right away because a glance at the raised bulwark showed me a number of gunners hiding behind the slight overhang all along the starboard scupper, and not a word was said out of any of them. They were waiting. Silently, and deadly, they awaited the command to fire. The burly mate who had almost knocked me down prepared a match in the sand bucket and I shivered.

Jack Muldoon's voice was powerful as he called from somewhere, probably at the side of the helmsman, "She's going to try to give us a run, men!" I ran to the bow and looked toward the sea where the sails of the other ship had taken on the blood red reflection of the setting sun, but my hopes grew when it appeared that she was intent on outdistancing us. Secretly, I prayed that she would succeed, but I knew enough about the art of sailing to doubt that my prayer would be answered. Our wind was dead astern, which meant we would have the advantage on her. If she'd stayed on course instead of quartering as she had, she might have had a chance. I wondered about the people aboard her, if it were a merchant ship heading toward the New World or one with passengers—men, women and children, in the process of giving up what they'd had in order to be free in a new land! My heart went out to them, for I didn't doubt for a moment that the pirates would kill them all, right down to the last baby.

I don't know how it happened that I found myself by Jack Muldoon's side, but suddenly he appeared from out of the gathering darkness and repeated what he'd said to me earlier, about going below.

"I'll not do it, for if you lose this battle I'll not be trapped inside a cabin," I screamed.

"We'll not lose this battle. You have nothing to fear from that quarter."

"How long before you come upon her?"

"A half hour, more or less." His teeth flashed white as he again peered through his glass, and his deep sigh was full of satisfaction as he said, more to himself than to me, "It's *The Nightingale*. Well, well! So we meet again!"

His excitement was so high that I felt almost as if I could

reach out and touch it. "Why are you so pleased?"

He looked down at me and his eyes picked up the ruby red glow of the lantern above him. They danced with unabashed pleasure. "She's a pirate ship. We had a little skirmish with her a few months back, but we'll best her this go-round, you can make a wager on it."

Again, his voice rang out over the ship. "*The Nightingale*, mates! They have her ship-shape and sea-worthy, and by the looks of her she's trying to put a distance between us. No doubt she knows who we are in spite of the flag."

I grabbed the sleeve of his doublet. "What flag? What are you talking about?"

"We don't run up *The Happy Jack* until we're about to close in, Garnet. It's been only recently that I sailed under *The Dancing Lady*. It's the way it is in my business. Less than four months ago, I was sailing a hermaphrodite under the name, *Charming Charlotte*. He's had a new name painted on *The Nightingale*. Had her careened and repaired, gave her a new coat of paint, but he didn't change her lines. Before long you'll see his flag run down, the other run up. At about that same time I'll have mine brought down and my true colors will go up there for Luis Cortez to see."

"Then he knows you're a pirate ship. Otherwise, he wouldn't be running."

"No, I doubt if he knows who I am, Garnet, for Luis wouldn't run from a good scrape with Happy Jack Muldoon. More than likely he thinks we're a vessel from the King's own fleet, and no pirate ship will risk an encounter with a member of the Royal Fleet if he can dodge it."

The half hour to forty minutes that the chase lasted was an eternity to me, but I stubbornly refused to go below to the cabin. I found my own excitement building within me as we closed in on our quarry; once I learned that we were chasing another pirate ship I no longer worried about the hapless crew and possible passengers. To me, a pirate ship was a pirate ship and since I was aboard *The Dancing Lady,* I had no choice but to cheer us on. In truth, I did have a choice, since *The Nightingale* was being pursued, had caused no trouble on her own. Yet something dark and dread within my nature had come to the foreground, and I was surprised at myself when I took a good look at my emotions. I was aboard *The Gentle Kathy* when she was taken over by a band of marauding pirates. Therefore, it didn't seem natural for me to want the man and the crew who had overpowered me to win the inevitable battle. Perhaps it was because I was familiar with the rag-taggle crew and at least felt temporarily safe under the protection of Captain Jack Muldoon. Maybe I was unwilling to exchange my precarious position for the unknown.

I swayed slightly as the helmsman heeled us to starboard, and the wind was loud in my ears. The water rolled higher and higher as the prow cut its furrow, and even in the darkness I could look up and see the canvas bellying out in a taut curve, I could feel the increased speed as they took the wind, and my exhilaration grew.

Almost before I knew it, the rigging of the schooner showed pale and ghostly under the moonlight. A few figures were silhouetted on her afterdecks and from the distance they looked as small as dolls. Jack Muldoon stood strong and free, his immaculate sleeves billowing in the breeze as he said we'd be upon the schooner within fifteen minutes.

Apparently he'd forgotten all about telling me to go below and my refusal to do so in the excitement, for he began to explain the movements of the crew: "Now the mates will be rolling the cannons forward to the closed port. They'll not raise the panel until the very last minute, though. As soon as we're within speaking distance, I'll allow Cortez first speak. Then we'll send forth a shot to inform the Captain to drop sail and quit."

By then, we were heavy on her quarter and banking into her wind. And every man on *The Dancing Lady* maintained silence. I doubted if they allowed themselves to take a healthy breath, for they were so quiet. We were two to three lengths from the schooner's stern when a voice sounded across the water, first hail. "*The Nightingale*, of Southhampton," came the call from the other ship. "Timothy Lancaster, Master!"

I felt as if a bolt of lightning had come near to felling me, for the hail made it clear that Jack Muldoon had lied to me when he'd said it was a pirate ship under the command of

Luis Cortez. I cried out, and for my pains Jack Muldoon clapped a hand across my mouth that was hard and hurtful.

"Lying bastard," he said fiercely. "Still thinks we belong to the King." The lilt of laughter and excitement was in his voice when he called back. "Happy Jack Muldoon, sailing the devil's craft, Cortez!"

As soon as the words were out of his mouth and carried across the water by the wind, the deck shifted under my feet and at the same time came a great, thunderous sound accompanied by an earsplitting yell of triumph from all hands. The cannon had been fired. A pale blue water spout appeared as if by magic on the schooner's bow. The figures, much larger now that we were nearer, appeared to jerk backwards, but not for long. Out of nowhere, what looked like a hundred men had appeared to join the others. Spurts of orange burst from their deck, when we were almost within hand-shaking distance, for the helmsman had brought *The Dancing Lady* alongside the schooner and already a number of Happy Jack's pirate crew were in the process of hurling up the grapnels and hooking them on the rail of *The Nightingale*. The volley of fire from the schooner took them by surprise. It was also accurate, and deadly, for before my eyes I saw three of Happy Jack's men tumble into the sea.

I screamed and Jack Muldoon roared at me. "Get down, Garnet!" He gave me a shove that sent me sidewinding, and I fell in a heap against the railing just in time to see our helmsman crumple and fall without a sound. Or if he made a sound I couldn't hear it above the steady blasts from what sounded like hundreds of fowling pieces, a truly deadly sound. But I heard the awesome thunder of cannon and instinctively knew it didn't come from *The Dancing Lady*. The next thing I knew, I was slipping downward, aware of deafening noise and blinding white light.

Someone bellowed. "Damn their eyes! They got us!"

Space. I thought I was hurtling through space, for my kicking feet could find nothing but air. Then I became aware of a wrenching pain in my shoulder and a crushing grip on my hand along with the determined voice of Happy Jack Muldoon saying, "Damn you, Garnet, give me your other hand."

I wondered why he hadn't asked me sooner, since all there was beneath me and the sea was the night and the air, but it was no time for me to be asking questions. Quickly, I swung my other hand to his reaching one and he hauled me up through the broken, splintered railing, angry and rough as he dragged me along, speaking to me through clenched teeth. "I told you to stay below. Now we're to be overrun by a crew of cut-throats and knaves. I'll get you to Aunt Becky, who always dons men's clothes just in case—why in God's name didn't you let me have your other *hand*?"

"You only asked me once!"

"The *hell* I did." We were running. Sounds of men falling, swords clashing, screams, curses, filled the pitch-black air.

"I guess I fainted then," I said as he dragged me down the steep and narrow stairs.

He spoke in my ear. "They outnumber us, but we still have a chance." He stopped outside Aunt Becky's tiny cabin. "Get in there. Stay in there. Do as she says." He was breathing fast and once he opened the door he gave me a push that sent me spinning into total blackness, but Aunt Becky's voice kept me from going into panic.

"Here," she said. "Slip into these. Hurry!"

"But why?"

"Don't ask questions." Her lips were so close to my ear that I could feel the warmth of her breath.

"Something is on my hand. Sticky." Instinctively, I lifted my hand to my face and smelled the scent of blood. "I'm bleeding."

"You'll do more than bleed at the hands of Luis Cortez if he finds you aboard and you a woman. Hurry, Garnet. We're father and son, Old Billy Beck and his boy, Garner."

My teeth were chattering as I yanked off the pale yellow gown and slipped into moldy-smelling breeches and blouse, a stiff leather jerkin. "Y-you m-mean y-you think they'll take over, then, the m-men of the schooner?"

"I think nothing of the kind, but it's best to be prepared, that's all. I've done this twice before, but I never had to stay in disguise very long, thanks be to God, for my nephew is not one to relinquish something once he has it."

Overhead was the sound of muskets and pistols being

fired and now and then the unmistakable thud of a body falling. After I was dressed right down to a pair of ill-fitting boots and stinking stockings so stiff with dirt that they were hard to tug on, I was quiet, and so was Aunt Becky. The clash of swords from above was a metallic accompaniment to shouts, curses and screams. I closed my eyes and prayed for deliverance. The clatter of footsteps outside the door came as a shock in the middle of my half-formed prayer for Jack Muldoon's survival and a whimpered cry of regret that he'd taken me captive in the first place. Jack himself burst into the little cabin, carrying a lantern. I gasped at the blood that dripped from a gaping wound in his throat, purple-black under the light.

Aunt Becky fluttered, raising her hands as if she would close the two flaps of skin, but he shook his head, looking grim. "It's over. They've set a torch to the ship. They're in the process of taking our cargo and within minutes I'll be forced to surrender."

Seven

When Aunt Becky and I came out of her cabin we collided with an evil-smelling man from the conquering pirate ship. He came from behind us as he dashed toward the stairs with a cask of rum on his shoulders. By some miracle, he managed to keep the barrel from falling, but he gave us a scorching round of curses for being there, in his way. Others were close by, roistering with glee as they plundered the grand cabin I had shared with Jack Muldoon. Their words were clear as they exclaimed over the furnishings, the jewels and clothing. More of their number were in the hold, to come staggering down the narrow hall, muscles straining under the boxes and crates they were taking as booty.

Muldoon was strict about lights at night since he had a healthy respect for fire. There were a few oil lamps aboard, but the majority of illumination after the sun went down was furnished by candles carefully kept behind gleaming glass. It was obvious that the marauding pirates cared little about the danger of an open flame, for they'd set down torches at every conceivable place. Aunt Becky and I skirted the one at the top of the stairs. If we'd worn gowns we would have been endangered by the tongues of flame that cast long, flickering bars of light on the deck. An oily stench from the torches blended with the pall of gunsmoke that continued to hang over the foredeck even though the last gun had been fired. As we hurried forward, the paralyzing sound of wood crackling as it burns blended with the shouts of men. When I turned around to look it seemed to me that they'd been hasty about setting the ship afire. The cargo of *The Dancing Lady* would take a long time to empty, for she, too, had been heavily laden. I wondered where Jack Muldoon was. When he spoke so urgently to us, he'd not surrendered, but he'd not hedged about his intentions to do so.

"It's only a matter of time before Cortez and his men seek me out," he'd said. Then he'd added forcefully, "Even though I would rather die than sign articles with the swine, I'll do it. It's that or burn with the ship, and I want the two of you out." Then he'd kissed his old aunt on the cheek and turned to me to cup my chin in his hand. For a long moment he stared intently into my eyes. I felt myself blanching under his gaze. He said, "Look smart, lad. And don't give up hope. I'll work out something to get us out of this, but for the moment, the fair winds are with Luis Cortez. You'll be given the chance to sign articles with him. Do it. The alternative is death."

Blood was everywhere, but even worse were the corpses strewn about all twisted in death. Minutes ago they'd been in mortal combat, now fallen in defense of their ship. Under Jack Muldoon's orders I had had little contact with the mates, but I felt a sense of loss as I recognized the dead. I did not want to join the pirate ship. Didn't see how I could possibly speak out with a clear "Aye" when I was put to the question.

As if she read my mind, Aunt Becky said, "Don't forget what he told us to do. You sign articles, and no balking."

"But—" I looked at her for the first time since we'd left the cabin and couldn't believe my eyes. She wore a three-cornered black hat, a patch covered one eye and over her paisley shirt she wore a gaudy jacket that did a good job of hiding her generous bosom. Her breeches were dark and loose, but they fit her all right. She seemed to be having trouble with her boots. They were worn and scuffed, and much bigger than she wore, for she was proud of her tiny feet. But she'd donned the out-sized boots by design, since no man would have delicate feet like hers. She also took pride in her hair, and had every right to. It was blonde with a goodly amount of grey in it, but it was thick and luxurious and hung almost to her ankles. I stifled a gasp when I saw her shorn locks peeking out from under the brim of her tri-corn hat. It looked very much as if she'd inverted a pot and quickly cut around the rim. A shockingly different style from the way I had always seen her, with her marvelous hair done up in two big buns at the nape of her neck.

The fear and excitement may have turned me fey, for I could not squelch the giggles that came over me. I tried to swallow them back, but they turned into gurgles, which she apparently misconstrued as stifled sobs. Speaking sharply, she said, "Now is no time for sniveling, Garner. Step lively, now. You're a big boy, old enough to know there's a loser for every winner."

A glance around showed me that no one was within hearing distance, so I whispered, "I'm not crying, it's your hair! And I was *laughing*."

She looked at me strangely out of the eye that wasn't covered by the patch and whispered back, "I just wish I had done a better job on yours."

A tentative touch with my fingertips caused me to stop dead in my tracks. Without my knowledge she had cut off my hair in the darkness as I dressed. But I hadn't felt a thing. The ends came to the middle of the back of my neck in some places. In other spots she had hacked it to my ears. "My God. When did you—"

"Be still," she cautioned as we almost ran headlong into the same burly-chested pirate we'd collided with below. He was empty-handed and on his way down, and he favored us with a scowl.

In my breeches, shirt and jerkin I felt naked, fearful that I appeared more feminine than I did in a gown because of the tight-fitting breeches that exposed every line of my legs. Footing was treacherous because of the spilled blood. It ran in a great stream from the dead and it was impossible to find a place to put my foot without slipping. When I fell, I went to my knees, which caused the conquering vermin from *The Nightingale* to laugh uproariously. Aunt Becky yanked me up, the picture of an exasperated parent as she shook my shoulders and shouted at me, promising to box my ears for being so clumsy. Once we were safely out of hearing of the pirates, I bemoaned my fears of not passing inspection. "Nobody will believe I'm a lad. One look at me and the Master of *The Nightingale* will know I'm masquerading."

"Nonsense. You're lucky enough to have a small and lean little arse and your waist is as narrow as any boy's. Even your love bubbles aren't as big as they might have been, and with the jerkin, you look flat in the front. Now, what we've got to do is take our places with the rest of the crew. You see? Already a number of Jonathan's mates have given their allegiance to Captain Cortez. There goes Lawson, helping to put our cargo into the boats that are headed for *The Nightingale*."

I moaned. Aunt Becky shook her head. "Better than dying, and anyway, it'll not be for long. My Jonathan will set things to rights."

Wishful thinking, I was sure, because the crew of the victorious pirate ship outnumbered ours by at least four to one. Jack Muldoon's crew was twenty-eight to begin with and Cortez had at least a hundred. By the looks of the dead, most of them were ours. From my point of view, there was no way Happy Jack Muldoon could extricate himself.

A tall and slender young man with a boyish face and merry blue eyes was issuing orders. He gave us an appraising look as he said, "State your name and skills, man."

"Beck," she answered in a deep voice. "And I was cook aboard *The Dancing Lady*. A mighty fine hand, if I say so myself. And this is me lad, Garner Beck. As hale and hardy a lad as ever ye'll hope to find and bright as the early mornin' sun, he is, work-brickle and quick." She shoved me forward and with a cuff to my jaw she ordered me to hold up my head and speak. "Tell him how strong you are and that you can lift a bale or box as well as any man." Turning back to the man who appeared to be the quartermaster, she spoke in a fawning purr. "And he's learned to take a 'and at the tiller, sir, even knows how to read a compass and chart a course. Learned by Old Cap'n Merryweather, who was childless himself and took this lad of mine to sea with him when he was nine year old, and me wife thinkin' she was a widder-woman, leavin' her with a boy to raise and believin' I was lost at sea."

The red-haired man looked at me out of his twinkling blue eyes and smiled. "How old are you, lad?"

"Fourteen, sir."

"Are you all your old father says you are?"

"Yes, sir."

"And you'll sign articles with Luis Cortez, harbor your loyalties only for him and his?"

"Yes, sir."

"He appears a bright enough lad," said the quartermaster, "for all that he looks undernourished and has a pasty color to his cheeks. He'll do. Now, you, Beck. Are you ready to sign articles?"

"Sure and I'm more than ready, sir," answered Aunt Becky with a vigorous nod of her head. "We were bested fair and square, and that's the truth of the matter."

The articles were set up in plain sight, a quill and pot of ink at the ready, but Becky had to explain what they meant to me when I hung back. Off the top of her head she put on a believable act as she squinted up at the quartermaster and said, "He was just a lad when I brought him aboard and Cap'n Muldoon let me do his signin' for him." She looked down at her feet, giving an excellent imitation of a man who was embarrassed, and reluctantly added, "I know it ain't right, but me and the lad are igorrant, so we'll have to make our mark like we did when we signed on *The Dancing Lady*."

Any fool could see that the quartermaster was out of patience, but his voice was strong and clear as he read:

"Article One: Share all prizes and share alike, save for the Captain's share and the Quartermaster's share, each getting two of all.

"Article Two: Fo'c's'le rules on disagreements. Word aginst word is settled according to the custom of the brotherhood. Duel to the death, quartermaster making the rules unless the majority of the crew speaks it differently. In that case, rules are set by the crew.

"Article Three: No shipmate will sack through a fellow shipmate's sea chest. Gentleman's honor prevails in this as in all things.

"Article Four: No crew member is to smuggle a woman aboard, on pain of death at discovery.

"Article Five: No man will steal from his shipmates. Anyone caught doing this deed will be flayed."

The articles were written clearly and in a passably fine

script. They were circled in black and the signatures went clockwise, round-robin fashion so that no man aboard would be more incriminated than the other—although I didn't understand the significance of the peculiar way of signing the articles until much later. I did understand the drawing at the top of the parchment, however. It was the Jolly Roger.

After the articles were marked with an "X" by us, the quartermaster ordered us to climb over the side, and minutes later we were aboard *The Nightingale* where we stood for orders by the Master, Luis Cortez. We were to go back and lend a hand to the taking of cargo from *The Dancing Lady's* holds. In spite of his name, Luis Cortez spoke the King's English as fluently as if he'd been born in London, but unlike the quartermaster, he was decidely not friendly. Icily, he said, "You signed articles with my quartermaster, and I'll warn you beforehand that I give no quarter to any man or boy. Get to your work and take care that you don't shirk. I take great pleasure in administering the cat to those who don't carry their load."

An hour and a half later, the schooner was well away from the sinking *Dancing Lady*. The flames were still burning bright enough to light up the sky before she went down. All hands were ordered to stand inspection on the main deck at eight bells, last watch. I was exhausted from carrying heavy casks and crates, from scurrying back and forth between the burning ship and *The Nightingale*. My teeth were chattering, but at least I had stopped referring to my "father" as Aunt Becky. If I addressed her as anything it was "Pa."

Cortez was resplendantly attired in a pale blue satin shirt with full sleeves and gathered yoke, a crimson sash at his waist and tight fitting breeches of dove grey velvet. His stockings were silk and his shoes were adorned with golden buckles. If I had met him on a social occasion I would have thought him handsome with his midnight-black hair and aristocratic features. But this was no social occasion. Long before we cast off from the raging inferno that was all that remained of *The Dancing Lady*, I had overheard the word passed from man to man that there would be a lesson in discipline at eight bells.

No one uttered a sound after Cortez motioned for silence, whether they were long-time mates of *The Nightingale* or just off *The Dancing Lady*. He stood on the bridge, relaxed of stance and casual of manner, his voice low and resonant. By standing high, he elevated his position, and I suspected he was aware of the inbred feelings shared by mankind since the beginning of history in which one man automatically gains advantage over many by the simple action of setting himself higher. Aside from that, he had arranged himself like an actor, with men standing by holding torches, he in the very center. His words were few. He reminded all hands that he was the undisputed master of the ship, that within him rested the decision of life or death for any miscreant.

"I am, however," he continued in his mellow voice, "a man of mercy." He paused for effect, or perhaps because he wanted to listen for a gainsay. None came forth. He smiled almost pleasantly, and lifted his right hand, one finger pointing, and his words were in direct opposition to the sound of his voice. "I could have ordered Jack Muldoon hanged. Instead, I will allow him to live after he has received his thirty lashes. Stand by to witness disciplinary measures and let the punishment meted out act as an example. That is an order."

My heart came into my mouth when Jack Muldoon was brought forward, his arms shackled behind him, the ugly wound on his neck all black and encrusted where the blood had congealed. When Cortez stepped to one side the cross behind him stood out in bold relief under the light of several more torches as the bearers settled themselves on either side of it. I felt as if all the blood had been drained from my own body when I saw that cross, for I was sure Cortez meant to crucify Jack Muldoon, that when he'd referred to himself as merciful he was making a gruesome joke. Hanging would be much kinder than the slow, barbaric torture of crucifixion.

Becky reached for me and held my hand tightly. "Nay, lad," she murmured in my ear. I had taken two steps forward without knowing it. If it had not been for her restraining hand, hard as steel and with the strength of two brawny men, I would have torn at the backs of those who stood in my way and gone to his side.

Jack was expressionless as they fitted his arms into the cuffs. He was face forward and stripped to the waist. I drew a long, trembling sigh of relief as I realized that he was not, after all, to be crucified. His feet were flat on the deck, not impaled. But the two stalwarts who advanced on him with the vicious cats wore cruel and evil grins as they flailed the air and I understood in that moment that he was not to be flogged on the back.

"Not—" Becky's hand was hard on my mouth. For a moment, I struggled with her, mindless as a runaway horse.

The leather thongs whistled as they were raised and then sent slashing down against flesh and bone, one torturer on each side of Jack. Long, thin ridges of blood wealed from chest to belly, from thigh to leg. Then again. And again. And all the while, Happy Jack Muldoon kept his eyes locked in on the man who was responsible for his torment. Luis Cortez.

I lost count as the back and shoulders of the seamen before me, the masts and jibs and spars began to blur together and go round and round, in the center a man who stood as still as death while the death-dealing blows descended upon his most vulnerable parts, from nose to loins, from knees to nipples. His breeches fell away in shreds and then the shreds that fell away were flesh. He smiled. Yes, as he continued to look Luis Cortez in the eyes, Happy Jack Muldoon smiled. I retched as I whispered his name. "Happy Jack Muldoon." Yes, he smiled as if he were indeed happy.

The swirling parts of ship and human flesh and blood merged into one and my legs turned to water. I prayed for the relief of oblivion, but even though I was falling to the deck my ears were unrelieved from the ghastly sound of his inhuman torture. A pair of strong arms held me upright. Not Aunt Becky's, because she was not as tall as I. Yet there was something feminine about the way the arms encircled me. Stranger yet, the voice that spoke in my ear was sweet and musical. A woman's voice for sure. "Stay where you are. He'll be taken down before he's dead and that's a promise."

Half turning, I saw the red hair of the quartermaster, tall, strong and manly, and knew he was holding me up. Then it came to me that it must have been my dead mother's voice that spoke to me, and I understood that I had once again received knowledge of what was to come, but this time in actual voice. Never before had I been impressed with an omen of portent that presented itself at the same time as the event in question. Still, there it was. A burst of sound. Luis Cortez went taut. His eyes were wide open and his features frozen in an expression of disbelief and surprise. A black hole was between his eyes and I saw it and knew it for what it was as he fell.

Part 2

Eight

With a wry smile the quartermaster watched the melée that followed the sudden death of Captain Luis Cortez. "Pandemonium," she said in her natural voice, and the way she pronounced the word made it clear to those around her that she enjoyed the shouts of jubilation, the hats tossed into the air, the loud laughter and ringing cries of triumph.

A moment after the first wild cries rang out, Philadelphus Fields strode forward, gave the inert body of Luis Cortez a kick and knelt to spit on his face. Then she removed his sword. Standing to her full height, she issued an order of command. "Haul him down from there! I am now the Master of this ship." As she spoke, the revelry dwindled and died, but the tall woman repeated her words, loud and clear. "I said to haul the prisoner down. I am now the Master of this ship, and I have issued my first order." Using the shining sword as a pointer, she gestured to the two men who had been set to the flogging. "Carry him to the Captain's quarters and put him on the bed." Her right hand went to her cap and a mass of auburn hair came spilling down around her shoulders as she turned toward Garnet Shaw and Aunt Becky, both of whom had followed her forward like sleepwalkers, tears of gratitude streaming from their eyes. Looking first at Garnet, then at the older woman, she lashed out another command: "The two of you will attend to Muldoon's wounds. In the cabin you'll find ointments that will soothe him."

Stunned silence marked the moment the quartermaster

revealed herself as a woman. It was immediately followed by even louder shouts of amazement, a thunderous yell in Garnet's ear, "B'God and Davy Jones, he's a female!"

Garnet tore her eyes from where the mates were releasing Muldoon's wrists from their bonds. Looking up into the magnificently beautiful woman's face, she said, "Then it *was* a living voice I heard instead of a phantom from the grave. It was you who spoke to me as you shored me up."

"Yes. It was I. I had to, else you stood to endanger us all by crying out at the wrong moment, or rushing to your lover's aid as you gave every appearance of doing."

"Then you knew all along I was no lad," Garnet breathed.

"Yes, I knew. It takes a woman to know another woman." The new Master's eyes blazed as she turned a radiant smile on Garnet. "Do not take me for a fool, or a weakling, however, for I am neither. Otherwise, I could not have carried this out. And please be so kind as to tell Muldoon that I will tolerate no attempts toward mutiny once he is on his feet again. I spared him from ruin, almost certain death, but—never mind. I'll tell him myself." Her business with Garnet and Becky Muldoon finished, she faced the adoring crew, her voice firm with authority: "You, there! Thomas Banks and Emmanuel Garcia. Three tots of rum for all hands and step lively. This is a celebration!"

The huzzahs rang out as Garnet and old Aunt Becky followed the mates who staggered under the weight of the mangled and pulpy Muldoon, who was lowered to the bed. Within moments, the door of the Captain's quarters opened and the new Master of *The Nightingale* entered. "How fares he?" She came and stood at the side of the bed, her expression unreadable.

"He'll live," answered Aunt Becky. "Thanks to you, Dell Fields."

The room was redolent of steaming mint tea that Garnet was feeding to Muldoon by the half teaspoon, and the pungent scent of eucalyptus oil was overpowering. Each time his aunt applied the ointment, Jack Muldoon winced. His face was almost unrecognizable with purpling flesh that swelled grotesquely on one cheek bone and the lacerations made by the tips of the biting thongs. One eye was swollen shut, with blood surrounding it. Yet even in his misery, Muldoon smiled—although it was a different kind of smile from that he had kept fixed on his face as he was flogged. His one good eye was liquid as he looked up at the woman who had sent Cortez to his death and his laugh was an explosion before he spoke. "My life is yours, Dell. Another twenty-two blows from that kind of punishment was more than I could have withstood. I was counting."

"And so was I, Jack. So was I." Dell Fields went to a row of cabinets, speaking as she went. "But your life isn't mine. I owed you, and I will be beholden to no man. Now we are even."

When she returned to the bedside, Dell handed an earthen jar to Becky. "Try this. It doesn't sting or burn, but it stops the bleeding as fast as the eucalyptus oil. And it heals this kind of wound in an amazingly fast time."

Jack Muldoon's blackened lips opened again and after he'd run his tongue across them to wet them, he spoke meaningfully. "You know your way around the Captain's quarters very well, old friend."

Coolly, Dell Fields answered, "Well enough. I was Ship's Quartermaster and nothing more."

"Then you fooled him into believing you were a man, just as you had the crew convinced. I recognized you the minute I saw you."

"Aye, but Luis Cortez knew me as a man. You had the advantage over him, having known me before."

"How did you get aboard and finagle your way into the late, unlamented Luis' graces?"

"Such curiosity," she answered. "For now, it's well enough that I did." Her voice turned hard as stone. "You will remember that you are my prisoner. Do not make the mistake of trying to undermine me as soon as you're well enough to stand on your own two feet. The crew eats out of my hand and they will continue to do so, for I have made no idle promises. No doubt it came as a shock to them when I let them know my gender, but they trust me because I kept my word and I did them a great service by ridding the world of a lying, thieving curse to humanity. So watch your step, Jack Muldoon. The eyes of all hands will be upon you."

"I'm no threat to you, Philadelphus Fields," answered Muldoon. "I'm helpless, and nigh unto bleeding to death."

"True, but there'll come a time when you'll begin to chaff under the command of a mere woman. I believe that was what you called me a few years back." She smiled and tossed her long mane of fiery hair. "And you've been deprived of your ship, your crew, and considerable wealth. Even though I have known you in the past as a man of honor, I also know your nature."

"There was no honor in Luis Cortez," he murmured.

"No. None. Even worse, he killed for the pleasure of killing. The screams of the tortured were music to his ears." Dell Fields moved toward the door. "You are lacking in manners. Will you not tell me the name of the girl who attends you?"

"Forgive me." To Garnet, he said, "We are in the presence of a great and gallant lady. Captain Philadelphus Fields. May I present my betrothed, Captain? Garnet Shaw."

The two young women nodded, and Garnet executed an awkward curtsey, feeling at a disadvantage in the tight-fitting breeches. Then Dell Fields put out her hand and Garnet put out hers. For a moment, Garnet felt ill at ease, but the taller woman's smile was kind. "I am very happy to meet you, Garnet," she said cordially. "And I am sure the Muldoon is in good hands, between the two of you."

Becky tipped back her head in order to look the Captain full in the face. "You've changed considerably, child. For my part, I think it's for the better. And I'm grateful as well as pleased to find you aboard the ship that captured us and brought us to our knees."

As soon as Dell Fields left, Muldoon grinned. He looked at Garnet out of the eye that wasn't closed shut and touched her face. "Don't look so frightened, dear. We could have fallen into a hornet's nest. Luck was on our side."

Garnet withdrew, taking the empty tea cup with her. "You call it luck to be in this shape. I'm surprised that you're capable of sane speech. And how does it happen that you're so friendly with the woman who just finished telling you that you're her prisoner? I don't know whether to count us lucky or not. She speaks out of a honeyed mouth one moment, and spits vinegar the next. Gets you an unguent on the one hand and makes threats at practically the same time."

"She's a corker, all right."

"A pirate! A woman pirate!" Garnet held the lanthorn close to the steaming teakettle.

"No more mint, I beg of you."

"Spice, then," ordered Aunt Becky. "Pour in a goodly amount of good, plain tea, lovey, and add cloves and cinnamon. There's more and plenty. Cortez was a heathen and a madman, but he had good taste in the complements of his quarters—spirit cooker and all."

"I am curious about that big woman," Garnet said. "Philadelphus. But you called her Dell."

"A shortening," answered Aunt Becky.

"And what did she mean when she said you were even?" Garnet's hands were just beginning to stop trembling and her face was still waxen. "I was afraid you would *die*, Jack Muldoon. What will happen to us now?"

"He's a strong one, my nephew is," fawned Aunt Becky as she applied the ointment to the tender flesh between his thighs. "Now stop worrying about our fate, Garnet. Our course is set and to me everything is clear. What we have to do is count our blessings. Thirty of those kind of lashes would have amounted to more than sixty, with a man on either side laying them on. Even my Jonathan would have given up the ghost. Dell Fields saved him, and no matter why. It's enough that she did, and even though she's as hard as ground long frozen under the winter blasts, she's got a heart inside her breast."

All through the night the two women attended to the battered man. At dawn, the old woman dozed, to awaken to a sharp knock on the door. Garnet opened it to find a foolishly smiling Jack Lawson standing there with a covered tray. "The Master says it's for Cap—I mean, for the prisoner," he said as he entered. "And she says for the two of you to come and join her at breakfast, soon as you've fed him."

"I'll feed myself," said Jack Muldoon. When Garnet pulled back the snowy napery that covered the tray, he smiled. "Figs and oranges from the hold of the late *Dancing*

Lady, I'll warrant, as well as the smoked fish and the makings for the batter cakes. Fit for a king, and who am I to complain that it was liberated from my own stores?" He fell to with hearty appetite, and even though he looked worse than he had on the night before, it was only because the scabs were forming.

The wind was up and the schooner was cutting hard under a sea breeze that filled her canvasses and brought an exhilarating sense of speed to Garnet as she made her way through the deck in quest of Captain Fields. McClintock, formerly with *The Gentle Kathy* and late of *The Dancing Lady,* gave her a broad smile as he told her the directions, then offered to take her there himself. "I'm glad to see you, McClintock," she said to the mate. "I feared you'd gone down with the burning *Dancing Lady.*"

"No ma'am. Me and Stanky and Jack Lawson came through the fight in fair shape. We didn't put up much of a battle when we saw we was outnumbered. Anyway, when all is said and done, I reckon there's not a lot of difference which ship you're sailing with as long as you're on the account with a bunch of pirates. But they're not all a bad lot, ma'am. They was hungry. Near starvin' to death on the rations they'd had under Cortez. Seems odd, though, to call a woman Master. Even though she be as tall as any man, she's still a woman."

"You referred to *me* as Captain," Garnet reminded the man.

"Yessum. But all that seems like it was just a dream because it was so short a time before we was taken over by Captain—I mean Mister Muldoon. Beggin' your pardon, ma'am, seein' the way things are between you and Mister Muldoon, but I've got to obey orders and Captain Fields said it plain that we was not to refer to him as anything but mate or mister."

"It's all right, McClintock. I understand."

He walked along at her side, his attitude hang-dog. "And I felt real bad about not bein' able to lift a hand to help him when they put him up there for the flailing. We'd all been told what to expect by word of mouth, but I never thought it'd be as bad as it was, and anyway, we kept waitin' for the shot to ring out. The one that killed Cortez. But you know, ma'am, it didn't come off as real-like. I mean, there we all was, every man jack of us with our eyes on that terrible thing. None of us wantin' to watch, all of us ordered to. All of us hopin' and prayin' the man with the gun would use it and quick—but it seemed like such a long time before it happened."

"It seemed longer to me, McClintock. No one saw fit to tell me there wouldn't be twice-thirty lashes."

"I thought you knew. I thought *everybody* knew!" The boy shook his head. "How come nobody told you?"

"I don't know."

"If I had known you were kept in the dark like that, I would have told you myself, ma'am."

"Thank you, McClintock."

"And here be the officers' mess, ma'am. Captain Fields, she's in there all by herself."

Garnet pushed against the swinging doors that opened into a small dining room. Half a dozen tables and chairs were placed closely together, but as McClintock had said, the Master of the ship was alone. Windows were open to the breeze. Dell Fields' hair rippled and blew as she sat at one of the small tables, a mug in front of her and a delicate little pipe in her hand. "Good morning," she said as Garnet entered. "But you're alone."

"Aunt Becky begs leave to stay with C—her nephew. He's able to feed himself, but she's weary from being up with him through the night, and asks your permission to rest instead of eating. If that's not all right, I'm to go back for her. With your permission, of course."

"She's an old woman and no doubt in need of more rest than you, but judging by the circles under your eyes you had little sleep yourself. Sit down, Garnet. Will you have coffee, or tea? I've waited to order, so we may enjoy our meal together."

"I've never tasted coffee, ma'am." Uneasily, Garnet seated herself across from Captain Fields, wishing Aunt Becky was with her. She felt awkward in the tall woman's presence, but at the same time she was vaguely irritated. "But I ...wouldn't mind taking a taste of it to see if I would like it."

The cabin boy came at a snap of Dell Fields' fingers.

"Bring the lady a cup of coffee. Then tell the cook to prepare the breakfast I ordered for two."

Garnet found it hard to keep her eyes off the little pipe in the Captain's hand. It was a pretty thing, with a curved stem and a bowl the size of a robin's egg and about the same color. Although she had seen men smoke, she'd not known women had taken up the habit, but she found the aroma of burning tobacco most pleasant.

"You aren't expected to wear breeches, Garnet," said the other woman. "As you can see, I'm glad enough to get back into a gown myself after several months of dressing as a man."

She was resplendent in a pastel shade of blue-green, somewhat darker in color than the smoking pipe. The velvet skirt was full, the bodice tight around her slender waist. Ruffles of heavy lace trimmed the sleeves and neckline. "It's a lovely gown, ma'am, and very becoming. I've an idea that you can wear any color you please with your fair complexion and such dark red hair. You look—different. And very nice."

"Thank you. As soon as Muldoon's wounds are healed well enough for him to be moved, you'll take the quartermaster's cabin. It's small, but big enough for two. My gear is there now, but I'll have it removed to the more commodious cabin where I'll sleep within a few days. Your gowns are in the hold and you may take them. I'll expect you to dress for dinner."

The cabin boy brought the coffee. It sent up a delicious fragrance. Garnet looked at it and her mouth began to water. "Is it to be drunk plain?"

"Some like sugar with it, or honey. I take mine as it comes, but in the evening I add a tot of rum. We've a cow aboard, and you might like it with cream or milk."

Garnet lifted her spoon, tasted and found the coffee bitter, which was a disappointment. "It doesn't taste as good as it smells."

Dell poured from a pitcher of cream, then added a heaping spoonful of sugar. "Now try it. You'll probably find it more to your liking."

After one taste, Garnet doubted if she would ever be able to get enough of the delicious brew. "Almost like chocolate," she said dreamily. "Much better than tea."

Dell laughed. Garnet looked up at her, a question in her eyes. "I'm not poking fun at you, Garnet. I'm thinking of the fit Cortez would throw if he saw us drinking coffee, lacing it with cream and sugar. Breakfast under his orders didn't deserve the name. A mug of tea so weak it had no flavor and a bit of hard tack, and it full of bugs. Ugh! Middle meal was thin soup. Five potatoes, three onions, a leaf or two of cabbage for flavor, all cooked together until they were mushy, then served up with the weevily bread, and that, mind, was enough soup to serve a hundred and more men. The evening meal was equally bad. Smoked fish or meat, most often cold. About enough for a good chew and swallow. Tea with a drop of rum, while Cortez dined in style, but even he had precious little luck getting the cook to do justice to the fine foods he had brought along for himself. One day we'd been without water for so long all our throats were parched, but he had an entire barrel in his quarters. Grudgingly, he offered me a cup under cover of darkness, after I went to his quarters. Next morning it rained. If it hadn't, I might have lost all I had gained, for I was as thirsty as a dog on the desert and sore tempted to run him through."

Garnet sat quietly during the other woman's bitter recitation. She wondered how it happened that Dell was aboard the pirate ship in the first place, how it happened that she'd come on as quartermaster, but she was afraid to ask.

"I suppose your Muldoon told you how we happened to know one another, and why I owed him?"

"No. He was too... that is, he was in a great deal of pain after you left and his aunt gave him a considerable amount of rum to ease him. It had a quieting effect."

Another burst of laughter from Dell Fields' lips, then, "Yes. It eases the pain but addles the brain."

Guardedly, Garnet asked, "Do you know him well?"

"At one time I did." The boy brought a breakfast of poached fish, sliced oranges and an odd looking bread that was almost burned on the outside and gooey in the middle. Dell Fields sighed as she pushed the food away. "I don't know what task I'll give you, Garnet, but you must realize that a ship can't carry idle passengers."

"You may be sure I'll pull my oar, Captain," Garnet said quickly. She wished the boy had not brought the badly cooked breakfast just then since she'd been about to learn at least a part of what she wanted to know, but she reminded herself to remember her place. The woman was puzzling. On the surface, she seemed kind enough, but there was something about her that kept the younger woman on pins and needles. "I'm a good hand with the needle. Mayhap I can repair sails, and there's always a bit of mending to be done aboard any ship."

Dell brightened. "Well and good, but we'll begin with something more personal. This is the only gown I was able to find that came to my ankles. The rest are made for women your size or smaller."

"Perhaps I can take two and make one."

"You speak well, Garnet. Like one who was well-born. How does it happen that you came to be aboard a pirate's ship? The Captain's woman, so to speak."

The fish, like the inedible bread, was raw in the middle. Although she was ravenous, Garnet couldn't eat it, but she ate the last of the sliced oranges and when Dell offered her more she didn't refuse, nor did she refuse another cup of coffee. In between mouthfuls, she spoke of her early childhood, the disappearance of her father, the time she spent with Captain Merryweather. Leaving out the part about taking command of *The Gentle Kathy* and planning to make the voyages and pocket the money herself for as long as she could get away with it, she concluded with as much of the truth as she felt was necessary about losing the ship to Happy Jack Muldoon. "And then, well—you know what happened yesterday."

"Do you love him, Garnet?" Dell Fields' blue eyes were unwavering.

Garnet looked away, flushing. "Sometimes I do and sometimes I don't. You see, I . . . have reason to believe he might have been instrumental in the death of my father, and I've even better reason to believe he killed the lady I told you about."

"Why?"

Garnet found the blue, penetrating gaze disconcerting. She wished she'd not mentioned those dark suspicions. But once she had started, she saw no way out of going on with it.

Slowly, with her lips often trembling, she spoke of finding the opals in the laquered box, and of the engraved initials. "So you see, Captain Fields, I have no choice but to believe that he was the one who slit her throat as she slept. How else would he have come by those opals? They were hers. I know they were."

"You say they were in the quarters you shared with him aboard *The Dancing Lady*?"

Garnet nodded. The lump in her throat was so big she couldn't speak around it.

"I'll send for them and take a look." Dell Fields concentrated on lighting her pipe. She doubted very much if Happy Jack Muldoon had killed the woman the girl's father loved. It was not his style to act as a hired assassin. She liked the girl and wished her no harm, but things had moved so quickly that she'd not had time to decide how she was going to handle much of anything, let alone the situation between herself, a former lover, and a young girl who was, as yet, an unknown quantity.

At an early age, Dell Fields learned what she considered two valuable lessons. The first was to recognize the time to take action when it presented itself. The second was to be careful about plans for the future, including many contingencies. She was capable of carrying on a surface conversation with Garnet Shaw while she devoted deep thought to more important things. The day before was ended, and no longer important to her except for the consequences.

The greatest factor which had served to gain her objective was the total hatred and fear every man aboard held for Captain Cortez. His disregard for human life was probably his most despicable trait, but his native cruelty, his obvious enjoyment at seeing suffering had tended to flame the fires of his already disgruntled crew. The men who signed on with him lived in mortal terror of being the butt of one of his monstrous jokes, or the object of his displeasure. Even in the beginning, Dell had been aware of the danger involved in carrying out her plans, but she had been willing to die, if necessary, to kill Cortez. Disguising as a man was hazardous, but the only way to get aboard his ship. First she gained the respect and good will of Cortez's crew. After that, she won them over completely by doing what she could to ease their hunger, seeing that the sick were cared for, and subtly playing upon their already festering hatred of their Captain.

The months had been exceedingly tedious for Dell Fields. By nature she was not a patient woman, and she had already waited many years to take her revenge upon Luis Cortez. There had been times when she was almost driven to end his life herself. But she restrained her impulses, knowing she would savor the satisfaction much longer. There was another reason why she had not put a bullet through Cortez's brain. The Master of any sailing ship needed the respect of the crew and Dell Fields preferred to gain that respect in a more positive manner than by using force. History had taught her that the leader who seizes authority can quickly be toppled by a newcomer with greater power, but the one who gains power by the choice of the people is less likely to be usurped. For that reason, she had seen to it that another had fired the actual bullet, and she was the only one who knew how much of her own iron will had been behind that fatal shot.

The sighting of *The Dancing Lady* came by chance. Luis Cortez was elated when he saw the outline of his old enemy's ship, but he had been no more overjoyed than Dell Fields, who realized that at last the opportunity she had awaited for so long had come.

Cortez, unlike the majority who plundered the high seas, felt no kinship to others in the brotherhood. The unwritten agreement to not molest a fellow pirate ship meant nothing to him. Plunder was plunder, and prize was prize. Other buccaneers left Master and crew with an empty hold to get back to land as best they could, but Cortez seized, slew, and set fire to his conquest. Further, no man who tried to defend his vessel escaped with his life, be it merchant seaman, cruiser, or any other legitimate seafarer. If Cortez needed the extra hands, he would prolong the execution of those who signed the articles with him, but it was merely a matter of time and the whim of the cruel Cortez as to when he would massacre the men who accepted their lot in good faith and became members of his crew.

"That's Happy Jack Muldoon," he had chortled to Dell Fields on the day before. Then he'd ordered his helmsman to pull hard away in order to appear as if he was trying to flee. With the fifty extra hands aboard that had recently been taken from *The Swann* he would have no trouble boarding *The Dancing Lady* and he had an extra advantage in surprise.

Dell did her share, as always, her expression never once betraying her seething emotions. She'd been almost overcome with joy when she realized the opportunity would soon be at hand to take command of *The Nightingale* by having Cortez killed. Cortez habitually made a ritual of putting the conquered Master to death. It was seldom a quick and merciful death, either. She knew he would go to great lengths when it came to the murder of Jack Muldoon. They were blood enemies and had been for many years, a situation that was known about and whispered about among the entire brotherhood. Cortez's fiendish nature would know no bounds when he devised the most exquisite of tortures for the man he hated above all others. More important for Dell Fields, she knew him well enough to be certain that he would lose himself completely in his enjoyment of whatever spectacle he prepared for Muldoon.

It was the first time the ideal moment had presented itself. To take a chance on murdering him at any of the past executions could have been fatal. Pistols and fowling pieces were not totally dependable, and neither was the loyalty of the men if the matter came down to being questioned about who put the idea in their heads to rise up against the ship's Captain. Any member of the crew would attempt to save his own hide by pointing the finger of guilt at the quartermaster. Until then, Dell had been afraid to risk exposure. Knowing Cortez would devote his entire attention to the torture of Jack Muldoon, knowing such a chance might not come again, she had made her final move. Even then, there was a chance that the marksman would miss, but Dell took the chance.

Muldoon's woman appeared bright and willing enough. She'd just suggested that Muldoon's aunt had considerable experience in food preparation.

"Yes, I'm sure you're right," Dell answered. "We've twice as many hands as we need, but they all have to be fed. I'll take it kindly if you ask her to report to me after she has rested. As soon as I can put into a port, I'll give the mates the freedom to sign on with another ship. Meanwhile, I must see to their well-being. Hungry mates don't make good hands, and even though we're in no danger of running out of supplies, food has to be prepared better than it has been."

As Garnet left, Dell Fields' blue eyes followed her appraisingly, wondering how much of her compliant nature was due to fear, and how much of it was genuine. "Wait," she called out. When Garnet turned around, she smiled. "I'll have the jewels you referred to brought aft for my inspection and I'll try to find out how they came to be aboard *The Dancing Lady*. I've not forgotten our discussion."

Nine

Out of deference for her age, Dell Fields was gracious to Becky Muldoon, and there was no pretense in her warmth and affectionate manner. They were in the hold, inspecting the stores. The new Master of *The Nightingale* held a genuine feeling of good will in her heart for Jack Muldoon's aunt. She liked and respected the dauntless old woman. "Well, what do you think?" She pointed to a barrel that sent off the smell of decay.

"Throw them all out. One bad potato in a bunch turns them all rotten, and by the stink of 'em, they've not been fit to eat for months."

"Cortez would have ordered the cook to put them on to boil," Captain Fields said with a shudder. "What about the turnips?"

"Some of 'em are wrinkled and too old to cook, but most of 'em will do."

"I've been hankering for a good meat stew." Dell's mouth watered as she envisioned a thick, savory stew with plenty of tender meat and vegetables. "There are plenty of carrots and onions, but it takes more than that to make a stew."

"If the beef isn't too far gone, perchance I could put together what you crave, substituting dumplings for potatoes," the old woman mused. "But this crate of onions has to go overboard." She wrinkled her nose and put up a hand to wipe the tears from her eyes against the stench. "And what is a stew without a few onions?"

"There's another crate of them that's not been opened."

"Then if they're good, you'll have what you want, Captain. Providing there's enough beef to use for flavoring, enough grease to make up some nice flaky dumplings."

"I'll order the steer killed. Or a sheep. Aside from my own hunger, I want the men to have enough to sate their appetites."

"You're wise, Captain Fields. A hungry man soon turns ugly. My nephew always sees to it that his men are fed hearty, and for that very reason." The old woman looked thoughtful. "But if I was you, I would have a sheep slaughtered instead of the steer. You've six of them and there's nothing any tastier than a good mutton stew."

"I'll leave that to you, Becky. Now I'll send a man down to bring up the vegetables, order another one to kill a sheep. You stay here to help the mate make a good selection, then I suppose you'll be busy in the galley."

The old woman gave the young one a shrewd look, tipping back her head in order to make eye contact. She was shorter than the average woman, but her attitude made it clear that she felt no intimidation and her words underscored that feeling. "I've no doubt that you want to speak to my Jonathan without an audience. For all of me, you've no need to take care to get me out of the way. I'd as soon you came out and said it plain. You've set the girl to sewing, so your path is clear. She's tractable enough unless she's crossed, but as nice a lass as you could find anywhere and she'll not make trouble, since she's smart enough to know the way the wind blows. Don't make the mistake of underestimating her smarts, though. She's your match, Dell Fields, but in a different way."

The red-haired woman's blue eyes flashed icy cold, but only for a second. Then she burst out in a hearty laugh and put out her hand to old Becky. "And I'll not underestimate you, either, Becky Muldoon. I was trying to be—what is the proper word—uh—"

"Tactful?"

"Yes. Tactful. But you understand there is much to be said between your nephew and me, so I'll take it kindly if you see to it that the young woman doesn't stop in the middle of her work and come to see how her lover fares."

Becky again looked into Dell Fields' blue eyes and spoke gently. "You're no longer the downtrodden lass of three years past, and you've learned to keep your feelings to yourself. Do you still scream out in the night?"

"I've not for a long while, but I still awaken at times in the throes of the old nightmare."

"Now that Cortez is dead, you'll no longer be tortured by the past. Now go. I'll stay here until the lad comes down to carry up the vegetables. Then I'll find Garnet and set her to work at scrubbing and peeling them."

"If your nephew was equipped with half as much common sense as you, Becky, there would be no reason for me to speak my words to him."

Becky grinned. "Chances are good that you'll get him to see the handwritin' on the wall, Dell."

"He'll see it, all right. But whether he'll read it the way it's written and take it to heart is another matter entirely."

"Well, if all else fails, you can always use your charms."

In spite of herself, Dell Fields blushed furiously at the idea of using her charms on Happy Jack Muldoon, then she blushed even deeper at the idea of allowing her emotions to color her fair skin. During all the time she had masqueraded as a man and acted as quartermaster to Luis Cortez she had never once betrayed herself by flushing like a woman, and there had been times when the conversation she overheard, even participated in with the crew, would have sent an ordinary woman into a swoon.

But she'd had a goal, she reminded herself. A promise to all she held dear to rid the world of Cortez, and she had undertaken just that, with an amazing singlemindedness of purpose. Absolutely nothing was allowed to stand in her way, but there were certain precautions she had to take. First of all, she had to learn the skills of a quartermaster well enough to not only get aboard, but to stay there, and in the end make herself practically indispensable to the man she hated with a consuming passion.

Secondly, she was forced to keep a certain distance between herself and the crew because of her sex and the danger of being unmasked, which was difficult with privacy at a premium on board an all-male ship. When nature called she had been hard pressed to find an opportunity to relieve herself without being caught with her pants down, but she had managed. The only natural advantage she had was her unusually tall figure. Everything else had come through applying herself to her craft and her pretense. But the time for pretense was over, she reminded herself as she knocked on the door where Jack Muldoon recuperated from his brush with death. So she would say to him what she'd come for and be done with it. Make sure he understood which course to follow and the consequences that would be his if he quartered when she wanted him to tack, or set sail when she wanted him to lean hard to leeward.

"Come in," he called out.

She entered and closed the door behind her, her features set in cold, hard lines.

"Sit down," he said pleasantly.

"I am in command, may I remind you? Therefore, I am the one who decides whether I shall sit or stand. And whether you do, incidentally."

After three days, Muldoon's scabs were beginning to flake off and the bruises were not as prominent, but he still bore the marks of his ordeal. Dell Fields was hard pressed to keep from taking back her words, but she remained firm as he painfully got to his feet and stood before her until she issued the command for him to sit at his ease. "You're still stiff and sore, I see."

"A little." His flashing smile brought back a semblance of his usual good looks. "But I understand one is much stiffer in death, although I can't say for sure whether there's soreness. I appreciate your kindness, Dell in allowing me to remain in the Captain's quarters. The three of us would have been cramped in a cabin of lesser size."

"Do not refer to me as Dell again, Muldoon. I am your Captain, and you are not to forget it."

His eyes sparkled with mirth. "Forgive me. I'll try not to make that mistake again."

At last she seated herself on a chair a few feet from the bed where he lay back against several pillows. "And don't attempt to make me the object of your misbegotten humor, either. I do not appreciate it."

"There was a time when you did...Captain Fields."

"That time is in the past." She regarded him silently for a moment. Then she spoke crisply. "I want you to know that I was taken by surprise when Cortez spied you out. When he told me he'd sighted your ship and ordered the helmsman to pretend to give flight, I was appalled. I knew he would swarm you and board you, if only by sheer force, and knowing what I knew of the bad blood between you, I also knew what would be your fate."

"God knows I'm perfectly aware of the way things were with the bastard. I don't hold you responsible for my being flogged, Captain, if that's what you're getting at."

"You're right. Even if I had wanted to jeopardize myself by trying to persuade him to let you off—which I didn't, by the way—my words would have fallen on deaf ears. The lust to see you whimpering and pleading for mercy was too high for any ineffectual words from me to have saved you. Anyway, if I had been so foolish as to plead your case he would have turned on me. No man who gainsays Luis Cortez would have lived."

"Except for me and thee," Muldoon said softly. "And you're no man."

"And I never once allowed him to guess that I disagreed with him in any thing."

"But you've gained your ends." Admiringly, Muldoon shook his head. "You know, a lot of people make vows. I'm talking about stalwart men. But you're the first person I've ever known who carried out to the end a vow of such proportions."

"And in the doing of it," she said with a partial smile, "managed to pay back a debt. I owed you my life."

"You owed me nothing, but I'm grateful and obliged that you were aboard."

She stood, strode to the cabinets that lined one side of the room and took out a bottle of wine. "In the morning, you will move into my smaller quarters with your woman. Your aunt will bunk down in the alcove above the galley. I am claiming the Captain's quarters as my own."

"Of course. You've been most kind to allow us to remain here these past three days."

She poured the wine into goblets. "These aren't silver. Nothing like as splendid as the ones that were taken from your ship. Plunder from another vessel, but lovely to look at and the devil doesn't care where they came from."

Muldoon nodded. She gave him one of the goblets and he took it, waited for her to take the first sip or make a toast or whatever pleased her. He wished she would sit down. A fine line of perspiration dampened his forehead as he waited for her to get on with it. It was highly unlikely that she'd come for the sole purpose of announcing that she was claiming the Captain's quarters and to remind him of his status. When she said nothing, but continued to stand over him, he grew agitated. As casually as he could muster, he said, "What are your plans for the future, Captain?"

"I will put you ashore at the Bermudas. You and yours, unless I can persuade Becky to cast her lot with me."

"It's doubtful if she'll agree to it, but there's no harm in asking. My aunt and I have been through a great deal together. She's grown to enjoy the sea and the excitement of the voyages. She's even taken on the speech of the mates."

"Yes. I noticed." A fleeting smile played about Dell Fields' lips, but she said nothing further.

Muldoon wondered what was on her mind. Wished she was as easy for him to read as Garnet was. At least, as apparent as Garnet was at times. "The Bermudas." He spoke without much expression in his voice. "Under the circumstances, I'm in no position to argue."

"No. You're not," she said drily. "And I am taking your breeches. Not the ones you wore when you were flogged, the ones your woman brought you to wear around the cabin." She bent forward and took them from the foot of the bed and folded them in her lap.

He looked at her, feeling hopeless and angry, but chose to ignore the business about the breeches. "I would consider it a kindness if you would allow me to stay aboard until you reach—wherever you're bound." Muldoon dreaded the idea of being put ashore in the Bermudas. It was under the dominion of the Crown. He guessed she planned to drop anchor in the Colonies where a man of his reputation would stand a better chance of remaining free. In Virginia or the

Carolinas, say. He closed his eyes for a moment as he visualized himself fleeing from the long arm of the law if she put him off in the Bermudas. The cluster of islands was too small for his liking and too thinly populated. A man of his bearing would create instant curiosity on the part of the natives, and he didn't relish the idea of being brought before the Governor and questioned. His name and description would have him on the gallows. "How long will it be, by your calculations, before we come upon them?"

Shrugging, Dell said, "A month. Six weeks. Three, if the winds hold and the sea is benevolent." She held her goblet aloft and fixed him with a freezing smile. "I'll drink to your continued recovery."

Since he was not expected to drink to his own health, he remained as he was, still holding his goblet while he tried to figure out what she would say next.

She took a small sip and looked at him again. "Now we will drink together, Jack Muldoon. To a successful end to this voyage. Calm seas and fair weather."

He drank, but he still waited, and not with an easy mind, although she emptied her goblet.

Standing again, she looked down at him and favored him with another wintry smile. He remembered another time, when her eyes had been warm and glowing in their bright blue depths. She was happy then, and content. A wife and mother with her missionary husband on the Barbados Islands. Tall and stately as she went about her duties of helping the man she loved convert the heathen to Christianity, a womanly figure and stunning to look at. Even then he'd recognized that her spirit was great. Her loving husband had respected her strength and intellect, and once, before he met his death at the hands of Luiz Cortez, the Reverend Wills confided in Jack Muldoon that his wife's spine was made of iron.

After her husband died her blue eyes were grey with grief. She was a long time lost in the passion of her sorrow. Muldoon came each day to the little hut where she had lived and loved. For days she sat like stone at the table, the light in her eyes dimmed. She had been more dead than living. In time, he liked to tell himself, he helped her find her way back into the land of flesh and blood, of laughter and joy, of rejoicing in the tang of an ocean breeze on her face and the touch of a man's hand on her breast.

"You will remain in your quarters after you've moved," she said, breaking into his reverie. "You may go on deck for an hour each day, for exercise and fresh air, weather permitting. And I will be at your side. I will also give your woman permission to accompany us."

"Then I am to remain a prisoner."

She nodded. "Yes, you are to remain a prisoner, but not because you were running a pirate ship, certainly." Her laugh was refreshing. Much like it had been in the old days, before her heart was broken. And her blue eyes were bright when she said, "After all, I've been plundering the seas myself for many a month. Long before I signed with Cortez. Learning the trade, you might say." She hesitated for a moment before she plunged the sword of necessity in. "It's a measure of safety for me. Your reputation far surpasses mine and there's not a knave aboard who wouldn't transfer their loyalty to you. Fair treatment, good food, plenty of water and enough rum to satisfy any man without turning him into a drunken sot won't hold a candle to your charm, your reputation or your diabolical skill when it comes to chicanery."

He grinned. "I bow my head. Whether in shame or pride, I can't say."

"And I—" Her eyes belied the stern mold of her mouth, and she had to swallow before she could get the words out, which gave him pause. Either she didn't mean what she was about to say or she was having a hard time spitting the words out, which he took as a sign that she wasn't sure of herself. But he merely nodded when she finally said it: "I don't find you appealing, so save your energy for the little girl you ravished in your usual high-handed way."

"I didn't ravish her. She was agreeable. Nor did I take *you* by force, Dell Fields. I mean, *Captain*!"

"Your attentions came at a time when I was down so low that I had no strength with which to fight you."

"Damn it to hell, you didn't fight at *all*! If I remember correctly, it was you who came to me. There in the hut, six weeks after your husband—"

"You were never one to listen, or to weigh matters. I came

out of emptiness. Because you'd made me laugh and talk. I wanted to live and needed your words about life being for the living. You aided me greatly, I'll admit that, but the night I came to your hut I wanted nothing but the comfort of your arms, although I received much, much more than that."

"If you didn't want me to make love to you, why did you return the next night?" In his anger and need to make her tell it the way he thought it had been, he had yelled at her, which meant he'd lost control. A damnable error, because that was obviously what she wanted. He could see that she was pleased by the coolness with which she smoothed her dress, the calculated way she put her empty wine goblet down on the chest at the side of her chair. For her to be in complete control was maddening, yet he admired her for it.

Her answer left him unmanned, however. In all of his life, he'd never thought he would be in such a position. Of course when he considered the alternative, which would have been certain death, he decided his situation was tolerable. Even so, he had never been so enraged in his life. Quietly, and without a trace of emotion, she said, "I was willing to accept your bumbling attempts at love-making in order to receive what I needed, which was a man to hold me close. At that time, I realized I needed the comfort of those arms in order to survive—and in order to gain my revenge on Luis Cortez, I had made up my mind to live."

He said, "Very well. I'll accept your orders and your wishes. You are the Master of this ship and I am your prisoner. And I'll not attempt to impose upon a former relationship, wouldn't dream of it now that you've made it painfully clear that it meant nothing to you."

"I didn't say it meant nothing. I was grateful. Still am. How did you acquire the opal necklace and matching earrings that reposed in a lacquered tray in your quarters?"

Caught off guard, he answered her truthfully. "Bought them from a down-and-out bastard by the name of Simon Moskowitz. Why? Were they yours? If so, you may have them back with my compliments, since you have them anyway."

"They're very beautiful," she said. "Perhaps I shall be generous, and give them to your little love."

When she was outside the cabin, Dell Fields walked with

her natural long-strided gait and took no care about keeping down the sound of her heels against the deck. Quickly, she turned and ran soundlessly back to the door, where she pressed her ear against the wood to listen intently. She heard words that would have burned the ears of a woman who was easily shocked. Then she heard the clink of glass against metal and the gurgle of liquid being poured. With an expression of mirth upon her face, she walked on tiptoe until she was well away. It was one thing to best a strong man in a verbal duel, but quite another to let him know she knew he had turned to the bottle for solace. Dell Fields was not, by nature, a cruel and heartless woman.

With Becky Muldoon's fine hand to guide the preparation of the food, a change for the better had come about in that quarter. The supplies that were taken from *The Dancing Lady* did much to add zest to the food that was served aboard, and experience had taught the new ship's Master that the mood of the crew could be accurately gaged by their mess. She was not without problems, however, for the schooner was too crowded for comfort. Men in close quarters, sleeping side by side with barely enough room for them to turn over without disturbing two others, were apt to grow short-tempered. Dell Fields was hard pressed to come up with a way to ease the situation. Although Cortez had given no thought to the discomforts of his crew, she gave it much consideration. Cortez made short shrift of shipmates who fought among themselves. He killed them, usually in privacy in order to keep the others from growing unruly—but sometimes in front of every man aboard, as a lesson in discipline.

Since the day they took *The Swann*, long before boarding Muldoon's vessel, Dell had worried about the crowding of too many men together for another reason. Disease was always a danger aboard ship, but with the scanty rations and maggoty, rotting slop Cortez had served, the chance of sickness was much higher. Ridding the stores of the decomposed foodstuffs and putting Becky at the head of the mess had done much to alleviate her worries, but there was no way she could increase the breathing room of the crew. At the moment, they idolized her. With single-minded purpose she had gone about the mutinous act that ended in putting a bullet through the hated, cruel Cortez, and she had done it at great risk. They knew it and they also knew that any one of them could have gone to Cortez to warn him that his quartermaster was taking steps to bring about an insurrection—which would have resulted in her death.

The fact that Cortez had not been a Captain who saw any reason to court loyalty in his crew was on her side. There were no men aboard who had been with him for any length of time. Those who were lucky enough to have survived his poisonous swill and raging, mindless temper, had had a belly full. Some left their measley share of the booty behind to jump overboard the minute they sighted land. New hands were quick enough to learn that the articles they signed meant nothing to Cortez, especially concerning the share of the plunder. Ten pieces of silver went to him for every one that went to the crew; this was his custom, and he thought nothing of shooting down any man who protested. Those who came aboard with high expectations soon dropped into the doldrums of hopelessness. Whenever a new batch signed on, the greenhorns were told quickly that they were fools, that Cortez used the lash for no reason at all, starved them and treated them like slaves. So Dell Fields had spent no time worrying about the sly song of a stool pigeon reaching Cortez's ears. The plan had worked, she'd come through it unscathed, but she was unsure of herself as she looked into the future.

Those first few days after the victory presented no problem, but she knew she was on her honeymoon. The men adored her, true; to them she was their savior and their reaction to learning her gender increased her advantage. Among themselves, she had been told, they referred to her as a saint. Many had knelt down to kiss the hem of her gown, and some had told her frankly that they'd doubted their chance of living long enough to see land under the command of Cortez. But due to overcrowding and boredom, she knew the honeymoon would not endure for long. In time, the men would begin to wonder if they'd shamed themselves by allowing a female to lead them, even though they'd not known she was a female at the time.

Putting an end to her charade was a choice she had made after much consideration. If she had continued to masquerade as a man she would not have feared losing the respect of the crew, but at the same time she would have been forced to continue in constant danger of being exposed. The vision of how she would fare at the hands of an unruly mob of renegades, long after the first flush of gratitude had paled, was what brought about her decision to show her hair at her moment of triumph. The added twist of a female putting down the tyrant served her well at the time. The men took great satisfaction in chortling together over the way she had bamboozled Cortez. But after the novelty wore away she was afraid they would conclude that she had bamboozled them, too—which alarmed her.

Muldoon's presence aboard was a definite threat. A born leader with a reputation for derring-do such as his could easily be her undoing, but she would not place herself in the same category as Luiz Cortez by eliminating him. Aside from that, she'd spoken the truth when she said she owed him her life. As she went about the business of the day she asked herself if there was another reason why the very thought of ridding herself of the threat of Happy Jack Muldoon was repugnant. At last she admitted to herself that she still felt a stirring deep within of the old spark that had existed between them. If not, she would not have gone to such pains to deny them vocally, nor to take pleasure from the barb she'd deliberately pressed home.

Dell Fields knew and understood herself better than most. After more thought, she was sure that she could hold her emotions in check. Being aware of her own vulnerability, she considered, was as good as a warning. More than once her well-formed lips curled in a secret smile as she went back in her mind and reflected on Muldoon's reaction to her renunciation of his charms. By coming out with it, she'd found his center of weakness. For a long time she had known the great store men set in their ability to satisfy a woman, but she'd been more than a little surprised to learn that Jack Muldoon was as prone to protect his balls as the next man. She had thought him so full of his own worth that he'd not be touched in the least by her statement. Well, she would be well rid of him when she sent him ashore at the Bermudas. At the same time she would rid herself of fifty or so of the crew by the simple measure of giving them a handsome share of the plunder she carried in her hold. She realized it would not take Muldoon long to get another craft together and the crew would be there for the picking, but that was nothing to her—although she had no wish to meet him on the high seas again. Not after she'd wounded his pride and trampled all over his ego.

Night fell and Dell Fields retired to the small cabin. It suited her just as well as the big one she would take on the morrow, but protocol demanded that a proper ship's Master enjoy the Captain's quarters, and to leave him there with his woman would be losing face with her crew.

Sighing deeply as she settled herself in for a few hours, she pondered the mysteries of men and their need to keep their manly image intact. In all of her life she had known but one man who had no fear of losing face or balls, and it occurred to her that with men, they were inseparable, which made her chuckle.

For a long time after the tragedy, Dell Fields was unable to keep her mind from picking over the threads of brutal memories. She tried very hard to mind the present and look toward the future as Becky Muldoon and her nephew advised her, but unless she was actively engaged in conversation with someone else, she re-lived the horror every minute of every day. Even when occupied in the give and take of conversation, the terror hovered in the back of her mind, ready to swoop down on her and devour her with melancholy the minute she was alone again. As the days and weeks passed, she was able to force her truant mind into daytime obedience, but when night fell and she slept, her dreams were vivid and remorselessly detailed as she experienced the devastating moments again and again and again.

It was Happy Jack Muldoon who helped her replace the thoughts of hopelessness with revenge. He'd said, "You can't get them back by grieving, but I know you can't force yourself to stop dwelling on it until you fill your head with something you *can* do. It's time to look toward the future.

Surely you don't plan to remain forever in this hovel and mourn your loss."

She recalled how she'd looked at him, the grief within so great that she often had trouble raising her hand to comb her hair. She was overcome with a great lethargy during those days when the shock still consumed her. As far as she was concerned there was no future. "I hadn't thought about it," she had whispered through pale lips.

"You must." She recalled how he had rubbed her cold hands and tried to revive some spark of life. "Before, you were more vivid and lively than anyone I've ever known. Now you're as pale as a ghost and even your flaming hair has grown dull. Do you think that your husband would appreciate the way you've let go? Why, he was as proud as a peacock of his saucy wife. I remember how he liked to remind folk of your energy. The way you would hustle and bustle about the place making bread, tidying things up, your apron whipping in the breeze while you hung out your clothes. We came back to the hut one day, Thomas and I, and he threw back his head and bellowed with joy at the sight of you as you carried the baby in one arm and a great pail of water in the other. Shoulders back, face eager to get to your next task, hair blowing out behind you in your headlong rush."

"No. Tom would never want me to fold up and give in. But don't you see, without him, without my baby, there's nothing *left* for me!"

"Don't you have a home? A mother, a father? Brothers or sisters you could turn to in your time of need?" That was before she came that night, to his hut. Before she became so hungry for the warmth of another human being that she'd gone to him, well knowing the way he felt about her, although in truth he'd never by word or deed told it plain.

"No, I can't go home."

"Then you're an orphan?"

"Not exactly."

He turned in exasperation. "What do you mean, not exactly? A person is an orphan or is not an orphan."

It was then she had told him her true name. "They wanted a boy-child because not a one of my mother's sisters had produced a male heir. There was the money and land, just waiting for the first grandson of my mother's father to be born. He sired fourteen daughters in wedlock and perchance as many more out of it. Nobody ever knew for sure. He died with a curse on his lips for his wife and all his happenstances because they'd failed to give him a boy. So he set up an instrument with a barrister that bequeathed his holdings to the first boy that was birthed by any of his daughters. I was it, and they named me Philadelphus, after my grandfather.

"I was a big baby. Much bigger than the others, with strong, lusty lungs and the appearance of one who had been outside the womb for a good two months, or so I was told. There was no resemblance between the husky baby that came to my parents in their late life and my sisters. All of them were fragile, most died at birth or in infancy. And there was the will of my mother's father, who was long dead by then. I'm sure it hung over their heads like an apple of gold, just out of their reach. The midwife was easily bribed into lying by the promise of a lifetime of ease once they got their hands on that estate. They borrowed another newborn boy-child of the neighborhood when they had to go to Pembroke for the inspection. They left home in poverty, wearing rags and afoot, but they came home in style, in a carriage. I was raised as a lad."

"But—" She was sure he'd been about to say it was obvious to anyone that she was all woman. The biggest, most delectable and exciting woman he had ever clapped his eyes on, he told her later, but at the time, their relationship had not progressed that far.

"I have a good idea what you're thinking, and when I told Tom he also doubted that they were able to carry off the deception for long. When I was thirteen, my girl cousins ganged up on me and—uh—satisfied their curiosity about the boy who lived in plenty while they did not. My mother shared what she could with her sisters, but my father was stingy and saw to it that she didn't give them over much. Blood is thicker than water, but when the little girls who had long been puzzled about the sissy-acting boy in the first place went running home to tell, the blood thinned out mighty fast. My mother and father were tried and found guilty of lying under oath and obtaining worth by fraud. They went to Bridewell and I was put with a good minister's family, which is where I met Tom, the oldest son. We were of the same age and I was the only girl in the house. The minister's wife was good to me, but she was the oldest of a family of five children, the only girl. All her young life she'd helped care for her little brothers. Then she had sons, and knew little about raising a girl. Perhaps the pattern was set long before I went to their house to live since I never felt quite at home with womanly chores. I hurried at my tasks because I was fearful of not being womanly enough, perchance."

"Then did your mother and father die at Bridewell?"

"No, they went to the New World, with many other felons. They sent letters a few times. After a few years, the letters came no more. So I don't know whether they're still living or not, but I often wonder. Of course I wouldn't dream of going to my relations."

"Come with me as soon as my ship is seaworthy again," he'd said. "I'm heading there."

But it was unthinkable for her to consider such a thing. She had known all along that he was a pirate, and she had accepted the faith of her foster parents. As Tom's helpmeet she was a fiery and devoted member of the faith. At least she had been until the day Cortez murdered her husband and her baby girl.

Lying awake, Dell Fields looked back into the past to the day she had first asked herself if she still believed the Word. She had embraced it and promised to spread it to every far-off corner of the world when she gave her vow to love, honor and obey Tom Wills, and she had been faithful about keeping both promises. On that day when Jack Muldoon offered to take her to the New World with him, she no longer believed in a just and kind God. She had done nothing to bring down His wrath, and yet He had not lifted a finger to save the two people she loved.

Turning over to search for a more comfortable position, Dell Fields refused to continue to look back. Talking to Muldoon had brought the memories of three years past flooding back, but she wouldn't allow them to overwhelm her. Deliberately, she sat up, lit her pipe and sat in the darkness, her mind busy with the present. Yes. Set Muldoon off at the Bermudas, the girl and his aunt with him, although she would make it attractive to the aunt to stay on with her. After that, she would make her way on to the New World. Turn away from pirating and purchase land. A land that was rumored to be beautiful, and where women could work it and own it, beholden to, or dependent upon, no man. After she was settled, she would try to find trace of her parents, but it was not her true parents that she wanted to find most. She would look for them, but it was Thomas Wills' mother and father she longed for and they, too, had gone to the Colonies. With Cortez dead she was free to look for those good people who had given her a home, given her their son. Until she had taken her revenge upon the murderer of her husband and child it was out of the question for her to seek her foster parents. Their ways were gentle, and they did not hold with violence. Instead, they held with peace and kindness, believing the meek would inherit the earth. Those ways had once been hers, and there were times when she longed for the comfort of the tenets. Maybe she would ask for forgiveness, now that she had purged her heart of hatred. In the darkness, she laughed aloud at herself, recognizing both folly and hypocrisy in such thoughts. For a little better than three years she had lived in burning hatred, thrived on the intention of killing. Now that the killing was done it was hardly sensible to expect forgiveness.

Nevertheless, she would try to find her husband's people, although she would never let them know of her sins any more than she would pray to a God she no longer believed in just to be on the safe side. She had done what had to be done and she was not sorry. Instead, she felt as if a great burden had been lifted from her, leaving her free to begin living.

After she emptied the ashes from her pipe into a bowl of sand, Dell Fields stretched out again and knew she would sleep. As she drifted off, her mind flickered for a moment on Garnet Shaw and she sighed. There were five years between them. She was twenty-one to Garnet's sixteen. There was an innocence about the younger woman that she envied. She hoped Muldoon would do nothing to remove that priceless luster.

Ten

Muldoon was so much improved on the fourth day after his ordeal that he was able to walk to the quartermaster's cabin unaided. Again, he took his morning meal alone while Garnet and Dell Fields kept each other company in the officers' mess. His Aunt Becky had been up long before the sun, he supposed, enjoying herself to the utmost as she hurried about with pots and pans.

As he finished his solitary meal of eggs, smoked meat and fried potatoes, topped off with apple fritters and a pot of tea spiked with rum, he looked forward with anger to another day of doing nothing. If only that contrary red-haired woman would let him come on deck. The bruises were quickly fading and the scabs all but fallen away but he was impatient and easily bored. Cursing, he paced the floor and railed inwardly.

Dell's high-handed decision to keep him naked was too much! He was half of a mind to walk on deck as he was, bare as the day he was born. The motely crew would see nothing they'd not seen before. They were all men. His aunt had dressed his private parts and neither Garnet nor Philadelphus were strangers to them, either. Grinning from ear to ear in spite of the sores that hadn't as yet healed on his lips, he took pleasure in visualizing the ire he would build in Dell Fields if he were to do just that. Now that he was feeling better, he doubted if she'd make good her threats if he did what he wanted. He had no intention of trying to coax her crew into accepting him as their Captain, hell no. He owed her that much. But damn it all, she had no right to keep him locked away as if he were a gibbering idiot, the family lunatic that had to be hidden away in the attic.

It galled him that she didn't trust him. Rankled with him that she'd seen fit to thrust into his hide by making that ridiculous statement about his ability in bed. He postured as he recalled the past, remembering no time when she'd left his bed unpleasured. After a while he was able to convince himself she'd said it out of spite.... Or fear, more likely. Come to think about it, she'd almost as good as said she was worried about his undermining her authority. The idea tickled him. It also amused him to consider the possibility that she still found him attractive, and he was sure she did. Any woman he had ever wanted had come to him, including Dell Fields. By the time Garnet returned to the room his spirits were much lifted.

"She's an interesting woman," Garnet said as she picked up one of the gowns she'd been working on for Captain Fields. Looking at the embroidery instead of Jack Muldoon, she asked, "How did it happen that you saved her life?"

"You didn't ask her?"

"I did, but she said she'd much rather you told me. Anyway, she's very busy."

"We were in the Barbados, about three years ago. Aunt Becky and I, that is. Had to take the ship in for a careening, otherwise we'd never have put in there. But we'd no choice, because the bottom of the vessel was heavy with coral. Made her sluggish when it came to chasing or being chased . . . well, it was a disreputable old whore in the first place, but the best we could do at the time. It was a frigate. Built like a box and cumbersome."

"Why did you happen to have an awkward ship like that?"

"Because we'd lost a round, just like I lost the last round to Cortez. In this business you don't win them all, you know. So we, ah, liberated the frigate and set out in her with a crew of five."

"Liberated it? But from where?"

"From where it was docked, just there for the taking if you don't count the people who lived in the palace by the sea. No doubt they owned the old tub, but since there was nobody around and we were getting tired of walking along the shoreline, we weren't in a position to pick and choose." Muldoon lifted his eyebrow and gave Garnet an oblique look. "Do you want to hear about how I happened to be sailing an old frigate, or do you want me to tell you how Aunt Becky and I happened to meet Dell Fields?"

"How you met Dell Fields. And saved her life."

"We put in to the Barbados to careen the frigate, as I said. It was a happy surprise to find a missionary on the island. His name was Thomas Wills and his wife and baby daughter were with him. We—ah, didn't exactly lie about how we happened to set down anchor in the harbor there, but we didn't offer any information, either. And just in case the owners of the old tub set up a hue and cry over her disappearance, we decided it'd be prudent to give her a new coat of paint and sort of—you know, change her lines a little. So we were hard at work. The preacher came to pay his respects and invited us to take a meal with him and his good wife. They lived in a hut, but it was ship-shape and spit-polish clean. A nice little family, and Aunt Becky was especially glad to have another woman to talk to. It'd been almost a year since she'd laid eyes on another female, so they drank tea and swapped recipes. Aunt Becky cuddled and cosseted that little baby to her heart's content. It was a pleasant time for her, and except for the hard work, it was a peaceful time for all of us, in the beginning."

Muldoon's eyes took on a faraway look, then they hardened.

Garnet asked, "Then, Dell Fields was on the island, too? As well as the missionary and his wife and child?"

"She was the missionary's wife. As happy a young woman as you'd ever want to find. Worshiped the ground her husband walked on and never gave a thought to anything but making her man happy and loving him, and they both adored the child. She was a pretty little thing, about a year old and a sunny disposition, which you'd expect in a baby when all she'd ever known was love. Blonde curls and dimpled cheeks, big blue eyes. The natives turned themselves inside out for Tom Wills. He did—a lot more than converting them to his faith." Jack Muldoon swallowed. "If ever I met a man I admired, it was Tom Wills. He ministered to the sick and taught them to read and write, but maybe it was a greater thing to write down their history, to make much of their own ways. It was as if he... gave the natives a great sense of pride instead of looking down on their customs and trying to make them over in what he considered the proper way. One time he told me he wasn't sure their ways weren't more proper than the ones he'd been sent there to force on them. He was a giant of a man, Garnet. I'm not talking about stature, but he was taller than his wife by a couple of inches. He stood head and shoulders above any man I've ever known, and because I happened to be there as a result of the blood-lust of Luis Cortez, Tom Wills died."

"Why did Luis Cortez hate you?" Garnet interrupted the thread of Muldoon's story because of the strange mixture of sheer hatred and abject sorrow on his face. The lost, haunted look in his eyes was more distressing than the hatred. Until she asked the question, she had a feeling that the man who had smiled through abominable torture a week previously was about to shatter.

"It's a long story." His voice had a strangled sound. "But I—suppose you have a right to know." He poured a mug of rum, swallowed half of it, then held the mug in his hands, to stare into it pensively. Before he spoke again, he tossed off the last of it, and she waited quietly, wondering if he was taking so long a time because he was making up a story that would sound plausible. At last, when she had just about concluded that he wasn't going to say anything, he gave her a crooked grin and said, "Would it suffice to say that I humiliated Cortez's sister? Insulted her and shamed her in the very worst way, and in public, too. There were over two hundred present."

"You ravished her, then? Ruined her?" Horrified, Garnet visualized him in the act of mounting a helpless woman in the presence of onlookers, the poor thing scratching and biting and screaming for help—but she could think of no way such an occurrence could have taken place, for if over two hundred people were there it stood to reason that they'd not have passively watched.

"Christ no," he answered. "By the left hind foot of God, I

did no such thing. That would have been impossible. Why must you always jump to the wrong conclusions, my dove?"

"I didn't know I did. You said you insulted her and shamed her. What else could I think?"

Sighing deeply, Muldoon leaned his head back against the pillows and said, "Damn all and more than that. If we weren't betrothed, I would tell you to jump overboard. You must have sense enough to realize that if I humiliated a young woman I also succeeded in dishonoring myself, so it's a story that's not easy to tell."

Garnet gave him a look of seething anger. Raising her voice, she said, "*You're* the one who said we were betrothed, Jack Muldoon—so high-handed you are and without a question as to how such a serious step sits with me! You took it for granted that I would swoon at the idea of becoming your wife. Well! Open up those jackass ears of yours and listen to what I have to say on the matter. I'm not sure I want to even consider it, and if you try to force me in front of a magistrate to say my vows, I will say no, I won't do it, when he asks me the question."

"By God!" He reared back in amazement. "You were flimmering and flammering about your damned ruination, saying I forced you and all that stuff and nonsense, so I thought you'd be pleased at the notion. I *told* you, I love you! What more do you *want* from me?"

"Not a thing!" Her cheeks were crimson, and her eyes were shooting little orangish flames. "What I want is something you can't give me. It's something I already have, and that's my self-respect. Unless I allow you to, you can't take that away from me, so I've decided to not allow you."

"You've been spending too much time with Dell Fields. Those are her words you're mouthing, not yours. She's changed you. Talked to you and filled all the sweet places in your head with a bunch of blather."

"No she didn't. I felt like that before we were taken over by Cortez, before you were put to the flailing, I just didn't say so."

"You're lying. Out-and-out lying. I saw the way you looked when I was up there with my hands tied behind me, those bastards lashing me with the cat. You were as pale as a ghost."

"Certainly I was, and I'll be the first to admit it. I would have felt that way about the lowest creature on this earth being subjected to that kind of brutal torment. The trouble with you, Jack Muldoon, you decide the way things are and that's the way they're going to be, always have been, always will be. You're not capable of realizing anyone else has the ability to think or make decisions."

"The trouble with you, Garnet Shaw, is cabin fever. You've been confined too long with me. Spent too many hours at my side, and until lately I've been unable to lift a hand to see to your happiness. That, and too much exposure to a woman who's more man than woman. It's not seemly for a woman to masquerade as a man for so long, and to get away with it unscathed!"

Garnet's voice was barely above a whisper, but each word fell crisp and cold, like the sound of a bell being run on a cold winter morning. "You—would—presume—to—speak—of—what—is—seemly?" The laugh that followed was devoid of mirth, and the sound of it enough to cause Jack Muldoon to break out in goose flesh. "And anyway, you're biting the hand that feeds you, the hand that saved you from certain death. What is it with you, Jack Muldoon? Earlier, you spoke of Captain Fields as a woman of great warmth and many other admirable attributes. Now you dare to say she's turned into something inhuman! Your tongue has surely split in two."

"And yours has come unhinged. It pains me to learn that you have the tongue of a viper." He peered at her intently, his eyes clouded with disappointment. "Before, you were so *biddable*!"

"Fash and fiddle! It pains you to find yourself in the same uncomfortable position that you had me in. I was biddable because I had no choice. I was your prisoner, don't you remember? Now you're hers, and you're straining at the chains." Garnet giggled. "How it must rankle with you to be confined to a room all day long without a stitch of clothing, allowed to go above only once a day, and closely watched at that!"

"You're damned *right* it rankles with me! She behaves as if I am a wild beast!" He stood up and paced the small quarters. "She has no right to degrade me in this manner. I tell you, she has nothing to fear from me, and it's only because I'm a man and she's a woman that she treats me so unjustly. She has all the fears and little sillinesses of womankind that plague the race. Unsure of herself, that's what. I am a man of honor! I've given her my word that I won't undermine her position and that should be enough." Out of the corner of his eyes, he caught her vivid smile and saw that she was having a hard time squelching it. "All right," he said impatiently as he stopped in mid-step. "It would be a kindness if you'd tell me what you find so amusing."

"You won't like it."

"Tell me anyway!"

"All *right*! The way your family jewels swing back and forth as you pace the floor is very—funny." For a trembling second, Garnet knew a surging fear that he would strike her. His fists doubled and his features turned rigid. But apparently he thought better of it. Instead of hitting her, he reached for a blanket and wrapped it around his waist, glaring all the while. After he was settled again in the chair, he gave her a melting look and spoke gently. "Garnet, my love, please forgive me. Every word you said was true. I strain at these fetters and I find it galling to be placed in the position of being confined to quarters and led around on deck by a couple of women. He took her hand and seemed to take solace in her encouraging smile. "Now I'll go back to where we were before we became immersed in a foolish quarrel."

Garnet listened quietly and asked no more questions. As the story unfolded, she became engrossed, then spellbound. For his part, Jack Muldoon was swept into the past, back to all the misery and disappointment of his early youth as he re-lived it:

Early in his childhood, Jonathan Muldoon absorbed the knowledge that he was not the only Jonathan Muldoon of Carrickfergus County, Ireland. Although he had searched his memory repeatedly, he couldn't remember ever having been told the way things were, but he could likewise not remember a time when he didn't know his father was Lord Jonathan Muldoon who had a legitimate son, Jonathan

Edmund, and a bastard son, Jonathan Cortez o'Muldoon, both of whom were known as "The Muldoon lads." Jack lived in a cottage with his Spanish mother and a serving woman. The other Jonathan was the Young Lord, and he was not referred to as Jack. He was four years older than Jack and he lived in the castle with his father and Lady Muldoon. There were other legitimate children. Two daughters and a much younger boy who was seldom seen about the estate except in the company of Lady Muldoon and a retinue of servants. Even then, the little boy was kept in a closed carriage and young Jack Muldoon knew there was something mysterious, something not quite right about the youngest son of Lord Muldoon.

When he was about nine years old, the carriage went by the place where Jack Muldoon was hunting and he was afforded a glimpse of a pale face, a head that looked swollen, and pale rolling eyes that had a witless appearance, a sick looking mouth that drooled. When Jack, the child, went home to his beloved mother he told her he had seen the lord's younger son. "No wonder they keep him hidden and won't allow him to go about like other children. There's something about him that's not—"

His mother had hugged him to her breast on that day and told him to have pity in his heart for the lad. "He was born with a big head and a deformity in his brain."

Now and then young Jack Muldoon happened upon his older half-brother. The young lord was amiable, a good marksman and born to the saddle. On one of their happenstance meetings, he appeared sullen, but hastily assured young Jack that his ugly disposition had nothing to do with their somewhat unusual relationship. "My father has arranged my marriage and I'm unhappy with his choice for my bride." He looked at Jack and frowned. "Sometimes I envy you. The old man won't give a damn whom you marry. I've been thinking about killing myself, Jack."

The young lord was nineteen years old at the time to Jack's fifteen. Over the years they had formed a cameraderie of sorts and Jack was appalled at the casual way the young lord spoke of taking his own life. "Nothing could be bad enough to kill yourself over it!"

"That's what you think." Jonathan Muldoon then went into a lengthy tirade about the solemn duties of the elder son of a lord. "And to make matters worse, there's no second son to inherit," he continued, "not actually, because my little brother was born with a defective brain. So there's no way out of it, old boy. I must marry my fifth cousin, Janet, and she's no more keen to take me on as husband as I am to take her for my wife. Like myself, Janet has given her heart to another. Also like myself, the one she loves is a commoner, which is unthinkable for a nobleman to even contemplate. Our fathers have everything all arranged. I like Janet well enough, and she's a nice-looking colleen, but damn it all, a man should have the right to choose his own wife!"

At fifteen, Jack Cortez of the Muldoon clan had no interest in the gentler sex. In all truth, he found girls tiresome and silly, except for his mother and his father's half sister, Becky Muldoon. But they were women grown, who did not squeal at the sight of a fishing worm, or spend hours in idle gossip and giggling. It came to him that there was a way to help the young lord solve his problems. "Let's run away to sea."

"You don't understand, Jack," Jonathan Muldoon said dejectedly. "I was born into duty." Then he had explained that nobleman are born with certain obligations, including the continuation of the line, the running of the vast estates, seeing to the welfare of the peasants who lived on the land and depended upon the master for the very bread they ate. "Then there are the bastards, like yourself," he continued unabashed. "And the mothers of the bastards, like your own. They must be provided for and looked after, just as my father has provided for all the bastard children of his father before him and their mothers."

The afternoon was a lesson in the way things were for Jack Muldoon. Before then, he had never given his lot in life much thought, and even then he was not offended by his half brother's casual reference to his own status of illegitimacy. Just as he was born with dark hair and liquid eyes that changed from dark, dark brown to an odd hue of blue-grey, he'd known for some time that he was born out of wedlock. The knowledge he gleaned from the young lord that changed the course of his life was that his father had actually stolen his mother. He had spirited her away from a magnificent, if run-down *casa* in Spain and promised to marry her, a promise he could not possibly have kept since he was already married to Lady Muldoon.

Confronting his beautiful mother, he looked at her with black rage. "Why did you not ever tell me, my mother?"

"Tell you what?" His mother had looked at him in surprise.

"That you are of noble birth, that the Lord Muldoon lied to your father when he said he would bring you to Ireland and make you his wife!"

"What on earth gave you that idea?"

"The young lord told me. He said you were brought from your own beautiful *casa* under the impression that you would marry Lord Muldoon, but after you arrived you found out you and your family had been lied to."

"Oh. Well, that was a long time ago, and the young lord's version is not exactly true. I am of noble birth, yes. The Cortez name is ancient and respected and one of my ancestors made himself famous when he sailed the seas and conquered a country across the ocean, which is New Spain. But my father was badly in debt. He faced a prison sentence in spite of his *casa* and good family name. I was the youngest daughter of five, each of whom had cost him several *lire* for dowry, and my brothers had long since died. Lord Muldoon offered to pay my father's debts in exchange for bringing me to Ireland as his mistress, and of course my father had to accept. It would have been a disgrace for him to go to prison."

"But not a disgrace to *sell* his daughter?"

"Come, now!" His mother shrugged her young son's ideals aside. "You must learn to be practical. A young woman without a dowry is less than nothing in Spain, and by the time I reached a marriageable age there was no dowry. I did not look forward to spending my years as a spinster, and I have not been unhappy in Ireland. I was given a great gift, my son. You."

Angry and disillusioned, young Jack turned to his beloved Aunt Becky, who had adored him from the moment he was born. To her, he railed and ranted against fate, against the complacent way his mother had spoken to him concerning the shameful way she'd been bartered. As always Aunt Becky sympathized and agreed with him, but she prudently advised him against going at once to his father and chopping off his head.

"You're a boy, not yet got your full growth, so you'd not stand a chance against him. And anyway, your mother is wise. She's accepted the lot of women, so she's better off than I am, for I've never been able to look at myself as an object put on earth for the pleasure of men. There's something out of kilter with the world, I'm sure. Women have as many brains as men, if not more, but it's the men who run things, and I would be a lot more content if I didn't feel as I do. Your mother is well fed and clothed. She has a roof over her head and my half brother no longer forces his attentions on her now that she's grown older. It's the young and unspoiled ones that command his attention, one after the other. He's like our father, the old lord, who died these many years ago and sired nineteen bastard children, me among 'em, and only two in the holy bonds of matrimony—your father and his sister who went into the nunnery. Sure and it's a shame nobody thought to tell you sooner, my lad, but the young Lord Jonathan didn't have his facts straight. Your mother came willingly enough, and willing she's been down through the years to live as she has. Faith, and I envy her, for she's not forever pained in her guts like I am with the injustice of it all!"

By the time young Jack reached the age of eighteen a number of things had taken place that helped him adjust to the way things were. Young Lord Muldoon married Janet and went to live in a palatial home in the highlands beyond Carrickfergus where the first Lord Muldoon of recorded history took his bride in the year 1401. A month later, Jack's adored mother died after a short illness. At her bedside were her son, Becky Muldoon, and the lord himself, who had been summoned by his half-sister when the end of the lovely Spanish woman's death seemed near at hand.

Evalina y Cortez looked searchingly into the eyes of the man who had brought her from Spain as she lay dying. Her voice was clear as she spoke to him: "My time is short. I make a first and final request of you."

Later, Jack wondered if his father was touched by the woman's suffering. On the other hand, he might have feared the cold fingers of death that seemed to hover about the room and reach into every crevice, a reminder of his own mortality. "Whatever you ask, Evalina, I will give."

"Give my son your name."

Lord Muldoon's eyes took on a flinty look. His jowls flushed a deep, unhealthy shade of red. "My dear, I—"

The dying woman sat up, a semblance of flash and fire in her eye. "Never, not once have I asked you for a thing until this very moment, and I will thank you to honor my request since it is the custom to keep the promise you give to those who have but a short time to live. I beg of you. Give my son your name."

"You're being very foolish. There's no stigma to being the bastard child of a man of nobility, woman. I shall settle a fine estate on him. Surely that will satisfy you."

"No. I beseech you to give him your name. You fathered him, and you have but one son to carry on the Muldoon name, since your second son is incapacitated and not likely to live. Jack is the eldest of all your bastards, and certainly the brightest. He is also dependable and you must look to the future when you are gone. There is always a chance that your other Jonathan and firstborn might meet with an early death, although I hope and pray such is not the case. But if he did, who would see to your vast estates and carry on the name of Muldoon into eternity?"

Exasperated, Lord Muldoon shook his head, but when the dying woman clutched his hand and looked at him with an unreadable expression in her eyes, he appeared to blanch, and soon he nodded. "Very well." He raised a hand as if he would ward her off. "Don't—look at me like that. I do not want the curse of a dying woman on my head. So be it. I will give him my name. Henceforth, he will be Jack Muldoon, and I will attend to the matter at once in order to make it legal."

Evalina fell back to her pillow, her features relaxed in the peace of death.

A month to the day later, Lord Muldoon took the legal steps that made Jack Muldoon his son by adoption. His Aunt Becky told him her brother did it out of fear that Jack's mother would come back and haunt him if he didn't carry out his promise, but Jack himself held little faith in the curses of the dead, and the change in his name meant little to him. He continued to live in the cottage with his Aunt Becky after his mother's death, but as he grew into young manhood his horizons were much broadened. He discovered the lure and excitement of women and he also grew to enjoy his status as the Young Lord Muldoon, whose pockets were amply lined with coin to be wagered at the gambling tables. No longer did he go about the estate in tattered clothes. His father supplied the money and his Aunt Becky saw to it that he was dressed suitably. Women swooned in his wake, flirted with him outrageously from behind their fans, and allowed him liberties that he'd only dreamed about in his early innocence.

Jonathan Muldoon the elder returned to the estate of his father three years after he was wed, and he returned alone, the carriage draped in crepe. Becky, who heard everything newsworthy that took place in the castle, relayed the news of the young lord's return to the family home. "His poor wife Janet was taken in childbirth, the bairn along with her. 'Twas her second, and he's come home in his grief and mourning with the first-born, poor young man, and him a widower, too, so sad, so sad."

The half-brothers met in the moors as they had in earlier days—by happenstance or not, Jack was never sure. He liked his half-brother and wished to convey his condolences, so he rode out to the place where they'd met in the same way when they were young.

"I'm sorry," he said sincerely. "Although I never met her, I know your loss is great."

"Janet was a good wife and a good mother. I miss her grievously," answered Jonathan. As they rode, they spoke of the past and the present and on Jack Cortez Muldoon's mind was the memory of the wistful way his half-brother spoke of his true love. He checked himself before he gave voice to his thoughts since it would dishonor the recently dead Janet to speak of the girl Jonathan loved, but didn't wed.

As if the other might have read his thoughts, Jonathan said, "My first sweetheart died this past year. Now once again I must allow my father to choose me a suitable wife."

Jack Muldoon spoke hesitantly. "He—gave me his name. Mayhap you knew?"

"Yes, I learned of it when I came home, and I'm glad," Jonathan said with a smile. "You've changed, Jack. Grown taller and broader in the shoulder and you've a certain style about you that you didn't have when I left."

"And Lord Muldoon has spoken to me of marriage. He... has chosen me a wife, but I told him I prefer to be choosing my own. Could you not do the same?"

Jonathan shrugged. "I could, I suppose. But it isn't worth the words we'd have if I stood up to him. If my darling still lived, there would be no question about it, but as long as he chooses one who isn't impossible to live with and she's not displeasing, I'll not gainsay him. I learned to love my Janet. Not in the way I loved my little lost love, but we worked it out well together, and she was a jewel among women." His eyes filled with tears and Jack felt awkward. He turned away in order to keep the older man from being embarrassed by his tears of sorrow. After enough time had passed to enable Jonathan to speak in a normal voice, he said, "I understand my father intends to settle a goodly estate on you. Take everything you can from him."

"Strange words from one who also stands to inherit."

"There is more and plenty for each and all of his children. My sisters will marry men of great wealth. One has already done so. But the husbands, both present and future, are as greedy as my father. They're cut from the same cloth, and at his death they'll fight me, with my sisters to back them up in their avarice, in their attempt to wrest the bulk of the estate from me. They'll not give a care to the bastard children he sired, to the poor, benighted peasants who have added so greatly to his coffers. My mother is a fool who has always taken the easy way out. The young lad won't live to see another fortnight pass. As you know, he was born weak and puny."

Jack waited, expecting his half-brother to say more, but nothing was forthcoming until a long silence had passed between them. When Jonathan did finally continue, it was in a near whisper. "The old man is sick nigh unto death. His days are numbered, I'm sure. Although I don't plan to give up the ghost myself in the near future, there's always that chance, so when he makes you the offer, seize it. There'll be nothing coming to you from anyone but me, and I can't guarantee you I'll be able to do right by you."

Although Jack Muldoon had never cared a whit about his father, he was startled at the old man's appearance when he was summoned to the great house. He had fits of coughing that left him weak and spent and his linen was stained red with the blood that came up. Fixing his bastard son with a shadow of his old imperious stare, he said between seizures of coughing that he had made arrangements for the wife he had chosen to spend a few days at the castle "She is a distant relative of your mother and a noblewoman of great bearing and fabulous beauty, but you must not startle the little dove. She has been brought up in a convent and knows nothing of the ways of the world. She is the daughter of a Spanish grandee; a maid of fifteen, lily-white of complexion, possessed with dark and impelling eyes." From his desk, Lord Muldoon withdrew an oval portrait in a gold frame. "This is what you have to look forward to, a treasure indeed, and you'll be the envy of all men."

The miniature painting was of a girl so ravishingly beautiful that Jack Muldoon was speechless. Never had he seen such enchantment. Very vaguely, the lovely face of the girl in the painting resembled his mother.

When he was able to speak, he said, "And she is a distant relative of my mother?"

"Yes. She is Luisa Cortez y Martinez, and she arrives on the morrow." After another fit of coughing that almost sent the old man toppling to the floor, he wheezed, gasped, then managed to add, "She doesn't speak a word of our tongue, but you'll have the pleasure of teaching her, eh?" The evil grin that distorted his already ravaged features was sickening to Jack Muldoon, but he did the proper thing. Kneeling, he took his father's gnarled hand and kissed it. Lord Muldoon gave his tall, dark son an appraising look. "Be outfitted in the best you have. The adorable child must not be offended by unsuitable dress, and mind your manners when you come to take tea with the rest of the family."

Jack Muldoon was barely able to contain himself as he rode as hard as he could to the cottage where he blurted out the surprising turn of events to his Aunt Becky.

"They always try to right their wrongs when they feel the breeze from the black wings of death," she said harshly, "and he's no exception, unless he's planning one of his monstrous jokes. But let's not look a gift horse in the mouth. You say you were taken with the lady's picture?"

"She is more beautiful than a sunrise. Lovelier than a rainbow. The absolute in perfection." He wished there were more ways to describe the stunning face he already worshiped and during the night he disturbed his rest by getting up and writing down the best of those that came to him.

Dressed in immaculate attire, Jack Muldoon made his way to the castle in a rose-colored haze of expectation, and his first sight of the gorgeous creature who sat demurely in the drawing room with his father did nothing to dim his joy. She was ravishing. The painting had not done her justice. After his father made the introductions, Muldoon was hard pressed to take his eyes off her long enough to go through the amenities. The only drawback to his absolute joy was the language barrier, but he made up his mind to overcome it immediately. He wouldn't wait for her to learn how to converse with him in his language—he would learn hers first. In a corner, a woman in black remained silent. "Her duenna," explained Lord Muldoon.

Daintily, the precious Luisa drank her tea. Modestly, she lowered her fantastically long eyelashes when she felt his ardent gaze upon her, and her alabaster cheeks turned rosy. The old man spoke to her in her own language, with the aid of a text book, but Muldoon suspected he sounded *gauche* although the girl answered politely as well as prettily.

Lord Muldoon turned to Jack after a painful ten minutes of difficult conversation with the girl in Spanish. "She says she will be happy to marry you and move to the New World with you."

Jack Muldoon opened his mouth and croaked, "New World?"

"Yes. Luisa is the love child of the *grandee* I spoke to you about yesterday, but her welfare is of prime importance to him. He wants her to go to the New World where her birth will not be known. And upon you, my son, I have settled an island. It is a virtual paradise, where roses bloom the year 'round and the bountiful earth gives up riches beyond your wildest imagination. I am doing this in loving memory of your mother, and because it is my duty to look after the well-being of my children." Tears filled the old man's eyes and he whined, "and because I am an old man and not long for this vale of tears. Before it's too late I feel the need to right some wrongs. You, too, will be accepted as a gentleman in the New World. You'll not go empty handed, and gold brings honor to even those who do not deserve it. The island is called Fairhaven and it's close enough to the Virginia colony to afford you the comforts of your needs, but not a part of it. I own it. The King gave it to me in payment for—certain obligations. You will be the Governor."

The wedding was slated for September, four months from the time Jack Muldoon was presented to Luisa Cortez y Martinez. He passed the time in a state of near ecstasy when he wasn't champing at the bit in his impatience for the allotted time to pass. The ceremony was to be held on the Cortez estate in Barcelona, after which Jack Muldoon and his beautiful bride would sail for the colonies. His father presented him with a lavishly outfitted ship, complete with crew, and Becky Muldoon made up her mind to accompany her nephew and his bride across the ocean.

The first-born son and heir of Lord Muldoon received permission from his father to accompany his half-brother to Barcelona since the lord's failing health would not permit him to go. Together, Jonathan and Jack Muldoon set out for the trip, accompanied by Aunt Becky, a few servants, gifts for the family of the bride and a goodly supply of gold.

Garnet looked at Muldoon expectantly. "You aren't going to stop there, I hope." She said it because he gave every appearance of doing so. After he reached that point, he had stood up, poured himself a fresh glass of rum and sat there staring moodily out the porthole.

As she looked at the back of his handsome head, Garnet wondered what on earth could have gone wrong to cause him to humiliate the poor girl in public. How had it happened, and whatever had brought about the bad blood between Luis Cortez and Muldoon? The set of his head, the taut look of his shoulders, kept her from voicing another protest at his delay, though. The blanket that covered his lower half no longer looked ridiculous, for some reason she couldn't fathom.

He turned and smiled, but it was a hard, forced kind of a smile that caused her to shiver. It looked very much like the one he'd had on his face when he was undergoing the punishment.

"We arrived on schedule and I was wined and dined. It was a sumptuous home and my half-brother and I were treated with utmost courtesy. They went out of their way to be hospitable with their smiling faces and bowing and pleasantries, which I understood was usual in Spanish homes. Such excesses of deferential treatment! The ladies kept to themselves except for the servants, who went about with their big dark eyes all smiling as they served the evening meal. My half-brother and I were put up in magnificent rooms with the finest oak furnishings. He was happy for me, Jonathan was. The wedding was to take place on the next day and I barely slept a wink in my excitement. Once I dreamed Luisa came to my room, but of course it was only a dream and I felt foolish because when I awakened my arms were outstretched. No high-born young lady shows herself to her bridegroom on the night before the wedding. Even if it were not considered bad luck, it would have been a breach of etiquette." He smote his brow as he referred to the preparations of the next day. Fine wines were served with the morning meal along with wondrously spicy dishes that he liked very much in spite of having never tasted them before. There was much back-slapping, the sound of violins, flowers everywhere. "It was a morning of extraordinary bliss in spite of my impatience.

"Then it was time. Luis Cortez, half-brother to Luisa, came to the rooms to escort me down to the garden. He spoke endearingly of my mother, who was his relative. And he spoke in English, too, almost as if he'd been born to the tongue. He'd gone away to school, he told me, in England, which explained his ease with the language. And he was to repeat the wedding vows to me in English.

"At first, I was somewhat taken aback at the size of the

family who had congregated together under the beautiful cork oak trees, but they were dressed splendidly for the occasion and there wasn't an unfriendly face in the lot of them. Jonathan was at my side as we made our way through the garlands of flowers. The day was golden and blue. Nature's blessing for our union, I told myself as I breathed in the heavy fragrance of gardenias and roses. The tables that had been set up and covered with spotless linen, some distance away from the flower-bedecked bower where my bride awaited me, were laden with food for the wedding feast. I looked at my bride and counted myself the luckiest man in the world. Her back was to me, and she wore a dazzling golden gown that caught the rays of the sun and formed a halo around her.

"The cleric looked down at me with a kindly smile and began the ceremony. A gentle breeze, scented with orange blossoms and other heavenly fragrances, ruffled the spun gold lace that fell in gossamer folds from her tiara. The breeze grew stronger and her glossy black hair, the same that I had dreamed about ever since I saw her, peeked out from under the veil. Enchanting curls. Cortez came to the place where the cleric asks who giveth this woman, and one of the men came forward. 'I do,' he said.

"Jonathan was standing close to me, nervous as I, and holding the ring. Cortez repeated the words, 'And whosoever has cause to say nay to this union, let him then step forward and say it for all to hear, else forever keep silent.' I felt my half-brother stiffen at my side, heard an exclamation not unlike a man in the act of being strangled. I glanced at him quickly, then toward my bride, and saw her glorious hair uncovered as the wind flipped the veil away from her face. Hair. Hair everywhere on her face except for a triangular patch of pustules on her cheeks. She looked like an adder, flicking tongue and all, with hooded eyes as they looked at me in the most godawful way! No nose except for a slight point above the snake-like mouth and not a tooth in her head. I saw it all in a quick, disbelieving look when she opened her mouth to scream, as she tried to gather the folds of her veil back over her hideous face."

"Good God!" Garnet stared at him. "You mean she had changed that much since you—"

"No! Of course not. The snake-woman was an entirely different creature. What followed next was a time of loud cries of protest, mostly from me. And Jonathan—well, Jonathan's face was white and sick-looking as he grabbed my arm and tried to yank me away from that terrible apparition that I had believed to be my darling. I can't remember what he said. Something about a terrible mistake, then something else about my father and his knowing all along what was in the minds of the Spaniards, maybe he'd planned it. A grotesque joke, or a final slap in the face to the memory of my mother. He was telling me to get out of there. So much confusion, and me in a state of numbness, barely able to move. But I remember telling whoever was interested that I would not marry that monstrous freak. At the same time, I felt a great pity for it. For her, I mean. To this day I cannot think of her as human. It seemed to me that God had made an awful mistake, and I had a feeling that she was innocent of the plot to wreck me. She suffered. I could see it in her heavy-lidded eyes and it came to me that she'd been hoodwinked just as I had. No doubt they'd told her I was enamored of her, poor creature. And a woman lives only to take a husband. It takes much longer to tell it than it did to live through it. We were only a few seconds in getting away from there, so the thoughts that went through my head were like lightning.

"Jonathan fell. He went down with a startled cry. One look told me he was dead, with a sword run through his chest. I tried to run, but I was surrounded by seven or eight wild-eyed men, each of them armed with dagger or sword. I was unarmed. A man does not go to the nuptials wearing a sword. But I grabbed one and began slashing about me, and I'm sure I ran one of them through, cut one or two more. In my demented state I was suffused with power. Leaped over the stone wall that surrounded the house as if it were a foot high. Jumped on a horse—God knows who it belonged to!—and whipped it into a mad gallop. They were after me within minutes, a whole pack of them, but I was fleeing from the gates of hell after having glimpsed paradise and they were running after me because I had brought dishonor to one of them. So I out-distanced them and headed for the harbor. Within minutes, we'd cast away while I told it all to Aunt

Becky. Nothing would do her but we must go back to Ireland. I mourned for Jonathan. Felt cowardly for leaving his body three in Barcelona, wanted to turn back, but she wouldn't hear of it. She took over the ship, but it wasn't hard for her to do so, for I was done in and laid out by the enormity of the trick that had been played on me.

"Aunt Becky went marching into the castle where she confronted my father and accused him of planning the whole thing. At first he denied it, but she was like a raving maniac. Don't forget that she had lost another nephew to death because of an old man's lust to pay back the memory of my mother for exacting his promise to give me his name. Oh, yes, that was what had eaten away at him, and Becky knew him well enough to guess at his insane reason.

"He turned on me, however, and blamed me for Jonathan's death."

"Unreasonable of him!"

Muldoon looked at her and shook his head. "Have I not told you there is nothing fair about this life? Well, there is nothing reasonable, either."

"The girl! Who was the girl? The one who was so lovely!"

"He had purchased her from the place I spoke of earlier. On the streets of London. Dressed her, bought her jewels and put her through her paces. My aunt ferreted out the information from the servants about the shameless way he purchased her. She was not a Spanish girl, but she couldn't speak a word of our language, just the same. She was an Italian peasant, poor child. And she lives there still, on the estate. Just one more of his discarded playthings, as my mother was."

"Then your father was not as sick as you had believed?"

"Oh, yes. He was sick, all right, and very nearly died. He lay between life and death for five full days, but he lived to laugh at me, and grew stronger with each passing day. The last time I went home was when I saw you, Garnet, for the first time. He was trying his utmost to sire another son by his second wife, a child of seventeen years. His lady died shortly after the poor idiot slipped away, and my father married again within three months."

"So you became a pirate. Did you do it to bring shame to your father?"

"No. I was on my way to the New World, Aunt Becky with me, when my ship was seized by Damon Rung. You've heard of him, I suppose?"

"He was hanged in Newgate, I think. Probably about a year ago."

"The very one. He took what we had in the hold and scuttled my ship. When you're faced with a choice of life if you sign the articles with a pirate or death if you don't, you sign. So I was one of the mates with the infamous Damon Rung when His Majesty's Navy took him off the coast of Egypt. They'd been laying back to get him for many a year, but I didn't fancy going to the gallows along with Rung. I told the truth. Said I was taken prisoner and forced to sign on with the rest of my men, but I could just as well have saved my breath, for it's a story most pirates tell in an attempt to save their necks. I escaped with the help of a good and true friend, name of Vincent Argan. It was Vincent they hanged on the day I saw you first, Garnet."

"God in heaven!"

He grinned. "But they didn't hang him. We'd fixed things up so he went through the trap-door, looking very much like the rope did what it was designed to do. A greased palm here, another one there, and it's possible to cheat the gallows. We were all set up to grab Argan, pretending it was his corpse, of course, to get him safely out of the country. Which we did, and that was why I happened to be there, in London Town at the time. Anyway, I was branded as a pirate. So I became one. Might as well run up the Jolly Roger in earnest seeing that I was hunted and hounded on all sides, and afterward it occured to me with some pleasure that in the doing of it I no doubt caused the old man a goodly amount of grief."

"And Aunt Becky agreed to come along with you."

"Yes. She was with me when we were there at the Barbados, where Cortez landed. I don't know how he learned of my whereabouts. Quite possibly it was by chance that he showed up there. Thomas Wills was with the natives when Cortez came ashore. They were building a hut, and Dell had left the little girl with her husband while she went to see about a sick woman. Aunt Becky went with her. We were working on the frigate when they swarmed us, and swarm us they did, which led me to believe they knew I was there. He'd sworn to avenge the wrong I did by not going through with the wedding. I was taken by surprise. Had no idea Cortez was on the island until I heard the screams and shouts of the natives. By the time I got to the place where they'd been peaceably working on a hut, Tom Wills was dead as were ten or twelve natives, who had tried to defend him. The rest of the natives had beaten Cortez and his men back and they escaped, except for a few who were slain by the enraged natives, aboard his ship."

"But why did he kill the missionary?"

Muldoon gave her a level look. "It was not Cortez's nature to ask a civil question, nor behave in a civilized way. Much later, we learned that he came ashore with armor gleaming, ready to do battle. His words to Tom Wills were to the effect that he meant to kill me. Wills, being a gentleman as well as a man of the cloth, begged him to be reasonable. Cortez, according to the natives who surrounded Wills, became enraged at the idea of a man—any man—asking him to be reasonable. His next action was to run Tom Wills through."

"And the baby?"

"She was with a few of the native children, who had been set to watch over her. Cortez lopped off her head, and his men killed two of the native children in the same mindless manner. As if it were a passing gesture, during the time they were being driven back to the sea."

"Poor Dell!"

"Yes. She didn't see him kill her husband, but she, too, had heard the commotion. She and Aunt Becky had left the hut where they'd gone to attend to the sick woman. They broke into a run at the sounds of the shouts and the fire from the pieces. She was about thirty yards away when she saw her baby's head fall to the ground and roll into a little swale."

"Such a horror for a mother to see. Enough to turn her into a madwoman."

"Indeed. And she was, for a while. First, she ran to the place where her little baby had fallen. And then she saw her husband's remains. After that, she began to scream like a demented person and she ran toward the sea, toward the ship where the murderer of her husband and baby had gone. She was a powerful swimmer, and God knows she would have made it to the ship, which was just getting under way, for she was propelled by all the furies of a mother and wife."

"You kept her from swimming out to the ship, then?"

"She wouldn't have stood a chance against Cortez and his men. She was temporarily deranged, and certainly not responsible for her actions. I'm sure she didn't stop to think of what she was about. They would have cut her to pieces as she tried to climb aboard."

"Then you brought her back to shore."

"Yes. And she hated me for it, for a long time, because she felt there was nothing left for her to live for—and I kept her from at least trying to take the life of the man who had killed so wantonly. But as I said, she wasn't responsible for her actions."

"Then, I suppose she began to make plans for the future. After a while, that is. Did you influence her in her determination to kill Luis Cortez?"

"Yes, I did. At the time, I was grasping for straws. The way she was, so lost and so tragically locked in on her grief, she'd never have survived. She didn't *want* to live, and when people don't want to live, they sicken and die."

"She's very vital. I mean, she is *now*. One would never guess that she had once given up on living."

"And she was just as vital before her own private world came to an end, but there you have it. We don't all have the capacity to love as Dell Fields loved, perhaps. If we did, there would be more suicides following the death of husbands, wives, lovers, and children. She had known a condition that she considered perfect happiness, which comes to only a chosen few of us in this life, and it was taken from her suddenly and most cruelly. Yet, there was the strength of her. A spark of it remained, even after I brought her back from the sea. Aunt Becky detected it, not I." Muldoon shrugged. "But now she's much as she was before, except for a certain flintiness that wasn't there before. The survival factor, I suspect. Her own method of working out a way to go on living."

"You were lovers, weren't you?" Garnet's eyes were steady on him, and she neither smiled nor frowned.

"Why do you ask?" His gaze was unflinching.

"Do me the favor of answering my question instead of asking me another to take its place. I sense something between the two of you in spite of the way she speaks to you and of you, as well as your own oft-times anger when you are in her presence."

"Very well." Muldoon continued to look at her unwaveringly. "We were lovers, in a manner of speaking. But I'll have you know it was not until after her husband and baby were killed. Dell Wills worshiped the ground her husband walked on, and he was a man who was above reproach, a man I admired above all others. We came together without design, not on my part, nor hers, certainly. I had no intention to besmirch her, but I wanted to comfort her. Then it happened. After a while, it was over."

"Did you love her? Do you love her still?"

"Not...as I love you. Not then, and now I love her not at all."

Garnet sighed. "It seems strange to be with the two of you, knowing that you've had us both. I wonder how you feel about it, yourself. Do you look at us when we are walking on deck together and feel like the cock of the barnyard?"

"Hell and all the nether regions, no! I feel like a damned animal being led around on a chain."

With an unreadable smile, Garnet said, "Comfort yourself with the knowledge that you don't have much longer to be put through the ordeal of being locked in your room except when you're taken for your evening walk on deck. Dell said we're making good time, and if the winds hold favorable we'll be at the island where she plans to leave you within a week."

"Oh, she did, did she? That's odd. When I asked her earlier, she said she didn't know."

"Well, she's done some charting."

Muldoon looked at Garnet as if he had been hit over the head. "What do you mean, the island where she plans to leave *me*? Has she asked you, as well as Aunt Becky, to accompany her on to the New World?"

"That she has, Muldoon."

"And by the sound of it, the fact that you said *me*, and not *we*, you're not going with me, then?"

"I'm giving the idea my most serious consideration."

Eleven

Garnet grew more and more relaxed in Dell Fields's presence as the days passed. She reflected on many things one afternoon when the two women took tea in the Captain's quarters. Garnet had just finished putting together a fourth costume from frocks that Dell had taken as booty from *The Dancing Lady*.

"You're a genius with the needle, Garnet," the Captain said as the younger girl put the embroidery hoops aside.

"And you'll look aboslutely stunning in this outfit. The cream-colored lace bodice was just the right size for you, and by using the lace on the skirt, I lengthened the brown satin in a way that made it look as if it were made that way in the first place. These are very becoming colors for you, Dell."

"The birds you embroidered on the skirt and petticoat add a great deal of charm to the entire effect. But you know, Garnet, sometimes I wonder why I bother. Do women dress themselves in finery in order to attract men, or because they want to be envied by other women?"

"A little of both, perhaps," answered Garnet. "Then, too, we must not lose sight of your plans for going to North America. Clothes do not make the woman or the man, but they go a long way toward presenting a good first impression. Or second, or third, for that matter. You'll want to put your best foot forward, and I'm sure you're doing the right thing by gathering together a suitable wardrobe."

The Captain gave Garnet a quizzical look. "Have you given the idea of accompanying me any further thought?"

Garnet frowned. "Yes, I've given the idea considerable attention. I believe I am growing to know and understand him a little better than I did before."

Dell Fields' laughter filled the quarters. "To hear you speak, Garnet, an outsider would believe there was only one male aboard. Or in the entire world, for that matter, the way you speak of him as 'him.' You refer to Muldoon, of course. You're in love with him."

"I don't know whether I am or not. But I'm sure I feel more at ease since you assured me he had nothing to do with the death of my father or the Lady Neilson. Are you quite positive?"

"Absolutely. At least as positive as one can ever be about anything. I know the man he purchased the opals from. A disreputable personage if ever one existed, but it's doubtful that he would murder. Muldoon confines his illegal activities to piracy, while the fence, Moskowitz, buys and sells stolen goods. Unlike Muldoon, Moskowitz is a coward. He purchases the ill-gotten goods from many a hired assassin, but he would never endanger himself by doing the actual bloody work of murder."

"Muldoon said he was down on his luck when he bought the opals from him."

"No doubt he was, too. I know the man well enough to realize that he has periods of insanity, in which he's unable to work at his trade of fencing stolen goods. When he's just coming out of a long period of lunacy, he's in dire need of monies, so he'll sell his goods for a fraction of their worth. It may interest you to know, Garnet, that Moskowitz is somewhere in the New World. Together, the two of us could be persuasive enough to make him tell us the truth as to whether or not he sold the opals to Muldoon." Dell went to the porthole. "It's growing very dark. I wonder if my clock has stopped." She went to the ornate clock that sat on an ebony table and bent down low to listen. Straightening, she said, "No, it's still ticking away. I do hope we're not in for a blow when we're probably only a day away from the Bermudas. But look. Whitecaps. The wind has climbed. Damn."

"Maybe it's just a little rain squall," Garnet said as she

joined the Captain at the porthole. "But it is very dark and gloomy, of a sudden. Yet this morning the sunshine was almost blinding, it was so bright. And the sea was as calm as glass." As she spoke, Garnet felt a little chill of foreboding, but as always when she got a glimpse of the future, she doubted herself. In a split-second, she'd had a flash of the coming storm, with forked lightning splitting a night-black sky and waves rolling over the ship that would surely send it to the bottom of the sea.

"A good man is at the helm," Dell said thoughtfully. "But the darkness is eerie. Especially for two o'clock in the afternoon."

As she spoke, the vessel lurched, sending both women against the wall. When they righted themselves, Dell hurried to lash down the sea chest where her growing wardrobe was folded. It was the only piece of furniture in the quarters that was not already secured. "I'm going above, Garnet. Perhaps you should see to Muldoon. Make sure everything is ship-shape and ready for a gale in your cabin."

The deck was already wet when Dell hastened to the helmsman, and a quick glance showed her that he was having no difficulty, as yet, at keeping on course.

"We're in for a bad 'un, Captain," said the man at the tiller. "Clouds over there toward the north are blacker than the inside of a well, and rolling fast. Seemed like she built up bad in a trice. Bright sunshine one minute, then all of a sudden came the squall."

Dell looked skywards for a second, then began to issue orders to bring down the sails. She'd seen the most terrifying sight a sailing craft can encounter on the high seas. A black and rolling cloud swirling counter-clockwise, and it appeared to be bent upon swooping down on the foaming, billowing sea. The craft was in the very path of it. "A cyclone," she shouted above the shrieking wind. Her voice had enough carrying power to reach the farthest decks and lowest hold as she ordered the crew to bring down the mainmast, batten all hatches, and drop anchor. From her quick calculation, they would be in the eye of the hurricane within minutes.

The mates performed their tasks quickly and efficiently— and they were just in time. All hands breathed a long and heartfelt sigh of relief when the wind screamed by a safe distance from where they were afloat, the ship tossing restlessly as it was held by the anchor. The black, whirling cloud dipped down into the sea, churned up the water for miles around, then lifted, spun around angrily for a few breathtaking moments, and sped well away. A shuddering silence seemed to hold the craft spellbound for a few moments following the departure of the whirlwind, and then the rains came down in a fury.

In their cabin, Muldoon scowled at Garnet. "Unseasonable. A hurricane like that is likely to come back. We'll be in for it again, mark my word. Get me my breeches, woman, and be quick about it. I'm a better hand at holding a ship steady in a storm than any man jack aboard, and no fool woman is going to keep me from that tiller."

"If she needs you, she'll ask," Garnet answered. But she was apprehensive, in spite of her calm voice.

Muldoon roared. "Get me my breeches, or by all the gods and their by-blows, I'll go above naked!"

"Helmsman Laramy is a good man," said Garnet. "I'll not get you your breeches until I'm ordered to do so."

Speaking through clenched teeth, Muldoon came to her, grasped her by the shoulders and marched her to the porthole. "Look out there, you little idiot! Those waves are big enough to capsize us, and they'll be upon us in seconds!" He flung her aside, grabbed a blanket from the bunk and ran toward the door, with Garnet close behind, shouting at the top of her lungs that he must stay where he was until the Captain asked for his help.

He flung the blanket around his waist and tied it at the middle as he sprinted forward, and she had no way of knowing whether he had heard her and chosen to ignore her. No matter, she decided on the spur of the moment. He was disobeying the Captain's orders, but she'd done her best. In all truth, she would feel safer if he was given a chance to put his hand to the tiller.

Happy Jack Muldoon almost collided with Dell Fields as she was running toward him. "Good," she yelled. "Laramy needs help! He's all but astraddle the tiller, but he can't hold on much longer."

"Get me my *breeches*," Muldoon shouted.

For four days and four nights the storm played a cat-and-mouse game with the ship and crew. For the space of an hour or a little more, there would be no whisper of wind, and out of the black sky of night an egg-shaped moon would appear for a time, but only for a time. Then the gales would tear down upon the craft and lift it—only to dash it back down against the rolling sea. It was an angry wind, that howled like a million banshees bent on destruction, and the rain pelted down in a fury. The ship heeled from side to side like a gigantic teeter-totter, while timbers groaned and the taste of certain death was in every mouth. Then the calm would come again. Muldoon ordered the anchor up when the storm was at its worst on the first night, but Captain Fields argued. He roared back, his voice a match for the wild winds. "We'll be kindling wood by first light of dawn if we stay tied as we are. I say to pull it up, Captain."

"And I say we leave it down," she screamed back, the driving wind and rain in her face.

"Then don't hold me accountable if you find yourself floating on a bit of flotsam by midnight. She'll get worse before she gets better, and we've just begun to see the mettle of this storm. Tied down as we are, we're like a chained dog trying to protect itself from a pack of wolves, and them free!"

"Up anchor," Dell yelled after a moment of silence. "And I'll hold you accountable if we split down the middle, Muldoon!"

On the second afternoon the storm abated for a respite of three full hours. Muldoon was weak from having fought the wind. His fingers were bruised and bloody, his arms ached, and his belly and ribs were sore from his desperate effort to keep the tiller steady. Staggering, he took shelter from the drizzle long enough to get a bowl of soup and a good, hot drink of buttered rum against the battle he was sure lay ahead.

Dell said, "But the storm is over."

"It'll come back," Muldoon swore. "And like an enemy in battle, it'll bring back reinforcements. Mark me. There'll be a new force behind the wind, and the rain will turn to ice. This is a May storm, and there's none worse."

Another hour passed by, calm and peaceful, the breeze as

benign as a wedding shower of rice, but Muldoon proved right. When the enemy returned, there were reinforcements a-plenty, with more than icy sleet in the driving rain. Hail as big as hen's eggs rained down, and each massive volley seemed hell-bent for murder. Again, Muldoon fought to keep the ship afloat, against overpowering odds. The wind gusted and shrilled. It screamed and bullied as it twisted the ship first this way and then that. By nightfall, the lightning was so bright that it could have blinded anyone foolish enough to be above without cause, and it was followed by claps of thunder that sounded as if they had come from the very bowels of the earth before they'd worked their way up from the boiling sea.

All night long, the water churned under an inky sky, but the hail stopped falling. In its stead was a rain of red water, like blood. It fell in a fury and didn't stop until a tremendous wave, big as a mountain, rolled over and sent the ship plunging down.

Garnet's scream was cut off in the middle as she clung, terrified, to the wildly rocking walls of the cabin.

"It's all right," cried Aunt Becky, who had been with her through most of it.

"We're going *down*!" Garnet felt the roaring in her ears, saw the midnight blue of the water as it rushed past the porthole.

"Don't you worry about a thing," cried Aunt Becky. "My Jonathan will get us out of this safe and sound."

The ship seemed to roll end over end. Garnet didn't know which way was up, which way was down. Then there was the sudden startling beauty of lightness and brightness, and she realized they'd gone down several fathoms, but come up again, and were once more on the surface of the sea.

She had no more than caught her breath when she heard Dell Fields' chilling cry: "Breakers dead ahead, Muldoon! *Breakers, I say!*"

Later, she learned that the wind had been dead astern, and that they'd been almost on the breakers before Dell saw them. The keel was already in the grip of the swell, and for the first time, Muldoon wasn't sure whether he'd win the battle.

"Never would have won it, either," he admitted hours later to Garnet and his Aunt Becky, "except for the sudden calm that saved us. It came out of nowhere, a strip of peace and quiet."

"In answer to your prayers, no doubt," Dell Fields said in an unusually soft voice.

"Me? Pray?" Muldoon looked at the Captain as if she had lost her mind.

"You did. I heard you. First you'd sing a seaman's chantey, then a pirate's. After that, you'd pray. You said all the names of all the saints, then repeated the Hail Mary, I don't know how many times."

Muldoon refused to believe her. He was still arguing the point when they dropped anchor on a golden, lazy day in mid-May, close to the harbor of Bermuda, almost five days later than Dell's calculated arrival. The storm had blown them far off course.

For the better part of the time it took to get to Bermuda, the crew was hard at the work of cleaning up and making the necessary repairs after the storm. Dell sensed a change in the attitude of the mates as they neared Bermuda, and she prepared herself for what she'd long feared—a showdown.

It came in the person of a big and burly man who was known as "The Swede," but Dell was doubtful if he acted without the encouragement of several others, whom she supected of watching from a safe distance, but hidden behind the crates that were lashed to the deck. When The Swede loomed up out of the near-darkness, the lantern that Garnet carried to light her way back from having locked Muldoon away after his exercise, caught the glint of a cutlass. Her first thought was for Garnet's safety, her second a surge of anger against Muldoon, who had insisted on a bottle of rum to see him through the night. "Get back," she whispered to Garnet as she looked at the towering Swede and estimated her chances of besting him.

Her voice then rose hard as flint as she ordered the Swede to drop his weapon.

The man laughed. Dell's eyes flashed an unearthly fire as she again commanded The Swede to drop the cutlass.

The Swede tood a step forward, brandishing the long,

wicked weapon. Growling like an animal, he said, "We're done with being ruled over by a woman."

Dell whipped a dagger from her pocket. It sailed through the air, small but deadly, to imbed itself in the Swede's arm. The cutlass fell with a clatter to the deck and the challenger expelled an unearthly cry as he rushed forward, roaring like a wounded bull. Dell's second dagger felled him about three feet before he was upon her, his ham-like hands curled with the intention of strangling her. He lay jerking on the deck, the hilt of the second dagger protruding from almost the exact center of his chest. His eyes were open wide and already beginning to glaze over in the agony of his death throes. As he breathed his last, a curse was on his lips: "May you kick a long time when they tighten the noose around your throat, Dell Fields." His blood, dark and bubbling like red-black ink from mouth and nose as well as chest, continued to pump during the moment of silence that followed his awesome curse. Standing straight and tall, Dell Fields spoke to the men who had waited and watched: "Next time, the first dagger will end the life of anyone who tries to best me, for I do not accept challenges."

Not a word was heard from the surrounding area. Slowly, Dell took the lantern from Garnet and held it close to her own face in order to show her features to anyone who happened to be looking. Her eyes glittered as if they'd been lit from some strange and ghastly source, and the quiet all about remained.

Garnet Shaw continued to walk along at the side of the undisputed Captain of *The Nightingale*. When she returned to Muldoon with his bottle of rum, she told him what had taken place, and she said, "Never before in my life have I seen such coolness, combined with such flaming rage. Her eyes were burning bright with some unearthly fire."

Muldoon said he doubted if Dell would be challenged again, and she wasn't. They continued westward and reached Bermuda without further incident.

Twelve

Footsteps sounded outside Dell's quarters where the ship was anchored in the harbor of Bermuda. She heard them with vague annoyance, because she recognized the nononsense tread of Jack Muldoon and she wished to have no further discussion with him. Their business was finished and she had been more than fair with him when she gave him a generous purse with which to purchase himself a vessel. No matter that the gold had once belonged to him since she'd taken it for herself when she claimed the plunder from *The Dancing Lady*. Before that, they'd belonged to another. She had also given Garnet the jewels that had been in the lacquered box and wished them all an abundance of happiness. Garnet had wished her godspeed, and so had Becky, who had not for a minute considered the idea of leaving her beloved nephew to travel on with Dell. Muldoon had merely said he would be seeing her, and wished her well. Which she should have realized, she told herself as she answered his knock, meant he was not ready to bid her adieu in spite of his appearance of going peacefully ashore.

Without a pretense of a welcoming smile, she greeted him frostily: "We've said all we had to say to one another, Jack. Surely you can't expect me to be more generous." She did not open the door wide enough for him to enter.

"If I inconvenience you, I'm sorry," he said with a semblance of a smile. "Yet I find myself in the humiliating position of having to beg you to change your mind. There's not a chance of outfitting myself on this damnable island.

I've searched high and low, but there's not a seaworthy craft to be had." He pushed against the door.

She sighed, opened the door enough to allow him entrance, and went immediately to the desk where she'd been toiling over figures. "The Bermudas are well-traveled. You'll be able to purchase passage to England or Spain, I should think. Once you're there, you'll have no trouble getting a ship."

"You know damned good and well I can't go to England. And it's not healthy for me in Spain, either."

"France, then."

"Change your mind, Dell. Let us go on with you, to North America."

"No." She fiddled with her quill. "Surely you're not thinking you'll find a craft there? Ship building is all but non-existent in the new world, I've been told."

He smiled. "Perhaps I could liberate one."

"If you're thinking of liberating mine, think again."

"The notion hadn't crossed my mind. You should know better than that. It's most unreasonable of you to drop us off here in Bermuda, though, as if we meant nothing more to you than a few kegs of rum."

"The crew should be returning within minutes, and we'll be getting under way within the hour." Dell lifted her heavy red hair from the back of her neck. The quarters were hot and humid. She gave him an oblique look. "The island is like a paradise to some. It's too hot for my taste, especially today. But Garnet seemed pleased enough at the idea of exploring it with you. I suppose it seemed exotic to her. And in all truth, the temperature is only uncomfortable a few days out of the year. Why don't you settle down here, Jack? Stop risking your neck by pirating. You could become a respectable person, and in no time at all you'd find yourself a power to be reckoned with. When I get to America, I'll stay. It's doubtful if I'll ever go to sea again."

"A respectable person? A powerful person? With my name and reputation, I'll be seized by the authorities and taken back to London to be prepared for the gallows!" His laugh was mirthless.

She shrugged. "Take another name. You'd not be the

first, nor the last, either, to pretend to be someone you aren't. You've a way with you, Jack Muldoon; you're a born leader of men. Why not put that attribute to a good cause? Think of the life of ease you could gain for yourself. Surely you could find one island out of the more than three hundred that are here, on which you would be satisfied. In no time at all you'd have the natives eating out of your hand. The coral is there for the digging, and you have to admit it makes a beautiful building material. You could become a banana grower. Live in a fine home and never know another moment of need."

"You jest. Fancy me as a banana grower, with heaps of rotting fruit all around me, while flies buzz around my head as I sit on the piazza of my beautiful home, starving to death while a native fans me with a palmetto leaf. Even if I didn't die of hunger, boredom would soon send me to my grave. And you, Dell—you'll never be content for long on land. The sea is in your blood, just as it is in mine. I ask you once more. Take us with you to America."

Her eyes were as cold as stone. "I don't trust you, Jack Muldoon. You'd find a way to take my ship from me."

"I swear on my mother's grave I wouldn't do such a thing. God's arse, the chance to do it has already come and gone. After I got us safely through the storm would have been the time, but I didn't lift a finger."

"Because you were too exhausted to do so," she said scornfully. "And I showed you my gratitude for getting us safely through the storm quite handsomely by giving you a generous purse."

"Who are you to talk about being under-handed, anyway? You tried to take my sweetheart as well as my aunt with you," he said heatedly. "And don't turn your profile to me, damn it. At least have the courtesy to look at me when I speak to you."

"I didn't go behind your back when I asked them, and it's true that I'm disappointed in their decision to stay with you. The girl is young, Jack. You'll hurt her deeply. And I think very highly of your aunt."

"I'll not hurt a hair on Garnet's head," he said. "I love that girl with all my heart and soul."

Again, Dell lifted her heavy mane of hair from the nape of

her neck. Her eyes were bleak when she looked at him again, and she spoke scathingly. "I don't doubt you when you say you love her, Jack. It's just that you have only so much room in your heart to love women."

He grabbed her, his patience evaporating under his anger. "And that's the real reason why you won't allow me to accompany you to North America, isn't it?" His arms held her in a strong grip as his eyes bored into hers. "You still care for me. Not much, maybe, but you've not forgotten those hours we spent in rapture. And you've a streak of integrity that won't allow you to take the pleasures that rightfully belong to another woman."

Coolly, she looked deep into his eyes, and her voice was brittle as ice when she spoke: "I am no longer a grief-torn girl, Muldoon, willing to melt at a glance from you. Or a touch, either. Get your hands off me or I will not be responsible for my actions."

"You need to be loved," he said roughly. "You're a woman, damn you! And you've known what it was to be enthralled in the bonds of love-making. The snow-maiden front you put on doesn't wash with me, Dell, not any more than your hurtful words of a few weeks back ring true. You said you'd been willing to accept what came in order to be held in a pair of living arms, four years ago, but you throbbed with joy at my touch. I remember very well." Overcome with his rage and his boiling need to prove himself, he bent her backwards, yanked up her gown and caressed the tender flesh of her thighs, his lips hard and searching on hers.

Dell struggled. Her knee came up threateningly as she wished to God she'd spoken the truth when she said her crew would return within the hour. She was all alone, and it was doubtful if anyone would set foot on deck for another two hours. Her hands lashed out at him and her fingernails clawed at his cheek, but he quickly subdued her by grasping both hands in his own as he walked her slowly but surely to the bed.

Once he had her where he wanted her, she aimed the toe of her pointed shoe at his groin, but it missed the mark and enraged him all the more. She swore, then her teeth came down hard on the lobe of his ear. He felt a momentary twinge of pain, heard her make a spitting sound, and parted her thighs with his knee, her gown already where he wanted it, bunched under her waist and out of the way of his bludgeoning manhood.

"I'll kill you," she screamed as he entered her.

Muldoon didn't hear her. He was lost in the sweet oblivion of driving deeply into her, one hand clutching her bountiful breast. After a few moments, his joy manifested itself as he laughed in exultation. In spite of the way she had fought him, he knew by her rhythmic response, by the utterly blissful expression in her eyes that he had been right all along about her. Which was why he was taken off guard minutes later when she arose from the bed, grasped a sword and began to batter him about the head and shoulders. Weak and spent as he was, he barely had the strength to fend her off, and the crazy, wild look in her eye as she raged about was enough to quench a roaring fire. It occurred to him that he could count his blessings, because her anger was so great that she hadn't thought to unsheath the sword.

To add to the nightmare of being beaten about the head and shoulders by a madwoman almost as tall as he was, Muldoon's attention was momentarily taken away from the fight for his life by an apparition. Surely, he told himself as he made awkward grabs at the sheathed sword, it was an apparition, for he'd left Garnet and his Aunt Becky at a hostelry, with orders to remain there until he returned. Then it occurred to him that no apparition would be able to imitate his Aunt Becky's raucous yells, or Garnet's shrill cries of dismay. Becky was demanding an explanation from someone about something, but Muldoon wasn't quite able to grasp just what it was she wanted to know about, nor was it quite clear as to whether her anger was aimed at himself or Dell Fields.

Garnet's face was pale as death, but she was very explicit as she spoke of Dell's torn gown and the state of Muldoon's breeches as they hung about his knees while he tried to pull them up with one hand and at the same time defend himself from another blow from Dell's weapon with the other. And he heard himself yelling, "This isn't at all the way it may look, damn it!"

Garnet was flying about the cabin like a miniature tornado. "Oh, it's not at all the way it looks! Imagine that!" With both hands on her hips, she stood in front of Muldoon and looked up at him with fire in her big brown eyes. "I suppose you're going to try to tell me your breeches fell down of their own accord! Or mayhap you took them down so Dell Fields could mend a tear, you rogue! And look at her, with her gown all ripped down the front where you manhandled her! You ought to be ashamed of yourself, you great big oaf!"

"But he's *bleeding*!" Aunt Becky put her hand out to touch Muldoon's bloody ear and let out an additional shriek. "He's *mutilated*!" Turning to Dell Fields, she looked at her in shocked anger. "You sliced a portion of his *ear* off!"

Dell stared at the older woman for a second. "No I didn't," she said. "I bit it off."

"The Lord save us and protect us," breathed Aunt Becky. "The poor boy is marked for life."

"Out!" Dell Fields advanced toward the outraged, protective older woman and the embattled Muldoon. "Get out of here, all three of you, before I do something drastic. I mean it." Her eyes were brilliant with something that looked suspiciously like unshed tears and her face was pale.

"He could die from a wound like that," announced Becky Muldoon as she took her nephew by the hand and attempted to drag him toward the door. "They say a human's bite is far worse than a dog's."

Muldoon's face was thunderous and he hung back, but under the circumstances he decided to let well enough alone and leave with his aunt and Garnet. He said nothing further while his aunt continued to prattle away about the scratch on his face, and how Dell had certainly changed for the worse through the years: she was ungrateful, unkind, and had no right to try to kill Becky's dear nephew who had never done a thing but treat Dell with great compassion. He tried to quiet her by making a shushing sound, but once Becky Muldoon was launched into a tirade against what she obviously thought was unfair treatment of her nephew, all heaven and earth couldn't have silenced her tongue.

"Garnet, my love?" Muldoon stood half in and half out of the doorway as he gave Garnet a somewhat diffident look and extended his hand toward her.

Garnet remained where she was, in the middle of the room. Her return gaze was definitely hostile. "Surely you cannot expect me to stay with the likes of you after this—dreadful performance!"

"I can explain everything, my love," answered Muldoon with a flash of his usual *élan*.

"I'm sure you can," Garnet said spitefully. "And you'll do a marvelous job of it, too. But I am not blinded by adoration of you, as your poor misguided aunt is. You'll be able to smooth things over well enough with her, but I know full well what took place here, and nothing you can do or say will change my mind. Leave at once, or I shall join Dell in performing mayhem upon you."

Becky turned and looked at the girl, puzzled. "You can't mean what you're saying, child. Why, it's as plain as the nose on your face that Jonathan was not to blame for anything."

"He raped her!" Garnet pointed to Dell's frock, which hung in tatters. "When a man rapes a woman he's to blame for it. Don't be so befuddled that you can't see with your own eyes that he overpowered her."

"Hah!" Becky tossed her head. "When a man has his way with a woman of Dell Fields' size it's because she wants him to! Jonathan will be lost without you, Garnet. He loves you *madly*! Surely you'll change your mind and come along with—"

Garnet shook her head. "Just leave us alone," she said wearily.

Becky wanted to say more, but Muldoon decided it would be prudent for him to make a hasty departure, especially after he saw that Dell had picked up a marble vase and looked very much as if she planned to throw it.

"If I live to be a hundred," Becky said to him as they fled *The Nightingale*, "I'll never understand human nature. Neither one of those girls behaved with an ounce of human decency." She patted Muldoon's hand. "But don't you worry, lovey, you'll find another nice girl. One who isn't as prone to temper fits as Garnet. Such behavior! Such unladylike words to come from such sweet lips!"

"I can't live without her," moaned Jack Muldoon.

"I wouldn't worry about it, dearie," said his aunt comfortingly. "She'll come a-running before they cast off, I've a feeling in me bones. Why, she's fair daft over you, and as soon as she's had a chance to calm down and think things over, she'll change her mind about going on to the New World with Dell."

If Muldoon heard his aunt's soothing words, he gave no sign. He was sunk in the very blackest of despair, broken by flashes of wonder as to what had caused him to behave so rashly. He had gone to beg passage with Dell to North America, yes. But her attitude had set him wild. And then...He groaned realizing he'd made a supreme ass of himself by mouthing those stupid words to Garnet about things not being the way they seemed.

Dell was trembling violently as Garnet helped her out of the torn frock and into another one, but her voice was calm when she said, "I hope you didn't act out of impulse and will end up wishing you'd not cast your lot with me, Garnet. It's not too late to change your mind, for we'll not be getting under way until some two to three hours from now. So please don't feel that you must stick with a decision that might be the wrong one. You love the Muldoon, and love has a way of easing a lot of weighty problems."

"I hate him!" Garnet stamped her foot. "If he hadn't left when he did, I would have given in to my desire to flatten his face. It was bad enough, what he did to you after your kindness. But to have the brass to stand before me and tell me things were not what they seemed to be! Oh!—he must take me for a prime dunce!"

"Don't be so hard on him, Garnet. In all truth, what transpired was not entirely his fault."

The younger girl looked at the older one with wide, amazed eyes. "Don't tell me you led him on. I cannot believe it when I look at the way he tore your frock, in spite of what his aunt said."

Dell managed a laugh. "I didn't lead him on at all—no, indeed! Quite the opposite. I repelled him, which drove him to madness. Now that it's all over, I can see my own attitude toward him had much to do with his reaction. If I had a chance to do it all over, I would not be as fiercely cold to him, but he took me by surprise by coming back aboard after we'd said farewell. He said some things to me that angered me greatly, but I should not have allowed him to bring me to the boiling point. When I lose my temper, I don't stop to act with caution."

"Strange that you find excuses for his unforgivable behavior, Dell," said Garnet.

The tall woman buttoned her bodice. "It's just that I don't want you to look back to this day and wish you had stayed with the man you love, my dear, out of some misguided sense of loyalty to me. You've just now stated that you hate him, but love doesn't die that quickly. It shows in your eyes how you feel about him, and Muldoon is not as bad as most men when it comes to comparisons. In fact, I would say that he's better than the average. He's no dullard, he has the ability to make a woman laugh, and unless he's out of his mind with anger, he's as kind and gentle as anyone I've ever known, save for one."

"I can do without him," Garnet said. "There are other men. I would rather be wed to a man I can trust and make do without the other attributes."

When the ship sailed, Garnet was with it, and not once did she look back towards Bermuda and wonder if Happy Jack Muldoon was watching the majestic sight. Instead, she looked up at the sails and marveled at the fiery red from the reflected western skies. As she looked westward, she prayed that they would find peace and happiness in the New World.

Thirteen

On the third day out after leaving Bermuda, the high winds that had been speeding *The Nightingale* ever closer to the shores of North America grew even stronger. Garnet and Dell were eating their evening meal when the speed of the ship increased. Excited, Dell said, "At this rate, we'll be there long before we hoped." She filled her little pipe and lit it, puffing contentedly as she reflected on the future. "I've heard so many things about this new land, and all of it sounds almost as if the place has been showered with magic. Apples and oranges growing everywhere, and free for the picking. The earth so fertile that it isn't possible for farmers to have a bad crop. And the *freedom*, Garnet! Just think of how it will be to walk about the beautiful streets without fear."

"Fear of what, Dell?" Garnet had reservations about the stories everyone had heard about the bountiful earth in North America, and the freedom and ease of living that was reputed to be the lot of everyone who settled there.

"Fear of walking about the streets as a female, and knowing no person will attempt to make us behave in a way that is expected," Dell answered. "Oh, I'm sure much of what we have heard is exaggerated greatly. That is, I doubt very much if the streets are paved with gold and the streams flow with milk and honey. But we'll not be bound by the old ways, the hidebound principles of England that dictate everything from the way a woman wears her hair to the shoes she wears on her feet. I've heard that women are free to own land, and have property of their own, that females do not have to be forever indebted to some stupid male for their very existence."

"And I've heard that all the Indians are not friendly," Garnet said with some anxiety. "I should hate to be taken captive by an Indian and forced to be his mate."

Dell smiled. "Oh, the Colonists have long ago settled their differences with the Indians, I'm sure. I was talking with a seaman who had been there many times, and he assured me that the Indians are glad to have the white man settle there. It was just in the beginning that there was trouble. I do hope it doesn't take me long to find my husband's people. The moment I arrive, I shall start asking around for news of their whereabouts."

Dell's idea of America included riches beyond dreams, mansions for everyone and a life of gaiety as well as ease. Her concept of the land itself was colored with the enthusiastic reports she had heard from those who had been there, or at least claimed to have visited that far-away land of reputed plenty. She visualized a narrow band of settled seacoast that stretched from the southernmost tip of the Carolinas to New York, but the map she had carried in her mind as well as the one she had with her aboard *The Nightingale* did not give the appearance of a land that was vast. For that reason, she believed she would have no trouble finding Tom Wills' mother and father or her own parents. "The early settlers suffered untold hardships, I'm sure," she said. "But the Colonies have been in existence for a long time, and it stands to reason that those who remained have grown closer together because of it. No doubt everyone in North America feels a kinship with one another. So even if we don't find my people right away, we will soon hear news of them." She puffed on her pipe and her mind's eye drew comforting pictures of rolling hills and fertile fields, of stately homes and teeming metropolitan areas where music filled the air and people lived the good life.

Garnet's notion of the New World was very different. She feared that they would find a vast wilderness, where savage red men lurked behind every tree, lusting for the blood and scalps of whites. Her idea of settlements consisted of two or three rough buildings, with little sign of the civilization of

London in the demeanor of the citizens, and she could not imagine any women or children living under such rude conditions although she knew there were many women among the million and a half settlers who made up the mass of colonists. "Knowing something does not make it easy to accept," she said.

Dell looked at her in consternation. "Whatever are you talking about?"

Garnet laughed. "I find myself doing that often, since we set sail from Bermuda. I'll be thinking something to myself and even though I've not said it out loud, I come up with the last part of the thought, as if I *had* spoken aloud. I was thinking about the women in America. I find it hard to believe they're there. Visualizing men in a savage and wild place like that is no problem at all, but perhaps you're right and I'm wrong. When we get there we'll no doubt find it beautifully civilized."

The younger woman's idea of the size of the land they neared was similar to Dell's. Brought up as she had been in London, she couldn't stretch her imagination to encompass a place that would be any bigger, and it seemed reasonable for Dell to assume that all she would have to do would be to ask around after her late husband's people in order to learn of their whereabouts.

"Muldoon's father gave him an island," Garnet said. "Did he ever mention it to you?"

"Vaguely," Dell answered, feeling uneasy to be speaking about Muldoon.

"It is called Fairhaven. He plans to go there after he outfits himself with a ship and crew."

Detecting a wistful note in Garnet's voice, she looked at the slight figure who sipped at her coffee speculatively. "You yearn for him. It was a mistake for you to leave him, I fear."

"Sometimes I am lonely for him, that's true." Garnet's dark eyes met Dell's blue ones. "But I'm not sure I yearn for him. Nor do I feel I made a mistake when I left him there. If he cares for me, he will find me. But even then, I'm not sure that I shall ever forgive him for having used you so deplorably." She looked toward the darkening sea, not wishing to continue holding Dell's glance. "Now that the ugly affair is behind us, I sometimes find myself wondering if you dislike him as much as you pretend to."

"I never said I disliked him." In spite of her usual aplomb, Dell was annoyed to find her hands trembling, and while Garnet had her eyes averted, she quickly dropped her pipe in a bowl of sand and hid them in her lap. Then she forced a lilting laugh and said, "In all truth, the Muldoon has a certain air about him—a quality that I find fetching at times. Of course I am not alone in my feelings toward the abominable rake-hell. Other women find him irresistible."

"He's had many women, then?"

"I really don't know, Garnet. But I rather imagine he's had more than his share. It's—actually, he speaks the truth when he tells a woman he loves her madly, because at the time he says it, he means it. Unfortunately, he loves very often."

"How does it happen that you know so much about him? And about his women?"

"His aunt is talkative. She doesn't have a chance to converse with women as often as she'd like because there aren't any on the ship, as a general rule. She's gregarious by nature, too. So whenever Becky had a chance to become engaged in conversation with me, she did so. Before—when we were together on the Barbados—she confided in me about her worries concerning her nephew, because I was a married woman and because she was so lonely for woman-talk. Then, after Cortez took *The Dancing Lady*, we renewed our friendship of the past."

"What a liar he is!" Garnet said. "He told me he'd seen me from a distance, and couldn't rest and barely slept until he'd had me."

Dell leaned forward and looked at Garnet intently. "He wasn't lying to you about that, I'm sure. When Muldoon wants something, he thinks of very little else until he gets it, and in this instance, he wanted you. Some men become obsessed with a craving for drink, or gold, or jewels. Muldoon becomes obsessed with a craving for a certain woman."

"Then, after he conquers her, he loses interest," Garnet said bitterly.

"Not at all. Muldoon never loses interest in a woman, no matter how many times he has possessed her. It's just that there's room in his heart for more than one at a time." Dell's hearty laugh rang out. "In that, I doubt very much if he's much different from any other man alive. It seems to be something they all have in common, a built-in need to make conquests; yet at the same time to lose none of their loves of the past."

"It seems to me," Garnet mused, "that the business of loving is very complicated, no matter which way you turn it. Human beings are poorly equipped in many areas, but in the matter of love, we seem to be impossibly handicapped. For instance, I do not, to this day, know whether I loved Muldoon or not, or whether I still love him."

To Garnet, Philadelphus Fields was a woman of great wisdom. Where Garnet had occupied her spare time by reading novels when she was a girl at home, Dell had read the works of the great philosophers. More than that, she had studied them. "How *does* one know whether one loves a man or not?"

Again, Dell's laugh filled the little Officers' Dining Room. For a moment, her face was suffused with such incredible beauty that Garnet's heart was wrenched, because after the flush of purest delight that crossed her features there came a lost, deeply pained look of sorrow. She was pensive for a moment, and when she spoke again there was more than a hint of anguish in her voice. "I don't know all the answers, Garnet. I can only speak of what I feel to be the way things are when it comes to loving. It's a part of the great scheme of God Almighty that causes people to love one another. Or nature, perhaps. And I believe it is necessary for one's well-being to love and be loved. It's the first time around that comes hard, because we're fearful of being hurt. I loved Tom Wills completely, which includes liking him as a friend and passionately as a lover. *Because* I had the privilege of loving my husband, I also loved my child, and I believe once a person learns how to love once, it's an easy matter to love again. In your case, you loved you father. You grew into young womanhood with the knowledge of loving. When Muldoon came along, it was easy enough for you to love him, since your emotions were already attuned to the emotion."

"But you said you felt it was the scheme of God, or nature, to cause people to love one another. Now you're saying it's necessary to learn it."

"Yes, for the first time. It's human nature for us to want to eat foods that are more nourishing than mother's milk, but we must learn how to get the food from the plate into our mouth."

Garnet nodded. Her thoughts turned inward. With Dell's help she now realized that a good portion of Muldoon's personality was similar to traits she'd admired in her father. "In a way, Muldoon *is* much like my father. His good side, that is."

"And he has many similarities to my husband. Not his dark side, of course."

The two women exchanged a long and thoughtful glance. Without uttering another word, they understood one another completely.

Dell had accepted the woman-thing that was deep within her very being; it had bothered her ever since she'd ordered her ship to leave Bermuda. Time and time again she had been tempted to turn back and find Happy Jack Muldoon. Tell him she'd changed her mind, that she would have him accompany her to the place where she was bound. In spite of his ignoble side, he was a man she could respect, and perhaps even more important, he was a man who was capable of rekindling the fires that smoldered within. He was exciting and intelligent, but most of all, he was interesting. Dell could not abide the popinjays who paraded about in their colorful dress, sniffing at their scented handkerchiefs as they strolled about town in all of their empty elegance. She would not turn back, but she looked at her desire to do so with honest eyes and accepted it for what it was.

Garnet understood much of what was going on inside Dell's mind. She realized that Dell Fields was also in love with Muldoon, but she did not resent it. Instead, she acknowledged it in the same way that she understood Dell would not turn back any more than she, Garnet, would want her to. It didn't matter what motivated either one of them to refuse to give in to the desire to go back for the man they both loved, whether it was pride, stubbornness or some other emotion that she couldn't name. They would not go back to Bermuda, but there was always time to come, and Garnet understood that both of their futures held room for Jack Muldoon's love and also the loving *of* him.

Jack Lawson had chosen to cast his lot with Captain Dell Fields instead of throwing in with Muldoon. He entered the dining quarters quietly, to ask if the Captain or Garnet wished more coffee. Dell said yes, she'd have a final cup before she made her nightly rounds, but Garnet, who felt about to burst with things unsaid, was restless. She said she wanted to walk about the deck to look at the stars before she retired for the night.

"Begging your pardon, ma'am," said Lawson, "but it's begun to mist a little and the deck is a mite slippery, so you'd do well to watch your step."

"Thank you, Jack," answered Garnet. In spite of the lad's willy-nilly tendency in the past to break his loyalties to her or anyone else at a drop of a hat, she had a certain affection for him, which was a part of her new understanding of life and human beings in general. When she arrived on deck she was glad of his warning, because the deck was as slick as glass. Carefully, she moved among the ghostly coils of ropes, the spars and booms, mindful of the fine mist that lay on the deck almost as if it had been swabbed down, but not quite, for the wetness underfoot was barely discernible; it was a fine, almost dewy substance that covered everything with a cool slick. She looked up into the sky and saw a faint glimmer where the moon sailed along behind looming, slate-grey clouds, and tried to calculate their position. Four, possibly five or six more days and they would be in America.

As she peered into the blacker darkness toward the west, she visualized the outline of the maps she knew almost as well as the back of her hand. South of where the ship sailed through the night was the Tropic of Cancer, north of them the fortieth degree parallel, which set them reasonably close to the thirtieth—which they followed because of the current. If they continued on as they were, they'd reach the southernmost tip of the New World, which was far from their destination. Dell Fields disliked the heat of the tropics in the first place, but more important, the people she sought were allegedly in the Carolinas. Which meant they would be forced to continue as they were until they reached the remarkable currents that flowed along the shore. Then, if the winds were kind, they'd drop anchor near the place they sought. Even then, the unknown quantity would still be with them, Garnet felt uneasily. At best, they would drop their sails at the exact spot Dell had her heart on. At worst, they would be several miles to the north or south of it, and it was the southern portion that Garnet most feared. Savage red men were terrifying enough to contemplate, but they would not be all alone in a strange new land if they reached the Carolinas, since other white men had long been there before them.

In the south, she'd heard there were tribes of natives who might, or might not, belong to the same race of Indians that roamed North America, but they were said to be much more dangerous, for she had heard they were cannibals. The idea of being staked to a tree while a number of naked savages stripped off the choicest bits of her flesh while she was still alive caused her great consternation. She took comfort in telling herself she had no way of knowing how much truth and how much fiction was in the tales she'd been told, and went to bed with the profound hope that no cannibals whatsoever existed in either North or South America.

The following day was gloriously beautiful. A sailor's delight, with a benevolent breeze and a sea so calm that it was possible to look down and see one's face reflected in the glassy surface. The sun was warm and golden, the sky the purest of blue and not a cloud in sight. During the midafternoon, a lavishly outfitted ship appeared on their north, the sails awash with the brilliant yellow of the sun. Garnet's first thought was of Muldoon, but she quickly told herself it was not possible for him to have found himself a craft and overtaken them. The beautiful ship at first appeared to be skimming along much faster than *The Nightingale*, but after a few moments of careful scrutiny, Garnet realized that the illusion of great speed she'd first noted was just that. An illusion, nothing unusual on the open sea. She heard the cry, "Ship ahoy," at about the same time she sighted it, and moments later she heard Dell's orders to the helmsman to keep on course, which meant they would soon be passing the majestic vessel, but would come close enough to speak with her passengers.

At the tiller, where she knew she would find Captain Fields, Garnet waited patiently for Dell to let her have a look through the glass. Moments before she put it to her eye, she was shaken with the conviction that the other vessel was becalmed. A confusing decision, considering the way the sails were set. *The Nightingale* was making excellent time, and since the strange craft was close at hand and in full sail, she should likewise be flying across the sea at the same rate of speed. The glass brought the ship close enough to allow her to read the name: *Celeste III*. Under Dell Field's orders, *The Nightingale* came within three lengths. Close enough for an exchange. Dell signaled for the quartermaster to do the speaking, which he did in a resounding voice that was loud enough, to Garnet, to be heard all the way back to the Bermudas.

No answer came from the *Celeste III*. Garnet clutched Dell's shoulders. "There's something amiss. It could be a trap. They could be pirates."

Dell shook her head. "I don't think so. I saw no one about. Did you?"

Garnet lifted the glass and swept it from stem to stern of the *Celeste III*. She saw no sign of life, which served to increase her apprehension. "They may be hiding, and at the ready to fire upon us."

"If they planned to fire on us, they would have done it long ago, when we first hove to," said Dell. She reached for the glass and looked for a long time at the glistening ship, brilliant under the sun, and gasped. "The sails. Look at the *sails*!"

When she handed the glass back to Garnet, she saw that the sails were in shreds. Instead of bellying out, trapping the power of the wind in order to send the *Celeste III* along at a good speed, the breeze blew the tattered canvas this way and that, and all the while the ship remained stationary, barely moving against the gentle force of the waves made by the approaching *Nightingale*.

Jackson, the quartermaster, spoke suddenly, chillingly.

"Tis a ghost ship, Cap'n. Unmanned and becalmed. I've heard of 'em, but in all my days at sea I never seen one of 'em before." He grinned. "God knows what treasures are in her hold."

"And God knows whether it's a ghost ship or not," Dell said. "Maybe there's sickness aboard." She frowned, weighing the possibility of increasing her own wealth against exposing herself, Garnet, and the crew of *The Nightingale* to some dread disease. Again and again, she swept the length of the strange craft with the aid of her glass, seeing nothing. Then, just as she was about to tell the helmsman to move away, she caught a glimpse of a human being aboard the *Celeste III*. "God in heaven! It's a lad! A young lad, and he appears mortally wounded." She had seen his face for a bare instant, and it was a blood-encrusted face, with one eyeball hanging grotesquely on his cheek. It was the way his one hand fluttered in a feeble wave that arrested Dell's attention—a kind of futile gesture that seemed to express both hopelessness and the final gasp of a human struggle for survival against great odds.

"We'll board her," she said decisively.

The boats went down. No sound came from the gleaming *Celeste III* as the men rowed hesitantly toward the silent, hulking ship. Dell remained aboard *The Nightingale*, her face expressionless as she watched six of her men cover the distance between the two vessels. Garnet was rigid with fear, expecting a fusillade from the other ship at any moment, but it didn't happen. The seamen threw up the grappling hooks and boarded the *Celeste III* without incident, and quickly disappeared over her side. Moments later came a resounding shout—"All dead, Captain! Every man aboard, dead as a man can ever get!"

He was wrong. The young boy who had struggled mightily to lift himself to the railing was not quite dead when Garnet and Dell found him lying in a pool of his own blood, but his wounds were mortal. Dell knelt and looked into his one unmangled eye, that was already hazy with approaching death. "What took place aboard this vessel, lad?"

His lips were white. Garnet doubted very much if he

understood the question that had been put to him, but his bloodless lips parted and one word came out along with his last breath. "Mutiny."

The deck was a shambles, with bloody corpses lying about in all the crooked, agonized attitudes of sudden and brutal death. Most of the blood had long since dried, and some of the bodies had begun to bloat. The Ship's Master sat bolt upright in a massive chair inside his elegant quarters, a bullet between his eyes. A cat, full grown and oddly marked, was at the Captain's feet, all lost and forlorn as she looked up at the two women and cried pitifully.

"Good Christ," breathed Dell Fields.

And Garnet wondered how it had happened that a mighty crew of lusty men could have ended life in a brawl that defeated them all.

The hold of the *Celeste III* proved a treasure-trove. Casks of rum, chests of gold and jewels that sparkled and glittered, were only a part of it. There were crates of food, tobacco and furs. "A King's ransom," cried Jack Lawson as he staggered under an enormous stack of soft pelts.

"No," answered Dell Fields. "A Queen's ransom."

Lawson's countenance fell. "Yes, Captain," he said in disappointment.

"But we'll share and share alike," added Dell with her lilting laugh. She looked at a crate of foodstuff. "We don't even know if they were going away from the Americas or heading toward it, for without a man at the tiller she could have turned round and round, many times over. Not that it matters. We'd be foolish to leave her to founder, and founder she would. It's strange that she's not gone down before now."

They were hours getting the loot aboard *The Nightingale*, and it took more time to find a place for the booty since they were already heavily laden. Then the treasures had to be lashed down, which took more time. The pale blue of dusk was just beginning to replace the rays of the rapidly setting sun when Dell ordered the masts set for sailing, and once again Garnet Shaw found herself alone on deck, the strangely marked cat in her arms.

Laramy, the helmsman, had spoken with knowledge of the cat. "Them is killer-cats," he had said as he backed away from it. "They come from Siam, which makes 'em Simonese, and they'll tear a man apart if they been trained to. They make better guard dogs than the meanest old dog you can find, and on top of that, them Simonese is unlucky to have around. They bring down the curse of Satan to anybody who goes around 'em and if it was up to me, we'd drown the bastid and be well rid of it."

Neither Dell nor Garnet would hear of it. They both were of the opinion that a cat, even a fawn-and-chocolate-colored Siamese with eyes that looked as if they'd been fashioned of glass, and dangerous claws to boot, should not be destroyed. Dell had seen evidence of rats aboard. "Anyway," she said firmly, "since it survived the fate of the crew on the *Celeste III*, it wouldn't be right to kill it." She named it "Sime," because most of the crew continued to call it "Simonese," and although its hoarse cry was unpleasant, it had the demeanor of a lithe and lovely baby.

Looking about her, Garnet drew a trembling breath as she tried to erase from her mind the memory of the brutality that lay in the *Celeste III*. She wondered how the mutiny had come about, in what manner the battle had raged until every man aboard was either dead or dying. Whatever had taken place there would remain a secret since no man had lived to tell the story. But she wondered and wondered, and as the pale blue of dusk turned to darker blue, and the purple of evening gave way to the total darkness of night, she had never felt lonelier. It was as if some of the horror that reigned aboard the *Celeste III* followed along in the wake of *The Nightingale*, and the icy fingers of the dead had somehow come aboard. When she could no longer abide being alone, Garnet went to seek out Dell for companionship and warmth.

"I was looking for you," Dell told her. "We'd best eat our supper while it's hot."

Garnet shook her head. "I had no idea it was meal time, for I was lost in my thoughts." Together, the two women went to the Officers' Dining Room, where the quartermaster awaited them.

"You're pale as a ghost, Garnet," said Dell as she seated herself. "It was the dead aboard the *Celeste III* that got to you, I suppose. Strange. You've been at sea for more than two years. By now you should have grown accustomed to the disregard certain men have for life."

"I think I've grown soft," Garnet said. "Living with Muldoon did it. I keep thinking about all that bloodshed. And worrying about something similar happening to us. Two women, with one the Captain of the ship. The Master of the *Celeste III* was big and brawny. He looked as if he were capable of quieting an uprising, but he's dead, along with the others."

"And I am a woman," Dell said with a wry smile. "So you're worrying about my ability to control an unruly crew, I take it."

"Not . . . really. And not because you're a woman." Garnet swallowed. "It's just that I don't want to have my life snuffed out aboard this ship, and we're a long way from land, with treasures in our hold that no doubt tempt many."

"I've promised to share and share alike," Dell said. "The men trust me because I've proven myself trustworthy. Calm your fears, Garnet. Mayhap you're feeling puny because you're in the family way."

If Dell had thrown cold water on Garnet, her reaction couldn't have been more surprised. "But I'm *not!*"

"And a good thing, too. "Dell said harshly. "Because if there's one thing we don't need, it's to be tied down with a baby. When we reach the Carolinas, we'll have plenty of problems to face without the added worry of a woman in a delicate condition."

She had already made arrangements to sell *The Nightingale* to the quartermaster, but first they would divide the contents of the hold. After that, they would purchase horses and a conveyance of some kind in order to travel about the land in search of her husband's people. As Dell spoke of the future, Garnet's period of gloomy foreboding was dispelled. By the time she settled in for the night, the cat at her feet, she was calm and able to sleep. The next morning proved to be as gloriously beautiful as the day before, and *The Nightingale* continued to make good time toward the shores of the Carolinas. Unexpectedly, the lookout's cry sounded at sunset of that day. "Land ho!"

Fourteen

Before anyone went to shore Dell Fields made good her promise to divide everything that was taken from *The Dancing Lady*—as well as from the *Celeste III*—among the crew, herself, and Garnet. There was other plunder that had been accumulated during the time Cortez was Ship's Master, and that was also equally divided. The only items that Dell specifically took for herself were the fine gowns, capes, ladies' shoes, and other finery that had been among the booty from the *Celeste III*—and no man argued about that, for the wearing apparel was tailored to fit a woman as tall as Dell Fields. Although there were only four gowns, two capes, one of fur and the other of soft wool, the clothing was made of the very finest fabrics and Dell had already satisfied herself that they fit her.

For going ashore, she selected a black silk on which Garnet had embroidered charcoal grey vines from hem to neckline. The shoes were black velvet, decorated with silver bangles, which went well with the luxurious black Cluny lace shawl. She put her fiery hair in braids, which were fashioned into a heavy knot at the nape of her neck; then over her head she draped a sheer black veil. Garnet gave her an appraising look, after Dell asked if she looked presentably ladylike. The younger woman said she did, but added, "Even draped in black, Dell, your vivacious coloring stands you in good stead. You're a handsome woman, and mourning enhances your beauty."

"The first purchase I make must be a bonnet," Dell said

with a great rolling of her eyes and her mouth all turned down to show her distaste. "But like it or not, I must present a proper appearance. It's been many years since I've had to bother with a bonnet." Her eyes misted over as she slipped her wedding band onto her finger. "And a long time since I've worn this, too. I had to take it off when I passed myself off as a man, but I kept it well hidden."

Garnet's frock was peach-colored watered silk, with an ice-blue underskirt trimmed in peach lace. She wore the Neilson opals at Dell's insistence, and a blue silk cape over her shoulders against the somewhat chilly breeze which defied the clear June morning. "I, too, must find a suitable bonnet," Garnet said as she looked at herself in the mirror in Dell's cabin. "Should I put my hair up?"

"No. Let it stay as it is, loose and curling around your face." Dell looked at her hands in dismay. "Lord save me, my hands take away from the effect I want to present as a lady, but there's not a pair of gloves in any of the boxes."

"There's a bit of mink fur in with my portion," Garnet said quickly. "I can easily fashion it into a muff. Perhaps we'll be able to find a pair of black gloves for you after we've purchased our bonnets, but a muff would hide your work-worn hands in the meantime, and it'd not look out of place at all, as chilly as it is."

"Such a bother," Dell answered. "But worth the effort. Have you seen Lawson?"

"Not since we divided the spoils."

"I ordered him to get himself rigged out in gentleman's attire since he insisted on staying with us, but I do wish he would hurry. I'm as nervous as a badger, so it would do me well to go ashore and get it over with quickly. Of course you know full well why the lad begged to cast his lot with us, even though I told him he would have to pretend to be our servant. He's hopelessly in love with you, Garnet."

"You're mistaken, I'm sure."

"No I'm not." Dell pulled the gown away from where it bound her slightly under the arms. "If he doesn't hurry, I will have this damned thing ruined, I'm in such a sweat. Lawson looks at you with such yearning I'm surprised you hadn't noticed." She began to pace up and down the quarters.

"Walking up and down like that will only increase your discomfort," Garnet said as she hurriedly turned the mink pelt into a muff. "My goodness, Dell, we'll not be lucky enough to find your mother and father-in-law the minute we set foot on dry land. Why don't you sit down and try to compose yourself?"

Dell sat down, crossed her legs and rummaged in the reticule she'd left on a table until she found her pipe. She filled it with moist, crumbly tobacco and lit it with trembling fingers, then took a long, deep drag.

"That's another thing," Garnet said from the bed where she sat as she sewed. "I'm not sure it is considered genteel for a woman to smoke a pipe. Perhaps when we find your husband's people it would be wise to wait around a bit, and see whether it is the custom in this new land before you light up." She bit off the thread and dropped the muff on the bed. The cat they'd rescued from the ill-fated *Celeste III* immediately pounced on it as if it were another animal.

"Stop that," Garnet cried as she retrieved her handiwork from the cat's claws. "And something else, Dell, you must watch your language. You've grown accustomed to the ways of men aboard ship, and you aren't aware of how often you swear. And—uh— ladies don't cross their legs, either."

"Damn me," Dell retorted. "You're right, of course. I should have been practicing genteel manners these past weeks." Frowning, she knocked the fire out of her pipe into the bowl of sand, her expression thoughtful. "I'll see to it that no stranger sees me smoking my pipe, but it's a habit I can't seem to break, even though the tobaccos have gone sour on me these past few days. Every time I light up I get to feeling blarmish. I'll send Lawson to a tobacco shop the minute we set foot on shore, though, for a new supply. Nobody will raise an eyebrow at the idea of a young gentleman buying tobacco." She drummed her fingers on the top of the table impatiently.

At that moment, Jack Lawson tapped on the door and presented himself to the ladies after Dell called out for him to enter. She gave him a warm smile and assured him that he looked every inch the gentleman in his fawn-colored breeches, red jacket, and ruffled shirt. "Your boots are a little the worse for wear, but never mind. We'll buy you some new ones as soon as we get to Charles Towne. And more presentable stockings, too. Those are downright dirty-looking."

The boats were down, Lawson informed them, and everything was in readiness for going ashore. "The mates, Captain Fields, they asked me to tell you they're mindful of the last orders you'll ever give 'em, and this is the last time I'll be callin' you Captain, ma'am. And they've asked me to bring you out with your eyes closed, for they've a surprise for you."

Dell arched her eyebrows. "A surprise?"

"Yes ma'am, Mrs.—uh—" Red-faced with embarrassment, Lawson looked to Garnet for help, unable to recall Dell's married name.

"Wills," Garnet supplied.

"Yes'm," said the boy with a gulp. "Mrs. Wills, the mates want to show their appreciation to you for all you've done for them. For bein' fair and square, and for helpin' them get out from under the clutches of Cortez, them that stayed with the ship, ma'am. So if you'll just let me lead you, and if you'll kindly close your eyes, it won't take long. Miss Garnet, ma'am, if you'd just take her other hand—there. That's fine, Miss Garnet, ma'am, and I thank you kindly."

"I must say," Dell remarked as she closed her eyes and allowed Garnet and Lawson to lead her out of the quarters, "that you're doing very well in the role of a servant lad. But don't overdo it."

Utter silence met her ears as she was led forward. For one moment, but only for a fraction of a heart-beat, she stiffened as the idea struck her that she might be willingly going to her death—and stupidly, too, since she had closed her eyes trustingly. She was, after all, a woman of wealth. It was true that she had held nothing back when it came to sharing the booty with the crew—except for the clothing, which fit her so well—but the chests they'd already loaded aboard the rowboats and taken ashore contained a goodly amount of gold that she'd acquired long before she joined on the account with Cortez, and many a man had met his death over a good deal less than that. Still, Garnet was her friend. And in spite of feeling slightly foolish, she trusted her crew. "When can I open my eyes?"

"Any moment, ma'am," answered Lawson. He winked at Garnet and grinned after she'd taken in the sight of the mates and responded with a quickly indrawn breath of disbelief. They lined the deck on either side, each man standing at attention and holding aloft a bouquet of flowers. Although they were not dressed uniformly, all of them had ransacked the contents of their own chests and come up with presentable apparel. A motley crew, some with eye-patches, a few with missing limbs, but they were all there to a man, and not a face but was wreathed in smiles.

At a signal from the quartermaster, a chorus of male voices began on a low, sweet note. In the beginning, the voices faltered and sounded a little ragged until they all were daring enough to join in, but by the time Lawson told Dell she could open her eyes, there was harmony aboard *The Nightingale*, and the sound of it alone was enough to bring tears to the eyes of Dell Fields. But as she listened to the words, she sobbed openly. It was obvious that the mates had labored long to make up a suitable chantey and put it to music, and the message was clear:

We love you to a man, Captain Fields,
And we'll miss you dreadful hard, Captain Fields,
But if God is good, and we all believe He is,
Then we'll someday meet again, Captain Fields.

We have journeyed over sea, Mrs. Wills,
Now you're leaving for the land and the hills,
But you've been fair and kind, though you
    leave us behind.
May God guide you as you go, Mrs. Wills.

The cadence grew more sprightly as the men burst into a well-known pirate's chantey that spoke of taming the wild seas, of sending the weak down to Davey Jones as plunder for his water-logged locker, and of impressing the strong of heart to the life of a pirate. It ended with reference to the habit of certain European governments of dubbing former pirates knights as long as they confined their plundering to enemies of their country.

Dell's eyes brimmed over again at the closing song, which was sung solemnly, and softly:

Fare thee well—
Fare thee well—
Love go with thee—
Love go with thee.
When you're gone.
Remember me.

The mates sang it as a round, and there wasn't a dry eye aboard as Dell slowly made her way from mate to mate, accepting their floral tributes along with several kisses pressed on her hands. By the time she was lowered into the boat, she was sobbing brokenly, and looking back toward the ship with a most miserable expression on her beautiful face. The men lined the deck, all but the quartermaster, who had already gone ashore to pawn himself off as the Master of *The Nightingale*, acting on Dell's orders. When he helped the women get out of the boat he bowed deeply and paid Dell an uncommonly high tribute by telling her she was a better Captain than any man he'd sailed under. "The old gent over there will take care of your baggage until you send Lawson for it—I've already paid him."

Dell thanked him and offered him her hand, which he kissed in a courtly manner.

She said, "Where did the mates get all these flowers?"

"Well, Mrs. Wills," answered the new Captain of *The Nightingale*, "it happens that it's a market day in Charles Towne, which is where you'll be after you round that bend in the road, yonder. And the men bought every posy the lassies were selling." He swallowed and took Garnet's hand, which he also kissed after another formal bow. "Ladies, the New World awaits you. I've noised it about that you are Mrs. Thomas Wills, a widow woman, and her young cousin, Garnet Shaw, traveling with a servant, Lawson, and in need of rooms at an inn. Godspeed, ladies."

"Godspeed, Captain," answered Garnet and Dell in unison.

To Lawson, the former quartermaster said, "Keep an eye out to the safety of these fine gentlewomen, both of whom frighten easily for they've been brought up in gentle ways, my lad."

"Yes, sir," said Lawson with a knowing grin.

"And if you give their secret away," continued the new

Captain in the same tone of voice, gentle as a baby and sweet as sugar, "if you let it drop that they've sailed the seas and pirated with the best of 'em, me and the mates you've left behind will be bustin' your head when we meet again."

"Yes, sir," said Jack Lawson, his grin suddenly fading.

The Captain turned and headed back to the ship. Except for the short excursion ashore that they'd had previously, the crew of *The Nightingale* would not be spending any time in Charles Towne, for the sake of keeping the image and reputation of the two women intact. Dell had decreed it so, explaining that it wasn't that she didn't trust the mates, but if they went ashore and filled their bellies with rum, they'd get loose-lipped and forget everything they'd been told—which was simply that the Widow Wills and her young cousin had booked passage on *The Nightingale* when it departed from England, along with the manservant, Lawson, and a woman named Nelly Belston, who was both chaperone and servant to the young widow. Nelly, sad to say, had sickened aboardship and died a week after embarking from England's shore. The fiction was necessary because a reputable lady did not travel without the company of an older woman.

Dell secured her veil more closely about her face after Garnet told her she could see the sparkle of tears.

"I don't know why I'm so heartsick," Dell said. "I guess it's because of the way they were, there at the last. To tell you the truth, I'll miss them, every one of them."

"It's because we've been through so much with them," Garnet said sadly. "When people share a lot of sorrows and dangers, they grow close."

At first glance, the settlement was depressing to both women, although neither gave voice to their feelings as they strode resolutely toward the business square.

"Brick," said Garnet. "So much red brick. I wonder if they manufacture it here in this place."

"But some of the buildings are of stone," Dell answered. "While others are flimsy affairs of wood, and not very well put together. Mayhap they're temporary." She looked at a group of men who had congregated under an enormous tree within the shadow of what appeared to be a public building;

then she looked away. As soon as they were safely beyond the serious-faced men, she whispered, "They speak in a foreign tongue, those men."

"Frenchies, it sounded like to me," said Lawson.

Dell directed him to go up to a substantial-looking man who stood in front of a butcher establishment and inquire as to where they could find a hatter.

"I feel foolish carrying this cat, Mrs. Wills," said Lawson. "Couldn't I just sort of put her down and let her follow along, kind of nice-like?"

"Cats don't follow along like dogs, you idiot," Garnet said as she reached for the Siamese.

After Garnet had the cat in her arms, Lawson went over to the butcher and engaged him in conversation, leaving Dell and Garnet on the street in front of a tea room. Apparently the market day was over—all but a few of the stalls that lined the street were empty of produce, and the rest of the merchants were packing up their unsold goods and placing them in wagons.

"I'm famished," Garnet said. "Let's go in and have tea and cakes after Lawson comes back. Then we'll go to the hatter."

"I could do with a spot of tea, too," Dell said. She looked at the lad and shook her head. "He's not one to ask a question and get the answer and leave the matter stand. Look at him, flap-jawed as they come. He *would* stand there and talk! And it's going to rain, too."

As if aware that he was being talked about, Lawson turned around and grinned. Then he touched his forelock, said a few words to the gentleman in the apron, and came back to the ladies. "He says there's a hatter on down the block, ma'am, and there's a fine inn where ladies will be safe from harm on the block opposite this one. Oh, yes. And them Frenchies, well, he says to me there was a colony of Huguenots that settled here in 1685, and now a thousand more have come down from Nova Scotia. Not Huguenots, exactly, but real close to 'em. Acadians, he says. Looks like they're about to take over from the Englishmen, if you ask me."

"The French," said Garnet carefully, "are extremely artistic people." She was afraid the foreigners knew enough

English to understand what Lawson was saying and didn't want to get them into any trouble. "We're going to have tea, Jack. As our servant, it wouldn't look well for you to join us, but—" The idea of asking him to stay outside while she and Dell went in and enjoyed themselves was upsetting; yet she was afraid the settlers would think they were a strange lot, to go into a public place for tea and take a servant along with them. Out of troubled eyes, she looked to Dell for the answer to the dilemma.

"He can go in," Dell said comfortably, "but he can't sit at the same table with us. Hurry! That rain is cold!"

The rain came down hard as the skies turned darker, and before they could get to the tea room a jagged streak of lightning lit up the square in blinding fury. It was followed by a loud clap of thunder that shook the very ground, and several horses reared and pawed the air at the terrifying sound.

At the entrance was a tiny black girl dressed in a red and yellow calico gown, beruffled and charming, but barefoot. The girl held a chain on which a monkey cavorted. "God in heaven," Dell said to the child who had plastered herself against the building and covered her eyes because of the thunder. "That thing is almost as big as you are."

"He's tame and won't bite, but Mistress said I must watch him outside because he's not house-trained," shrilled the frightened child. "She will be out directly. She *promised*!" Big tears swam down the tiny face for a moment. "On'y she been in there for over an hour, and now the storm will kill me for sure! And monkey, he gets fractious when it rains and Mistress knows I can't handle the little devil. It's the thunder. Scares him, and when he's scared he turns mean as sin."

Dell bent and looked into a pair of almost black eyes that were fringed with sooty lashes so curly that they indented the skin of the eyelids when the child looked up. "Tell me your mistress's name, dear."

The child turned ashen at another crackle of lightning. "She's Mistress Cathcart, ma'am. Maybe she forgot I'm out here with the monkey and all on account of she forgets a lot of things."

"How adorable," Dell murmured as she entered the tea

shop. "I doubt if she's more than four years old but her speech is as precise as any adult's. Oh, Garnet, do you suppose she's a—one of those— I mean, do you suppose someone *owns* her? That the Mistress Cathcart she spoke of purchased her just as if she were a cat, or a dog—or a monkey? I've heard of such ungodly practices taking place here in America, but I didn't know they bought and sold little *children*!"

Garnet cringed at the fire in Dell's eyes. "Dell, don't go into a rampage, I beg of you. If slavery is the custom here, we'll not be able to change it, especially not right away—just off the ship and complete strangers!" She was thinking back to the time Dell was challenged by the Swede. The same fire was in Dell's eyes as she marched, dripping wet, into the tea room and asked in an imperious voice if Mistress Cathcart were in the room.

Scurrying maidens laden with trays stopped in their tracks, but not one voice was heard in answer.

Looking around, Dell squared her shoulders and headed for a grey-haired lady who appeared to be the proprietress. "Perhaps no one heard me," she said in a deceptively pleasant voice. "I am asking after Mistress Cathcart, madam."

"She's not here," said the plump, middle-aged woman.

Another deafening volley of thunder followed a streak of lightning that brightened every window in the tea shop to a dazzling glow. Haughtily, Dell said, "But she left a little blackamoor outside, and it's beginning to storm."

"It's just a little ole nigger wench," said the woman. "It won't melt, God knows. And the rain won't hurt it a bit since all those nigger wenches smell awful strong. Mrs. Cathcart isn't here. She was here about an hour ago, but she left. Ask anyone you care to, my good woman, and they'll all tell you the same thing."

"By what door did she leave, then?"

"Good heavens," said the plump woman, plainly put out at the idea of a stranger kicking up a fuss about a little black girl. "How would I be knowing which door she left by? I've got my trade to keep an eye on, so I wouldn't be having the time to watch the doors."

"Is that child a slave?" Dell's voice was cold, hard, and flinty.

"Well, my heavens above," answered the proprietress. "It certainly isn't the blood child of Livonia Cathcart! Dear me, madam, if you're going to raise a ruckus, I must ask you to leave, for I run a respectable establishment, and my customers are not accustomed to being upset as they enjoy their refreshments."

A number of well-dressed ladies who were seated at the small tables seemed to be enjoying the spectacle of the tall, outraged woman in widow's weeds as she spoke angrily to the proprietress. They tittered at her next spate of words, although some of them pretended to be shocked. Dell said, "To hell with you, and all of yours. And if you should happen to see Mrs. Cathcart, kindly tell her I have taken her baby-girl slave *and* her goddam monkey to the inn where I'm stopping."

"No need to use unsuitable words, madam," admonished the proprietress. "And I will have you know, since you seem to be a stranger, that it is a punishable crime to take the property of another. You could go to jail for stealing a slave. Or a monkey, for that matter."

"I'm not stealing her, you old bawd, you," yelled Dell. In her anger and impatience, she snatched the veil from her head. "I said I'm taking her to the inn. If the Cathcart woman wants her back, she can come and get her." With a quick glance around the room, she took in the entire patronage when she said, "You're all my witnesses. The little girl is barely more than a baby, and I'm taking her out of the storm."

A small, dark-eyed, ivory-skinned woman stood up and took Dell's hand. "Which inn, madam? I shall relay the message to Mrs. Cathcart, and with great pleasure."

Dell looked at Lawson, who had remained transfixed throughout the entire exchange, open-mouthed and wringing his hands. "McSwane's," he blurted. "Or McSwene's, maybe."

"McSwaney's," said the little woman who had spoken to Dell. "It's my guess that Mrs. Cathcart will come to claim her property in about an hour. I will be there myself, as your witness in this, for you are indeed a fascinating woman, and what you said is quite true. You've stated your intentions and you are not stealing Livonia's pickaninny."

Garnet didn't say a word. She didn't give a hoot about her own reputation, but Dell had been explicit about never, under any circumstances, wanting her dead husband's people to know anything about the life she had led since his death. She'd said, "They're so good and so gentle and kind, Garnet. Their response, if they'd known about the heinous way Luis Cortez murdered Tom and my baby, would have been to pray for Luis Cortez's black soul. In time, they'd forgiven him. Been truly compassionate. Not I. Under those dreadful circumstances, there could never have been any turning of the other cheek, and I'll never be sorry I was instrumental in his death. Never! Nor do I regret the way I've lived during the years I planned and waited and schemed for it. But my mother and father-in-law brought me up in their faith, and their hearts would be broken if they ever so much as dreamed that I . . . have sinned. So I must put on a great act and be a pure and virtuous lady, for their sakes. After I've seen them and paid my respects, we'll settle down and build a house somewhere in America, and I'll try to go back to behaving as if I had been continuing in the ways of virtue." Garnet understood and respected Dell for her consideration of the man and woman who had been mother and father to her, then mother and father-in-law. But as they went out into the raging rain storm, she hoped and prayed that Mr. and Mrs. Wills were nowhere near Charles Towne, for Dell had certainly shown her colors inside that fusty little tea shoppe.

She was still showing them as she instructed Lawson to take care of the monkey, handed him the chain and whisked the little girl up in her arms, to run pell-mell through the rain-swept streets of Charles Towne in the direction of McSwaney's Inn.

Garnet ran as fast as she could, holding the yowling cat in her arms, while Lawson struggled with the monkey. Even the driving rain and the earth-shaking thunder didn't drown out the shrill chatter of the monkey, and when it wasn't chattering it was shrieking.

Drenched to the skin, the tall, flaming-haired woman and the small dark-haired one clattered into the Inn, with Lawson right behind them, a bare few minutes after they left the Tea Shoppe. The women went to stand gratefully in front of the blazing fireplace at the end of the room while a rosy-cheeked young man gave them a startled look. Dell's teeth were chattering because the rain was cold and penetrating. "See to our rooms, Lawson," she said over the top of the little girl's head. "She's wet through and through, and I want to get her good and dry as soon as possible."

"But what'll I do with the monkey?"

"Give me the damned chain," Dell said impatiently.

"No, you have the child," Garnet said. "I'll handle the monkey." She took the leash and looked in horror at the ugly thing as it climbed up her skirt following another clap of thunder. The cat arched his back and spat, his chocolate-colored ears laid back and his blue eyes shooting dangerous sparks. The monkey looked at the cat, climbed back down Garnet's skirts and hid his wizened face in the folds of the material. The cat relaxed, and under cover of Lawson's voice as he made the arrangements about rooms, Garnet whispered, "Dell, please. Your language!"

Five minutes later, Garnet and Dell closed the door of an upstairs room, and in short order, they'd stripped the child down to the buff and wrapped her in a blanket. The cat rested majestically in the exact center of the bed and barely flicked an ear when the knock sounded at their door and a voice followed to announce that their trunks had arrived. Lawson led several men in with trunks, chests, and crates. After the men had departed, he said, "I don't much cotton to that monkey."

"Well, the cat doesn't like him, so you'll have to keep him in your room until the woman comes to claim him," Garnet said. She wanted him to hurry with his leavetaking so she could get into dry clothing, now that her things had been brought.

"What if the owner don't come?"

"Then we'll figure something out," snapped Garnet. "We'll give the little varmint away. Go and change your clothes, Lawson, really! You're soaked, even more than we are, for we didn't have to go out and get our belongings and see that they were delivered."

Dell had chosen the rocking-chair, where she sat contentedly rocking the child, both of them mother-naked under the blanket. She appeared totally unconcerned about monkey, cat, Lawson, or Garnet as she looked down at the quiet, happy little girl who snuggled against her so trustingly.

As soon as Lawson left, Garnet found suitable wearing apparel for herself and Dell, and as she dressed in the warm and dry clothing, she reminded Dell that the little one's mistress would be arriving soon. "So you ought to get dressed, Dell."

"Why?" Dell's blue eyes were as clear as a midsummer sky.

"Because the woman will be out of sorts and you'll be wanting to put your best foot forward."

"I've already put both of my big feet in my mouth." Dell's rueful laugh filled the room. "So much for my high-handed notions of making a good impression on the citizens of Charles Towne. I'm sure word has gotten around town that I'm daft. Now that the worst of the storm is over, those women have probably rushed forth to tell everyone they ran into about the crazy lady who raised hell at Mrs. Nettle's Tea Shoppe. The clerk down there—he looked as if he had a tender heart, and I hope it's not just the way he looks, because I wouldn't want to be thrown out. Still, I'd probably do it again. This little child was terrified. A woman has no right to leave a baby out in a storm."

Again, a knock sounded at the door. Flustered, Garnet called out, "Just a minute, please." Then she went to take the little girl from Dell, whispering, "Hurry and get dressed!"

"It's Mr. McSwaney, ma'am," called a cheery voice. "I'll just be leavin' some nice tea for you, and all you have to do is open the door. And there's a lady soon to be coming up to visit, name of Mrs. Lightfoot. Said to tell you she's the one was in the tea room, come to witness for you as she promised."

Dell giggled as she yanked on a purple underskirt, a lavender gown embroidered about the hem with violets. "So much for my widow's weeds," she said as she allowed her wealth of auburn hair to fall about her shoulders. "With one black dress and it as wet as can be, I can hardly be expected to wear it. Lord, Garnet, I don't care much for the heat of the tropic lands, but if this is the way the Carolinas are in June, I can't say I favor the weather here, either. First the damp, cold winds of early morn, then this storm, and that rain was *cold*!"

Garnet opened the door and found a stand with a tray. She brought in a sizzling hot teapot complete with a crocheted cozy and three cups, saucers and spoons. There was thick cream, sugar and a lemon that looked as if someone had had it hanging about the place for several days, but the flaky scones more than made up for the condition of the lemon. "And look! Marmalade and butter aplenty," Garnet cried. She'd had no marmalade or butter since she left England.

After a gentle tapping at the door, Garnet opened it to find the little lady in the hall. "Come in, please do," she said politely. "How kind of you to come."

"I keep my word," said the woman as she accepted the chair at the table where Garnet had put the tea. "And even if I didn't, I'd break my neck to see Livonia Cathcart get her come-uppance." Mrs. Lightfoot took her tea with sugar only, and politely refused the scone, since she'd already filled up, she said, on sweets at the tea shoppe. "Mrs. Nettle was fair in a nettle, too," she said with a dimpled smile. "She's a cousin to Livonia Cathcart and everyone in town knows Livonia uses the tea room as a front so she can go dallying with Ned Breidenbecker, the blacksmith, and him with an invalid wife. To say nothing of Livonia's husband, who would take a dim view if he knew of his wife's carryings-on. But until today her little secret has been safe. She goes into Prue Nettle's tea room by the front door and leaves her little slave-girl in front, so if her husband passes by in his buggy he'll know of his wife's whereabouts. But *imagine* leaving that little thing out in a storm! And with that filthy monkey! Cathcart himself is kind to his slaves, but Livonia is kind to nobody but herself. That woman ought to be horse-whipped."

Dell stirred her tea. The child was sleeping soundly in the

bed, the Siamese cat snuggled close to her and sleeping also, but not as soundly. His ears twitched with regularity. "How often, Mrs. Lightfoot, does this fiendish woman leave her slave in front of the tea shoppe while she goes gallivanting off with the blacksmith?"

"Why, every day. Winter and summer."

"But no one ever saw fit to rescue the child, I suppose, from unseasonable weather. Do you have much cold weather here in the Carolinas?"

"No, it's never cold, but she's been out in the storm before. I take her to my house when I see a storm approaching, but I always see to it that she's at her post when it's time for her mistress to return. You see, I live across the street from Mrs. Nettle's establishment. I have no choice but to get the little thing back to the front of the shoppe in time for her to be there when Livonia comes back. My husband keeps the accounts of the big Cathcart lumber company and furniture factory." She gave Dell a direct look. "You were in mourning."

"Yes. But my gown was wet, and this was the first thing my cousin found when she opened the trunk. Forgive me. I am Dell Wills. My husband was a missionary, and he was murdered by a—savage. My baby daughter was killed by the same person. I'm afraid I was quite beside myself when I saw the unfortunate child so frightened of the storm, because of my own daughter, I suppose." For a moment, Dell lowered her eyes and touched a piece of linen to them. Her eyes were tragic when she looked again at Mrs. Lightfoot. "But that was no reason to use the name of the Lord in vain, if that's what I did. Most unfitting behavior, for a missionary's wife." Turning to Garnet, she said, "And this is my dear cousin, Garnet Shaw. We've come here in search of my husband's mother and father."

Garnet acknowledged the introductions, inwardly amazed at Dell's stunning acting ability. Without saying a word that wasn't true, she'd somehow managed to convey the impression that the deaths of Tom Wills and her baby daughter had occurred recently, which just might account for her wild and unruly behavior. When Mrs. Lightfoot looked shocked and offered her sympathy and made little comforting sounds, Dell protected herself from further inquiries by saying she could not bear to speak another word of her loss, that she'd only said what she had in order to keep Mrs. Lightfoot from thinking she was a woman of low morals.

"On the contrary, Mrs. Wills," said that good lady. "I admire you immensely, and even though I may endanger my husband's position with the Cathcart Company, I'll witness for you anyway."

"I mean to keep the little girl," Dell stated firmly.

Fifteen

Livonia Cathcart reminded Dell of a wildcat with its tail caught in a trap. Without so much as a by-your-leave, she burst into the room with a snarl and an outraged yowl. Her first words were both accusation and threat: "I'll have the law on you for taking my property!"

Dell looked up from where she was sitting in the rocking chair, her expression mild as milk, her voice sweet as sugar. "Mrs. Cathcart, I believe." She smiled, glanced at the sleeping child on the bed, then turned toward Garnet, who sat quietly with needle and thread in a corner. In this way, they had set the stage for the woman's arrival, and Mrs. Lightfoot was not in sight. Nor was Lawson, who had the monkey with him. Five more ladies had arrived just minutes before the irate mistress of monkey and child, and they'd gone gladly to the adjoining room after McSwaney suggested letting Mrs. Cathcart have enough rope to hang herself before they all trooped in; perhaps the Charles Towne ladies wouldn't even be needed.

Cordially, Dell said, "Won't you have a chair, Mrs. Cathcart? No need to get yourself all in a stew over a little misunderstanding."

The plump, blonde woman tossed her head and rushed to the bed, where she held her hands out as if she would snatch the little one up. "No misunderstanding about it," she shouted. "You stole my slave-girl and my monkey, and Mrs. Nettle has summoned the constable. He'll be coming any minute, and I intend to swear out a warrant against you."

"Don't you touch that baby," Dell said softly. "Lay a hand on her and you'll walk out of here as bald as an onion." Her hearty laughter filled the room. "I wonder how your husband would react to a bald-headed wife. To say nothing of the blacksmith or other stray men you've bedded."

"How dare you threaten me!" The Cathcart woman spoke boldly, but her expression gave away her inner fears and doubts. "And just who do you think you are, to come into town and destroy the peace and quiet in this way?"

"I know who *I* am," Dell answered with a lazy smile. "*You're* the one who is apparently laboring under the misguided notion that you're Mrs. God Almighty. Now, I don't care how many men you want to dally with, Mrs. Cathcart, but I imagine your husband would be mighty interested in how you spend your time when he thinks you're in the tea shoppe."

Mrs. Cathcart took a deep breath, opened her mouth and squinched her eyes shut.

"No use in screaming, Mrs. Cathcart," Dell said sweetly before the woman could begin what she intended. "And don't think you have me over a barrel. You're not going to swear out any warrant, but if the law is on its way, you'd better shut up and listen instead of wasting time having a screaming fit. Now, I intend to buy that precious child from you, fair and square. Whatever your husband paid, I'll give you double the amount. And you can have the monkey back. You see, I don't have any husband who depends for his living on working for the Cathcart business, so I'm not afraid of you on that score. And I'm not afraid of going to jail, because if I do, Mrs. Cathcart, your husband is going to have his eyes opened about you. I know things that'll frizzle his hair."

Livonia Cathcart opened her eyes, expelled her breath and turned a ghastly shade of grey.

Quietly, Dell continued: "That little girl was scared to death of the storm, but she didn't dare run for shelter, and after I took off her wet dress, I found out why she was afraid to disobey you. Those scars on the backs of her legs go mighty deep, Mrs. Cathcart. And that bracelet around her ankle is so tight that it's bitten right into her skin. Branding her would have been a sight kinder, for a brand would have healed in time."

"I didn't know she'd outgrown the bracelet," whined Livonia Cathcart. "And she had those scars on her legs when my husband bought her for me."

"Is that a fact?" Dell stood to her full imposing height, her face calm, but her eyes bright with anger. "Melly was given to you when she was two weeks old. It says so on the bracelet that tells her name and says you own her."

Mrs. Cathcart gave Dell a frightened look, but she held onto her aplomb with both hands, and managed to speak huffily. "How do you know so much about me?"

"Why, maybe I've got a bit of magic about me," Dell said. "On the other hand, it's possible that some of the other ladies around town don't much care for the way you mistreat an innocent child who was sold to your husband with the promise that she would be treated with kindness since she's half white, fathered by a respected colonist and all."

"Who told you such terrible things?"

Dell threw back her head and laughed. "Now, wouldn't you like to know? Come on, Mrs. Cathcart. Tell me how much it cost your husband to buy a baby girl. I'll give you twice that, as I mentioned before."

"He paid three hundred dollars."

Dell shrugged. Footsteps sounded in the hall and once again came a thunderous knock accompanied by a loud voice demanding that the door be opened in the name of the law.

"Open the door, Mrs. Cathcart," Dell said sweetly, "while I count out the money."

A portly gentleman entered belly-first and looked around the room. He touched his forelock to Mrs. Cathcart and cleared his throat. "Now which one of these women stole your property, ma'am?"

"It was," said Livonia Cathcart in an almost inaudible voice, "a misunderstanding, Constable. I'm sorry I inconvenienced you, Mr. Stringer."

The constable cleared his throat again, swept Dell with a glowering glance, then turned the same kind of look on Garnet. "You're the womenfolks that got off the ship this morning, isn't that right?"

Both women nodded and smiled.

"The Captain, he said you was gentlewomen. Nobly born,

or somesuch. We don't hold with nobility, here in Charles Towne. You might as well get that straight right off. And we don't hold with no shenanigans, neither, such as walking into a place of business and causing the proprietress a heap of trouble. You went and took that there pickaninny from where her mistress had told her to stay put, and we don't hold with nobody coming along and interfering with slaves or anything else that belongs to proper colonists like Mrs. Cathcart, here. You had no call to go and do what you did."

Mrs. Cathcart began to jabber an explanation, making things up as she went along: "This lady, I mean the tall one with the red hair, well, she sent word by her servant that she wanted to purchase my little Melly, and I said to him that Melly should be there in front of the tea shoppe. And—uh —he said she would come and get her, we'd make the arrangements about the payment later on—after this lady had found accommodations, the serving man not at the time knowing exactly where this lady would be stopping. And so you see, I—uh—did as I said, and left Melly there. And where I made my mistake, Mr. Stringer, was in forgetting to tell my cousin, Mrs. Nettle, about our arrangement. And then—well, when I returned from—paying a call on a sick friend, there had come a dreadful storm as you well know, and Mrs. Nettle, my cousin, was just beside herself on account of thinking someone had stolen my little Melly. And—then I just completely forgot the conversation I had previously had with the servant this lady sent; you know how I am, dear Mr. Stringer, just as silly and forgetful as can be, dumb little old me!"

Dell and Garnet exchanged amused glances. Mrs. Cathcart scooped up the pile of gold coins Dell had placed on the table, dropped them in her reticule except for five or six, which she held out to Stringer with considerable simpering and eyelash fluttering as she said, "I would take it as a great pleasure if you would accept this small token of my appreciation for your touble. The fact that everything was just a silly little old misunderstanding because of my own poor, befuddled mind has nothing to do with it. Anyway, I've been wanting to contribute my share to the building of the church you and your missus have worked for so tirelessly."

"Well, now!" The Constable broke out into a broad smile, pocketed the coins, and bowed deeply to all three women, saying that he certainly was glad to see there was no trouble. "It was a pleasure to have met you ladies," he added in his rumbling voice in spite of having been introduced to neither Dell nor Garnet. "And it is always a pleasure to feast these old eyes on a lovely blossom such as yourself, Mrs. Cathcart, especially seeing that you're a good Christian, true and pure."

As soon as that worthy man was safely out of earshot, Livonia Cathcart demanded the names of the women who had tattled on her. "Not that there's a word of truth in those vicious lies."

"Speaking of lying," Garnet said, addressing the woman for the first time, "you're very poor at it. The man obviously knows there was no time for anyone to have sent a servant to speak to you about purchasing Melly. But money talks, as you know quite well. It also answers. Perhaps you would be wise to conduct yourself in a less dangerous manner for a time."

"Just give me the monkey!" The woman tapped her foot impatiently. "You just give me that monkey, and as long as there's advice-giving in the air, I'll give the both of you some. You're not wanted in Charles Towne, and my husband practically owns it."

Lawson didn't use the connecting door to bring in the monkey. To do so would have exposed the ladies who had waited in the next room, all of whom had promised to come forth and have their say if Livonia Cathcart refused to sell Melly to Mrs. Wills. And since Livonia Cathcart had been persuaded to sell, there was no use in bringing down her wrath on them. He stepped in from the hall.

"It amuses me," Dell said to Garnet after everyone had left, "to think of how she'll forever wonder which one of her acquaintances told. Maybe it'll drive her loony."

"Might drive her a little closer to the brink," Garnet said, "but she's already marched down that road a good ways. You know, though— we've no room to talk about anyone else's lunacy. Here *we* are, with a child, a cat, and Jack Lawson." She shrugged her shoulders. "Oh, well. At least we're not saddled with the monkey." She directed Lawson to go and find a doctor who would come to the inn. "He'll have a tool he can use to get that abominable bracelet off Melly's ankle."

Dell winced. "And on your way back, Lawson, please stop at a tobacconist's for a supply of smoking tobacco. I've thrown out the canister I had aboard *The Nightingale* because it made me sick to smoke it."

Garnet stood up and straightened. She held up the frock she had been sewing for Melly, a confection of pink and gold. Dell broke into a pleased smile and shook her head as she marveled at Garnet's expertise with the needle. "She'll look like an angel in it. Oh, I do hope she won't suffer when the doctor removes that ugly bracelet, but as you and I both saw, the flesh around her little ankle has already been rubbed raw."

"It's an abominable practice," Garnet said. "We should awaken her. If we don't she'll be wide awake tonight."

With tenderness, Dell brought the sleeping Melly awake, after which Garnet went down to the clerk to ask for a pitcher of water so they could give the child a bath. When Lawson arrived, Melly was parading around the room in her new gown, her hair braided in pigtails and tied with a pink ribbon, a gold locket Dell had just given her around her neck.

"Doctor couldn't come," Lawson announced. "His missus said he was sick in bed. So I stopped at the goldsmith's who will be along in a few minutes. And here's your tobacco."

"You're not telling all there is to tell, Lawson," Dell said as she looked at Lawson appraisingly. "In all truth, the story of my taking Melly has swept through town, and the doctor refused to come. Or did he tell you he wouldn't treat a slave-child?"

"Neither, ma'am. The doctor's good wife told me he was sick abed, unable to get up. But he heard us talking and came into the room where we were, wearing his night-shirt. He was bleary-eyed and barely able to stand, but not from sickness. He was drunk and belligerent with his wife, saying he was able to tend to his business. But I didn't think you'd want an old stumble-bum to take care of the little one, ma'am. The goldsmith will have a steadier hand, and he's equipped with the tools."

Dell was satisfied. The goldsmith came, and Melly began to cry the moment she understood what was to be done, but the man was quick and efficient as he stripped the pin from the bracelet, then spread the offensive thing in order to get it off with as little discomfort to Melly as possible. She screamed only once, and that was when the strip of metal pulled away from the raw and festered skin.

"She's a little princess," said the goldsmith after Dell had dried Melly's tears and comforted her. Then he took two tiny bits of shining gold from his bag. "If you'll permit me, Mrs. Wills, I would like to give this little girl these ear bobs. Her ears have been pierced already, but since it appears a long time since she's worn ornaments in them, they'll soon be growing together."

"Why, thank you," said Dell, amazed at the young man's kindness.

By way of explanation, the goldsmith said his heart was wrenched each time he saw cruel treatment of slaves, having been indentured himself as a child. "Mr. Moskowitz brought me here, and I had no choice in the matter. An indentured servant's life is little different from that of a slave, and when your manservant told me about the manner in which you took the child, I wanted to stand up and cheer you."

"Moskowitz is here in Charles Towne?" Dell and Garnet exchanged glances.

"Not at this moment, ma'am. He returns on the morrow."

"Well, now. My cousin and I will be glad of an opportunity to speak to him about a certain matter," Dell said. "Meanwhile, allow me to pay you for your services."

After the goldsmith left, Dell warned Garnet not to mention anything to Moskowitz about the earrings the goldsmith had given to Melly. "He didn't say that he slipped the gold out of that filthy old curmudgeon's supply—but that's something indentured servants do as a kind of token gesture against the men they're indentured to. But *imagine*! Finding Moskowitz here, in Charles Towne." It was obvious that Dell's hopes were high concerning the matter of finding Mr. and Mrs. Wills, now that she and Garnet had blundered onto the notorious London fence.

They kept their rooms at McSwaney's Inn for almost two weeks, and although Dell spent most of her time asking after the whereabouts of her husband's people, she found not one soul who could give her news of them until the very last day of their stay in Charles Towne. It was the doctor who steered her toward Williamsburg, in the colony of Virginia.

"Good people," the old doctor said. "The salt of the earth. Mr. Wills was poorly and I treated him as best as I could, but his health was failing. I discouraged their leaving because I feared he would not survive the journey. They settled here as if they planned to stay, and that was right after they came over from London. I believe they had friends in Williamsburg."

Dell was grateful to the doctor for his information, just as Garnet was relieved to know that Muldoon had told the truth about the way he happened to be in possession of the opals, which she wore to Moskowitz's establishment at Dell's urging. She undid the clasp, removed them from around her neck and gave them to him, saying nothing.

He looked at them, nodded, and then looked back at Garnet. "Beautiful. Very beautiful. Do you wish to sell them, madam?"

"No, I want them appraised," she answered carefully.

"For what reason?" The old man's gaze pierced her with an unreadable look.

"I was thinking of making out a will, and I would like to list everything of value that I own."

"I see." The old man nodded. "Very well, but you know, of course, that my time is valuable. I can tell you a good bit about this necklace, but not for nothing."

"Then tell me. I shall pay you well."

"First, I must see the color of your coin."

Impatiently, Garnet demanded to know the amount he wanted. When he told her, she gave it gladly. Tipping back his head, he said, "That necklace came from the home of a nobleman whose name I will not divulge. She was murdered as she slept in her bed. The assassin took the opals from her neck after the dread deed was done, but when he brought them to me at my London establishment, I had no way of knowing they were stolen. The assassin was paid to eliminate the lady's life, not to take her possessions. He has since gone to the gallows for another crime. I watched him hang myself, less than two months after I bought this necklace and the matching earrings, among other bits of jewelry he offered."

"His name," she pressed.

"His name was Foy. William, or Wilburn Foy."

Blanching, Garnet clutched the table that separated her from the old man. It was several seconds before she could settle herself enough to ask if the man remembered to whom he had sold the opals, for she was busily putting things together in her mind. Foy. Her would-be suitor. Dame Clements' nephew, who killed Lady Nielson, and possibly her father. Now that it was out in the open, she wondered why she'd not realized all along that Foy was a criminal. Her instincts had told her to avoid him, but she'd never known why she'd detested him so violently until that very moment. Even though Moskowitz's reputation was unsavory, he had no reason to lie to her.

"One thing more—to whom did you sell the opals?" As she asked, she put down several more pieces of gold.

"A dashing young fellow who is the son of a lord. Young Muldoon, Jonathan Muldoon, though most folks call him Jack."

The conversation gave Garnet a profound sense of relief. Throughout the entire time, Dell had not spoken a word, and neither had Jack Lawson. They left the little building in silence, but after they were well down the street, Lawson gave Garnet a mild rebuke: "You should have known, Miss Garnet, that Captain Muldoon would never have committed the crime you suspected him of. For shame that you could have given the idea room inside your head!"

"Remember your station, Lawson," commanded Dell. "It is not for the likes of you to tell a lady what doubts and worries she held within her heart."

"Yes, ma'am. Only—"

"Only what?" Garnet had turned the full force of her magnetic brown eyes on him. Earlier, before they'd set out for the goldsmith's, she had told him the entire story of the disappearance of her father and the murder of Lady Neilson, and she'd learned that he'd overheard enough of the conversation that had taken place between herself and Captain Merryweather to guess at her notion that Muldoon was behind the ugly work that was done. "Why should you defend the man who took over my—that is, Captain Merryweather's ship? You were there throughout the boarding and seizing, and you knew that Muldoon took me against my will."

"Yes, ma'am."

"And you were well aware of his black and murderous ways. A pirate. That's exactly what he is, and you know as well as the next man that a pirate has no respect for life."

"Ah, but Captain Muldoon is a man," answered Lawson. The way he pronounced the word, *man*, showed respect and admiration. "A pirate, yes," the lad continued. "But there's a world of difference between a man who hires himself out as a murderer and one who does it in the course of his business." He looked down at the little girl who walked along with her hand trustingly in his. Melly had immediately captivated Lawson and turned him into her willing slave. "Begging your pardon, Miss Garnet, and yours too, Mrs. Wills, but I must say that I have a deal more respect for a man like Happy Jack Muldoon than I have for the trull who mistreated this innocent child... for all that she's the wife of a respected man."

"If you care so much for Muldoon, then," Garnet said spitefully, "why don't you go to the Bermudas and ship on with him? Or go to his island out there beyond Charles Towne and await his coming? It has a name. Fairhaven. And that's where he's bound."

"No, ma'am. As long as I'm allowed, I'll continue to cast my lot with the two of you," answered Lawson. "I figure I owe you both. You spared me after I went along with the others who wanted to relieve you of the good Captain Merryweather's ship and goods. I'll not forget that you allowed me to live after the attempt was made to overthrow you. And I'll not forget that I owe my life to you, too, Mrs. Wills. If you hadn't seen to it that the earth was rid of Luis Cortez, I would have long ago been shark bait."

It was obvious to both women that the lad was sincere. It

was equally plain that he admired Muldoon enough to imitate him. Lawson had spent a great deal of his share of the spoils from *The Nightingale* on spotless white breeches, shirts, and waistcoats similar to Muldoon's. He tried to walk as Muldoon walked, and now he had taken to having his hair barbered in the same carefree style that Muldoon affected. His attempt to be a duplicate of the older man was sometimes humorous, often sad, for the boy would never reach his goal.

He was not exactly short of stature, but neither was he tall. He was freckle-faced and had features that were neither good nor bad. Except for his immaculate white clothing, he would never be noticed in a crowd, for he had nothing about him that was commanding or interesting. Yet both of the women had remarked that he was beginning to show some valuable traits. He was thoughtful and kind. And since Melly had been with them, he had turned scholarly. The four-year-old asked him many questions, and young Jack Lawson was determined to give her factual answers in spite of his own lack of knowledge. He was a reasonable hand when it came to ciphering, but the written word came hard.

During the two weeks they spent in Charles Towne, Lawson spent all of his spare time poring over the books he purchased at the store. When he didn't know a word, he hounded Garnet or Dell until they not only told him the meaning, but the proper way of saying it. Just as Dell admitted freely that she was addicted to tobacco, Lawson said he was addicted to book-reading. Unlike Dell, however, he could pursue his habit as much as he pleased as long as it didn't interfere with his duties. Dell grew edgy as the days passed because even the fresh tobacco made her queasy. She craved her smoke after a meal and before she retired for the night. But a second or two after she put a flame to the tobacco in her little pipe, she put it out with a sigh of regret and an expression of angered perplexity. It was unfathomable, she complained, how a small comfort that her entire being cried out for could turn on her in such a baffling manner.

Eight days after they arrived in Williamsburg, Dell Fields fainted dead away on the floor of a bootery where she'd gone to inquire after her mother and father-in-law. Even after she regained consciousness, the hot and crowded room was spinning.

"What has happened to me?" She looked up into a pair of ancient eyes, milky with an opaque film, and a countenance scored with lines. The face was so old that it looked neither masculine nor feminine, but a mixture of both. A world of compassion was in those eyes, but when the old mouth moved and a sound came out, the words were in a foreign tongue.

Dell looked up into the sea of concerned faces, afraid. "Garnet?" Memory was coming back to her. She'd been standing in front of a little counter, conversing with the shoemaker, and Garnet had been with her.

"I'm here, Dell." Dell turned her head and was washed in a sea of gratitude when she realized that her head was cradled on Garnet's lap.

"I swooned?" Her voice sounded strangely weak.

"Yes, but you'll be all right. It was brought on by this oppressive heat."

"Everything went black," Dell said, her voice thin and weak.

"But you're going to be all right," Garnet said.

Dell's eyes moved to the face of the old, old person who knelt down and continued to speak in a strange language.

"Please," Dell said when the shadowy syllables came to a stop. "This person is trying to tell me something, but I don't know the language."

A woman tittered. A man coughed. In her confusion, Dell tried to sit up, but a pair of frail hands that she realized belonged to the old one who was peering at her so intently pushed her down.

The shoemaker appeared in Dell's vision. His face was red as if he felt great shame in what he was about to say. "She is my great-grandmother and she speaks only Basque. She says you will be soon to get a baby-one."

"Oh, no," Dell said. "She is mistaken. I was—it was just—it was just the awful, unrelenting heat of the day. I'm sure she means well, but what she is saying is quite impossible." Again, she tried to sit up, but just as firmly, she was pushed back down.

"Tell them, Garnet, that I must be up and on my way," Dell said in a firmer voice.

The shoemaker looked distraught. "My great-grandmother, she say you stay down on back for three days, then you be all right, carry the baby you will soon to get all the way to the birthing."

"How absurd!" Frantically, Dell looked around the shoemaker's establishment. "I cannot stay *here* for three full days! And at any rate, your great-grandmother is mistaken!"

"She not mean you stay here on floor for full three days, missus," explained the man. "She say you get taken out of here by strong men and not walk on own feet. Got to inn where you must rest. And my great-grandmother is never mistaken. In Basque country, she be midwife for sixty year and now midwife in Colonies. She see all signs in ladies who soon going to get babies." He said something to the old woman, who spoke back with a number of gestures. The shoemaker translated. "She say only this time, at the now and here is to be careful. After three days, pouf! You back again in health very good. Is dangerous time for you just in now."

Before she was aware of what was taking place, strong men lifted Dell from the floor and carried her outside. She closed her eyes against the blazing sun as she was taken across the street and down two squares to the inn, a part of her feeling as if she were dreaming the whole thing. Behind her were the footsteps of what sounded like a hundred people, most of them women. They laughed and chattered, and called cheerily to others who were going about their daily business. She overheard them explaining joyfully that the tall, red-haired one was going to get a baby. Children ran along with the entourage, and they too took up the happy cry. When Dell risked a quick look around her, she was reassured that at least a few things in her world were operating normally. Garnet's hand was holding hers. She could hear Melly's excited questions concerning the strange turn of events that had taken place in the bootery. "Is Miss Dell really and truly going to get a baby? Where will she get it? Will it be soon? What color will its hair be? Will it like me? Will it want to take my golden earrings? Will we buy it at the baker-man's? Why must Miss Dell be carried? Is she sick?"

In between each question, Lawson's voice sounded, patient as always, but stumbling at times. Dell smiled. By the time her bearers had transported her to Holloway's Inn and all the people who had come along to make sure she was safely transported had reluctantly left them on the outside of the building, she was hard pressed to contain the bubbling bursts of laughter that threatened to explode from her throat. But she controlled herself long enough to thank the serious faced men who placed her gingerly on the bed, and maintained her silence until they had departed. Then she said to anyone who was interested, "I've never heard of anything so foolish in my life."

Garnet opened her mouth to answer, but Dell lifted her hand and pointed to Lawson. "Go to your room. I have some things to say to Garnet that are of a private nature."

The lad was so pale that every freckle on his face stood out very clearly. "You gave us all quite a turn, Mrs. Wills, ma'am." He put Melly down on the floor.

"*I* didn't turn," announced the child. "She didn't give *me* any turn."

"Not that kind of a turn, Melly," said Lawson.

"I want a turn," cried Melly. Even though she had been with them less than a month, Melly had grown accustomed to having her own way. She didn't know what was meant by giving someone a turn, but she didn't want to be left out of anything.

"Later, Melly," said Lawson with a fond pat on the child's head. "I'll come back in a moment and give you a turn around town."

As soon as he was out of the room, Dell said, "It was the *heat*, Garnet. The midwife is dead wrong. My flow is upon me at this moment, and it was the same last month."

Garnet stared at her, uncomprehending.

Dell spoke crossly. "Don't you know anything? When a woman is going to have a baby, her courses come to an end until the baby is born. That was the way it was when I had my precious little lost baby. It is the way of nature, understand? The blood goes into the making of the baby."

"I didn't know." Garnet smiled. "If you were a cow, or a horse or sheep, I would have more knowledge about it. No one ever told me anything about such things. Mating, yes. I've long been aware of the mating of animals, and after Muldoon, I...But is it always a thing that happens? I mean without fail, do the flows stop when one is going to birth a human baby?"

"*Always*," Dell said firmly.

"That's not what the old woman said. When you were unconscious, she explained everything to her grandson, who then repeated everything she said to me." Garnet's eyebrows came together as she tried to recall each word that was spoken. "According to her, some women do not show the signs until after the first two or three months. I suppose the cessation of the courses are one of the signs she meant. And she said that during the regular time of the flow, a woman who does not show the signs must take every precaution to be quiet. That she must not walk about, or work. At the time, the words meant little to me, for I was so frightened when you fell so heavily to the floor, without a shred of warning. But now—well, doesn't it make a little sense to you? What she was saying?"

"Fash! Certainly not!"

"You look angry. And also very strange. I suppose you would dislike having Muldoon's baby very much, in which case you must do the exact opposite of what the old woman instructed."

"Oh, I can't—No! I mean, *yes*! I dislike the idea of having a baby by *anyone*! Right now, I mean, when I am not—I don't have a husband and I've told everyone in Williamsburg I am a *widow*. I was talking to the good wife of the man who owns this inn and she was delighted to tell me about a young girl who was put into the stocks for the crime of having a baby out of wedlock. Mrs. Holloway pointed out the stocks to me and said that was where the young girl was forced to stand for twenty-four hours, with her head sticking through a little hole, her hands tied behind her back. The children pelted her with garbage."

"You've not said how long you've been a widow," Garnet reminded her. "Not here, nor in Charles Towne. And you've taken great care to wear mourning attire."

"Yes, but—"

"But if you don't want the baby, you can easily rid yourself of it," Garnet said matter-of-factly. One hand was behind her back, where she had her fingers crossed. "All you have to do is get up and walk around."

Dell gave her a scathing look. "You're being very foolish to take the prattle of an old, old woman seriously. I've had no sickness in the mornings and almost from the beginning when I was going to give birth to my daughter, I felt a tenderness in my breasts. Within a week after she was conceived, there were certain subtle changes within my body that let me dare to hope that I was going to be a mother. None of those things have manifested themselves, therefore I know I am right, the ancient midwife is wrong. But no. I would not deliberately miscarry. Not even Muldoon's child."

"You got sick when you smoked your little pipe," Garnet said.

"It's the fault of the tobacco, you idiot! Strange, isn't it? I mean, it is grown right here in the colonies, yet it has something wrong with it."

"Yes. Like the mixture you kept in the canister aboard ship. Gone bad, you said."

"I believe you actually *want* that old woman to be right, Garnet Shaw!"

Swiftly, Garnet left the foot of the bed and came to stand close to her. "Oh, Dell. Philadelphus Fields Wills! If you could only see the way you look. The rapture in your eyes is almost hurtful to see in spite of your barbed words, the cross sound of your voice. Speak the truth! Down deep in your heart, you hope the old woman is right."

"We have Melly," Dell said, "and already I adore that little imp. She's wrapped all three of us around her finger."

"And she knows it, too. But surely there's room in your heart to love another babe."

Holding her hands over her eyes to hide her hot and salty tears, Dell spoke through her sobs. "Not once, since I lost my baby girl, have I ever thought of having another child. I filled my mind with nothing but plans to avenge their deaths. There have been other men, aside from Muldoon. Not many, but—there have been times when I've wanted to die from loneliness, and...but I did not conceive. But—no. I'll remain quiet for three days, just in case. I'll do it to please you, Garnet, because it's clear that you feel I must. Afterwards, I'll get up and go about my business. We must not give up on my search. Garnet, you're so very apparent. Every emotion you feel is as easy to read as—that sampler on the wall. You would be very hurt if I didn't carry out that foolish Basque woman's instructions."

Sixteen

Three days later, Dell arose from her bed, irritable after prolonged inactivity.

"I'm not going to fall on my face, Garnet! Stop hovering over me, will you?" She felt the room whirl for a moment, but she was determined to get back on her feet. "Being confined to bed is unhealthy for a woman who has been accustomed to strenuous acitvity, you know." Dell sighed. "But I did what you wanted."

Melly danced around the room, pleased and happy because her adored Miss Dell was back to normal. During the past few days she had spent most of her time with Lawson in order to allow Dell peace and quiet in the daytime. Garnet had brought Dell her meals, forced her to use a cumbersome bedpan and acted the part of nurse.

"Really, I feel quite fit," Dell said as she walked determinedly across the room to a chair. "It's just that it'll take me a while to regain my strength."

"I know my letters," Melly said. "Lawson taught me. A, B, C, D, E, F, eleven. Is that good?"

"That's fine, sweetheart," Dell said.

"Come, Melly," Garnet said, "we'll go downstairs to the tavern and have breakfast. And we'll bring Miss Dell hers."

"I'm starved," Dell said dramatically. In spite of the trays that Garnet had brought to her during the time she spent in bed, hunger pangs and the idea of something more substantial than the milk sop and soft cooked eggs was very appealing to her. But when Garnet brought a tray with ham, fried potatoes, quince jelly and biscuits, Dell took one look and heaved.

"Oh, my God," she said after Garnet had washed the tears from her eyes that came from the bilious attack. "It's true! I think I shall die. Take it *away*! The smell of that ham is... Oh!" After another fit of dry heaves, she tottered to the bed and covered her face with the bed covering. For a full week, Dell suffered with morning sickness far worse than she'd had when she carried her first baby. Her sickness left promptly at seven o'clock each evening, and she ate everything she could between seven and midnight.

The Basque woman came on the morning of the eighth day, less than an hour after Garnet went to her and begged for her help. She was accompanied by a plump great-granddaughter who instructed Dell to drink a cup of liquid that looked vile, but smelled faintly of mint. "Grandmama says to sip slow," said the girl. "One sip, then lie back on pillow. Then you take one bite of dry bread, here. Then the tea, just one sip. Then the dry bread. It stops the sickness."

By then, Dell would have gladly tossed down a gallon of clabbered milk, which she detested, or anything else that might help. The taste of the tea was not unpleasant, and a calming sensation followed the first taste.

The young woman instructed Garnet in the preparation of the brew and promised that if Dell drank a cup every morning upon arising and ate one half a crust of dry bread, she would suffer no more. The remedy worked like magic. Every morning, Garnet prepared the tea and Dell gratefully drank it. Within a few days she was strong and healthy enough to resume going about the village of Williamsburg in quest of her husband's people.

The innkeeper's wife had asked around during Dell's illness and that good and gossipy woman seemed about to burst with her news, once Dell was up and about again. "The Wills man died," she said, assuming a pious expression. "Died just a day or two after they got here to the settlement. And the widow went on up to the East. An odd one, she was, or so they say. Belonged to a strange set of folks that held with an odd belief, and wanted to be with others of her kind. Etienne LeMonte's woman, Mercy, says she knew Mrs.

Wills well. Mercy LaMonte says she'll give you a letter of writing Mrs. Wills sent to her some months back, and it'll tell you right exactly where she's at, there in the cold lands where foolish folks settled."

The news of Dell's condition had quickly spread about the village, and the innkeeper's wife was curious about the exact date of the death of Dell's late husband, which she asked about slyly:

"Your poor, dead man. What happiness he would derive if he only could have lived to see his baby. And when was it you said he left this earthly coil?"

Dell, knowing very well she'd never breathed a word of the exact time of her beloved's death, was undisturbed by the craning neck, the eager eyes of the woman. She answered, "Just before we set sail, which is why I came. It's natural for me to want to be with his parents. Doubly so now, that I find I am with child."

In private, she told Garnet they would have to hurry about journeying to the Massachusetts Bay Colony. "That dear, good woman must never know about my condition, and a few months hence, it will show. We'll stay a month with her, then find a place to live where we'll be safe from prying eyes and wagging tongues." By her own calculations, Dell doubted if she was more than a month and a half along. She was slender as a sylph at the moment, but experience had taught her she'd not be slender much longer.

Before they left Williamsburg, Dell went to pay her respects to her father-in-law's grave. The preacher accompanied her to the burying grounds, where she placed a wreath at the marker and knelt, for a moment, in silent grief. The preacher was a kind and thoughtful man. "Mr. Wills was not a member of my flock," he said, "but no matter. He was a godly man, and in all truth I've never known better Christians than the Willses. I was sorry to see Mrs. Wills leave Williamsburg, but I can't say as I blame her since most of the residents looked upon their faith as intolerably wrong, even sinful. A sorry state, indeed, when one considers the reason this New World was settled."

Until she had actually gone to the graveyard where Tom's father was buried, Dell had been unable to accept his death.

"I would be very proud," she said to the preacher, "if I could give my Melly and my babe a home foundation as solid as Mr. and Mrs. Wills gave their children, and later, to me." She wanted to buy or build a house within walking distance of Tom's mother, but of course that was out of the question. The Wills' religious persuasion negated a widow's marriage since they believed that those who were joined in holy wedlock were bound eternally, even after death. Which was why she wouldn't take Garnet's suggestion that she pretend to have married again and was once more a widow. She would keep the knowledge that she had turned her back on the faith from her mother-in-law, just as she would not let her know of the baby she carried or any of her past activities. Never would she cause the woman who had been like a mother to her a moment's pain.

When Dell took the vows, the idea of preceding Tom in death or having him precede her was not frightening, because she believed with all of her young heart as his parents and he did: the wife or husband goes on to prepare a place in heaven for his spouse. But when Tom was murdered, Dell felt she had lost every shred of the faith she had so willingly embraced. Now and then she experienced a twinge or two of longing for the solid ground of the faithful, however. In the Wills home she had been taught to hold no human in bondage, for the act of enslaving another was an abomination unto the Lord. Her high-handed manner of rescuing Melly was instinctive, and so was her inability to accept the plight of the other slaves who abounded in the new land; but she had common sense enough to know she was incapable of leading all the slaves into freedom. Yet she often found herself wishing she could do just that.

Other changes were taking place within Philadelphus Fields Wills. As the days passed while they waited for a ship that would take them to the Massachusetts Bay Colony she found it more and more difficult to make practical decisions, and she was prone to emotions that she considered weak and undesirable. Tears filled her eyes at the magic beauty of a single rose. Melly's swiftness at learning the lessons Lawson taught her caused Dell to react with unabashed sobs of pride and tenderness. When Garnet put together a few garments for the baby, Dell was so touched that she wept for an hour.

"Soft," she confided to Rilla Mayfield, who would accompany them on their journey, "I'm turning soft as butter. Before, when I carried a babe, I was not prone to weeping spells and periods of foolish weakness, so why on earth do I find myself behaving so this time?"

Rilla Mayfield was a spinster who would never get a husband, not even in a land where men far outnumbered women. She was born lame, had lost all her teeth before she was sixteen, and was further hampered by a speech impediment that caused her to talk as if she had a mouthful of hot soup. At forty, she had resigned herself to living out her days with a brother and sister-in-law who resented her presence, so she'd jumped at the chance to accompany the rich and beautiful women wherever they decided to go. Dell had promised her a lifetime position as nurse to the little ones and chaperone to herself and her "cousin." Then she'd said, "It's possible that my dear cousin may marry, of course, seeing that she's much sought after by the young men, but I will always provide for you, Rilla. As long as I live."

It was true that young women didn't customarily travel alone, but Dell's reasons for adding Rilla Mayfield to her household had nothing to do with custom. She had learned that Rilla did all the household chores for her sister-in-law, which included the cooking, cleaning, sewing, spinning, and carding—as well as the care of the eight Mayfield children. She was also expected to pick bayberries during the season, and spent many hours each day at the hard labor of making the bayberries into candles, which was the family business. She'd had the look of a starveling about her when Dell saw her at the candlemaker's. After a few discreet inquiries around Williamsburg, Dell learned about the woman's hard life at the hands of her brother and his wife, so she'd made the offer. After being with Dell and Garnet for only three days, she was already beginning to fill out, but she could not answer Dell's question about her strange behavior.

"Law me, Missus," she said in her ill-formed words, "the Lord works in mysterious ways. My brother's good wife came off different with each one of her youngins. Sick all through the first one. Wasn't hardly able to lift her head off the pillow for nine full months, but she was sweet as blackberry wine. Turned sour as vinegar with the second one, but never knew a minute of sickness. Acted crazy as a bedbug when she carried her third, and got as fat as a pig, too, for she ate all the time. But when the fourth one came along, she never knew a day when she was hungry, and I'll never forget how she worked herself half to death, like she was driven by the Divvel himself. Each time she got cotched she got different, and I'm thankful I'll be well out of it the next time around, for the last time was the worst of them all. She spent the whole time wringing her hands and praying to die, she was that miserable with a burning in her chest."

To Garnet, Rilla said that she could see nothing odd about Mrs. Wills' behavior, and in private, Garnet said she surmised that the true ways of Dell Wills had come out with the acknowledgment of being with child.

"She was different, then, was she? Before she got cotched?"

Garnet smiled. "She tried very hard to show herself as a woman of great strength and power in order to survive. After a while, I think she fell into the habit of presenting a hard, cold mask to the world... but now that she no longer has to maintain a mask, she's probably relieved at the idea of being womanly."

"Well, I've seen a sight of women go through the long months of waiting and the birthing at the end, but I've never in my life seen one as pleased as Mrs. Wills. Nor as lovely, either."

Dell glowed. Her complexion had been flawless to begin with, but with the passing of each day she took on an ethereal look more intent than that of the day before. Some of the Williamsburg women were displeased with the threat of two single and beautiful woman in their midst. Dell received numerous proposals of marriage in spite of the fact that everyone in town knew she expected a child. Garnet also received offers of marriage. Dell paid no heed to the Williamsburg men who flocked around them. She was of the opinion that the swains were primarily interested in the gold inside their chests and none of the swains interested Garnet.

Garnet was impatient to board the ship that would take

them to Boston Harbor, and thence to Roxbury, to Dell's mother-in-law. Her desire to be gone increased after a maiden and her mother stopped her on the street and asked if she and the red-haired women were soon to depart Williamsburg. Their murderous expressions and hostile attitudes made it clear that the women in the village resented the attention the newcomers were getting from the male population.

The journey aboard *The Sprightly Lassie* passed without incident. Both Garnet and Dell remained close to their cabin while Melly delighted crew and passengers with her antics, Rilla Mayfield and Lawson in attendance.

It was late afternoon when they left the ship and went immediately to a livery stable where they rented a conveyance that would take them to Roxbury. Now that they were growing closer to the reunion she had longed for, Dell's spirits were even higher than they'd been before. Her color was vivid as they entered the outskirts of the village. "I can't wait, " she said excitedly. "I do hope she lives in the village proper, for I think I shall burst if we're directed out in the country." Intently, she looked at the cottages that lined the tree-shaded streets and wondered if they were passing by the very house she sought.

The town square bustled with activity in spite of the lateness of the hour. It was a clean and neat place. Not as up-to-date as Williamsburg, Dell remarked, but she was impressed with the looks of the place. "They're an industrious people," she said with approval. "Exactly the kind of place in which Tom's mother would choose to spend her widowhood."

Lawson brought the horses to a stop in front of the town hall. Even though the dark of night was not quite upon the land, the windows in the sturdily-built meeting place already glowed with candle light. People were entering the building, and Dell said it was an ideal place to ask directions to the Wills house since so many townsfolk were assembled there. "Do be as quick as possible, Lawson," she said. "This one time, don't become involved in a conversation. Just ask direction to the Mrs. Thaddeus Wills house, thank kindly whoever gives it to you, and come back."

After Lawson had disappeared inside the town hall, Dell tapped her toes against the carriage floor. He returned with a tall, thin man dressed in black. Quickly, the two men walked to the carriage.

"This is the Reverend Sanders," said Lawson. He sounded as if someone had a hard grip around his throat.

The Reverend stood ramrod straight on the ground while Lawson climbed up and took the reins. In a rasping voice that dripped with venom, the preacher addressed himself to Dell: "Mrs. Wills was an undesirable, along with the others of her peculiar beliefs. They had built themselves a settlement to the east of town where they practiced their ungodly rites and spoiled the air for miles around. Last week, a group of worthy citizens took matters into their own hands and rid this peaceful place of the stench of those who defiled the name of God by fornicating out of wedlock and other sinful deeds. Mrs. Wills—vile woman!—had taken in a man who was not her husband. She tried to excuse her wickedness by saying the man was old and sick, that she gave him shelter and succor out of the goodness of her heart, but we knew her kind just as we knew the ones who came here before her. Even now, the pollution of their lustful and sinful ways hangs like a pall of brimfire over this peaceful village. The meeting tonight has to do with God's work that was done in dealing with these Philistines."

Dell leaned forward, stunned. Most of the words the man had spoken were a meaningless jumble to her, but one phrase burned into her brain. She spoke it. "Rid this peaceful place? In what manner did the godly citizens act, pray tell me?"

"They burned them all out," thundered the Reverend Sanders. "Those who escaped the work of the righteous and God-fearing are scattered to the winds." The horrible man raised his fist. "And there, by God's will, they shall perish! No man in his right mind will take them in."

"You killed them!" Dell's scream rent the air. "*Killed*! My husband's mother was a good and true Christian, and she was *murdered*!" Together, Garnet and Rilla Mayfield restrained her from jumping out of the carriage and attacking the man.

Garnet took command. "Whip the horses, Lawson!" She

cried out the order as she struggled to keep Dell inside the carriage. Lawson applied the whip and sent the carriage away at a great speed, but the sound of the wheels against the road and the fast clip-clop of hooves were not loud enough to obliterate the threatening words of the preacher, who shouted that no friends or relatives of those who called themselves the Gentle Christians were welcome in Roxbury. As they sped out of the village, Garnet could hear the man's voice for a long, long time.

"They're crazy," Lawson said. "He told me God had spoken directly to him and ordered him to slay the sinful and set fire to their homes. He was the ring-leader in the burning and slaughter, I'll bet you anything."

"Go toward the east," Dell said. "I want to see that place where she lived. If she survived, we'll find her."

Lawson wanted to find an inn where the ladies and Melly would be safe for the night while he went in search of the ruined settlement, but Dell would not hear of it. Obediently, Lawson took the fork in the road that would carry them due east. Within a half-hour, they came to a devastated area that lay dark and desolate under the light of the full moon. Not a cottage had been left standing, and there was no sign of life. Dell insisted on getting out and walking among the ruins. There had been seven small houses, but nothing was left of them save for a few collapsed roofs that had fallen in upon the burning buildings.

"England," Dell said in a voice so hollow that it brought goose flesh to Garnet's arms and the nape of her neck. "This is a harsh and ugly place, for the people who have settled here have made it so. I want my baby to be born in England. But first, we must search high and low. Tom's mother may be wandering around in the wilderness, lost and hungry. Homeless and confused. We will wait until daybreak, then we'll go through the rubble, piece by piece. If she died in this carnage, she must have a decent burial."

"I will search," Lawson said firmly. "You are not strong enough to withstand the sight of—whatever remains."

Dell lifted her head heavenward, and the sound that came out of her throat began low and deep before it rose to a high, piercing scream that filled the moon-bright night, then fell gradually to a lower note before it arose again. There, under the moon, Dell keened and wailed, while the others stood by helplessly, understanding without knowing how they understood, that this mad, eerie expression of her grief and disappointment was necessary to the woman who stood among them and mourned her dead.

They had passed an inn some few miles before they reached Roxbury, and that was where Lawson took them. Dell did not protest, but when morning came, she refused to allow Lawson to go back to the settlement of the Gentle Christians without her. Rilla remained at the inn with Melly, but Garnet went with Dell and Lawson, carrying shrouds against what they might find.

Bare moments after they arrived at the scene, they found the remains of Mrs. Thaddeus Wills. In silence, Dell directed Lawson to dig a grave. In silence, she and Garnet wrapped the frail fire-blackened body in linen. When they placed the body in the ground, Dell whimpered. Garnet uttered a simple prayer, and the three of them solemnly returned the mounded earth to the hole. Before dusk fell, they had found five more bodies, each one of which they wound in a shroud, then buried.

"We will come back," Dell said, "with markers for their graves. But we'll not go to Roxbury. We'll get them in Boston. When I am once again in England, I will rest easy, for we will have done our best for the mortal remains of good people and true."

They were on their way back from Boston, the conveyance heavy with tombstones and all their possessions, when they were overtaken by highway-men. Lawson was killed outright as he fought manfully to send the horses charging through the mass of men who had stopped them with firearms. Rilla Mayfield was shot in the chest. She expired within the hour, while Dell attempted to staunch the flow of blood that seeped from her chest and Garnet attended to Melly. The child appeared to be nigh unto death from the piece of metal that had smashed into her shoulder. She rallied shortly after the Mayfield woman died.

Lawson lay sprawled on the ground. They had dragged Rilla Mayfield to a shady place under a tree where they worked over her. Melly was weak and feverish. Her eyes were glassy. Garnet said, "We'll have to bury them."

Dell didn't answer.

"We have nothing but the wrecked carriage," Garnet said. "They even killed the horses."

Dell stared off into space.

Garnet put out her hand and touched Dell's cheek. "Oh, please! Can't you see that I can't do what must be done without your help? For the love of God, listen to what I'm saying!"

Dell sat down on a fallen tree trunk and hummed tunelessly.

"We have nothing," Garnet cried. "They took our gold, our clothing! Dell, don't just sit there! We have Melly to think of. Your unborn baby!"

Dell picked a few pieces of grass, which she braided carefully. All of her attention was riveted upon the way she crossed one stem over the other, then repeated the process.

Part 3

Seventeen

As I vainly tried to get some kind of response from Dell, it occurred to me that I had come full circle. A few years ago I was penniless and knew not which way to turn. This time, the situation seemed worse, for at least after my father's disappearance I had been responsible for no one but myself, and I had been in the land of my birth. Looking back, I realize I was very close to the breaking point as I stood in the road where the highwaymen had taken two lives and left us bereft of all our possessions—which included a way to get back to Boston. I was sorely tempted to sit myself down at Dell's side and join her in the insane braiding of grass. If it had not been for Melly, moaning softly from the pain of her wound, I believe I would have given up the never-ending fight for mere existence. But she was little and hurt, and she depended on me. Dell, too, needed assistance, and I was mindful of the life which was growing within her as I told myself firmly that I couldn't just stand there all day long and look at Lawson's body.

For a young man who was built on the slight side, he was uncommonly heavy as I dragged him out of the road, my emotions so devastated that I could not even find relief in tears. Back at the scene of the burning and killing of the Gentle Christians, the soil had been well tended, and digging a grave had not proved difficult. Anyway, Lawson had done most of the work. Looking down at his face, relaxed in death, I was reminded of Dell's casual statement that the lad had loved me. If he had, he'd never spoken of it, but he'd given his life to protect those of us who lived through the horror of being accosted by highwaymen, and as I tried to dig a hole into the unyielding earth with a stick, I found myself remembering all the many acts of kindness he'd performed, but especially his unswerving devotion to the mite of a girl who had come to us. The sound of my voice came as a shock when I realized I was talking to him, and him dead. "Lawson, oh, Lawson, if you could only help me now."

My back ached and I was weak with fatigue by the time I had made a shallow indentation into the stubborn ground. It wasn't deep enough. Wild animals would find him and I couldn't abide that. I rested for a moment, and again tried to arouse Dell from her strange withdrawal. She remained as before, apparently as witless as an infant as she braided, then re-braided, long spears of grass. When I was once again digging into the ground, my senses froze in terror as I heard a horse approaching. The rider seemed to be bent on getting wherever he was going in a hurry, and was upon us before I had a chance to do any more than wish I had taken Dell and Melly deeper into the thickets where they'd not be seen.

He was a tall man with a russet-colored beard and hair to match, and I drew a breath of relief when he took a look at the battered carriage, cast a glance toward the dead, and dismounted, his expression saddened and appalled at the sight. I was standing above the place where I was trying to dig a grave, and I was so morbidly confused that all I could do was stay where I was as he advanced toward me.

"Mistress, what has taken place on this spot? Surely a young woman such as yourself is not responsible for this carnage!"

Taken aback, I shook my head and immediately burst into tears. "We were stopped by men with firearms. They killed our servants, and badly wounded the little girl. Then they took our gold, and all of our possessions, and shot the horses before they left."

The man had a pick and shovel tied onto his saddle. He said he was Isaiah Mathew, of Roxbury, as he removed the tools and went at once to the place where I had struggled with my ineffective stick. "You're too small to set yourself to such a task. I didn't know there were foot-pads abroad; I've heard nothing of it."

Roxbury! I wondered if he had taken part in the massacre where Dell's mother-in-law and all the others were murdered.

"I'm Garnet Shaw," I answered. "From England." Dell's profile was turned to him. She didn't appear to be aware of his presence. "And this is my cousin, Dell Wills, and our... Mrs. Wills' adopted daughter, Melly," I added as I gestured toward the child. "My cousin has suffered so greatly from the shock of seeing our servants murdered that she... has turned mute."

The man gave Dell an understanding look. "It happens that way to some of us. 'Wills,' you said. A Mrs. Thaddeus Wills lived over yonder." He pointed toward the ruined settlement. "I'm heading there. When I returned to town I learned of an awful thing the townsfolk did. My brother was married last week, and I was in Boston for the wedding. When I returned, I was sickened at...But you don't need to hear of sad and brutal happenings. You've enough worries of your own. I'm sure the names are coincidence." He made short shrift of cutting away the roots that had stymied me, and soon had a fitting grave where poor gallant Lawson would rest through eternity. Before I hardly knew what he was about, he had lifted Lawson into his arms and was carrying him toward the grave. "So young, this lad. It's a pity and a waste for a man to die when he is in the bud of his youth."

"He was more to me than mere servant," I said. "We'd been together through a good deal of strife."

"There are coins in his waistcoat, Mistress Shaw," said Isaiah Mathew. "I heard them jingle when I lifted him. You said the highwaymen took all you owned, and even though it may seem an indelicate thing to do at a time like this, the poor lad will not be needing his gold and you will."

I could not speak over the lump in my throat. With great tenderness, the stranger went through Lawson's pockets and found several shillings as well as a gold dragoon, which he gave me. Then he lowered Lawson into the ground and immediately bent to the task of digging again.

After the dirt had been mounded and tamped down over both graves, Mr. Mathew looked at me out of earnest blue eyes and asked if I could describe the highwaymen, but I could not, for they had all worn stockings over their faces, with round holes cut out for eyes and mouth. "There were many of them. Sixteen, I think," I said. Maybe fifteen or seventeen. It happened so quickly, I couldn't really—"

"No matter. Now we must talk about getting you back to... England is a long way and passage is costly. Your cousin will probably take a few weeks to recover from her shock, and the little one needs the attention of a doctor. There's a doctor in Roxbury, which is not far from here."

"No, I can't go there. The Mrs. Thaddeus Wills you spoke of—she was the mother of my cousin's husband. And you've no need to go to see about giving them a Christian burial, for we were on our way back from doing that. We learned of the tragedy after we came into Roxbury, which was where we planned to visit with Mrs. Wills."

"It was the devil's own shameful deed was done that night," said Mr. Mathew. "I knew Mrs. Wills well. The man she sheltered and fed was very old, and dying. He had lost both his legs in a scrap with the Indians. Arrows had pierced them both. There was no wrong-doing in that house. She meant only to make his last days comfortable." He looked at me oddly. "So you buried them. You and the lad, the other ladies. Was there—will you be kind enough to tell me if there was a girl of about fourteen, with hair the shade of mine among the dead?"

I shook my head, for I had seen no young girl who answered to that description. "The dead were middle-aged, or beyond."

"My sister. She was not well enough to travel to Boston with me for my brother's wedding, and since she was young and pretty, I felt she would be safer with the good folk at the settlement than to stay alone in our house in town." He looked very relieved.

"We saw no young people at all, and we searched the wreckage well enough to make sure we'd left no one for the beasts to find."

"I dare to hope that my sister escaped into the wilderness, then. I must begin my search, but I can't very well leave you here all alone, with a wounded child and another woman who is not quite—"

"You've done more than enough," I said. "My cousin is tractable, I think. We'll walk back to Boston. Between us, we can carry the little girl when she grows tired of walking. I had the papers for ship's passage in my pocket. The robbers took my jewels, but I'm sure they did not notice the deep pockets on my frock, otherwise they'd have taken the papers." I also had a few coins inside my bodice and Dell never went anywhere without a goodly sum of silver and gold in the belt she wore around her middle.

Before the young man would allow us to set out toward Boston, he insisted that I get Dell to her feet. She sprang right up with a merry laugh on her lips, and dropped to the ground the grass she'd been braiding. I told her we must walk to Boston. She nodded, smiled, and began to trudge along as if she hadn't a care in the world. The most heart-rending thing about the oddness of her was that she seemed to have forgotten all about Melly.

"You have been very kind," I said to Isaiah Mathew. "At a time when your own heart was heavily burdened, you took time to do something that would have taken me hours and hours without help or tools. I am grateful. So very grateful. And I pray that you find your sister soon, and that she is well."

"Godspeed, Mistress Shaw," he answered.

During that long, hot trek toward Boston, I thought about Isaiah Mathew's kindness. It was soothing. Far more restful than to consider the future, which loomed before me like a big, black void.

Eighteen

Dawn on Christmas Day was breathtakingly beautiful, with a cerise sky above the burning sun that rose to bathe all of Fairhaven Island in a pink-gold haze. I awakened when it was still dark, to replenish the wood in the fireplace. Once I was up, I decided against going back to bed, mindful of the tasks I had set for myself on that day. There was a goose to stuff and bake, sweet potatoes to roast, bread to make as well as the Christmas pudding I had promised Melly.

In all truth, we had not fared so badly as I had feared we would when I decided we would go to Fairhaven. Muldoon was a lot of things, but he was not one to bear a grudge, and even though Dell had set him and his aunt off in the Bermudas, I doubted that he would turn us off his island if he came and found us there. Dell was in no position to gainsay my decision. She continued to be removed from herself and either could not or would not speak when I kept after her during the voyage back to the Carolinas. So our choice of abode was up to me and I settled on Fairhaven because our supply of money was scant and what little we had would be needed for food and clothing instead of a place to live.

The island was not where I had believed it to be, which was hard by Charles Towne. When I made inquiries of the officials concerning an island that had once belonged to Lord Muldoon, but had been settled on his son, Jonathan, I was directed to the settlement of Awendaw, close to Bull Bay. According to the maps, the island I sought lay close to Georgetown, and a narrow stip of land that extended from the island like a pointing finger was less than a mile from Cape Romain Harbor, which gave me heart. The village of Romain would be less than a half-hour away, by row-boat.

The land agent asked questions I was not prepared to answer, but I muddled through with half-truths, claiming kinship with Lord Muldoon and lying shamelessly, but firmly, stating that Young Lord Muldoon had given us leave to settle on his island but I had lost the papers to highwaymen. His attitude was one of disinterest, more than anything else, and he let me know that he cared very little about the holdings of titled gentry. "The settlers at Romain call it Shipwrecked Sailor Island," he said. "But if it pleases you to say it is Fairhaven, it's nothing to me."

I was ready to build some kind of crude shelter, but to my pleased surprise I found a little hut already there, sufficient for summer and fall but apparently long unoccupied; and by the time winter came the three of us had made it snug enough to withstand the cold.

The settlers at Romain Village told me the hut was built years ago by a shipwrecked sailor. He'd died there, a hermit and an eccentric, seldom coming into the harbor village except for supplies, and never saying any more than he had to. They also made allusions to his ghost, which was believed to roam about the island for more than ten years after he died. If so, I never saw it, nor did I hear the unearthly shrieks and cries that were said to frighten anyone foolish enough to spend a night there. As far as I was concerned, I was glad the shade was said to reside there, since the fear of it kept undesirables away.

With the few pieces of silver and gold that had been in Lawson's possession, together with the shillings that were inside the lining of Dell's bodice, I purchased necessities. The goat gave milk and I taught myself to make cheese. We had chickens for eggs, and one cock. I bought the pair of geese because they were cheap, and I hoped we would someday have goslings. I planted a vegetable garden and was rewarded with a fine crop of corn, potatoes, turnips, beets and beans. There were some strange looking fruits that grew on the island, but although they were pretty to look at, I was afraid to chance eating them. They were red in color, about the size of a small plum, and heart-shaped. There were also berries that I recognized, which made fine jams when combined with the sugar I bought on the mainland. It was necessary for me to be very frugal with the money I had left after purchasing such things as a rowboat, pottery, cutlery, pewter spoons and bedding. Throughout the summer we slept on the ground of the hut, our beds made of fragrant pine needles. Melly complained. Dell said nothing. During those first few weeks, I often looked speculatively at Melly's gold earrings and considered bartering them for dress material, but I was holding them out as the last thing to go. A kind of cushion to fall back on, if needed, but I also didn't want to cause the child the grief of losing her precious ornaments. God knows she had little else to take comfort from during those first bleak weeks, and even though the highwaymen had relieved Dell and me of our jewels, they'd not touched Melly's.

When we were equipped with the bare necessitites for survival, I still had enough coin to purchase two lengths of dress goods as well as an assortment of embroidery floss.

It shamed me to wear my frayed and soiled gown into the village in order to show the two beautiful costumes I had created, but I had no choice. My work would sell itself, and before I could even think of sewing something for myself, Dell, or Melly, I had to get the money for my work. I had no trouble selling the gowns to the women of Romain.

Each time I rowed across to sell my wares, I had good luck. After I made a sale I invested in more cloth, embroidery floss, beads, bangles, and other findings. I felt a great sense of accomplishment on the day that I was at last able to afford to buy goods to make frocks for the three of us, and Melly's proved to be an asset. I took her with me to show her off and to give her an outing. By then it was late October, and the poor child had not been off the island in all that time. She was vivacious and charming in her orange watered silk and the very minute the good matrons of Romain clapped eyes on her garments, they ordered something similar for their own children.

The day Dell came back to herself, I was cutting out an order for three sets of pantaloons and shirts for little boys, and my work was in progress for girls' clothing. During all that time, Dell had not uttered a single word, and I was beginning to grow accustomed to her silence. Melly talked incessantly, and she continued to beg for books when we went to Romain, which she chose as a treat over sweetmeats. It pleased me to listen to Melly's voice as she read aloud. Dell sat, as usual, on a pallet on the floor and stared off into space. When Melly came to a word she mispronounced, I was startled to hear Dell correct the child. In my surprise, I dropped the scissors.

Just as if she'd never fallen into silence, Dell said in her old, teasing way, "Garnet, you're so careless! You could have cut off your toe!"

Looking down, I saw that one point of the scissors had just missed my foot. It was my turn to be speechless. I stared and stared at her. Melly did, too, but she regained her senses quickly. As she ran to Dell, her little face was aglow with happiness. "Miss Dell! You talked!" The child flung her arms around Dell and smothered her face with kisses. Dell responded by hugging Melly tightly to her breast and laughing and crying, both at the same time.

After a while, she said, "I've been away."

My legs had turned to water, so I had to sit down. "Yes," I said. "You've been away."

"I was here..." Dell looked thoughtful. "I mean, I've not *really* been gone, but a part of me was missing. It isn't that I've not been aware of all the things that have taken place, but I couldn't force myself to speak, or to lift a hand to help you." She frowned as if she were trying to figure out how to explain what had happened to her, how she'd felt. After a while, she said, "I can't describe it. I've felt as if I've been hamstrung, although I knew I was free. And each time I tried to utter a sound, my throat closed up and my tongue refused to work. Is it October?"

"Yes, Dell. It's October," I answered.

"The baby. It will be born in December, if I've reckoned right. You've done well, Garnet, taking care of a madwoman and a child." She stood up and began to pace restlessly around the tiny space, speaking of the winter to come, the work that we must do on the hut in order to close out the cold and the rain. After so long a time of silence, she was slightly prone to babbling, but I understood that she was trying to catch up on all the things that had gone unsaid for so long.

That evening after we finished our supper, it was Dell who jumped up and put the water on the hook in the fireplace to heat for the dishes. "It's only fair that I do the housework, Garnet, now that I'm well. You're the breadwinner."

She wanted her pipe. I promised to bring her tobacco and a new pipe when I went into town again; then I suggested that she accompany me. She said it would be a while before she would be ready to talk to other folks. Before we went to sleep that night, she announced that she would name her baby Thomas, in memory of her husband, and Garner, after me. Then she said she had dreamed she would have the child on Christmas Day.

For Christmas dinner, we had the goose, sweet potatoes, corn, and a prune pudding, a welcome change from our standard fare of seafood, hominy, and turnips or beets from the hole I had dug where I stored root vegetables. Melly's gifts were few, but she was happy with an orange, glazed pecans, bonbons and the baby doll Dell and I had made for her in secret.

Keeping anything secret from Melly took the patience of Job and the magic of a wizard, but working together, we'd managed. Dell had cleverly fashioned a head, feet and hands out of papier maché. After the parts were sufficiently hardened, she boiled onion skins with which she tinted the skin. Beet juice gave the cheeks a blush as well as the rosebud mouth. The hair was sparse, as befitted a newborn babe, and looked very realistic after Dell had stained it with tobacco juice, but the eyes were absolutely marvelous. There were wisps of lower and upper lashes, brows, and even a tender pink tear duct at each corner. For the eye color, Dell experimented with all sorts of vegetable dyes until she'd made a pair of eyes as dark brown as Melly's own, or mine. After the doll was assembled with a cloth body stuffed with sawdust from the mill in Romain, I dressed it in a lacy christening gown and wrapped it in a blanket. When Melly first saw it, she said, "Is it little Thomas, born already and wanting me to love him?" It did look almost as if it would begin to cry at any moment, for it was that realistic. Which gave me an idea. Since Dell was talented at making heads, hands and feet, why wouldn't the mothers and fathers of the children of Romain be willing to buy these cunning babies for them? It was too late for this Christmas, but there were birthdays, and we could charge at least a shilling for each one, providing it was outfitted.

That came later, of course. Dell was once again her old strongwilled self. She had no doubts about her baby being born on Christmas Day and she was so positive that I believed her. I was elated when I saw the dawn come up so bright and cheery. To me, it presented a good omen. I was not superstitious about the ghost of the shipwrecked sailor, but I accepted the bounty of nature, and the day promised to be perfect for the birthday of Christ as well as Thomas Garner.

The twenty-fifth of December came and went, and Dell slept serenely through the night. By then we'd been able to purchase a proper bed, which was a welcome change as the weather turned colder. I didn't sleep because I expected her pains to start and I was more than apprehensive. I was afraid I wouldn't be able to cope with childbirth.

Without consulting Dell, I had made arrangements with the midwife in Romain Village. I would fly a red flag in the tree that faced the mainland if I needed her. The piece of bright red cloth was ready and waiting. I had a length of rope tied to one corner and I had already practiced throwing it up to catch the rope on a branch and had grown rather proficient at the art.

On the twenty-sixth day of December, Dell awakened, rosy and lovely, the picture of one who has rested well. She said, "You look like the wrath of God. You're not coming down with the fevers, I hope."

"No, but I hardly closed my eyes all night long. I was afraid you'd begin the birthing."

"Oh. Well, it just goes to show that you can't depend on dreams."

On the last day of the year, a strong gale blew in from sea. We were snug and warm in our house, and we complimented ourselves for having the foresight to chink all the cracks in the logs of the new room we'd built and for taking pains when we built the fireplace. By midnight, the howling wind sounded like a pack of wild animals, but we were comfortable under our warm bed coverings, Melly between us. Sometime in the night, I awakened and put logs on the fire against the penetrating cold winds. Not a peep was heard out of Melly or Dell, and I was very quiet as I crept back to bed. When I awakened again, I had dreamed that Sime the cat was outside and crying to get in, but there she was, at the foot of our bed as always, giving me a baleful look out of her dazzling blue eyes because I touched her with my feet as I scrambled up, mindful of the cold and afraid the fire had gone out.

Melly stirred in her sleep, but Dell was already out of bed. I assumed she had gone to the privy. Again, I heard the cry that had awakened me, and it did sound similar to Sime's low-pitched yowl. Without stopping for shoes or a wrap, I dashed outside to the privy, alert to the frightening idea that had haunted me ever since Dell had recovered her senes: I feared she would go out of herself again when her baby came. If so, she was likely to do almost anything with it. Not that she'd ever been violent during the time her spell was upon her, but she did some peculiar things. On one occasion she turned a plate of shrimps upside down on the floor. And once she had taken all the eggs I had gathered from the hens' nests and dropped them into the sea.

She was not in the privy, nor on the path that led to it. Fortunately, I looked in the original hut the hermit had built before I began a search of the island. There she was, the babe at her breast, as pleased with herself and life as anything I could imagine.

"Isn't he beautiful, Garnet?" Her voice was a croon.

Still near hysterical from my fright, I said, "Why the devil didn't you call for help? You could at least have let a person know that your time was upon you!"

"Oh, I didn't want to disturb you. I knew everything was going to be all right. Garnet, you look like a *demented* person! Really!"

I raised my voice. "Well, how would you feel if you got out of bed and couldn't find *me*?"

"Hell, girl! I would have figured you were in the other part of the house."

Laughter overcame me, and Dell laughed, too. The hermit's fireplace crackled with burning logs, and Dell's attitude was matter-of-fact, as if everybody got out of bed, gave birth to a baby, then went about the business of cleaning up after it before settling down in our one and only chair to rest a bit.

Thomas was a big baby. We had no means with which to weigh him, but we guessed that he would tip the scales at eight or nine pounds, and he was beautiful. A thatch of midnight lay in ringlets all over his head. His face was red, which took me aback until Dell assured me that the redness would fade, but his features were perfect. I could see Dell in the shape of his mouth, the arch of his eyebrows. And I could see Happy Jack Muldoon in his nose, the set of his eyes and the dimple in his chin. "He has the best of the both of you," I whispered when she handed him to me and I looked at all that tiny perfection in wonder. To me, he was a miracle. No matter that he wasn't born on Christmas Day, I was so bemused with him that I was halfway willing to believe that he was the Messiah, returned to earth.

Melly worshipped Thomas, and Dell loved her son beyond all reason, although his birth marked a new relationship between herself and Melly. In the beginning, she had been overly indulgent with the little girl and affectionate to a great degree. When her strangeness settled over her, she seemed unaware of Melly's existence, but once she was herself again, she was as loving and motherly toward Melly as before. But after Thomas was born, she loved the little girl even more than she had. For my part, I sometimes was almost alarmed. My own words would come back to me after I had been holding that adorable baby, and I blushed at the realization that I sounded downright silly when I fawned over him. I reminded myself of Becky Muldoon as she spoke to her nephew.

We prospered. Dell worked several hours each day at doll-making, and soon we were sending dolls, gowns, nightwear, and other garments all the way up to Boston and New York City, and as far south as Savannah. The ship captains would stop by on their return trips with good, solid cash in return for our goods. Dell enlarged upon her efforts and produced doll houses for the children of the wealthy who lived all over the expanding colonies, and she equipped them with exquisitely-made furnishings, right down to rugs cut from woolen scraps for the floors and tapestries and paintings for the walls. The little dolls that inhabited these elegant houses were carved from wood, and they had moveable joints so they could sit on the tiny sofas or at the little dining tables. I dressed the dolls in fashionable garments, just as I sewed costumes for the larger papier maché dolls Dell made, and of course I continued to supply the growing market with ball-gowns, shawls, fancy nightdresses and all manner of clothing.

Thomas was a-year-and-a-half old and Melly was almost five the summer that Dell said, "We are respected and respectable. Our new house will soon be complete, and I am especially glad for our children. I like to think of them growing up as the children of women who have earned the respect of the colonists."

"But are you content, Dell?" We were alone, because Melly and Thomas were out of hearing distance. They were playing with some scraps of lumber the working men had left after they had stopped working on the nice house we were having built.

Dell looked out into the sea. "Content? Yes. I'm very content. Are you?"

I nodded. There was nothing that I wanted. Dell always referred to the children as "ours." We were making a substantial place for ourselves, but more important, we were forming a solid foundation for the children's future. Muldoon had never appeared during all that time we had been there. We'd known we were taking a chance at putting a good deal of money into the building of a proper house, but neither of us felt he would object—if he ever happened by. After all, Thomas was his own son. Anyway, the island was big enough for several families. If Muldoon showed up with a wife, we would either sell him our house or not interfere with him if he built himself a home elsewhere on the island. If I felt a wrenching of my heart when I considered the idea of

Muldoon appearing out of the blue with a woman on his arm, I ignored it.

We did not lack for male companionship. Once each week, a ship would dock at Cape Romain Harbor and the crew enjoyed a visit to the island. They purchased doll babies, doll houses and fancy garments for wives, sisters, sweethearts and children. The ones who were not married were attentive to Dell and me, and we enjoyed the mild flirtations as well as the more serious ones.

In spite of the original name of Fairhaven, no one ever referred to our island in any way except Shipwrecked Sailor's Island. We had found the struggling green shoots of grape vines the hermit once tended and with care we coaxed them into producing grapes once again. We also came upon a rose garden. It was gone to weeds and overgrown with tangled briers, but we enjoyed working in the out-of-doors as a change from our regular work, and before long we had nourished the roses back to their former glory. We planted a formal flower garden and made it into a place of beauty, and of course we continued to work at the vegetable patch. To our surprise, our island became known far and wide as a little piece of heaven, and by the time we'd been there three full years we were beginning to be visited by hordes of curiosity seekers. After another year, we were forced to hire a guide and charge admission, which paid the wages of the young lad who rowed over each day from Romain. The visitors were so many that they took us from our work, which continued to flourish. Merchants were now coming to order from us, and they marveled at the workmanship that went into our products.

Both Dell and I had many suitors. None of them were quite what I had in mind when it came to taking a husband, but I knew in my heart that I would someday wed. My plans did not include leaving the island. I wouldn't dream of leaving the children, whom I adored, and I could not think of parting with Dell. We were as close as if we'd been born to the same parents.

Melly was a regular little actress, and she was growing into a young beauty. She had taught herself to play the dulcimer, and she had a singing voice that would rival the angels. She was the high point of the tour of Shipwrecked Sailor's Island as she stood by the gate of departure to bid the tourists goodbye.

Our hired quide seldom bothered Dell or me, but on a soft afternoon he asked permission to bring a visitor into the parlor. "He says he met you once before, Miss Garnet, and by your leave he would like to renew the acquaintance. The name is Isaiah Mathew, and his sister is with him."

Naturally, I put aside my work and ordered cold drinks brought to the parlor, and I did nothing to hide my delight in seeing once again the tall, russet-haired stranger who had acted as a good Samaritan on that long-ago day when he'd buried Lawson and Rilla Mayfield.

When he entered with the pretty girl at his side, I stood and held out my hand. "We meet again, Isaiah Mathew," I said with no pretense at hiding my pleasure.

"My sister, Eveleth," he said.

She was a pretty girl who looked much like her older brother, and I was glad to learn that she had survived that awful night of the burning and slaughter. Mr. Mathew spoke of finding her in the wilderness, hungry but otherwise in good health after she'd escaped from the ire of those who dared call themselves champions of God as they committed their savagery upon good people.

Mr. Mathew made no bones about how he happened to come to the island. He'd heard tales of the two lovely cousins who had made a life for themselves on Shipwrecked Sailor's Island. "They speak of you in Boston and New York, Garnet Shaw. The widow who makes doll babies, the younger cousin who fashions garments for the young ladies. I chanced to get into conversation with a sea captain, who spoke of you in such glowing terms, and it occurred to me that you might be the ladies who were there at the side of the road all those years ago. One tall and red-haired, the other small and dark, both beauties. I've searched high and low for you, Garnet Shaw, and cursed myself a thousand times over for letting you get away from me before I learned of your destination."

At my blush, Eveleth Mathew rebuked her brother for speaking so boldly. "But it's true what he says, and pray forgive him, Miss Shaw. He was smitten badly, but that's no cause for him to behave in such an untoward fashion."

Isaiah asked if he could have the honor of coming back to call on me. I said he was welcome. When he came back the following day, he was alone, and he wasted no time before proposing marriage. I said I would have to consider the matter, and it was true when I told him his confession of love had taken me by surprise. But I did admit that I had often paused to give thought to the man who had shown such kindness to us on that dreadful day outside of Roxbury. He had moved away, into Boston, after the debacle. His sister was to be wed within the month, and after her marriage he would be free to settle where he chose. He said, "I would not find it hard to be known as the husband of one of the devastating women who live on Shipwrecked Sailor's Island, Miss Garnet. If you would only allow me to, I could be of great assistance to you and your cousin. It is a peculiar life you live. Surely you do not find it natural for you to have reached the age of—"

"I will be nineteen this year," I told him.

"Other women of your age have already begun a family."

Amused, I said, "You are getting along in years yourself, Isaiah Mathew. You must be all of five and twenty! Very soon you will be all stooped over with age, and your beard will be grey—as well as your hair."

"I beg of you, Miss Garnet, do not toy with me. I tell you, I have nearly lost my senses over you."

"But are there no fetching young ladies in Boston Town, sir?"

"Of course there are. But it's you I want. Ever since I found you there at the side of the road—lost, frightened and trying to dig a grave with a stick—I've never been able to look at another woman with any real interest. You have no idea how many miles I've traveled. I even went to England, and asked everyone I saw if they knew Garnet Shaw, because you said you were Garnet Shaw, of England."

"I've often thought of you, too, Isaiah," I answered truthfully. The idea of having a handsome and thoughtful man at my side was pleasant, but there were many reasons for me to hesitate. Dell and I had begun our life in the New

World with a lie—saying we were cousins. It was doubtful if he would turn away from me for that, but there *was* my background. I did not see how in the world I could look this kind and gentle man in the face and tell him that I had been loved by a pirate, that I had not objected except in a very small way, and that I had once killed a man. It wouldn't be right to marry him unless I was truthful, though.

But there was something else. Isaiah had kissed me. It was a pleasant enough kiss, but I had done him the disfavor of comparing the sensation with the one I had when Muldoon kissed me all those years ago when he'd put his mouth on mine inside a London chocolate shoppe. My response had been shameful. I wondered what manner of woman I had become, to even compare a wild and lawless pirate to a good, industrious man like Isaiah Mathew, but I didn't want marriage without love—and I was afraid that I still loved Muldoon. At least a part of me did, and as long as that was so, it wouldn't be fair to accept another.

Still and all, an incident had occurred a few weeks earlier that had disturbed me greatly. Our children had been invited to the mainland to attend a birthday party for the Governor's daughter, It began to rain shortly after our servant rowed them across, which meant there would be no visitors to the island. I was tired, and decided to go to my room for a nap. Perhaps I had been asleep fifteen or twenty minutes when I was awakened by the soft touch of a hand on my upper arm. I had been sleeping on my side, with my face to the wall. Just awakening from a deep sleep, I first told myself I was dreaming, for no one was in the house but Dell and myself. But I was not dreaming. Again, I felt the touch of a hand on my upper arm, and it moved in a most caressing manner, toward my bare neck, where it lingered. My second thought was of the ghost of the shipwrecked sailor, although we'd never been bothered with the slightest sign of any mysterious happenings. Cautiously, scared out of my wits, I turned over and stared up into Dell's face.

I spoke her name, probably as if I disbelieved that she had actually entered my room and touched me in that very personal, almost seductive manner.

Her eyes glowed as she looked down at me. "Forgive me, Garnet," she said huskily. "But you were so beautiful as you slept. I—long for the touch of—"

Thoroughly alarmed, I sat up and asked, "The touch of what?" My voice sounded cold and harsh, compared with hers, all soft and low.

She sighed. Then she said, "Just the touch of another human being who isn't a little boy or a little girl. I'm a human being, with natural desires. I yearn for love."

Then she lit her pipe, sat down in the chair across the room and spoke of business matters.

The incident had left me feeling uncomfortable, although I tried not to dwell on it. As a young girl at home, I was an avid reader of novels, and of late I had been reading the classics, which included references to Sappho. But Dell? No. I could not allow myself to believe that she was interested in me as a lover. Even so, I found myself recollecting instances of looking up from my work and finding her eyes upon me, and they'd had a strange look in them at times. A look that I could not fathom. I had always known that there was a certain secretiveness about Dell. She had spoken of having casual lovers, but she'd not said their names. She'd been a loving and dutiful wife, had loved her husband, Thomas Wills, with all her young heart and soul, I reminded myself. And certainly she was female. She had given birth to a baby after being with Muldoon only one time—while I—for all I knew, I might be unable to conceive.

Which was another reason I put off giving Isaiah Mathew an answer. He would want children. But I couldn't very well tell him I doubted if I could get with child. At least, I couldn't tell him until I had made a clean breast of my past.

Whether or not I would have eventually married Isaiah Mathew is something I will never know. After he left, Dell was in a jovial mood. She had met a man she was seriously thinking about taking as husband, a man named Jefferson Good. There was a radiance about her that evening that was similar to the way she'd been when she first learned that she was carrying Muldoon's baby. She said, "He reminds me a good deal of my poor, dead Tom, Garnet. Not in looks, for he's Tom's exact opposite, but he's somewhat taller than I, and he's of the same turn of nature. A real man, who has no fears about proving it."

Jefferson Good had come to the island to purchase one of

Dell's famous dolls for his sister's daughter. I had met him, and it came as no surprise to me to learn that he had fallen in love with her. She'd fairly bedazzled him, and it was obvious to almost everyone, including Melly and Thomas. They both wanted her to marry him, and brought the subject up every hour of every day for the next week. The children wanted me to marry Isaiah, too.

Mr. Good was to return on the following Sunday, and so was Isaiah Mathew. Dell and I talked over the subject of how we would work out a partnership arrangement if we both were married, and we were amiable, as always, when we discussed business. She had almost come to the conclusion that she would be happy with her Jefferson Good when fate blew in on the gales of a hurricane and made it impossible for either one of us to marry.

The day had started out with a red sun. By noon, the breakers were crashing like thunder as they moved in on the island, but we had weathered worse storms, and after we'd battened everything down, we settled in to wait it out, just as we'd done before. The force was lessened greatly by the time night began to fall, and that was when we looked out and saw the men—and a ragged, tattered, cut-throat lot they looked—swarming toward the house, their ship listing badly, hung up on a sand bar.

All alone as we were, save for two servants and the lad who took visitors through our vineyards and gardens, we didn't stand a chance against them, for they were seventy to eighty strong, loaded with muskets, swords, and other weapons, and woman-starved right down to the last puny little mate. He was the one Dell picked off with the shot from her fowling piece. He fell dead in his tracks, but the others moved on in a sea of deadly intent, and not a man jack of them paid heed to the few that we killed as they surged forward.

Nineteen

It was almost a full twenty-four hours before the thieving, murderous, raping crew of the *Rolling Ruthie* was drunk on wine from our cellars and their lusts satiated. Still drunk, they staggered to the *Rolling Ruthie*, found that the tide had risen enough to free her bottom from the sand bar, and sailed away.

I had been used without mercy—treated as a piece of meat, a knife at my throat while several of the brutes stood in line and made obscene noises, impatient for their turn. It was a time of madness, of ugly, cruel acts that were vile and more animal than human.

For several moments after they left, I lay where I was, on the floor of my room after they called a halt to their depravity. I ached from head to foot, was bruised about the arms, throat, belly and loins, and quite unable to do anything but moan feebly and attempt to get to my feet. Each movement brought an involuntary cry of pain, but I could not give myself over to the luxury of tears of shame. There were the children to consider. My heart hammered as I tried to swallow down my fears for Thomas and Melly. I knew Dell had been used as savagely as I, and feared for our serving women. Several of the contemptible creatures had carried Dell off amidst a great shout of victory, just as they'd carried me off. I was taken to the dining room, and now and then, in the midst of my own misery, I could hear Dell screaming and cursing, so I knew she was close at hand, probably in the sitting room.

Dizzy and sick, my torn garments barely covering me, I dragged my abused body toward the children's bedchambers, my pulse pounding as I tried to prepare myself for the very worst. I fell into Thomas' room and collapsed on the floor, too weak to take another step, but still suffused with hope. Dell was there, and she held what appeared to be an unscathed little boy in her arms. I couldn't say a word, but Dell understood what I wanted to know. I shall never forget the rush of gladness that filled me when she said, "They came into his bedchamber, took a look at him and went on. He locked his door, but they didn't come back."

"Melly!" I shrieked our daugher's name. Such a little beauty, and bound to be a tempting morsel for the brutes.

Thomas, who spoke quite plainly by then, said, "Don't worry, Mama-Garnet, Melly got away. She sneaked out. Told me she was going to Romain for help. It was sometime in the night. Before that, she hid from the bad men."

That child!—that precious little girl, so terrified of storms but willing to row across the water for help in spite of the lightning and thunder that had sounded all through the hideous night and well into the day.

"The fiends!" Dell cried. "I managed to kill another one when he was in his cups. I only wish I could have rid the world of more."

Both our serving women had been put to the same kind of brutal treatment. We found them cowering in their rooms, where they'd been when they were assaulted. They were bruised and half out of their minds—but still strong and healthy, and I felt they would recover from the disaster. As soon as we found the lad who took the tickets and guided the visitors about the island, we would waste no time in taking baths and putting a good face on the matter. It was over with and done. Dell's mind had not cracked right down the middle as I had halfway feared, and except for looking anxiously landward for Melly, we felt the worst was over.

The material possessions the filthy crew had plundered were nothing compared to the fear that haunted both Dell and me. The lad was fair as a girl, and he had golden hair. His beardless face and gentle ways could have brought him to ruination under the hands of those who had swept in from the sea, for the uncouth animals would make sport of such a boy, and they would not have hesitated to use him in a most horrifying way.

I offered a small prayer of thanksgiving when the lad appeared from a little cave where he'd gone at the first sign of trouble. There he'd lain silently, throughout the entire time. He sobbed and hid his face when he came out, saying he was sorry he'd not tried to help us in our need. "But I was afraid!"

"It was good that you thought of the cave," Dell said comfortingly. "If you hadn't, they'd probably have killed you with their perverted lusts."

A quick look around the grounds was enough to tell us the cutthroats had laid hands on everyhing of value they found. Not a keg of grog was left in our wine cellars, not a bottle of wine or a cask of rum. Our keeping room had been plundered to the bare walls. Smoked hams, baskets of sweet potatoes, turnips, barrels of molasses and jars of honey, all gone. The bedchambers had been looted of anything of value. Jewelry, combs, even clothing, they'd taken most of it. They'd trampled the beautiful roses to the ground. Viciously torn every bud away and stomped it into the mud. The grape vines were slashed, the vegetable garden demolished.

"But they didn't touch the children," Dell said. "And we still have the house as well as the long room where we work." Lengths of dress goods were missing, most of the findings had been taken, but we could build again, and we *would* build again, we decided. But in the future we would hire guards to patrol the island.

Again and again we went outside to scan the water for signs of Melly. At last the row-boat appeared, and she was accompanied by several of the friendly citizens from the village of Romain.

We had bathed the stink and the filth from our bodies by then, and it was with a great shout of welcome that we all ran down to the shore to greet our visitors. The settlers at Romain were a good lot. They joined forces whenever disaster came to any one of them by forming a house-raising party for a family that had been burned out, or gathering clothing for the homeless families, and it was always share and share alike when any family was in need. When death came to a village family, every citizen lent a hand in the laying out of the dead, grave-digging, coffin-building, and providing food for the bereaved. Through the years Dell and I had done our share when it came to helping those who had suffered tragic losses. We supplied the destitute with food from our keeping room and clothing from our stores, and it was heartwarming to see Melly arrive with our good neighbors.

The Reverend Tracy Pinchot was the first to come ashore. He took our hands in the same way he did when he met us on the streets of Romain, to invite us to Sunday meetings. "My dears," he said, "the news of this terrible thing has shocked every man and woman in Romain. You have a brave girl, here, in Melly. She risked exposing herself to those derelicts by running to the boat, and I know you both join me in praising God that she was delivered from their evil." His hazel eyes were kind as he looked deeply into mine, then Dell's. "Do you require the services of a physician? Wanting to prepare for the worst, I saw fit to bring our own Doctor Thompson."

We assured him that we were all right, and so were our two serving women, Honesty Jones and Aretha Horning, both of whom went down to the shore with us to greet the Romain citizens. Everyone appeared pleased to see that we had suffered no irreparable damage, but they were appalled at the destruction of the island. The good pastor suggested that a crew of workers come the next day and take steps to put our damaged vineyards back in order. The heavy rains had made it far too muddy to attempt such a thing right then, but there were several volunteers who mentioned the names of others whom they were sure they could depend upon to help us in our need. Provisions were in the rowboats, enough to see us through until the morrow, when we would be recipients of food and supplies from the combined keeping-rooms of the village.

Our good neighbors helped us clean up the shambles that the intruders had made of our house, and we gathered together before we went to bed on that night to count our blessings. All of us agreed that things could have been much worse. The Reverend Pinchot asked Amos Bledsoe and

Hiram Clay to stand guard with him through the night, which gave us a sense of security. Even though taking steps to patrol the shores after the rape and pillage occurred was somewhat like locking the barn door after the horses had been stolen, we knew we would sleep better knowing we were protected. The thieving, brutal seamen had defiled our bodies and made off with a goodly supply or our worldly possessions, but they'd not included our gold in their loot. Dell had buried it long ago, for safekeeping, and only she knew where it was.

Because I was utterly exhausted, I had no trouble going to sleep that night, but each time I drifted off I awakened with a jerk and a sense of panic. During those times when I did sleep, I re-lived the horror of being forced to submit to the knife wielding pirates in my dreams. Regardless, I awakened the next day feeling rested enough to turn my hand to the cleaning-up to be done.

By eight o'clock in the morning, our two serving women, the lad, Dell and I and even Melly and Thomas were hard at work on the house. First we'd served breakfast to the good men who guarded us as we slept. They were just about to get into the rowboat for the return trip to the village when several villagers rowed in.

Dell was saying something to young Thomas about the goodness of the people who lived in Romain when I made note of an oddity in their mannerism as they came ashore. Their expressions were grim, and each one of them, men and women alike, came forward with their arms crossed in front of their waists amidst a chilling quiet. The spokesman was Rupert Wattle, the village tanner.

The tanner held a paper, which he peered at nearsightedly as he read it. My first reaction to the words that came pouring from his pursed-up lips was that the people of Romain had decided to play a prank on us. Impossible to lend any serious credence to such nonsense, I thought, as I glanced first at Dell, then at Honesty Jones and Aretha Horning. The document, for it proved to be a true instrument, duly drawn up and signed by a Notary Public, made my hair stand on end:

> *Be it known,* (the tanner read), *that the citizens of Romain have considered the matter of the four women, herein listed as Dell Wills, Garnet Shaw, Aretha Horning and Honesty Jones, and do accuse all four of them of lewd and lascivious behavior, having consorted with persons unknown, alleged to have been men of the sea. It is further stated that the above-named women are accused of committing the further crimes of drinking spiritous decoctions with the aforementioned men, of catering to their carnal desires and of altogether comporting themselves in an undesirable nature.*
>
> *Be it known that after due deliberation on the part of the peers of these women, the citizens of Romain have taken steps to remove the three minor children from the dwelling house of alleged debauchery so that these children will be safely housed with God-fearing Christians until such a time as these four women have been duly tried by a jury of their peers.*

Reverend Pinchot was the first to speak. He walked toward the fish-faced tanner, his expression frozen in shock. "Now, wait a minute, Rupert. What have you people been thinking of, to draw up such a disgraceful paper as the one you've just read?"

The pastor was met with hostile eyes and frigid silence. He tried again: "This is an affront to justice. An outrageous act against these women, all of whom were victims of a heinous crime. Have you all lost your senses? What kind of people would get together and make such serious charges against the very victims of crimes that were perpetrated *against* them?"

Along about then, it occurred to me that not a one of the folks who had come over on the day before were among the group of thirty or more who had come to back up our accuser.

The tanner gave the preacher a scathing look. "You're no better than they, to defend them. And you a man of the cloth! We've long known, Mr. Pinchot, that you were not fit to lead our flock. You came to the island at the bidding of yon child." He gestured toward Melly. "Went crying through the streets in an attempt to roust good citizens from their Holy Day in order to come to this island where evil and wickedness had been done. By your paying attention to a young girl of color alone, you showed us what several of us have long suspected you of, sir. We've been discontent with your services almost ever since you came among us to head up our church because of your outlandish notions that the nigras are humans, that honest and true Christian men have no right to use them as God has provided, as slaves. And you've caused dissension among our young by your modern notions that women should have privileges that any pious man considers blasphemous. It was more than the righteous could bear, sir, for you to stay here on this island where fornication had been done and guard these filthy women. You are hearby given notice that you are no longer the preacher of our church." Rupert Wattle lifted his hand. "Seize the children! Seize the scarlet women! The women shall be cast in irons, the children placed in good homes."

Dell sprang into action. As long as I live, I shall never forget the pale, shocked look of her face, her bright and angry eyes or the cutting edge of her voice. She stood tall and straight, a fowling piece in her hand. "There will be no seizing of anyone." With a meaningful gesture with her pistol, she turned to the tanner. "You'll do well," she said coldly, "to get back in those boats and go on about your business. You make one move toward the children or anyone else, and I'll blow your frigging head right off your shoulders."

Wattle was obviously a born rabble-rouser, but it was quickly apparent that he was likewise a born coward. He turned deathly pale at the sight of the pistol in Dell's hand, urging his followers to move in on her, assuring them that she wouldn't use that weapon, they had nothing to fear. But as he spoke, he backed toward a tree. Before he could get behind it, Dell let loose with a blast from her weapon.

The tanner stared down in horror as the ground rose up in a great spray of earth about an inch from his boot. Still speaking quietly, Dell informed him that she'd not aimed for his foot, she had sent the ball where it had gone in. Then, before anyone could get his breath, she said, "See that yellow leaf on that sassafras tree? The one that's bigger than all the rest, and more vivid yellow? Watch it."

Every head turned to the tree, and a second blast rang out that neatly took the leaf away. "You will all get off this island," Dell said as soon as the reverberation was stilled. "Get back into your boats and leave me and mine in peace. As the reverend said, we were the victims of a heinous crime, and I do not intend to stand accused of anything by *any* of you." Without looking at him, she added, "Reverend, you're welcome to stay. You are too, Mr. Bledsoe, Mr. Clay. I don't know what took place among the residents of Romain to cause the likes of Rupert Wattle to be chosen spokesman for all, but you tell the villagers that Dell Wills is a woman to be reckoned with."

Neither Bledsoe nor Clay stayed, but both of them looked as if they would like to. They had wives and families in Romain. The preacher remained, but the lad who had long worked for us as a ticket-taker and guide queued up with the others.

We stood in silence as the rowboats left the island. Dell threw back her head and breathed a long, drawn-out sigh. Then, speaking to me, to the children, the two serving women and the preacher, she said, "I should have known it couldn't last. We tried our best to be good citizens. We've worked hard for years, caused no trouble to any man or woman, tried to do what was right." She sighed again. "I'm going back to sea. I'll take my share of the gold that's buried and buy a ship." Her eyes met mine. "Garnet, you are free to go with me as you please, or stay and take your chances with the rabble that just left, but mark me well, they'll be back, and they'll cast you in irons, for they've chosen a fool for their leader."

Aretha and Honesty looked across the expanse of water that separated us from Romain. Dell spoke to them: "You are marked women. You heard the accusations. You are also welcome to come with me." She took the kind pastor's hand and looked him in the eyes. "You, too, Reverend Pinchot."

I did not ask if she planned to take the children. She was the blood mother of Thomas, and through her actions we had Melly. She would never leave them, nor could I bear to part from either one of them, and in some strange way, I accepted the destiny that had bound me to Dell.

I wanted to know how it happened that Dell had the pistol in her pocket. Her answer was typical: "If I had been armed, instead of having to reach for a gun, I could have killed enough of those pirates to scare the rest of them into turning back to their ship. I will never be without a weapon again."

She also told me that Rupert Wattle had made improper advances a few weeks earlier. Then she laughed and said, "It's said that there's no fury like that of a woman scorned, but if Wattle is any example of a scorned man, I'll warrant the maxim fits both genders."

Reverend Pinchot was with us when we boarded the next ship that stopped by the island, but he left us in Boston Harbor. Aretha and Honesty stayed with us.

No sounder ship was ever built than the *Sea Hawk*. Three masted, it had a double bottom and a reinforced bow, sheathed and filled in the regular manner for protection against any *teredo*. We carried a heavy armament consisting of ten four-pounders, eight swivel guns and ten musquetoons as well as small arms. Provisions were on the heavy side due to Dell's firm belief that mates who sailed on full bellies were better seamen. There was rum, thickened juice of malt, dried yeast, pressed hops, plenty of meal, lard, and a great supply of fresh vegetables. The meat was on the hoof, including two milch cows and numerous squawking chickens. We were bound for the southermost tip of North America where we would lay in a goodly supply of citrus fruit, which was said to stave off that deadly scourge of seafaring folk—scurvy.

Agatha Strong answered a notice we placed in the *Boston Newsletter* stating that we had need of a tailor or seamstress. She didn't turn a hair at the idea of sewing breeches and waists for women. Each day she came to our rented rooms above a Boston furrier's shop and took her place at my side. She seldom said anything, but worked steadily without complaint and turned out a good day's work. Saturday she took her wages and never failed to return the Monday morning after Sabbath, neat as well as punctual. When we'd used up every scrap of goods, she gave me a searching look, cleared her throat and uttered the longest speech I had heard out of her during the weeks we sat side by side at our task: "Mistress, would there be a place for me in the ship? I've a yen to go to sea. Seems right exciting to think of a crew of women sailors."

"But I thought you were a lifelong resident of Boston," I answered. "Established here and probably suffering from no lack of friends."

"Aye, I've lived here long. No friends, though. No husband, either. He beat me and I tossed him out."

We had done nothing that would call attention to going to sea with an all-woman crew aside from hiring Agatha. Dell had done most of the recruiting. Brothels had provided us with a number of mates. I was never able to bring myself to ask Dell how she managed to approach so many and find out they were discontented with their lot in life. But we'd recruited women from other walks of life as well. Spinsters and widows added to our growing number. Then there were those who had come over from England, Ireland or Scotland, married by proxy to a settler but willing to do almost anything to flee from the bridegrooms they could not abide. Julia Coats was typical. Her legally wedded husband met the boat, identified himself as her husband, and took her home to hitch her up to a plow before he bothered to show her the inside of her new home. Her sister Nan fared well, she told us. Nan's husband was goodness itself, and she loved him on sight. But Julia jumped at the chance to leave the husband who whipped her when she didn't pull the plow to suit him.

Kindness Dawes was another proxy bride. After her new husband met her at the boat, he took her home and introduced her to his three other proxy brides. When she objected to such an arrangement, he knocked all her front teeth out. "T'was drear and dree," she said of the household she gratefully fled in exchange for life at sea. "Drear and dree to be livin' in that house with all those women, each o'oon to be used for breedin' purposes. Said Oy to himself, ye kin beat me till Oy'm black and blue, Oy'll not do it, for Oy was riz' up in a good home and me dear ole popper lessoned us from the Good Book every night afore bed, and it's plain to them as 'ave the faith that more than one wife is against the teachin's."

If she had a second name, Marmara had never heard it.

She was brought over on a slave ship with her parents, both of whom died at sea. At around thirty-two years of age, she was taller than Dell, as powerfully built as any able seaman or roustabout, and educated, having been purchased by a kind inventor. From Marmara, Dell learned of the improved hearth that Mr. Irving had invented for the ship's galley. Marmara had seen the hearth demonstrated and spoke of the greater flexibility of such a thing as opposed to a regular apparatus. Since Marmara was to preside over our galley, Dell had the improved hearth installed. Marmara was a source of other information, as well. She knew of a machine that would turn stinking water fresh and sweet, another device that would extract potable water from the sea. It was invented by Doctor Priestly, the famous chemist. Dell and I chose the one that extracted salt from sea water.

Marmara would have nothing to do with the new and widely acclaimed product referred to as "portable soup." It was a gelatinous mass of meat marrow and bits of lamb or beef that was compressed into bars which could be boiled with pease or oatmeal. Marmara said it would rot a man's guts, so Dell and I figured it would likely do the same to a woman's. We did, however, lay on a few kegs of fermented cabbage as well as a marmalade of carrots that was allegedly a hindrance to the scurvy. The fresh citrus we planned to bring aboard was said to be a far better preventive, but when the oranges and lemons were gone we'd have the marmalade to fall back on.

It was an opportune time for us to be getting under way. The colonists were in a turmoil, some of them loyal to England and prone to point out neighbors and kinfolk as traitors to the King. The Federalists were also inattentive to anything that didn't have to do with gaining American independence. A week before we were scheduled to sail from Mystic, where we had the *Sea Hawk* built, five members of one family were wiped out with the plague, but the horrifying event was barely newsworthy enough to merit a small notice in the *Boston Newsletter*. A dread disease, capable of killing every man, woman and child in the colonies was insignificant compared with the growing malcontent among the colonists.

Dell wasn't questioned when she registered the *Sea Hawk*

and stated her business as a merchant ship and scrawled "Philadelphus Fields" on the papers. So once again, she'd succeeded at masquerading as a man. Big, brawny Marmara was at her side in the attire of manservant. Privately, we were in joint ownership of the *Sea Hawk*, but I refused to go to the registry and sign my name for fear of being caught at practicing deception. No matter how I tried to constrain my womanly figure I could not look and act like a man, and deception was punishable by death in some of the colonies.

In groups of twos, threes, and fours, the crew of the *Sea Hawk*, came aboard. For the most part, the women had never set foot on a ship before in their lives, but even I was in awe of the gigantic proportions of our vessel. She was four hundred and sixty-two tons, with a lower deck of a hundred and fifteen feet and a thirty-eight foot beam. The hold had a depth of fourteen feet, and the 'tween deck space would accommodate a crew of an even hundred. As it happened, only eighty women were aboard when we sailed majestically out of Mystic Harbor. The sea was clear and the winds favorable, so we lost no time in setting sail.

Our first stop was the Carolinas, where we would exchange our cargo of goods manufactured in the New England colonies for tobacco, cotton, and grain. From the Carolinas, we steered hard toward the West Indies where we'd take on sugar cane before setting sail for Europe.

Aside from young Thomas, the only male aboard the *Sea Hawk* was Doctor Fearnot Waring, who had signed on in good faith and was given a small cabin for his own use. We were well under way when he realized he was surrounded by females, a condition that brought him into such a rage that he all but foamed at the mouth. "I've been duped!" he roared as he ran back and forth in search of Dell.

Doctor Waring was a short and pompous man, with a round little belly and a penchant for strong drink. He was reputed to be a tolerably good physician when sober, but he'd been run out of a village near Mystic under threat of being tarred and feathered. In no condition to operate, he'd amputated a man's healthy arm and left the crushed one dangling, to which the man's six brothers took instant umbrage. Dell, always capable of extracting the most unusual and helpful information when necessary, learned of the incident and got word to him that the *Sea Hawk* was in need of a surgeon.

I was with her when he found her, agitated and all three of his chins trembling with indignation. "I demand to be taken back to Mystic this very instant," he said. "I'll not be ship's doctor to a bunch of fool women. You should have told me, Captain Fields, that your crew consisted of females!"

Dell looked down at him, amused. Obviously, he was still laboring under the misconception that Captain Philadelphus Fields was a man. In her natural voice, she said, "Doctor Waring, I don't recall that you asked the gender of our crew."

The rotund little doctor stamped his foot and screamed, "You too! God in Heaven, to think that I should have come to this!"

Still smiling, Dell waited until he had calmed down a little before saying, "And this is my co-Captain, Garnet Shaw."

The doctor did a lot of dancing and prancing and brow-smiting. He was also beginning to show the strain of being denied spirits, complete with trembling hands and a certain agitated look about the eyes. We refused to let him go ashore when we reached the Carolinas, knowing he wouldn't return, since we felt it necessary to have a doctor aboard. After a while he appeared to grow reconciled to the way things were, although he often walked around with a rather dazed expression, repeating to himself in a tone of wonder, "All of them. Women. How in tarnation did they do it!"

It was a good life. I realized how very much I had missed the rolling motion, the thrilling sight of sails in full mast, the often placid but sometimes treacherous, always changing sea. We did well that first year. No two ways about it, we were well out of the war between Great Britain and the colonies. Except for the doctor, everyone aboard was of one mind. We felt that war is absurd, and felt if the colonies gained their freedom from the Mother Country they'd do so with the blood of their young men. If England maintained the colonies as a possession, her victory would be gained by the bloodshed of *her* young men. Death is the only victor in the final analysis, we agreed. And since we were women, we wanted to see an end to all wars. After all, it was our sons and loved ones who fought them.

Doctor Waring was almost violent in his disagreement—as violent as he dared to be in the face of eighty armed women. He made snide remarks about the inability of the female mind when it came to matters of importance. He was a friend of Paul Revere and he'd also written several articles that Thomas Paine had published concerning the colonists' cause. I said I believed people had a right to freedom, but if men were as brilliant as they were reputed they should have found a more sensible method of obtaining it than killing and getting killed. Doctor Waring informed me that all women were cowards at heart, that if progress had been left to the gentler sex, the human race would be extinct.

I wondered what he had on his mind the following day when we were fired upon by a pirate ship.

Twenty

There were three casualties from the attempt on the part of the pirate ship to seize us and board. Sarah Jones, former indentured servant to a wealthy tobacco grower in Connecticut, was our helmsman. She lost three fingers, but Doctor Waring took care of the stumps as soon as the battle was over and Sarah counted herself lucky that she'd not lost an arm—or worse. Aretha, our former serving woman, now First Mate, suffered a broken ankle from cannon recoil. The third casualty was Sime, our cat. She received a mortal shrapnel wound from the marauding vessel. Melly was inconsolable. We gave Sime a burial at sea that befit an aging seaman. The child was not old enough to accept consolation in knowing that death came quickly and mercifully. Sime had been sickly for a long time and showed signs of a great deal of suffering from old age.

Dell was in her element during the skirmish. With red hair flying, she ordered round after round of volleys to crash into the mouldy old tub whose crew of cut-throats would dare attack us. They soon turned tail and ran. Dell wanted to chase them down and finish them off, but the majority spoke out against it as pure folly so we took the matter to a hasty vote. Dell conceded gracefully, but her motion to train the crew rigorously against the time when we would fight a real battle carried. The doctor objected, but he had no vote. After that, a part of each day was devoted to drills in which each woman would take her position against any enemy we might encounter upon the high seas. Once each week we actually fired our war machines just as if we were in the thick of an attempt to take us. Even though a mock confrontation was not the real thing, Dell held fast to her belief that a vessel must be prepared to protect herself at all times, and it wasn't long before our all-female crew was as fast as any when it came to manning the positions and readying for attack.

The weather was fair for several weeks, and we hove into ports where we went about our business just like any other merchant seamen except for the hog-tied doctor, who continued to object to his circumstance. He ranted and railed, but to no avail. Quite often he would single me out to, as he said, attempt to reason with me. On those occasions his speech would turn flowery and tedious as he pointed out facts that he considered scientific about the damage females did to themselves when they tried to compete with men. "It's a man's world, Garnet," he would say. "Women were made by God Almighty to act as handmaiden for men, who are superior in every way. You women are plying a dangerous trade, and sooner or later you're going to be overtaken by pirates, or members of the King's fleet, or ships of the colonists. These waters are full of smugglers, too, and everyone knows that a smuggler has no room in his heart for sympathy."

More than anything else, the doctor resented being aboard while the colonists were fighting for their freedom. He also raved against being thrown among harlots, thieves, runaway slaves and indentured servants. I suggested that he train Marmara in the healing arts. She was educated, had a natural flair toward medicine and wanted to learn. The inventor who had once owned her had died. She was sold along with the rest of his estate to a coppersmith who flogged her for the crime of reading one of her master's books—in spite of the fact that her master required her services every night in his bed. Over the years he had sired three sons by her and she had seen each of them sold into slavery when they reached the age of ten. When she ran away she relieved the coppersmith of a considerable amount of his cash.

Tall, attractive and strong, Marmara had every qualification, but Doctor Waring refused to believe that a black woman was capable of studying medicine. He was of the opinion that Negroes lacked the ability to reason, which placed them in the same category as any other animal. No matter how many times I pointed out the folly of his refusing to train her, since we would gladly turn him loose once we had a female doctor, he remained firm in his belief that she couldn't learn.

"But look at her," I would say, exasperated with a man so narrow that he could look at a fact and refuse to believe it. "Listen to her read."

He would listen, but turn away, saying she had memorized the words.

We plied our legitimate trade as we had planned from the beginning, but as the months passed, we began to occupy ourselves more and more with smuggling, which had been our original—but secret—aim. Doctor Waring knew of our dangerous habit of taking on articles from the colonies that were intended to be brought to England. The Mother Country felt she had every right to the produce and manufactured goods from the colonies, but the colonies were of a different opinion; and we were willing to risk getting caught in exchange for the profit we made from taking indigo, cotton, tobacco, and other goods to countries willing to pay a fair price.

We had a profitable year. Shore time was a pleasant vacation from the confines of the ship, but most of us were glad to get back on board since we never dared venture ashore unless we were dressed as men, which was risky.

In early January of 1776, Dell was standing alongside the tiller when she let out a great whoop and holler that brought me running to her side. "Take a look through this glass," she said to me, greatly excited. "If that isn't the *Rolling Ruthie*, I'll eat it from stem to stern."

I took the spyglass and peered intently at the vessel that lay far astern to starboard, a ghostly outline under the cold morning's sun. Flakes of snow were spiraling about in the biting wind, so cold they brought tears to my eyes and a stiffness to my fingers. Bit by bit, I made out the name of the awkward-appearing vessel and through chattering teeth, I mouthed them. "*Rolling Ruthie*, yes. But they'll never attack us."

"Of course they won't. Those filthy cowards would never attempt to fire upon a ship as big as ours." Dell's scornful words brought an additional shiver up and down my spine that had nothing to do with the frosty morning. "They're a crew of devils with a stripe of yellow down their backs, but with bravery enough to attack an island where unprotected women went about their work. They ravaged and robbed us—well!" Her grin was a death's mask, almost hideous as she poised like a granite statue with a mane of long, flowing red hair, savoring the revenge within her grasp.

I wasted my breath when I said, "Let's not disturb them. What good will it do us?"

The look she turned on me was enough to make my hair stand on end. "Maybe it won't do *you* any good, but it will serve me well to tear the bastards asunder. Had it not been for them, we'd be there still, leading the good life."

"But there were other things that entered into our leavetaking," I argued.

"Yes, but that filthy crew was the beginning of it, and I'll not rest until I've relieved them of their plunder. What's the matter with you, Garnet? Well you know that whatever they carry as plunder is rightfully *ours*!"

"I'll not be a part of murder," I cried.

She grinned again and spoke icily. "What I have in mind is not murder. They didn't kill us, so it wouldn't be sporting to do them in." Turning, she shouted to the helmsman to give chase to the *Rolling Ruthie*, then clattered below to make sure the children were safe and snug in their cabins. After that, she ordered every hand to the battle, a vivid and graceful sight as she signaled expertly to the rigger to use the wind to our advantage as we advanced on the *Rolling Ruthie*.

No doubt the knaves we chased paid scant attention to the *Sea Hawk* once they'd satisfied themselves that we were not a part of his Majesty's Fleet, bent on boarding and taking them as pirates. To them we probably looked like a harmless merchant ship, and at the beginning of our pursuit they were apparently unaware that we were advancing until it was too late. Our powerful sails caught the wind and bellied out as we kept on a northeasterly course and cut through the deep cold of the ocean as if we'd been pushed by the hand of God.

Dell collapsed her spyglass with an abrupt motion that gave away her growing tension as she shouted for all hands to be ready for fire. By then she'd tucked up her hair under a cap and presented the appearance of a strong man who had no doubts about his ability to be very much in control as she gave the quartermaster the final orders.

A cheer arose from the crew as we neared our quarry. Julia told off each command in her hearty voice and the entire mood aboard was one of tense expectation. The small arms had been brought from the hold and the fully-armed crew lay prone and at the ready along the starboard scupper, where they would surprise the crew of the *Rolling Ruthie* since they were hidden behind the bulwark.

I took position behind a cannon, my cutlass clanging against metal as I fell on my knees to ready the match in its sand bucket. All the rest of the cannons were manned by our stalwart women, and from my position I could see Dell with her teeth bared, a swaggering look about her as we closed the distance between us and the *Rolling Ruthie*.

The ungainly ship began to heel to starboard as it tried to out-race us, but it was a useless attempt. The water boiled noisily past us as we skimmed along as sprightly as the wind itself while the prey was like a box loaded with rocks, square-rigged and awkward as a colt just learning to walk.

Suddenly Dell raised her flag. I stood in order to calculate the direction of my shot and so did the others at cannon. We were on the *Rolling Ruthie's* quarter, near to blanketing her wind when Dell shouted the command to fire, her voice cutting through the cold air loud and clear. I held out my hand for the match and it was handed to me silently by Doctor Waring, who muttered curses along with reminders that it hadn't been too long ago when we'd spoken of the sorry business of war and killing. But he did hand me the match. I applied the match, and the sputter of the powder was a mere whisper against the roaring winds and the shrill, bloodthirsty cry that burst from Dell's lips. My cannonball hit first, a direct and powerful strike to the *Rolling Ruthie's* foredeck. The others followed quickly, a business-like sound that resulted in quickly turning the *Rolling Ruthie* into a foundering mass of ruptured wood. Our grapnels were tossed away, our boats lowered, accompanied by an ear-splitting din among the women, all of whom had turned into savages—myself included.

We took them easily, with hardly more than a token of resistance after another volley from our cannons. They were a shifty-eyed lot, and lazy to boot, judging by the disreputable condition of their ship. We had them aboard the *Sea Hawk* before they realized the'd been bested by women. Dell grabbed me and marched me forward to where she had them lined up against the railing. With us were our two former serving women, and Dell whispered a quick command. "When we're four feet from the bastards, we'll show them our hair."

It must have been a dreadful shock to the pirates. No doubt they thought they'd been lined up to have their heads lopped off, and it's a fact that several of them were bleating for mercy as we advanced. We stopped in our tracks and took off our caps to allow our hair to fall free. Stunned, the pirates stared and stared.

"Women," muttered their Master. "We was taken by a band of females, mates!"

Dell threw back her head and laughed heartily. "The same women you fiends raped and stole from, back on Shipwrecked Sailor's Island, but we've reinforcements as you can plainly see." With the tip of her cutlass, she grazed the cheek of one barrel-shaped man she'd described to me before, the one who had brutalized her more than any of the others. "I've a special duty for you," she said sweetly. "And I've had many a day to dream up exquisite methods of revenge."

I should have known. Dell had turned over heaven and earth in order to avenge the deaths of her husband and daughter, so it followed that she would not rest until she had brought down the men responsible for our leaving the island.

She kept her promise and didn't put the men to death, nor did she flog them or otherwise punish them by inflicting physical pain. Instead, she derived great pleasure in watching them perform the most odious tasks she could think of. They carried the contents of our chamber pots from our quarters, but only the liquids were thrown overboard in the ordinary manner. The solids were carried by hand.

Perhaps the most cruel torture of all was her decision to make the captives bathe us. Dell drew an inordinate amount of pleasure in forcing the men to prepare the bath water, then watch us undress. Then they were made to strip down before they knelt to act as bathing servants. She taunted them by pointing at their loins after she stepped from the bathing tub, great bursts of laughter filling the air. For two weeks the men of the capsized *Rolling Ruthie* were tormented, tantalized, and humiliated. After that we put them off on an island, bereft of a stitch to protect them against bloodsucking insects or a weapon with which to defend themselves against unfriendly natives.

Doctor Waring was beside himself at such goings-on. He begged and pleaded with Dell to turn back, saying she was meting out cruel and inhumane treatment to the prisoners. For answer, she faced him squarely and spoke in the cold voice of old: "You've never been gang-raped. They're lucky to get off with their lives."

Before the *Rolling Ruthie* sank, we dispossessed her of her cargo, and among the booty we found a few of our own possessions. The Captain's quarters yielded trinkets, and his bed was draped with my coverlet.

A strange unrest came over our crew following the taking of the pirate ship. At first, it was subtle enough to be barely noticeable, but after a while it came out in the form of unrest and discontent that was manifested in little squabbles among the women. In time, it was necessary to bring the problem out into the open in order to avoid further breakdown in discipline. Dell and I called a meeting and put the question forth to our mates. Point blank, we asked what was causing malcontent, why a bunch of heretofore industrious workers had suddenly turned slovenly.

Marmara spoke up at once. To a woman, our crew wished to no longer operate as smugglers and sometimes merchant seamen. They had enjoyed the conquest of the *Rolling Ruthie*. The fight and the takeover had thrilled them, and besides, they could see the wisdom in pirating. There were no monies to lay out for goods that we'd deliver elsewhere, and what we took we would keep. To put it flatly, they wanted to turn pirates.

Dell looked at me. I shrugged. Wherever she went, I would go. Whatever she did, I would do. It was agreed, and the flag that she had raised when we fired upon the *Rolling Ruthie* became a red one. We could not refer to ourselves as members of the brotherhood, that time-honored euphemism for pirates. Among ourselves, we knew we belonged to the sisterhood, but Doctor Waring called us lawless, seagoing vixens.

Privately, I said to Dell, "A year, and no longer. Then we'll settle down to respectability."

"Two years," she parried.

"A year and a half," I said firmly.

"Agreed." We were on deck, alone. Her eyes relected the mysterious depths of the sea and her voice was bitter as she said, "Where can we settle down to respectability when the year and a half that we've agreed on is up? We've no place to lay our heads. I wanted Thomas to be born in England, but that was not to be, which was just as well. The English are a sorry lot, at best, and if I had to take sides in this ridiculous war I would be partial to the colonists. But even they have not dealt kindly with the likes of us, and as far as that goes, few men who've ever been born to this grungy old world will give any woman an even break."

My chance to ease out of an unlawful life still hovered in the very air that surrounded us, along with the fog. The hangman's noose is always the threat in the background of any brother of the blood, and even though I had never heard of a woman pirate being hanged, it was reasonable to assume that such a fate would be a woman's even though I had seen few other signs of equality in the battle between the genders. God knows why I didn't try to talk her into selling out to the others and settling on any one of the islands where gold could pave our way. I think I didn't because of what she left unsaid, and I gave her my hand on it.

Dell was not one to rant and carry on, but I could read her at times and I felt I knew what she was thinking. It had been no fault of her own that her parents had pawned her off as a boy child in order to gain an estate. But they'd done it and been caught and sentenced to jail, which had disrupted her life at an early age. Then she had fallen in love with Thomas

Wills, had married him and done everything humanly possible to establish herself as a virtuous woman. Husband and child were brutally slain, a cruel reward in exchange for living the good life. Then she'd taken revenge on the murderer of her loved ones. Lived a life that was not in the least respectable, yet she'd flourished. Once again, she'd set about atoning for her sins. She had yearned to see her beloved mother-in-law, but found her victimized. Even then, she'd not given up on the human race. She'd settled down on the island and turned her talents to making an honest living. Then rape, and later the threat of losing the children to the pious people who had looked upon the sinned against as the sinners. Mayhap she halfway believed she was fated to the life of the lawless, since every time she turned to goodness and the pursuit of respectability she was smashed in the face. It's possible that I, too, had those self-same feelings deep down inside my own soul, but alongside the tragic life of Dell, my sorrows were pale indeed.

Instead of speaking my thoughts on that subject, I said, "You talked the rest of the crew around to piracy. Admit it."

She smiled as she nodded and said, "It was my true intention from the start. As soon as we decided on taking to the sea I knew we'd not stay legitimate long." Then she drawled, "Anyway, the chances are good that we'll one day run into Muldoon. It's a big and lonely ocean, but there's always a chance that our ships may some day come within speaking distance. It would please me greatly for Muldoon to have a chance to see his son."

Enigmatic woman, Dell Fields. It was the first time she had mentioned Muldoon in the same breath with her son, one of the very few times she had mentioned him at all, yet there was a definite softness to her voice as well as a kind of yearning that was echoed in my own heart.

Twenty-one

We did not meet Happy Jack Muldoon on the open sea, but we met other ships, many of which we pirated—but not all. We were not so foolish as to take on the warships that were plowing through the waters on their way to fight the colonists; we gave them a wide berth. Our plunder was growing steadily and after several successful months at sea, all hands grew restless with the monotony of the fare, and the closed society of women without a man to liven us, save for Doctor Waring.

Our ship's doctor finally gave in to our pressure to teach Marmara the healing arts. He did it as a bargain after we promised to let him go free once Marmara's skill was satisfactory. His continual harping and complaining was beginning to get us, but his slimy way of insinuating himself into a position where he was close to me had become the bane of my existence. Several times, he begged me to become his wife. Each time I refused, he grew even more amorous. There was nothing offensive about him, but he held no appeal whatever for me. I explained as kindly as I knew how that if I ever married I would want to love my husband. For answer, he insisted that he would make me love him.

Wanting to be rid of him became an obsession with me. He would come upon me when I was least expecting it and slip his hands around my waist. In exasperation, I slapped him soundly one time and spoke stingingly. "You're a nothing! I've had the best, and I'll settle for no less. If you touch me again, I'll have you thrown overboard."

The best that I referred to was Happy Jack Muldoon, and I no longer tried to tell myself any differently. Truly, I might have married Isaiah Mathew had it not been for the horrid day of the rape, for I had seriously considered him. There was plenty of time for me to wonder how he had felt when he came again to the island and had found us gone, and I regretted that I had not written to him or explained—kind man that he was—why we left so abruptly. I'm sure Dell's thoughts were often on the only suitor she had not turned away, too. And after a time it came to me that the reason we had both been attracted to the men we might have wed was because of their resemblance to Muldoon.

It was being back at sea that brought his image to mind, I told myself. And I looked for him in every port, found my heart hammering with excitement each time we passed another ship.

Trinidad was reputed to be a place of great excitement and intrigue, and we had made up our minds to go there for a full month of rest. We were on our way there when we came upon a sitting duck. The moment we sighted her sails a great cry went up among the mates. The excitement of a pending battle far and away superseded the shore time in Trinidad.

"Sail ho!" The cry sounded at dusk, far up in the rigging, and all hands were of the same mind. *Take it*!

Dell was not too interested in the sloop. There was a look of laxness about her, even from a distance. But the majority voted to move in on the craft, to seize her and board. One more prize before Trinidad.

The order was given, and we covered the distance between us in good time, followed by the speaking, which we politely gave to the other vessel. By then we could see the fading letters on her side enough to make out the name, *Bridewell's Baby*. From across the slight distance came a healthy bellow, "*Bridewell's Baby* of Long Island in the Colonies. Rolf Cammer, Master. What ship?"

"The *Sea Hawk*, out of the Carolinas, under the joint mastership of Shaw and Fields," Dell called back.

The battle was over almost before it began since the other vessel was no match for us. All through the first few moments when the startled crew of *Bridewell's Baby* attempted to hold their own, Doctor Fearnot Waring swore in accompaniment to our fire. He hated the idea of taking another ship's cargo. Despised the very idea of a band of women being able to do such a thing, and he let everyone know his feelings at the slightest opportunity. Mostly, however, he trembled in fear during these exciting battles.

Captain Cammer swore he was carrying sugar and other foodstuffs in his hold. When he realized he had been taken over by a bunch of women, he looked very foolish, but apparently he decided he wasn't going to allow the situation to remain so. We had long ago stopped masquerading as men except for wearing breeches. It was too much trouble to keep our hair up under our caps, our breasts tied down. Before then, our greater strength and dedicated manner as well as our skill with weapons had proved enough to keep a conquered sea captain nervous, but quiet, as we went about our looting. Not so, Captain Cammer. One look at the screaming, brazen women who swarmed aboard resulted in a mighty oath from him, followed by, "Avast, there, mates! Are we to stand by and allow ourselves to be taken by a bunch of biddies?"

He should have kept his mouth shut. Doctor Waring tried to tell him we were mild as milk as long as our captives did as we told them, but we were all vixens when crossed. Cammer paid the doctor no heed and ordered his mates to advance on us. Sheer folly! We had no recourse but to fire on them. I swear, the stupid Captain believed we were too spineless to use our weapons in a face-to-face confrontation! I hated to fire, but I did it. The Captain fell with an expression of surprise on his face, along with several of his men. The rest dropped their weapons and held out their hands, which we were quick about lashing together, then making them fast to the bulwark. Swaggering and boastful moments before, those who still lived turned to lumpkins who begged and howled for their lives.

The fetid stench from below rose up in a nauseating roll as I opened the hatch.

"Rotten onions," speculated Dell.

"Spoiled potatoes," argued Julia.

"I'll wager you both," shouted Marmara, "that it's mutton, and long ago gone bad."

About a dozen and half of us descended into that dark and steamy place. We had taken a slave ship. What looked like hundreds of them lay naked and suffering, their raw backsides festering with sores that oozed, manacled together so close they couldn't move away from their own wastes. Those were the ones who had survived. Several dead lay among them, most of them already putrid and badly bloated. Men and women. Little children. Babies. I took back the remorse I'd felt over shooting down the resisting Captain.

The slaves wore an expression of utter hopelessness. No doubt they believed we were just another band of murdering slavers, and for all they knew we would treat them no better than had Cammer. There was no resistance from any one of them as we went about the dreadful business of sorting the living from the dead. The ship would go down, the dead slaves and dead slavers with it, but God willing, we would get these poor, starving survivors onto the *Sea Hawk* first, along with the crew that hadn't resisted. We would not murder the crew in cold blood, but we would set them off at the first chance. The slaves would be returned to Africa, but first we would have to learn what part of that country they had been taken from.

For three days following the taking of the slave ship we battled a raging storm, and we were already short on rations. Due to our decision to anchor at Trinidad we'd not taken on a goodly portion of foodstuffs. For this reason, we stinted the crew of the capsized *Bridewell's Baby*, and not out of a hard-hearted decision to punish them, although Doctor Waring accused us of starving the men out of meanness. I made note that he didn't offer to share his more bountiful rations while he bombarded us with his tirade about the right of white men to enslave men and women of color.

He grew near rabid as the days wore on, exhorting us, and me in particular, with his patriotic fervor. God was on the side of the colonists, he shouted vehemently. Slaves were needed to help supply cotton and tobacco and crops to provision the Army. Africans were not humans, had no souls, could not think or reason as far as he was concerned. Therefore, they'd not suffered at the hands of the slavers, had not known a moment's sorrow or grief at their plight because "they didn't know any better," and his most deplorable statement concerned their reaction to lying among their dead and in their own urine and feces: "They don't know whether anyone is dead or alive, and they're accustomed to filth." He said we were traitors to the colonists' cause for stopping the slave ship. I came very close to beating his head in for him. If we'd not reached St. Paulo de Loanda when we did, I might have done it.

After we had divested ourselves of the slaves, I turned to Dell and said, "Let's leave the good doctor here in Africa."

She held out for Trinidad, where he could easily book his way back to the colonies.

The journey from St. Paulo de Loanda to Trinidad was a seafarer's dream. Blue skies and a swift and favorable wind took us there in amazing time. We spilled into the rowboats and rowed eagerly toward shore, a weary crew and every one of us looking forward to an entire month of any diversion that appealed to us.

On the second day ashore, Dell and I took our children to the marketplace where we were purchasing exotic cloth for our darling Melly and selecting fashionable wear for our Thomas, when I felt the skin at the nape of my neck prickle. Upon turning around, I looked straight into the strange-colored eyes of Happy Jack Muldoon. He shoved his way through the throngs that surrounded us, courteous as any nobleman, but determined to get where he was going.

Right there, while hundreds of people looked on, he took me in his arms and kissed me soundly.

I responded... Oh, God! How I responded! I could have swooned out of sheer delight as I clung to him and tasted the heavenly honey of his lips. At last, he drew away from me and breathed five words: "You'll never leave me again!"

Twenty-two

We were married the next day. It was as if all those years of separation had never been. As if Muldoon had never betrayed me by seducing the woman who had saved his very life.

It was not that I forgot the ugly scene that Aunt Becky and I came upon so unexpectedly that day aboard the *Nightingale* when Muldoon told me so foolishly that things were not at all what they seemed—oh, no. But I was able to put the incident in proper perspective. Growing older had granted a certain mellowness to me, perhaps, but aside from that, there was another, and a very wonderful reason for me to look back without anger. If he had not gone back to argue, only to end in having his way with Dell, Thomas would never have been born. Even though Dell was his natural mother, in a unexplainable way, he was also my son.

No man has ever been as proud of his son as Muldoon was of Thomas. "If only," he said in sorrow, "Aunt Becky would have lived to see him." His aunt had died a year earlier, of the fevers.

We had an enormous amount of catching up to do, but there was no thought of anything but love-making during those first deliriously happy days after we were wed. Again and again, my husband swore that he would never let me out of his sight again as long as he lived. Nor would he hear of parting with Thomas, or Melly, whom he adored and claimed as his own adopted daugher.

Over an extravagant supper at a tavern, Dell, Happy

Jack, and I discussed the future, both children in the care of a member of French royalty who had fled, along with her family, to Trinidad. The French Revolution was keeping apace with the American one, and numbers of French people were flooding into Trinidad in order to escape execution. Muldoon had made a handsome profit at providing the means for these wealthy and titled French men and women to leave their native land. It was a dangerous vocation, but Muldoon had always thrived on danger.

The supper over, Muldoon ordered another bottle of champagne. After it was served he spoke of the future. "I suggest that we remain here in Trinidad until after the war between the colonies and England is over. The Americans are going to win it, of that I've no doubt. When it is safe to do so, we'll go there to live."

"Where do you propose to live, Muldoon?" Dell asked the question drily, a wry smile on her lovely face. "On your island? We can't go back there." Grimly, she described the events that had led us to seek refuge on Fairhaven Island, then brought him up to the time we left it.

"We did well," I told him. "Over the years, we built a house and developed a good trade in clothing and dolls. It was a beautiful place, Jack." Then I told him of our fate at the hands of the crew of the *Rolling Ruthie*, the incredible behavior of the citizens of Romain.

He looked as if he'd been slapped.

"It's true enough," Dell said. "We were the victims, but somehow the people of Romain took it into their heads that we were to blame. And they were going to cast us in irons and take the children from us. Make us stand trial for lewd and lascivious behavior." Her wondrous laughter rang out. "So we picked up and left. Had ourselves a ship built and went to sea with a crew of women and a doctor, the only man aboard save for Thomas."

Muldoon had heard tales of the warrior women, the pirates in petticoats. "You've become a legend, my dears." He looked thoughtful as he poured more wine. Then he made a statement that left us both with open mouths and disbelieving stares. "You could not have built a house and done all those things on Fairhaven Island. Once each year,

I've voyaged to Fairhaven, and not once did I see any sign of human habitation. As islands go, it's not a bad place, and last year I put up a crude hut." He wanted to know the exact location of the island. After we told him, he was doubly sure that we'd sought a haven on the wrong island. "Fairhaven is off the coast of the Carolinas, not far from Williamsburg. The dolts were misinformed, or else they deliberately misinformed you."

"It was always known as Shipwrecked Sailor's Island," I said. "Even after we'd been there for a long while, nobody called it anything but that, and it wasn't of great importance to us."

"Well, we'll go to Fairhaven," he said. "The three of us, with the children. There we'll start life anew. The war can't drag out much longer. The King was under the impression that his fleet and his soldiers would make short shrift of the colonists, but that hasn't proved the case. He's growing more and more in disfavor with his subjects as each day passes, and the cost has been incredible. So that's where we'll go. I want my son and daughter to grow up on land, go to school, and contribute to the world in some great way."

Dell said, "If you think I'm going to be a part of an America where people go out on slaughtering parties and kill the innocent and dedicated, think again, Muldoon. To say nothing of fanatics who would put two women on trial after they've been raped!"

"All of the settlers aren't like that, Dell. You just had the misfortune to run into a few who—"

She interrupted him. "The few speak for the many. No, indeed. Anyway, I don't want to be the spinster aunt, shoved off into a corner somewhere. Not in the colonies or anywhere else."

He raised his eyebrows. "I doubt very much if anyone will ever consider you a spinster or an aunt. We'll draw up an agreement among us. Share and share alike in any endeavor we settle on. Anyway, you'll have nothing to fear. Not with a man in the family."

"I've made a success of my life on the sea and I'll continue to do so," she said, adding acidly, "and I don't need a man to protect me."

"Thomas and Melly are growing up without the companionship of other children," he said, raising his voice. "What kind of life do they have? Looting and pirating is a poor example for them. I'll not allow you to take my children back to sea. One of these days you're going to come up against an adversary you can't overcome, Dell. *Then* what'll happen to the children?"

She stood up and yelled, calling the attention of all the rest of the patrons to our table. "*Your* children? Hah! Melly is mine and mine alone. And I had Thomas without help from any man—or woman, for that matter. I was kind enough to consider your feelings, Muldoon, knowing you'd take pride in siring a son, but you've no right to high-handedly decide his future, and even less when it comes to Melly!"

He stood up and yelled right back at her, unmindful of the titters and gasps surrounding us. "You're losing your temper because you know I'm right! I don't give a damn if Thomas was sired by a werewolf and you picked Melly out from under the hen's nest, you know I speak the truth when I say you're not giving them a fair shake in life!"

I slammed my hand down on the table, but didn't stand up. The two of them were making enough of a spectacle. "Both of you," I said, "sit down and shut up. I'm not the natural mother of either one of those children, but I've shared in their upbringing and I will not part with them." With a sinking heart, I looked at my husband for a long, long moment. Then I looked at Dell. "I have longed for a life such as we had on the island, before we were forced to leave. There we knew peace and tranquility, and the children had a place where they could run and be free. They have a right to an education, they need to be with children their own age. But if I must choose between husband and children, I will not hesitate. I, too, will return to the sea."

Dell and Muldoon both sat down and looked at me, saying nothing. I chose that moment to suggest an alternative to living in the colonies. "What of your father's estates? He made you his legal heir. Could we not return to the estates that are rightfully yours? Surely he cannot still be living!"

"He's dead, all right, but I'll have nothing to do with the lands, the title. It can go to wrack and ruin for all of me, and my half-brother's surviving son felt the same way. He long ago left Carrickfergus and Muldoon Manor for a life in the colonies. No, if you fool women insist on living your lives out at sea, so be it. We'll form a company, the three of us. Hire a respectable crew of good men and true, and run a profitable shipping business. Right now, we could make a killing by furnishing the colonists with weapons, which we could get in Spain."

"We already have a respectable crew," I said angrily.

Muldoon smiled and managed a courtly bow even though he was sitting down. "Forgive me, my dearest. I cannot gainsay you on that."

We agreed, then, to use the *Sea Hawk* as a merchant ship, and legitimately supply the colonies with weapons and other necessary articles.

After that decision was made, we continued to enjoy our holiday in Trinidad. A few days before we were to sail for Spain, Marmara came to the rooms Muldoon and I shared to deliver a devastating message. With the exception of herself, our crew had deserted us. They'd taken their shares and purchased a ship of their own. Slipped out of sight at daybreak.

It was some weeks before it occurred to me that Muldoon's fine hand had been at work in bringing about that little *coup*, but when I asked him how he had persuaded the women to set out on their own, he denied that he'd had anything to do with it.

I never believed him, but I was never able to get my hands on proof that he was instrumental in their defection. When we shipped out for Spain, Marmara was our only woman mate, and she was a fine ship's surgeon. Muldoon treated her with every respect, which was her due.

Although the three of us were to have an equal say in all decisions, it soon became apparent to me that the men aboard looked to Muldoon for the final word in matters of importance. If Dell made note of the inclination of the mates to respect my husband's leadership above ours, she said nothing of it.

After a few months, I was surprised and delighted to learn that I was with child. For that reason, I cared very little about such minor things as authority, because even though I suffered with no nausea the way Dell had, I grew weaker with each passing day. At the end of the sixth month, it was all I could do to get out of bed each morning and take a little stroll around the deck. Marmara perused the medical books Doctor Waring had sold to us and could find no reason for my exhaustion. She made worried noises about getting me to a proper doctor, who might know more than she did.

Dell was an angel on earth during those days when I was too weary to raise my head from my pillow. When I neared the middle of the seventh month, she told Muldoon we absolutely must live ashore until after I had delivered and was back on my feet again.

He came to me and held both my hands in his, his expression tender and loving. "Dell says we must find living quarters ashore, where we'll be close to a regular doctor. How do you feel about it, my love?"

I told him I had no feelings about it, one way or another. We were two days out of Jamaica, heavily laden with armaments and heading for the colonies.

Muldoon kissed my eyes, my cheeks, my lips, and held me close. "Then we'll pull into Fairhaven Island. Even though most of the able-bodied men in the colonies are fighting the English, we'll surely find a few good carpenters, and we can put the crew to work with the roughing-in of our house."

"Why bother with building a house?" It seemed more sensible to me to rent or buy one that was already built.

"The English will mount a final thrust in an attempt to win the war," he said. "They'll not waste men and ammunition on a single house in the middle of a lonely island, which will make it safer for us." He went on to speak of the way the existing one room cabin could be enlarged enough to accommodate a family the size of ours. "We'll keep it for a home base, and we'll not stint when it comes to making it a place of beauty and luxury. I'll build you a castle, my heart, my own beloved. You were so wistful and so beautiful when you spoke of how happy you were when you and Dell were on the island you'd been led to believe was Fairhaven."

"That will be nice," I said, forcing a smile. "It will be a place where we'll have roots. When we're on the high seas, we can think of it as a haven, a welcoming fortress. Maybe someday we'll live there the year 'round."

He laughed. "And I shall become a gentleman farmer."

Tears misted my eyes as I spoke of the vineyards and rose gardens destroyed by the men of the *Rolling Ruthie*, and I tightened my grip on his hand. "We can make it a place of beauty as well as serenity." It struck me that I wanted very much to set my feet on solid ground, to keep them there. My condition may have made me more emotional than usual, but it came as a relief to actually feel a strong desire for something, and I began to look forward with ever-increasing anxiety toward the time when we would drop anchor.

I don't know exactly when it was that I realized my husband and Dell were lovers. It may have been shortly before I learned I was with child, or shortly afterwards. Nor do I know how I knew it, except to say that it was something akin to the sudden bursts of knowledge I had experienced as a child, even into my young womanhood. The last time I was warned in advance of a dire happening was when I foresaw the death of Lady Neilson. After that, the gift left me, never to return again until one night after I had known the rapture of Muldoon's love-making. The knowledge that he also gave Dell that kind of bliss came to me full-blown, without warning. Suddenly, I *knew*. My head rested on his shoulder. His arms held me in the close embrace that I loved so well and had longed for down through the years in spite of refusing to admit to my secret self that I ached for his caresses. Then it came in a blinding light. I may have moaned, for Muldoon kissed my lips, then asked me if I had been disturbed by a dream.

"No," I answered slowly, sweetly. "I don't think so, but maybe I was."

His heavy breathing told me he had fallen into deep slumber. I was very careful not to make another sound or movement that would bring him back to wakefulness, for I wanted to inspect the revelation from all angles in an attempt to divine how I intended to deal with it.

I felt oddly peaceful. Not in the least angry or jealous, which led me to wonder why. There was no doubt in my mind that they were lovers, so it followed that I must be lacking in some very basic emotions to find it impossible to dredge up the slightest feeling of woe. My lips curled and I found it hard to keep from breaking into laughter. Then I sobered and told myself not to be ridiculous, I had no way of knowing for sure whether such a thing were true. But I *did* know! And I didn't care. For some mysterious reason, the idea seemed to settle inside me as right and fitting.

My thoughts returned to how they might look upon their relationship, which again threatened to overcome me with mirth. Dell could hardly be expected to come to me and say, "By the way, Garnet, Muldoon is still a marvelous lover." Nor would my husband be likely to mention offhandedly, in the manner of speaking of what would be served for dinner, that he was sleeping with Dell now and then. It occurred to me that they would both be surprised if they knew my true feelings. Not only did I not care, I rather liked the idea.

Soberly, I asked myself how I would feel if he had turned to someone other than Dell, and I was alarmed at the searing sense of outrage that came over me. With quickened breath and a sheen of sweat on my brow, I visualized myself killing them both—my husband and his strange lady-love. Recalling Dell's flighty behavior during her pregnancy, I assumed I was being affected by the workings of some strange chemical inside my body that made me feel good about the idea of husband and dearest friend being lovers, but boiling mad about the same thing happening beween him and another woman. Sleep overtook me, my last lucid thought being that I would probably feel differently after the baby came.

Except for a squall, and later a period of utter stillness that left us becalmed for the better part of four days, the rest of the journey toward the colonies passed without incident. We neared the shores under cover of darkness and with extreme caution, and not a sound was heard from ship nor crew. The unloading of our cargo was the most dangerous part of smuggling supplies to the colonists. We knew better than to go near any well-marked harbor, for the British fleet lay in wait for operations such as ours. Fog, deep and impenetrable, enshrouded the coastline. Far from being an enemy to smugglers or pirates, for is a great blessing.

Especially such a one as that which covered the Atlantic seaboard that night. The anchor went down with barely a splash, and very shortly one solitary figure rowed toward Holden Beach. We were anchored off Folly Inlet, all masts down and every hand wide awake as we waited for the furtive return of our scout, knowing he might have fallen into the hands of the British.

An hour and a half went by before the boat appeared alongside and a half-whisper came up from the silent sea that all was well. Before the first rays of the morning sun lightened the sky, our cargo was unloaded and we were off, sailing north, destination Fairhaven, and everthing went off without a hitch—far and away the fastest and least hazardous delivery of contraband we ever made.

My spirits dampened as we neared Fairhaven Island. I stood on deck and watched as we approached, trying not to compare it with the island where Dell and I had prospered. The true Fairhaven Island was a bleak and unfriendly looking place, with a rough little cabin set down in the very midst of it, and nothing but a tangle of leafless trees surrounding it. The day was cold and drear, with a greyness overcasting land and sea. Happy Jack assured me the weather gave the place an unfriendly look when he noted my gloom, and swore the island was a virtual paradise for the major part of the year.

Later, we learned why we were unmolested by warring factions from either side as we straggled ashore; the British campaign was centered around the Hudson Valley under General Burgoyne, who had come down from Canada by way of Lake Champlain, where he was to be met by General Howe. St. Leger was to have left from another point in Canada through the Mohawk Valley where he would join the other two. Impassable roads, loss of supplies and unexpected attacks by Indians weakened Burgoyne, and the detachment he sent to Bennington to seize supplies was defeated by the fighting Americans. The American army was in front of him as well as behind him. Howe failed to meet him and he lost battle after battle until he was forced to surrender at Saratoga to the American General Gates. Howe had taken it upon himself to capture Philadelphia before he met with General Burgoyne, thinking he had plenty of time to lay the rebel capital low before joining forces with the other general. He took Philadelphia, but his losses were heavy and the battle at Germantown, where the American General Washington attempted to drive him out, delayed him until it was too late for him to join Burgoyne. It was not until much later that the British turned their attention to the South.

Muldoon had no way of knowing that the main thrust of the war was being carried out in the North, and he feared for the ship, which could be claimed by either side. For that reason, he saw us safely settled into the hut he had previously erected on Fairhaven Island, left half of the crew to begin work on an addition, and said he would head south where he would find a place to safely leave the boat. It wasn't until the fourth day after he left that I was again visited with a vision. Dell and I were poring over the sketches we'd made for the house when I saw my husband in the thick of battle. Everything came to me as clear as day. I straightened, shrieked and clutched her hands in my agitation. "He lied. He's joined the revolutionists, which he planned all along."

"You're imagining things, Garnet," Dell said in an attempt to soothe me.

"No I'm not. I *know*!" For the first time in all the years of our close affiliation, I told her of my fleeting glimpses into the future. I had not mentioned them before because they had stopped, only to begin anew as my pregnancy wore on.

"I don't believe in such things," she said. "You're overwrought, and prone to imagining things."

"I'm not in the least overwrought," I insisted. And then I told her that I knew she and my husband were lovers.

She did not deny it, but she begged me to forgive her. Truthfully, I looked her in the eye and tried to explain that I had not been offended. "In fact, I rather like the idea. He is amorous enough for the two of us, and I think I've known all along that you love him, even as I've known I do. And after all, you've shared your son with me, as well as Melly."

"You're a strong woman, Garnet. Stronger by far, than I."

Our relationship remained unchanged. Within a month our house was enlarged enough for comfort, although it would be a long time before it remotely resembled the castle my husband had promised me.

He returned, a ghostly figure with a festering wound in his chest, and although I was tempted to rail at him for lying, I did not. He had served with General Washington's Army at Valley Forge and he'd come back for the rest of the ships crew, all of whom he seduced into joining the fighting on the side of the colonists.

Darkness was beginning to fall when he came to me and said they would be leaving at dawn. I laughed and said, "You're a marvel, you are, considering that you've talked dedicated seamen into taking up arms on land, but you always had a silvery tongue, Muldoon." Then, because my time was upon me and I was bound to not keep him at my side out of a sense of obligation, I laughed again, and gave him my blessing. "I'll not try to tame you, Happy Jack Muldoon, for you're a man who will always do what you must do. I'm pleased enough that you've allowed Marmara to treat than nasty wound. Now, go to Dell, whose arms have yearned for you as much as mine."

He turned a sickly shade of puce, and his mouth worked soundlessly.

I sat up in bed and glared. "I'm not a fool, Muldoon. I've known from the beginning that one woman isn't enough for you, and I'm hardly in shape to cater to your needs."

"But I love you, Garnet," he cried.

"I know you do," I answered testily. "But you also love Dell Fields, which is all right with me." Before another pain tore through me, I was determined to get in another statement: "But if you turn to yet another woman, I shall kill you and her both. Two of us are enough. Now I've had my say. Go to Dell. I want to sleep a while."

Looking slightly dazed, he turned on his heel and left.

Marmara, who knew my labor had started, came to me after my husband left. She gave me a cup of tea which eased the pain enough to keep me from crying out. All through that long and tortured night, I often found myself thinking of Dell getting up in the middle of the night while Melly and I slept. Of her going into the shipwrecked sailor's little hut and giving birth to Thomas. But she had said I was the stronger of the two of us.

As the night wore on, Marmara increased the amount of

powders she put into my tea and I managed to endure the pain until the last, when my cry cut through the night like a knife. I feared it would awaken everyone on the place. Panting and sweating, I looked at Marmara and ordered her not to allow my husband inside the room. He came, my scream no doubt rousing him from bed, but Marmara refused to let him enter. He called to me from behind the door, begging to be let in. Gasping and writhing as a wave of agony enveloped me from head to foot, I looked at Marmara and shook my head. She yelled at him to stay where he was. He threatened to break the door down. Again, I shook my head. The pain was so great that I feared I would never live through it, and I didn't want him in there with me dying. There was no malice in my actions in spite of the way they may have seemed to him.

Release from the wrenching pain came as a miracle. I had given birth. I looked at it, all slimy and still, and clapped my hand over my mouth.

"Stillborn," Marmara said. "I'm sorry. It was a boy."

Before I could gather my senses together, another pain grabbed me. While I shuddered under it, a second baby was born. Everything speeded up; at the same time, it slowed down. The bed lifted and fell, the ceiling looked as if it were twirling around, and the next thing I knew, I was washed, dressed in a clean white linen bedgown and two tiny babies were making little cooing sounds, one on either arm. I had given birth to triplets. I mourned the loss of the one who struggled so hard to live, a boy who was perfectly formed and perhaps a shade more beautiful than the other two. They were very small. About half as big as Thomas at birth, but they were strong and healthy, each with a lusty pair of lungs, and long before they were three hours old they proved that they'd been born with the ability to show their tempers.

Muldoon was an absolute idiot as he hovered over the tiny boy and girl. He'd postponed going back to war until I was delivered, and though I hadn't wanted him with me when I was in labor, I was glad to have him there later on. He shed tears and looked at me as if I had presented him with a miracle. "But they are just like little people," he said in awe.

Dell, her own eyes shining, asked, "Well, what did you expect them to look like—little puppies?"

"I am starved to death," I announced. Then I looked at my husband and at my friend and my throat felt near to bursting with love for them both. "The girl baby is going to be named Della; the boy, Jonathan. The two of you may argue all you please over their second names, but do not attempt to change my mind for me. I didn't know I would have three babies all at once, and my heart aches for the loss of the third one. Long ago, I made up my mind to name my baby after you, Dell, if it should be a girl, and of course a boy would be Jonathan."

I wanted to beg my husband to stay with me, to not return to the dreadful fighting that was going on up North under the command of General Washington, but I kept my silence. He felt he had many reasons to lend a hand to the Americans and he did not hesitate to name them. "You, my darling, must live in a land of the free, and that's cause enough for any man to fight for his country, but I have more than one person's future to think of. Thomas, Melly, Della, and Jonathan will inherit a great nation. They could become statesmen."

"And Dell," I said, "will find a way to help with the running of it."

He nodded. I smiled. He took my hand. Knowing he felt ill-at-ease over my knowledge of their love, it was the only thing I could think of to help him, for I could never find the words to express exactly how I felt about it, except for that one time. Even then, I did not know how to say it the way I felt it.

When he went back into the battle, Muldoon saw where he could be more advantageous to the cause by turning the *Sea Hawk* against the British. It went down under terrific fire, with all hands aboard who had not already been killed by the enemy. The news came to me at a time when I was all alone on my island except for the two older children and the babies. Three days earlier, Dell had gone back to sea. She would never have left me if she'd known I would have no one with me, but Marmara was there, dependable and good as always. We had no servants because everyone was doing what they could toward supplying the starving troops with food and trying to keep them in clothing. We had knitted and sewed until our hands gave out and our eyes burned. We had coaxed the unyielding ground into shape and gave all we could to the soldiers from our harvest of vegetables. In spite of my former lack of interest in the war between the colonies and Great Britain, I, along with Dell and Marmara, had been caught up in patriotic fervor as the war raged on, and knowing Muldoon was somewhere with the Navy served as a whip to press us into backbreaking work. Melly, almost a young lady, was showing a great talent with the needle. We worked at the sewing of uniforms well into the night, and began all over again at dawn. Dell had worked as tirelessly as the rest of us, but by the time little Della and Jonathan were six months old it had become increasingly clear that she was restless and anxious to get into the thick of things.

She would begin conversations by saying she could handle a musket as well as any man and better than most. My answer was always the same: "There's no place in the Army for you, Dell. We're doing all we can."

Or she would say, "If we're to stay here for the rest of our lives, I should be doing something more worthwhile than planting a vegetable garden and raising hogs." At those times, her blue eyes would get a faraway look in them that always reminded me of a reflection of the sea itself. No matter that I reminded her of how important a side of bacon or a fine, rich ham could be to starving soldiers. She butchered the hogs, cut the meat and tended the fire under the smoke house. She milked the cow, churned the butter, and made minor repairs around the house. When it was time to take the victuals to the supply house, it was Dell who rowed them across, risking being fired upon by the British. But it was not enough, and it came as no surprise when she came to me of a crisp and frosty morning decked out in breeches and boots, a quilted weskit over a leathern shirt. With her glorious hair tucked under a hat, she gave me a smart salute. "Now tell me. I'm as good a man as I ever was, don't you think?"

"I will ask you once more to not attempt such foolishness again, Dell," I said quietly. Then I added, "We're no longer young. Shouldn't the foolhardy behavior of our youth remain in the past?"

"Oh, Garnet!" Her voice was the cry of a wild thing being

tortured. "I'm not—there's something lacking in me. Maybe I was born in a twist and when I outgrew it on the outside it stayed hidden inside me. I'm not like you, nor am I the same as any other woman I ever knew. Once I was, to be sure. That was when I was young and happy with my Tom. But ever since, I've been all mixed up inside, sometimes more man than woman, sometimes more woman than man. I can't stay here on this island doing woman's work when there's fighting at sea. That's where this war will be won, mark me. I'm going to Muldoon. And the *Sea Hawk*, where I'll help beat the British back all the way across the ocean."

"You'd leave your own Thomas, you'd leave Melly?"

"*For* them, I'm leaving. Don't you understand?" Her eyes flickered for a moment, and she added, "They're as much yours as mine. Always were. Anyway, I'll be back."

"If you'd been my blood sister, Dell, I couldn't have loved you more," I said slowly. My heart was hammering wildly. "What we've shared has been far and away more than mere friendship. Sometimes I think we were fated to go through life side by side. That's one of the reasons why I accepted the way things were between you and Muldoon. What happened to make you all twisted on the inside was back there on the Barbados, when you saw your husband and your babe cut down. But don't lie to you and me both. You want to get into the thick of it because you crave the sea and the excitement of battles."

She stood very still for a moment, her face gone ashen. Then she smiled and held out her hand. I pushed it aside as I put my arms around her and she put hers around me. "My blessings go with you," I said through my tears. I felt her body tremble from head to foot. She turned. I shouted, "Don't turn back, for if you do I shall hog-tie you!"

She didn't turn back.

That afternoon a frail old man rowed over from the cove to ask Marmara to come and attend to his wife. "She took a sick spell right sudden-like," he said. "Fell right down in her shadow, and looks at me plumb barmy out of her eyes. Cain't utter a word, but I think she knows me." He wrung his hands and tried hard to not be taken aback by Marmara's tallness, her blackness. It was not the first time white folks had come begging for the services of the doctor woman. Every doctor around the area was serving on land or on sea, and in spite of Marmara's color and her lack of a bona fide degree, she had earned considerable respect for miles around. The first to send for her were families whose slaves had fallen sick. She went, did what she could and came home before she went into a screaming rage against slavery. After the last white doctor in the village had been pressed into service in the Army, white people began to come out to the island to ask for her help. Again, she went and did what she could. The struggle for independence was no deterrent to disease, childbirth, or injuries. After a while, she no longer ranted at the mad injustice with which she was treated. Instead of raving and railing when the white people she ministered to showed her out the back door, called her nigger, or even more hated, "girlie," she began to see the humor in it. A week or two before the old man came for her, a one-legged veteran of the Battle of Brandywine rowed over. His wife had been in labor for four days.

"She almost didn't make it," Marmara said when she finally came home. "But you can be sure that the poor bastard who was bowing and scraping and calling me ma'am on the way over sang a different tune on the way back. He said it was a shame all that book-learning had gone to waste on a big nigger wench. Bless his heart, he doesn't know any better." Then she almost fell to the floor, overcome with laughter.

We had fallen into the habit of repeating those words among ourselves when an incident of outrageous proportions occurred. An eleven-year-old girl once came for help because her mother was badly burned. She went, applying her own strong back to the oars as she tried to comfort the frightened child. When they reached the village, the little girl ran down the street as fast as she could, anxious to get back to her suffering mother. Marmara followed the child through the front door. One of the neighbors took umbrage at a biggity nigger coming into the front door of a white person's house, but her abusive tongue was quickly hushed by another neighbor who had better sense. Turning to Marmara, the other woman said, "Bless her heart, she doesn't know any better. Seeing that you're a doctor makes all the difference."

So Marmara was away when a raggedy sailor came to tell me the *Sea Hawk* had gone down. "It was a bloody battle, ma'am. I was on the *Carradine* and we lost all but two men, and I'm one of them."

"Come in and let me give you some soup and a bit of rum," I said.

He came inside and seated himself at the kitchen table. "Ma'am, you don't seem to understand what I'm trying to tell you. Your husband was the commander of the *Sea Hawk*. I came to give you the sad news that he was killed in action."

Thomas was doing the milking and Melly was at the wash house. My babies were sleeping and even if they'd been awake they were too young to understand what was being said. Carefully, I ladeled out thick and steaming soup for the seaman, cut off a few slices of bread and poured him a tot of rum. Then I seated myself across from him and said, "No, I'm sure you're mistaken."

He looked at me and wept. "Ma'am, I would give my other arm, and gladly, if I knew I wasn't sayin' the God's truth."

Not having noticed that he had only one arm, I quickly changed the pewter spoon to the other side. Then I buttered his bread and shifted the mug of rum to the left of him. I was not going to believe that my Happy Jack Muldoon was dead. For some reason, it seemed to me that as long as I refused to accept his death, he was still living.

"There's another fellow in the rowboat, ma'am," he said. "But I was the one that had to come and tell you about your husband."

I went ouside and called the other man in. He wasn't a man at all, but a lad about the same age as Thomas. After I had fixed the sailor boy his meal, I said, "My son will be coming in from the milking any minute. Not a word to him of his father's death, for it isn't so, and I'll not have him upset."

"But ma'am—" began the one-armed man.

I silenced him with a look. They finished their meal without another word. Thomas came in with the milk and I poured them both a big mug of it, which they drank delightedly.

Marmara came home. She said the woman had suffered a stroke, that she could do nothing for her, but she might linger on for a long, long time in a helpless condition. With effort, I kept my roiling emotions in check. We sewed woolen mufflers by candlelight until we could no longer keep our eyes open, while Thomas kept up a steady barrage of statements designed to wear me down until I agreed to let him join General Washington's troops. I nursed my babies and kept telling Thomas absolutely no, he was too young to go to war. He was still arguing with me when we went to bed. Not once had I allowed myself to behave in a manner that was any different from usual. I clung to the conviction that as long as I believed Muldoon lived, he was living.

The human mind is a strange and marvelous work of art.

Twenty-three

For a full week, I went about my business as usual. Only once did I give in to the gripping fear that the sailor had his facts straight, but none of the others saw me break down. I went to the shore where I stared toward the north and I spoke to Happy Jack Muldoon, my husband, my love, my life, and I cried out. "You can't be dead! I have loved you all these years. Loved you enough to share you with Dell. Loved you enough to let you leave me and go to fight in a war that I didn't at first believe in. Damn you to hell, Muldoon, you come home to me! Do you hear me?"

I had started out in a calm voice as I cast my voice seaward, but by the time I was finished I was screaming, and clawing at my face and tearing my hair. To the gently rolling waves, I shrieked, "If you'll just come home, damn you, I'll tell you I *love you*!" The wave of regret over not having come out and said it before almost crushed me. I looked up at the sky and saw a cold, disapproving look in the blue. My words came back to me. They hung there in the cold sunlight for what seemed to be several minutes, but of course that was foolishment. Once spoken, words are not prone to hang around in the air. My children depended on me, there was work to be done. I couldn't stand there with my feet sunk in sand as the waves lapped in, each one higher than the last. The water was icy cold and up to my knees, but I was driven to call to my love one more time. Shivering, I raised my voice and sent it out over the shimmering, mysterious Atlantic before I turned back toward the house.

Along toward evening of the eighth day that had passed since the sailor came, I heard Thomas shout from the outside where he was feeding the chickens. I was churning, and the butter was about to come, but I ran outside without a thought to butter or anything else. Muldoon had returned. He was leaping out of the rowboat, Thomas running toward him with both arms outstretched. I was glad Thomas saw him, for that meant my husband was there in the flesh, and it was not just another of the frustrating dreams that tormented me each night. I ran and tripped over a stone, which sent me sprawling. But I was quickly up and running again. For the second time, I knew the blessed joy of my husband's arms around me after a long, long time. It hadn't been as long as the first time, but the past eight days had seemed like years to me.

Over supper, I told everyone about the one-armed sailor who had come to report that Muldoon went down with the *Sea Hawk*. For a moment, a stunned silence came into the kitchen.

"But you never said a word," said Marmara.

"I couldn't," I said. "If I had given it voice, it might have been true."

Only those who love understand such statements.

We had our own private reunion much later that night, long after we learned how Happy Jack Muldoon had been blown into the ocean and gone down so deep that he'd almost touched bottom. When he bobbed to the surface, the battle still raged. A piece of wood appeared. He grabbed it, hung on and stayed under, allowing the current to take him where it would. His knees were scraped by rock before he had any idea he was close to shore, but he was; and he said he lost no time in climbing up the rugged, rocky cliffs and flinging himself down, glad to be alive.

Content and warm and luxuriously loved, I put my head on his chest and whispered, "Did you hear me calling to you?"

He held me closer. "When?"

I told him about the day I came close to losing my mind, when I called to him. He said he'd not heard me and I was a shade disappointed, but I didn't let him know. He was never one to believe in the ability of a woman's love or any other kind of unseen force to be felt a long distance from where it began.

When morning came, he wouldn't go to the kitchen for coffee as he usually did upon first awakening. Instead, he pulled me back down in the bed and held me so close that I could hear the thunder of his heart. His voice rumbled under my ear as he said, "Last night when you told me about Dell, I had little to say. About her leaving, I mean."

"Yes. But there were so many things to talk of, I'm afraid I paid little attention. And anyway, there's nothing can be done about it." I took out the letter she'd sent me almost six months earlier, saying she was going to sign on with another ship instead of the *Sea Hawk*.

"I didn't want to spoil my homecoming," he said. Then he sat up and pulled me up, putting his hand under my chin in a way that forced me to face him. Very quietly, he said, "Dell is dead."

"No," I whispered. But just as I had known the seaman was wrong about Muldoon, I knew Muldoon was right about Dell. Otherwise, he would not be looking at me in that broken way, and speaking to me in that soft and grieving voice.

"That's why I was so late in coming home. If it hadn't been for Dell, I would have been here sooner. You remember Doctor Fearnot Waring?"

"Of course." The icy fingers of foreboding clutched at my heart.

"She was masquerading as a man."

"Yes, I knew."

"He... recognized her. Went crying through the streets of town that a traitor was in their midst. She was seized. And hanged. After rotting in the gaol at a Long Island village for all that time."

"But—"

He was quiet for a moment, his eyes all soft and hurting as they looked into mine. "I tried to stop it, Garnet, as soon as I heard the mad, excited word of the hanging of a red-haired woman that was to take place on the village square. But I was too late. They were cutting her down when I got there."

"Doctor Waring," I said between frozen lips. "I'll kill him."

He took my hand. "No you won't, my love. I already have."

Before he came home, he'd made arrangements for Dell's body to be brought to the island. The most difficult task that lay before us was in the breaking of the news to the children, who had adored her in a very special way.

Dell's grave is carefully tended. Her mortal remains rest in eternal peace alongside the stillborn babe, first of my triplets. Our island blooms and it has truly become a paradise. On Dell's other side is my daughter, Evalina. She died of smallpox a day before her first birthday. Although I go often to the family burial plot, I do not commune with the dead who are buried there. I see to it that flowers bloom on the two small graves and the bigger one out of honor to the memory of those who are there, under the ground.

Melly is a beautiful young woman now. She is engaged to be married to a fine gentleman who plans to take her to India, where she will live the life of a queen. Thomas will soon enter West Point. He has grown into a handsome young man and still has the best of his mother *and* his father in him, both physically and spiritually. A year after my little Evalina died, I gave birth to twin boys, and two years later I had another little girl. Life is good. Muldoon seems content to be a gentleman farmer, but just as I don't know all there is about myself, I know less about the secret places within his his heart. He is a loving father and a loving husband. Our children are growing and thriving.

Marmara lives in Charles Towne where she practices medicine without a license since she was refused entrance into any of the medical schools in the country. Now and then there is talk of having her prosecuted for attending to the needs of the sick, the injured, and women in childbirth, but nothing ever comes of it.

America is a country, independent of Great Britain. Sometimes I look into the future and try to visualize future generations of the odd mixture of Muldoons, Fields, and Shaws. I wonder where they will go, what they will do with their lives. Often, I have an idea that Dell is with us in spirit, but I do not mention these inner thoughts to anyone, not even my husband. Most of the time, I think of her as tamping tobacco into her little pipe, of looking toward the sea, of laughing her marvelously lilting laugh or puffing thoughtfully as she plans a new adventure.